Simply Magic

KATHLEEN KANE

St. Martin's Paperbacks

ISBN: 0-312-96984-8

Printed in the United States of America

St. Martin's Paperbacks edition/May 1999

St. Martin's Paperbacks are published by St. Martin's Press, 175 Fifth Avenue, New York, N.Y. 10010.

10 9 8 7 6 5 4 3 2 1

To my mother, Sallye Carberry, for going above and beyond the call of motherhood time and again over the years.

For sticking with me through dented fenders, broken hearts, and that ugly fifteenth year. For crying together at old movies, and laughing at each other's jokes. For travel stories—especially "The Incident" (and let's not forget the twenty bucks you owe me from San Francisco).

But mostly, for years of making magic happen for your family.

Mom, you are the heart of us, and the magic is in you.

Prologue

He felt naked.

Strange how not wearing a badge for the first time in ten years could affect a man.

"I sure am gonna miss all of this," Riley Burnett muttered. His horse shook its head, black mane flying, and Riley laughed shortly. "Yeah, I know. Makes me a stupid man. Hell," he went on, letting his gaze rake across the stark, wide-open Texas landscape. "What kind of fool actually *likes* living in a saddle day after day with nothing to call home except a ragged bedroll?"

Him.

Damn, how was he going to survive living in town again? Surrounded by people? Trapped for days on end in one spot with no chance of hopping on his horse and seeing new country? The center of a storm of gossip again, with the town biddies flapping their gums and whispering from behind their hands.

He shuddered at the thought.

"Hell, Demon," he told his horse, "even *you'll* go crazy locked up in a stable all day every day."

It had probably been a mistake to ride all the way to Texas just to turn in his badge. He could've mailed it to the man taking over his territory. But damn it, Riley had wanted one last ride. One last time to remember what it was to be a free man. A man with no responsibilities beyond the job at hand.

And as long as Erma Hightower had been willing to step in and watch over Becky in Rimshot for him, he hadn't been able to resist the urge.

Now it was done. Riley Burnett, U.S. Marshal, was officially retired. As of two days ago, he was just Riley Burnett, saloon owner . . . and *father*.

He shook his head and rubbed the back of his neck. Father. Hell, what did he think he was doing? He was no kind of man to be raising a kid. When he'd received that telegram saying his folks had died, he should have cabled right back, telling Rimshot's one and only lawyer to find his daughter a good home.

For the kid's own sake.

But that hadn't been a real option, then or now. Riley saddled his own broncs, settled his own problems, and he would take care of the child who was his responsibility.

God help her.

As he rode around an outcropping of rock, he pulled back on the reins. The animal stopped instantly and Riley leaned forward, folding his hands atop the saddle horn.

"Well, now, where'd *he* come from?" he asked himself as he squinted into the dying sun.

A small wagon lay drunkenly to one side, its rear wheel obviously broken. The owner of the cart stood helplessly beside it, shaking his head and glancing from the spare wheel lying on the ground beside him, to the broken hub, as if expecting it to leap up onto the axle by itself.

The little fella had a helluva problem. There was no way one man could replace a broken wheel all alone. Riley glanced again at the sun, lowering on the cloudless horizon, and knew he'd be making camp here tonight.

"Well, shit," Riley muttered and started his horse down the slope. The short man turned at his approach and Riley called out, "Need some help, mister?"

"Yes, thank you."

A heavy accent from somewhere other than Texas colored the man's voice. But that was nothing new in these parts. There were always lots of foreigners out west, looking to build new lives.

Riley gave a last, careful glance around before dismounting. After all, it didn't pay to take chances. This fella could be just the bait in a neatly laid trap. Then he looked into the little fella's eyes. Clear, shining gray eyes stared back at him and, in those eyes, Riley read all manner of things . . . not a one of 'em bad.

"What d'ya say we unload that wagon of yours, to lighten it up some, and then we'll get that new wheel on, all right?"

"Of course," the man responded and hurried to the back of the little cart. Between the two of them, they emptied the thing in minutes, stacking the man's possessions on the ground. He smiled to himself. Bolts of fabric lay beside hammers and saws. Knives, ropes, and baling wire leaned against a stack of hair ribbons and long johns. A tinker, he thought. A traveling man who carried his shop with him wherever he went. A man a lot like himself, drawn to the open spaces and the freedom to do as he liked.

Well, he corrected himself mentally, the tinker was a lot like the *old* Riley Burnett. Shaking off the sharp pang of regret ricocheting through his insides, he walked to the listing side of the wagon. "Now," he said, "when I lift up, you yank that bad wheel off. Then I'll set 'er back down, we'll grease up the axle and do it again. Should have that fresh wheel back on in a few minutes."

The man smiled at him and Riley noted how those gray eyes looked almost silver in the twilight. Odd, how they seemed to capture the little bit of light available. Oh, now he was getting fanciful when all that was needed were a few muscles.

Riley bent his broad back to the side of the tiny wagon. He'd always been a big man, able to move most anything once he put his mind to it. The cart was no different. In no time at all, the task was finished. Kneeling on the hard-packed earth, Riley tightened the bolts on the wheel hub, gave it a last slap of satisfaction, and stood up. Wiping his hands on his jeans, he grinned at the man watching him as if he were some kind of miracle worker.

"You're all set, mister." He tossed a quick look at the now-lavender sky overhead before returning his gaze to the man in front of him. "You can head on out if you want, but I'm fixin' to camp right up by those rocks yonder. You're welcome to share my fire."

"Thank you, but I must be going on," he said in that singsongy voice of his.

Riley never had been much for needing the company of others, in fact, had preferred to be on his own. So why was he feeling a bit disappointed that this little fella was going to leave so soon? "You need help gatherin' up your things?" he asked, shooting the tinker another quick look.

"No, I can manage. You have done enough, I think."

"It was nothin', mister," Riley told him.

"But it was," he said softly.

Riley shook his head. "Out here, folks tend to help one another when needed."

"I must thank you," the tinker went on as if Riley hadn't spoken.

"You already have. Don't you worry about it." With that, he walked to his horse's side and stepped up into the saddle.

"I offer you a gift," the man said quickly.

"Ain't necessary."

"But it is," the man said so solemnly, Riley turned to look at him. Those gray eyes of his now shimmered with a strange silvery light and seemed to sparkle unnaturally.

Even the air around them suddenly seemed heavier, thicker. If he hadn't known the sky above was a clear, deepening blue, Riley would have sworn a storm was rushing in.

"My gift will come when you least expect it," the man told him seriously.

Riley shifted uncomfortably in the saddle. "I told you, mister."

"But with this gift comes the risk of pain and even, perhaps," he added in low, ringing tones, "a price. A terrible price."

"That's some gift, mister," Riley said with a low whistle. "If it's all the same to you, you keep it for yourself."

A deep-throated chuckle rose up and fell around him like autumn leaves. "Oh my, no," the tinker said finally. "I'm afraid this gift is not for me."

"Don't sound like I want it, either, partner."

A long silence followed, heavy with the stillness of the air just before a cyclone sets down. The small hairs on the back of Riley's neck stood straight up. The other man's form was becoming more indistinct in the vanishing light. It was almost as if he weren't there at all anymore.

Foolishness. Of course he was there. Couldn't hardly talk if he wasn't there, now could he? But what was all that about pain and a price? Sounded more like a curse than a gift to Riley. Besides, he'd had all he could take here lately of surprise gifts. "Look, mister, I don't need—"

"But you do, my friend." The voice sounded far away, yet at the same time, it was as if it echoed inside Riley's mind. "You need this gift more than you know."

Hell, no wonder the man's eyes had sparkled so strangely. He's loco. Slipping off into the night just to spook a man? Gifts that came with pain and a price? No, thanks. But, he told himself, there was no sense arguing with a man so clearly deranged.

"Whatever you say, mister."

"Hear me, my friend," the man said in a whisper of sound.

The horse beneath him shied and Riley couldn't blame the beast. He suddenly wanted to be well away from there himself. Instead, he was caught by the voice that seemed to hold him in place and by the memory of the light in those silver eyes.

"Watch for this gift. Watch carefully."

"Yeah, sure I will." Ride out, Riley, he told himself. Spur your horse and ride out.

"And pay the price, my friend. Pay it gladly."

Damn it, this was just too blamed strange. "If I don't?"

The voice came again. This time, it was so soft, so indistinct, Riley had to strain to hear.

"If you don't," the little man warned, "the gift will be gone and no amount of regret will bring it back."

Just as he'd thought earlier. Sounded more like a curse than a gift.

A whisper raced through him. "One man's curse is another man's gift, my friend."

He sat perfectly still for another minute or two, stunned by the fact that the tinker had somehow read his mind, and hoping the voice would speak again. Explain all of this nonsense.

But there was nothing more. No sound. No voice. Nothing. Finally, Riley gathered up the reins, wheeled his horse around, and rode off. The hell with camping here, he told himself. He'd make another few miles before stopping to sleep. He wouldn't be able to rest easy until he had some distance between him and the little man who had apparently vanished into the desert night.

Chapter One

A small group of street hooligans surrounded a horse and cart and their owner. Each of the dirty urchins took a turn at taunting the little man with graying hair wearing poorly patched trousers and shirt.

Stunned, Phoebe Hightower stood stock-still a long moment, staring. No one was going to help him.

The late afternoon crowd streamed past the altercation, heads bowed, gazes averted. Then she looked back at the small man surrounded by his tormentors and made a decision. Clasping her tightly furled, slightly worn parasol in her right hand, she jumped into the center of it all. Swinging the sharpened steel tip of her weapon indiscriminately, Phoebe had the young toughs jumping back and away.

As the brief battle waned, her bonnet slid down onto her forehead, partially blocking her vision, and she was forced to peer at her last remaining opponent out of one cool blue eye.

"You're crazy, lady!" the boy yelped just before he took to his heels.

Exhilarated both by the exercise and the clear victory, Phoebe grinned and lowered her weapon. Drawing one long, deep breath, she reached up to rearrange her fallen bonnet before turning to look at the victim of those boys.

Small and wiry, the man was bent over, picking up a few of his belongings that had been shaken loose from his cart.

Since the man still hadn't looked at her directly, she spoke up. "Are you all right?" she asked, slightly out of breath. "Did those boys hurt you?"

"I am quite unhurt," he answered in a soft, deep voice.

There was almost music in his words and she wondered idly where he was from originally. St. Louis had its fair share of immigrants from around the world, notably the Irish. But they stayed mostly in their own section of the city, known locally as Kerry Patch.

He slowly turned around to face her and Phoebe was instantly caught by the power of his eyes. So light a gray as to be nearly silver, they shone brilliantly in contrast to his weathered, swarthy skin. He seemed ageless, both elderly and young all at once. There was an obvious strength to him that belied his small stature and an innate dignity seemed to radiate from him.

"My thanks for your help," he said, inclining his head slightly in a courtly half-bow.

"Not at all," she replied and found herself staring deeply into those eyes of his. Really, they were a most remarkable color. "It was nothing."

"Ah, but there you are wrong," the little man said with a half-smile. "It was much indeed. And in return for your kindness, I have a gift for you."

A gift? She shook her head. Phoebe didn't want payment for helping him and told him so.

"Please," he said and again she heard the soft lilt of music in his words. Extraordinary.

"No, really," she began.

"I offer you four wishes," he said, interrupting her neatly, and his statement was so surprising, Phoebe couldn't think of a thing to say in response.

"Four," he went on, taking advantage of her silence, "because three is customary and five wishes really are too many for any one person, even one so remarkable as yourself."

Wishes? Ridiculous, of course. And yet, he seemed so sincere. He obviously believed what he was saying and Phoebe considered the possibility that her new friend was, as her former cook might have said, a cookie or two short of a dozen.

As if sensing her withdrawal, the little man locked his gaze with hers and Phoebe again perceived the power lying within. How odd. Even the air around her seemed heavier, as if a storm were brewing.

"Please," he said softly. "You will do me the honor of accepting my gift?"

Well, really, she thought. What harm could it do? Not that she believed in that sort of thing, of course. If wishes really came true, she would be at home now, sipping tea and reading her books. Instead, she was here. Near the wharf, looking for a likely victim.

Victim. Oh, it shamed her to her soul even to think the word. But what else could she call the people she'd stolen from over the last few months? She cringed inwardly even as she tried to soften the truth. Was it stealing to take something so small as not to be missed from people who weren't harmed by the taking? Was she a thief if all she stole were warm clothes, food, and an occasional dollar or two from an unguarded till?

Yes. She was.

And wishing things were different changed nothing. Still, the man was only trying to be kind.

"Very well," she said. "I accept your gift. And thank you."

The little man positively beamed at her. Then, with a quickness she could hardly believe, he scrambled up to the seat of his cart and gathered the reins in his hands. Just before he smacked the leather straps in the air over his horse's back, he reminded her unnecessarily, "Four wishes only, no more, no less."

She smiled, then, at his cautionary glance, steeled her features into seriousness. "I'll remember."

"And kind lady, be careful as you speak them."

"Be careful?"

"As with anything in this life, where there is joy, there will be pain."

"I don't understand." Was he trying to warn her against using the wishes he insisted on granting her?

"Heaven demands a price from us all, dear lady. With my gift, I can do no less."

She had no doubt at all that when her time came, heaven would have a good deal to say about her petty thievery. But until then, she would continue to do as she must.

"You want to be *paid* for your gift?" she asked.

He drew his head back and smiled at her. But it was a sad smile, somehow, containing more secrets than she could ever have guessed at. "Not I, dear lady," he said. "I am but a tinker."

She was beginning to doubt that very much. There was something about him that set him apart from the dirty city street where they stood.

"Take care, dear lady," he said quietly, "to wish only for what you must have. Wants and needs are very different things."

With that remarkable statement, he gave a snap of the reins and his horse lumbered off, joining the stream of traffic flowing along the street. In seconds, he was lost to her, almost as if he had vanished into thin air.

Wants and needs, she thought. Yes, they were different. She wanted a blazing fire, a cup of tea, and perhaps a baked chicken. She *needed* to find a warm coat for Simmons.

"What a strange man," Phoebe muttered, already turning her gaze over the crowd hustling past her. Quickly, she spotted a well-dressed woman carrying a basket over one arm. And out of the basket peeked two thick loaves of fresh bread.

Phoebe's mouth watered and her stomach rumbled. Burying her self-recriminations deep in the pit of her hunger, she fell into step behind the woman, keeping a discreet distance as she followed her home, waiting for a chance to snatch what she needed.

It was a long walk, leading from the downtown area to a neighborhood that had once been lovely but now looked more like a tired old dowager. Finely dressed, but wrinkled with age and neglect. As the woman went in the front door, Phoebe hurried around to the back, hoping she wouldn't run into any servants.

But when she peered into the kitchen window and saw the woman she'd followed set the loaves of bread onto a table in front of three small, obviously hungry children, Phoebe gasped and took a step backward. Mind racing, heart twisting, Phoebe realized that her intended victim was no better off than she herself was. Worse, in fact, since this woman had children to worry over.

It seemed that Phoebe wasn't the only person in St. Louis trying to maintain a genteel outward appearance against impossible odds.

Shame reared its ugly head and spilled hot tears down Phoebe's cheeks. Pulling in a shaky breath, she swiped them away and hurried from the yard. She couldn't very well steal the bread right from a child's mouth, could she? And at that thought, she was forced to wonder how many others there might have been. How many times had she taken food from someone she thought wouldn't miss it? And how many of those people had had a need more desperate than her own?

With her conscience screaming at her, Phoebe scurried back out to the street. Hugging her completely inadequate shawl tighter around her shoulders, head down into the fiercely blowing wind, she started for home. She couldn't do this anymore, she told herself firmly. She had to find another way to survive.

Something else to sell. Though heaven knew, she'd al-

ready sold everything of value in her house save the walls
and the floorboards.

Wishes indeed, she suddenly thought with a tearful
snort of disbelief. If wishes came true, would she be in
this predicament? A shiver that had nothing to do with
the cold snaked along her spine and Phoebe shivered.

Late that night, settled in her bed, Phoebe tucked the lay-
ers of blankets up under her chin and stared across the
room at the cold hearth of the massive brick fireplace.
How long had it been since flames had visited that
hearth? How long since she'd felt truly warm all the way
to the bone?

Phoebe's stomach knotted as her memories of the past
year scrolled through her mind. Losing her father, then
finding out from his solicitor that her home was mort-
gaged to the roof and that there were several dozen creditors ready to pound her door down.

The sharp slap of betrayal rocked her anew and she
gritted her teeth against the feeling. She'd done all she
could. Fired the servants, all but Simmons, her butler,
who simply refused to leave—thank heaven. She'd sold
most of her possessions, and the furniture she'd kept had
slowly found its way into the fireplace grates. She'd even
taken out advertisements in out-of-town newspapers,
looking for a job. Certainly the education her father'd
given her made her qualified for several things.

Yet there were no offers. No response at all to her
search. And so she was back where she started. In an
empty home that held only memories of past grandeur.
And thanks to her thieving, she didn't even have her pride
to keep her warm.

Phoebe drew a deep breath and blew it out again,
watching as the air from her lungs fogged and misted in
the frigid room. Every day the temperature dropped a bit
further and winter hadn't even officially arrived yet.

If things continued as they were, she and Simmons
would never survive the coming winter. And, remember-

ing the faces of those children she'd seen earlier, she simply refused to keep stealing to get by.

"I just wish we could go somewhere. Start over," she whispered into the darkness. "Preferably," she added with a shiver, "somewhere warm."

A wish? She stopped herself.

Just for a moment, she entertained the idea that a wish really could come true. But an instant later, she dismissed the memory of the tinker and his "gift." She was too old for dreams and wishes.

Chapter Two

"More tea, miss?" Simmons reached for the dark brown teapot in the center of the whitewashed table.

"No, thank you," Phoebe said and watched him pour himself another before continuing to read the front page of the newspaper. She gave silent thanks that the older man had no idea just how she'd been managing to keep food on the table recently. If he ever found out that she'd resorted to theft—well, she didn't even want to think about it. Simmons had been more of a father to her than her real sire ever had been. He'd taught her, loved her, consoled her, and in general been a better parent than most children ever know. All the while maintaining what he considered the "proper" relationship between butler and mistress.

Sharing a table with her hadn't been easy for him at first, but once she'd convinced him it was far more economical to heat only one room, he'd surrendered.

As the meager fire in the cast-iron stove began to seep warmth into the room, Phoebe turned her concentration onto the classified section of the paper, spread out before her. Surely there was *something* she could do to earn money. Something legal, of course. And entirely respectable. She was determined not to go back down a larcenous road.

"Clerk, banking teller, laborer, bartender, hmm . . ."

She read the list aloud, wondering if Simmons was listening. "Why is it all of the jobs are for men?" she muttered. It seemed that women were fit only as schoolteachers and . . . Well, the remaining occupation open to women was one she was ill-equipped for—even if she were of a mind to try.

Phoebe knew she was too tall and too thin, except for an embarrassing wealth of bosom. Her dark brown hair didn't glitter with threads of gold nor did her blue eyes shine with innocence and naivety. As noses went, hers was unremarkable, but her mouth was too wide and her lips too full for true beauty. Or so she'd once heard a prospective suitor Father had dragged home remark.

Getting back to the business at hand, she ran one finger down the list of employment opportunities and stopped briefly on a small ad. "Schoolteacher needed. Must be widely read and well versed in grammar, the classics, and mathematics." Smiling now, Phoebe's spirit lifted. "This could be it, Simmons," she crowed. Hopefully, she continued, "We require a patient applicant of good character." She paused, looked up at Simmons and smiled. "That's me."

"Good character," he said with a nod, "certainly. Patient?" His lips pursed as he shook his head.

"I can be patient," she argued.

"And I can sing," he countered. "But not well."

Phoebe ignored him. Going on, she read, "Must be willing to relocate to Wyoming."

"Good gad," Simmons muttered darkly.

Phoebe sighed as she read the last line. "Males only need apply."

"Saved by gender," the butler said.

Disgusted and thoroughly disappointed, she sat back in her chair and scowled at the newspaper. "Men."

"What about them?"

"They run the world. However haphazardly."

"Some of us," he corrected her, "do quite nicely."

She leaned forward, braced her elbows on the table,

and propped her chin in her hands, pointedly ignoring Simmons's frown. "And some of you keep all of *us* from working at all."

Both of Simmons's gray eyebrows rose high on his forehead. "Is this going to become another stimulating lecture on women's rights?"

Tempting, she thought, but her heart wasn't in it. "No," she said on a sigh.

A bell broke into the silence and she glanced toward the door separating the kitchen from the hall leading to the front of the house. "Who could that be?"

"I'm afraid," Simmons said as he stood up, "I'll actually have to open the door to find out."

She followed right behind him as he moved down the hall. Inside her, a curl of anxiety twisted in the pit of her stomach. Terrified that somehow, someday, a police officer would discover her occasional bursts of criminal activity, Phoebe lived in dread that she'd be hauled off in chains.

Simmons's steps quickened, almost as if he were racing her to the door. Sometimes, she didn't know what she'd do without him. Now was not one of those times. His British accent thickened on command and he used his sharp tongue readily to dole out his opinion on any number of things. With his tall, thin frame and gray-flecked black hair, he could have been anywhere from forty to sixty.

And Phoebe couldn't imagine ever having the effrontery to inquire.

He opened the door and a blast of icy, damp air shot down the hall. Seeing the messenger on the stoop, Phoebe relaxed.

"Wire," a young voice announced.

"Brief and to the point," Simmons commended the messenger and snatched the envelope from his hand. Then he closed the door and handed the telegram to Phoebe.

"A telegram? For me?" She stared at her own name,

printed neatly across the front of the envelope. No mistake, she thought and noticed that her hands were trembling. Well, whatever for? There couldn't be more bad news. Her creditors had already been dealt with. She had no more family. And if she was about to be arrested, the police wouldn't send her a wire announcing the fact. Then what . . . ?

"Aren't you going to open it?"

She looked briefly at Simmons, then nodded. Swallowing back a tide of nervousness, she tore it open. Unfolding the telegram, she read the few lines once, twice, and then a third time.

Surprise and relief flickered to life inside her.

"What is it?"

"Great-uncle Steven died," she said.

"Again?" Simmons commented wryly.

She should feel bad, she thought, almost guilty about her lack of grief. But in her defense, she hadn't seen Steven Hightower since she was eight years old. Just before he disappeared somewhere out west. There'd been no word from him and the suspicion was that he had died years ago.

Apparently, though, he not only hadn't died, but had prospered. "He's left me half-interest in a business. A hotel," she added, still not quite willing to believe her good fortune.

"Mr. Steven?" Simmons said. "A hotelier?"

"Apparently," she told him, waving the wire for emphasis.

"And where might this illustrious inn be located?"

"A place called Rimshot, Nevada." She lifted her gaze to meet Simmons's.

"Rimshot. Very cosmopolitan," he said thoughtfully.

"It's in the west."

"I deduced that much."

"It's warm in the west," she said quietly.

"It's reputed to be warm in hell," Simmons pointed out. "But I wouldn't recommend living there."

But she wasn't listening.

To be *warm* again. Wouldn't that be lovely? To move someplace new. To begin again, where no one knew her. In a flash she remembered everything she'd ever read of the west and her mind conjured up images of starry skies, echoing with the cry of a coyote. She smiled to herself, then a moment later, frowned. Hadn't she only last night wished that she might have a new start somewhere? Hmm. She looked down at the telegram. Coincidence? It had to be. She'd been wishing for a job, not a hotel in the western desert.

Laughing silently at her own foolishness, Phoebe dismissed the ridiculous notion of wishes coming true. It didn't matter how or why this had happened. All that mattered was that it had.

"Well, Simmons?" she said, looking up at him. "Are you ready to be a cowboy?"

Those eyebrows of his arched high on his forehead as he said, "The proper response to that question, according to the dime novels you used to hide from your father, is, I believe, 'Let's mossy along.'"

Her lips twitched. "I believe the right term would be *mosey*."

"How foolish of me." He inclined his head before turning abruptly for the stairs. "I'll just go to the attic and retrieve your trunks."

She watched him go, then turned her gaze back to the wire that had just changed her world.

When she was a little girl, she'd secretly read everything she could find about the wild west and cowboys and Indians. She used to dream every night about driving a wagon into the great frontier. It wasn't until she was much older that she'd finally let go of those dreams in the face of reality.

And now *this*.

It was a chance she'd never thought to have.

To forge a new life.

A life that would be built beneath the hot, glittering sun of the western sky.

ONE MONTH LATER . . .

Snow flurries dusted through a small stand of pines, whipped around the bare, pale trunks of the aspens, then shot down Main Street, rattling windows and sending the citizens running for their hearths.

Riley Burnett watched them go with a shake of his head. What they were running from, it was taking all his self-control to keep from running *to*. How many times had he tracked some outlaw through blizzards? How many nights had he spent huddled under an overhang of rock beside a tiny speck of fire? Damn, it had been good. Being on his own. In the wide open. Not a soul to be seen in miles of riding. Pitting his own strength against nature and winning time and again.

He grimaced tightly. Now look at him. A townsman. A shopkeeper in the very town where he'd grown up. The very town he'd escaped from as soon as he was able. Standing in a train station, waiting for what was left of the world as he'd known—and enjoyed—it to come crashing to an end.

A small hand tugged on his pants leg and he reluctantly looked down into the tiny, upturned face of the daughter he hardly knew. A stirring of affection warred with the completely helpless feeling that hadn't quite left him since the first time he'd laid eyes on her.

And mixed in with all that was a small worm of doubt. Every once in a while, he caught himself examining little Becky's features, trying to decide if her mother had been telling the truth when she'd named Riley as the father of her baby.

Lord knew, Tess hadn't had more than a nodding acquaintance with Truth during her lifetime. She'd always been more than willing and able to twist a story until it suited her. He just didn't know what to believe. And he cursed his dead wife for that doubt.

"Up!" Becky demanded, lifting both arms to emphasize her request.

But he supposed Truth didn't really matter when it came down to everyday living. By law, Becky was his daughter. His responsibility. After all, it wasn't her fault that her ma had been the town slut.

Becky frowned at him, her pale eyebrows drawing down over eyes as blue as his own. But then, he reminded himself, Tess had had blue eyes too, so that was no proof.

As far as he'd noticed, the child didn't have much of a vocabulary. In the month or so she'd been with him, she hadn't even come up with a word for him yet. And he couldn't really blame her. Almost three years old, she'd been torn away from the only people she knew, her grandparents, and left with a man who didn't even know how to comb her hair without making her screech like a scalded cat.

Which, he told himself, accounted for the fact that her hair now looked like a rat's nest. Any time Riley came at her with a brush, she set to crying and squalling loud enough to wake the dead. So he just didn't brush it at all anymore.

"Up," she said again.

Sighing, Riley bent down and scooped her up. Cradling her easily with one strong arm hooked beneath her bottom, he stared into her eyes. "You're every bit as stubborn as me, aren't ya?"

She threw her head back and giggled.

"Maybe your ma wasn't lying after all," he muttered and wished to high heaven he could know for sure. But Tess hadn't been a woman to let a marriage license slow her down any. Every time Riley was out on the hunt, she'd been doing some hunting of her own. And he heard about it all from the town gossips.

She smacked him with one little fist.

"You got your ma in you too, I expect," he added thoughtfully.

Tess Harris hadn't been the easiest woman in Rimshot. But she'd damn sure been the prettiest. When they were growing up, Tess had every fella for miles in any direction buzzing around her. Riley had had to whittle the crowd down one by one until, finally, he won her favor and they celebrated in a hayloft. Then she'd turned up pregnant and between her folks and his, there'd been no way to avoid a wedding.

Riley grimaced tightly in memory. He hadn't been the first man to take Tess to a hayloft, he remembered. Nor had he been the last.

But then Becky was born and everything really went to hell. Tess let him know she wasn't interested in a squalling brat and was even less interested in a part-time husband. So Riley gave her what money he had and told her to get out. By that time, he was tired of being married to the town scandal. Her folks up and moved to San Francisco, so Riley's folks took their granddaughter in.

And if his parents hadn't been killed in a carriage accident a couple of months ago, everything would have gone on just fine and dandy.

Of course, if he'd never jumped into that haystack with Tess, then none of this would have happened at all, and he'd be a happy man, alone and out on the hunt.

In his arms, Becky shivered and he shook his head at the too-thin coat she wore. He'd been meaning to get her something warmer.

He yanked the collar of her coat up higher around her neck, wrapped his arms around the toddler, and glared at the stationmaster. Too cheap to throw another log into the wood-burning stove, old man Malloy kept his station damn near as cold as the outside.

Then Riley looked back at the little girl he hardly knew. And what did that say about him? His own daughter . . . probably . . . the only family he had left, and she was as much a stranger to him as the damned female coming in on today's train.

"So, Burnett," Malloy called from behind the safety of his desk, "the new boss arrivin' today?"

Riley shot him a long, slow look. "Partner," he corrected. "Not boss."

"Sure, sure. That's what I meant."

Partner. Hell, Riley didn't want a damned partner. He worked alone. He *liked* alone.

"Never thought I'd see the day when some female would be runnin' our saloon," Malloy said with a laugh, clearly enjoying himself.

"She'll be running the hotel. The saloon's mine," Riley told him. And once she hit town, he planned on offering to buy his new partner out. He didn't have the slightest idea why Steve would give half the business to a relative he hadn't seen in years, but he damned sure wasn't going to have to pay the price for Steve's sudden burst of family feeling.

A distant whistle caught his attention and Riley turned to look through the windows down the line of track. Didn't do him any good, though. Between the dirt clinging to those windows and the powdery wall of white flying past, he could hardly see the end of the platform.

"Right on time," Pete Malloy muttered as he stomped past Riley on his way to the double doors. "Durned if we ain't gettin' better and better at keepin' to the schedules. You just wait and see," he went on, "Rimshot's growin' so fast, we're gonna have trains stoppin' here two, three times a day."

Great. Not bad enough he was trapped in this damn town, Riley thought. But it was growing so fast, in a year or two it'd probably be a real *city*.

Another long, mournful blast of the coming train's whistle followed this statement and Riley blew out a disgusted breath. What the hell had he ever done to Steve Hightower that had merited *this*? But he knew the answer to that. Five years ago, he'd helped Steve out of a tight spot and, in gratitude, the older man had made him a silent partner. Riley had never figured on actually running the place.

And he damned sure wasn't interested in working with some spinster from St. Louis. But hell, no city woman was going to be able to stand the rough life she'd find in Rimshot. As that thought settled firmly in his mind, he smiled to himself. Why, he'd probably have no trouble at all convincing Phoebe Hightower to sell out her share of the business. Chances were pretty damn good she'd be *begging* him to buy her out inside a week.

Then all he'd need was the money to do it.

Lord knew, his folks hadn't left much money. And after selling his father's tailoring shop to a new fella from back East, there'd been just about enough to order in some fine new whiskey for the saloon. Just like always, cash money was scarce and, though he'd managed to hold on to some of his marshal's pay over the years, it wasn't enough to throw a party over.

But maybe he wouldn't have to *buy* out his new partner. He chuckled and the little girl in his arms echoed the sound. "Well, now, Becky," he murmured as he tugged her woolen jacket closer around her, "we'll just make sure Miss Hightower gets a good long look at the town, then sit back and wave good-bye as she hightails it out of here."

"Bye-bye?" Becky repeated and wiggled five little fingers at him.

" 'At's right."

The small wooden building shook and trembled as the train roared alongside. White clouds of steam rose up around the engine and mixed with the snow flurries that had seemed to thicken some in the last few minutes. A last scrape of metal on metal as the engineer set the brake and then Pete Malloy was pulling on his jacket and opening the station door.

A blast of cold air twisted into the room as if it had been waiting for its chance to get inside. Riley grumbled, tightened his hold on Becky, and stepped into the wind-whipped whiteness.

His cheeks stung with cold and he thought for a minute about taking Becky back to the relative warmth of the station house. But the thought of leaving the child to wander around on her own was worse than the idea of carrying her through the cold, so he didn't.

Marching quickly along the wooden walkway, he glanced up at the train doors as he passed. Only a few people were getting off the train and he didn't figure he'd have much trouble identifying his new partner.

A big-city spinster couldn't be that hard to spot.

In fact, Riley'd done some speculating on just what Phoebe Hightower might look like. In his mind's eye, he'd painted a picture of a small, cronelike woman, staring at the world from behind a thick pair of spectacles and jumping at every loud noise.

"Ah," a man said in a clipped British accent. "The desert."

"Very funny, Simmons," a woman snapped.

Riley chuckled and kept walking closer to the voices drifting to him out of the snow.

"Wear your hat, miss," the Englishman warned sternly. "Mustn't get sunstroke."

A real funny fella, Riley thought.

"Simmons," the woman said, "could you wait until we're out of the weather before starting this conversation?"

"Of course, miss."

What was a prissy-sounding fella like that doing in Rimshot? Riley wondered absently as he continued along the platform.

"Where do you suppose the hotel is?" the woman asked and Riley's steps faltered slightly.

"I doubt we'll have trouble locating it, miss," the Englishman answered.

Suddenly, as if wiped away by a giant, unseen hand,

the snow flurries died, giving Riley a clear view of the woman he'd been listening to.

Lifting the hem of her dress clear of the platform, she drew in a long, deep breath, as if finishing a race. The ugliest hat he'd ever seen, some kind of straw with lavender ribbons and a stuffed bird on the brim, sat atop upswept brown hair. A long gray cape covered the rest of her right down to her ankles, but it was her face that caught his interest. There was an eagerness in her expression as she raked the small, unimpressive station with a pair of interested, sharp blue eyes that didn't sit at all well with Riley.

And when those blue eyes landed on him, he knew. He was never sure just how he knew. But in that one instant, he was certain that *this* woman was his new partner.

Silently, he cursed Steve Hightower to a long, uncomfortable eternity in hell.

She didn't look away, merely held his gaze with hers as if waiting for him to answer a question she hadn't asked.

"Miss Phoebe Hightower," he finally said, already dreading her confirmation.

"Why, yes," she said, driving the last nail into his coffin. "I am."

"Figures." He hefted little Becky a bit higher in his arms and wondered why he'd been blessed with the only spinster in the world who didn't look as she was supposed to. Her pale skin was dusted with color, whether from the cold or excitement, he didn't know. She had a wide, handsome mouth and she held herself straight as an arrow, marking her as taller than the average female. But it was those eyes of hers that demanded attention. Even as he watched, their color shifted, from the soft blue of a summer sky to the dark, swirling violet of deepening dusk.

Damn.

"You," she said, one dark eyebrow lifted into a high arch, "I take it, are Mr. Burnett?"

"That's me." Though he wished to high heaven he was anyone else at that moment.

"A pleasure to meet you," she said. "If you'll help with my bags, we can be away and out of this snow."

"Fine." He stomped across the few feet of space separating them, handed Becky to the woman, and said, "You take her."

Clearly startled, Phoebe held the child at arm's length, looking as surprised as she would have if someone had tossed her a snake.

"Perhaps it would be better—" she started to say.

"Lady, I can't carry your bags and Becky too," he snapped, reaching for a carpetbag, only to have his hand slapped aside by a man who looked old enough to be his father. "Mister," Riley said quickly, "you best go about your business and leave me to mine."

"Ah, western hospitality," the older man said in that sharp English accent Riley'd already heard. "As warm as your desert sun."

"Simmons," Phoebe warned.

Riley straightened up and looked at the man.

"Mr. Burnett," Phoebe said, and he glanced at her. "This is my butler, Simmons."

"Your *butler*?"

Riley simply stared at her. A city woman in Rimshot was hard enough to believe. A city woman who traveled with her own butler was really going to make news.

"Mr. Burnett," Phoebe said with enough exasperation to let him know it wasn't the first time.

"Yeah?"

"Perhaps it would be best if we continued our conversation out of the snow? Your daughter appears to be turning blue."

Riley shot a look at Becky and noticed her lips trembling. What kind of father didn't notice that his own child was freezing to death? As he stood there, Phoebe

Hightower, clutching Becky to her, started down the platform, headed for the station house. Grumbling under his breath, Riley bent down and managed to get three of the heavy bags away from the butler before turning and marching right after her.

Determined to reach her destination as quickly as possible, Phoebe marched through the tiny station, out the front door, and onto the street. She looked around her briefly before spotting the two-story building with the word *hotel* scrawled across the front in faded red paint. Then she stepped off the boardwalk into the muddy slush that sucked and pulled at her shoes with every step. It was as if even the ground were trying to keep her from going any farther.

By the time they reached the Horseshoe Hotel and Saloon, Phoebe was exhausted. Not only from the three-day-long train ride and the walk in the snow, but from the fear of dropping the child she held so carefully.

She'd seldom been around children and on those rare occasions when she had, she'd never actually held one. Yet, the child was blissfully unaware of Phoebe's fears. The girl snuggled in close, burying the top of her head beneath Phoebe's chin in a way that felt somehow . . . right.

More right than anything else had so far.

She'd wanted warmth. And come to the so-called desert to find it. Yet, as Simmons had rushed to point out, she'd been greeted by a snowstorm and was colder now than she'd been in St. Louis. The first glimpse of her partner had not reassured her in the least.

A big man, he wore a black hat pulled low over his eyes and a heavy coat that only added to his imposing size. His mouth was a grim slash across his face and even the child he had held in his arms hadn't been enough to mask the vague sense of danger that surrounded him. Plus, she suspected he was no happier with her than she'd been with him.

His expression surly, he'd looked at her as though he'd

expected her to sprout horns. And the way he'd thrust his child at her as if the girl were a box of groceries . . . Feeling the first flicker of indignation blossom in the bottom of her stomach, Phoebe fed the small bud by taking a good look at said child.

The girl was dressed in a coat more worn than Phoebe's own cape. And her *hair*. Frowning, her gaze swept across the top of the girl's head, noting every snarl and tangle. The poor thing looked as though she hadn't been near a hairbrush in weeks. Didn't the man even give his daughter *cursory* attention?

Apparently not.

The little girl turned her tiny, heart-shaped face up and looked at her through milky blue eyes. A surge of gentleness rippled through Phoebe and even as it did, she tried to distance herself from it. Instinctively, she knew she was going to need all of her wits about her in the next few minutes. Best not to have them muddied with warm, cuddly thoughts about this poor, clearly neglected child.

With that thought in mind, she bent down and set the little girl gently on the floor. When she straightened up again, she took her first, real look at the property Uncle Steven had bequeathed her.

It was almost enough to have her running back to the train station.

She shuddered violently and clutched desperately at the folds of her cloak. As her fingers grabbed hold and squeezed at the frayed fabric, Phoebe forced herself to take it all in.

Faded wallpaper adorned the walls. It appeared to have once been patterned paper, but now, even the color was indistinguishable. Stained by cigar smoke and heaven only knew what else, there were occasional bare patches and even one or two long strips of paper that had tried to escape the wall they'd been slapped against.

A wall of windows fronted on what she supposed was the main street and her gaze snapped unerringly to the one broken pane, where a sliver of glass trembled under the force of the wind pushing past it.

Through a wide double door, she could see a larger room and she crossed the floor to peer inside. This, then, was the tavern. At least a dozen tables were sprinkled around the big room. The few customers seated at those tables stared at her in obvious curiosity. She nodded absently to them and continued her inspection. On one wall was a long bar behind which a large, beefy-looking man stood, eyeing her warily. As well he might, she told herself hotly. The only thing that appeared to have seen a dust rag in recent times was the mirror hanging behind the bar, reflecting the images of the bottles lined up neatly in front of it.

Disappointment welled inside her. Somehow, she'd expected so much more. First the weather had disappointed her—who would have expected snow in the desert? Then her new partner. And now finally, her inheritance itself.

The word *hotel* had conjured up images of fine buildings with elegant furnishings; she'd even imagined a quiet *salon* adjoining the hotel where gentlemen would retire with brandy and cigars after a fine meal in the hotel restaurant. She looked down at the sawdust-covered floor of the saloon and just managed to smother a sigh.

She should have known better. Hadn't she read all about western saloons? But still, one would have thought that in all the years since she'd read those dime novels, some positive changes might have taken place.

Then again, she told herself, it was a place to start. To forge her new beginning. To bury her past and look to the future. Her gaze dropped to the layer of grime on the closest table. As a matter of fact, she could simply gather up the accumulated dirt off the furniture and use *it* to bury the past. There was certainly more than enough to accomplish the task.

A bustle of movement and noise rose up and Phoebe turned toward the double doors. As she watched, Simmons entered the dimly lit saloon, followed closely by Riley Burnett.

Simmons stopped dead just across the threshold and muttered, "Good gad."

Mr. Burnett hadn't taken three steps before he dropped her luggage with casual disregard, then fixed his hard gaze on her.

"What have you got in those? Bricks?"

"Books," she replied.

He snorted. "Figures."

"Good *great* gad," Simmons whispered and Riley turned to look at the butler's shocked expression.

When he was facing her again, Riley asked, "Since you didn't bother to wait for me, how'd you know where to find the place?"

"It wasn't difficult," she told him. "This *is* the only hotel in town." Of course, there couldn't have been much reason to have more than one hotel. The entire main street was only long enough to boast about a dozen storefronts, not counting the tiny church huddled apologetically at the end of the street.

"She does have a point, Riley," someone in the saloon pointed out.

"Ah," Simmons noted quietly. "A champion."

Riley frowned first at the butler and then at the speaker, but Phoebe spared the slight man a nod of the head and he actually blushed to the roots of his swiftly receding hairline.

Yanking his black hat off, Riley crumpled the brim in his hand and stalked across the room toward her. "We need to talk."

She tilted her head back, to get her first good look at the man she'd be working with from now on. Great thunder, he was big. His blue eyes bored into hers and Phoebe told herself to stand firm. Her gaze drifted across his strong jaw and firm chin even as her mind warned her to begin this partnership on an equal footing. She noted the way his blond hair brushed the top of his shirt collar in back and reminded herself that she was a woman alone. Riley Burnett was clearly not an easygoing, good-humored man. She'd yet to see him smile. Perhaps, though, he was hoping to intimidate her. And if so, he mustn't succeed. It was up to her to ensure that this partnership worked. To see to it that he treated her not as a woman, but as a businessperson.

Her gaze finally met his again and she felt a tiny, almost imperceptible frisson of something extraordinary weaken her knees. She ignored it.

"Yes, we do need to talk, Mr. Burnett," she said, squaring her shoulders. "There are several points we need to discuss."

"You bet there are."

"About the changes that will have to be made."

He looked at her strangely. "Like what?"

She heard the scrape of chair legs on the floor and knew every customer in the saloon was leaning in, listening avidly. "Well . . ." she hedged a bit since she didn't really want to talk to him in front of an audience. "To begin, we might repair the broken windows."

"Lady," he said, folding his arms across a remarkably broad chest, "you haven't even been here five minutes and you think you can tell *me* what needs to be done?"

It was the tone of his voice more than his words that annoyed her. Dismissive. Patronizing. She replied in kind. "Apparently, I have to. Since as you've just pointed out, you've been here longer than I and you obviously haven't noticed."

Barely muffled laughter rose up and was quickly hushed.

"Patience," Simmons muttered.

Phoebe nodded halfheartedly. She wasn't at all sure that patience would be a virtue around Mr. Riley Burnett.

Riley's features tightened and he shoved one hand through his hair. Then deliberately, he turned his back on her and stalked across the room to the bar.

"Mick," he ordered. "I need a drink."

"Beer?" the barman asked, flicking a quick look at Phoebe.

Then Riley, too, looked at her before shaking his head and saying, "Nope. Whiskey. Strongest we got."

Chapter Three

❧

Riley picked up the glass and tossed the drink down his throat. A river of fire roared through him. His eyes watered and he told himself that one of the first changes to be made around here was stocking some decent whiskey. By the looks of his new partner, he was going to be needing it.

Setting the empty glass back onto the bar-top, he stared into the mirror at the familiar faces watching him. Every man in the bar was waiting with bated breath, hoping for a war and eager to be in the front row. Scowling, he let his gaze wander, first to the older man standing beside Phoebe. A *butler*, for God's sake. In Rimshot! And leaning against that butler's knee was Becky, her thumb in her mouth, her hair standing straight up, and her frown directed at him.

He sighed, then turned his head slightly to look at *her* reflection. Almost completely covered as Miss Hightower was by that long gray cape, she might have been carved out of stone. She was staring at him and he damned near shuddered with the force of her glare. Apparently, the new woman in his life disapproved of drinking. An unfortunate trait for the co-owner of a saloon.

Suddenly disgusted with the whole situation, he turned around to face her from across the room. Bracing his elbows on the bar behind him, he thought, *Damn* Steve

Hightower, for what had to be the hundredth time. Damn Fate for sending him back to this tiny little spit-in-the-road town. And damn all self-righteous spinsters who stuck their noses where they didn't belong.

Running this place and getting used to a daughter and being trapped in a town no bigger than a good-sized corral was going to be hard enough as it was. She didn't have to make it harder by looking at him through disapproving eyes. Hell, she didn't know him well enough to be disappointed in him. She could at least have the decency to wait a few weeks before deciding he was worthless.

"Mr. Burnett," she said, and every head in the room turned toward her.

And he *hated* being called *mister*. *Marshal* was all right. *Burnett* would do. Hell, even *son of a bitch* had its time and place. But *mister* was so goddamned 'upstanding town council member'–sounding.

Gritting his teeth against the thought of that particular indignity, he said tightly, "It's Riley."

She clasped her hands together neatly at the waist, giving every impression that she was calm and completely at ease. Riley wondered if he was the only one who noticed that her knuckles were white.

"Very well. Riley." She glanced briefly at the faces of the men looking at her before raising her gaze to meet his again. "Is there somewhere we could speak privately?"

Privately. Well, he could suggest they move up to one of the bedrooms that had, until a month ago, been occupied by several . . . *ladies*. But a former marshal could hardly be running a bordello, so now those girls were living in the old sawmill, and fixing it up real nice, Riley had heard. But though he would dearly love to see the expression on Miss Hightower's face when he suggested it, he told himself that purposely trying to get her goat wouldn't solve a damn thing.

And she was right. They did need to set a few things

straight, and he'd rather not do it in front of a bunch of curious cowboys.

So instead, he said, "Yeah." Then he walked the length of the bar to a closed door near the foot of the narrow stairway leading to the second floor. He paused, hand on the knob, and looked at her. "We'll talk in here," he said and stepped inside without bothering to see if she was going to follow him.

Of course she would follow him. Phoebe drew a long, slow, deep breath and tried to ignore the curious stares of the men watching her. She steeled her features into what she hoped was a blank mask. None of these strangers needed to know how disappointed she was in her new home. The Horseshoe Hotel and Saloon was not at all as she'd imagined—*hoped*—it would be. Even the weather had disappointed her. She'd been expecting bright sunlight and desert heat. Instead, a distinct draft shot up from between the floorboards and tickled her legs.

But disillusioned or not, it was all she had.

She'd sold her house in St. Louis and, after paying off the mortgage, had barely enough money left for her and Simmons's train fare west plus a bit extra. Not only was there nothing to go back to, but she had no way of getting there, even if there was.

No, this was her home now.

Phoebe slanted another surreptitious look around the room and, this time, refused to shudder. By heaven, Phoebe Hightower would not be beaten by a tumbledown building and a layer of dust thick enough to plow.

Squaring her shoulders and drawing herself up to her full height of five feet and seven and three-quarters inches, she half turned to Simmons and somehow managed a smile. "I won't be long."

"I'll be waiting," he said, with a glance down at the tiny girl clutching one of his pants legs. "Or rather," he amended with a shrug, "*we'll* be waiting."

Phoebe spared a quick glance at the child, who appeared to be as neglected as the Horseshoe Hotel. But at least the girl looked well fed. A ripple of shame trembled through her as she recalled the faces of the hungry children she'd seen on the day her larcenous career had come to an end.

And though she hadn't stolen a thing since, Phoebe hadn't been able to forgive herself for what she had so briefly become. How many children like this one had she deprived of food through her own desperation? How many people had gone hungry or cold because of what Phoebe had considered petty thievery?

A flush stained her cheeks. She felt the heat of it and hoped no one else would notice. What she'd done, she couldn't undo. She knew that. But staring down into Riley Burnett's daughter's eyes, Phoebe also struggled with a sense of indignation. She would never knowingly dismiss a child's needs. Yet . . . clearly, Mr. Burnett spent even less time with his daughter than he did with the business that seemed to be falling down around his ears.

The child looked like a waif.

"Miss Phoebe . . ."

Startled out of her thoughts, she looked at Simmons. He winked at her. "Tally-ho!"

Nodding, she smiled at him, silently thanking him for reminding her there was business at hand. If she and Mr. Burnett were indeed going to be partners, then it was imperative that said partnership got off to the proper start.

He needed to be aware right from the beginning that Phoebe Hightower would not be dismissed as easily as his daughter apparently had been. She reached up to straighten the brim of her one good hat before crossing the floor in a brisk walk. Her heels sounded out loudly against the wooden planks, since the layer of sawdust atop them was a thin one.

At the open doorway, she paused briefly before stepping into what turned out to be a room hardly bigger than a good-sized broom closet. But at least it was a *warm* broom closet, she told herself gratefully with a quick look at the potbellied stove in one corner. A blackened tin coffeepot sat atop its grimy surface, but the fire in its center reached out for her, welcoming her.

Phoebe stepped closer to the stove so that Riley could close the door behind her, and as she moved, she barked her shin against the leg of one of the two chairs squeezed into the "office." She winced and glanced quickly around the small space. Crammed into the impossibly tiny area were a desk and two chairs, all of which were nearly buried beneath mounds of loose paperwork. There was only one window and it was placed too high on the wall to see anything but the gray sky outside. Frowning slightly, Phoebe turned her head and caught sight of a particularly vulgar painting. A boldly voluptuous woman, tied down in a most uncomfortable-looking position atop a charging black horse.

Needless to say, the woman was naked.

Burnett cleared his throat and Phoebe tore her gaze away from the painting to look at him. "It was Steve's favorite picture," he said. "That's why he kept it in here. So he could look at it all the time."

Her estimation of late Uncle Steven slipped a bit. Then, searching for something to say, she remarked, "It's not a very good painting."

"Don't you recognize her?" he asked.

Deliberately, she looked back at the canvas and this time tried to concentrate on the woman's face. "Should I?" she asked at last.

Riley reached in front of Phoebe to straighten the hang of the picture. "That's Adah Isaacs Menken on her 'wild untamed stallion of Tartary.' "

"Tartary."

"Yep."

Phoebe shot him a look from the corner of her eye. He was smiling and watching for her reaction. "You're joking with me."

"No, ma'am," he said, waved her into a chair, then took a seat himself after tossing a pile of papers onto the already cluttered floor. "Ol' Adah cut quite a swath through the mining towns in the west. I once knew a man who stood in line eight hours just to watch that female get tied onto her horse and gallop off the stage."

Fascinated, Phoebe looked back at the painting. Miss Menken had been a pretty woman, but Phoebe had no doubts it was the woman's other notable attributes that had assured her success. She didn't remember ever reading about the woman, though. "She actually allowed herself to be tied, unclothed, to a wild horse?"

"Insisted on it, from what I hear." Riley propped one booted foot up on the corner of the desk, dislodging yet another pile of papers. "All part of a play she used to put on called *Mazeppa*." He leaned back, flicked a quick glance at the portrait again before chuckling. "If you can believe it, she was playing the part of young Prince Ivan."

A smile twitched at the corners of Phoebe's mouth despite her effort to prevent it. Her firm, no-nonsense, businesslike approach was rapidly dissolving, but she couldn't help it. "She played a man? Dressed, or rather, *un*dressed, like that?"

"And made herself quite a lot of money doin' it too."

Amazing, Phoebe thought. The western states truly were a world apart from the one she'd known. Why, a woman disrobing on the stage of the St. Louis Opera House would have been run out of town. Here, she was a popular performer. Strange how different two parts of the same country could be.

A small tingle of apprehension assailed her as she realized just how out of her depth she was in this place. And yet apparently, Uncle Steven had not only found a way to fit in here, but to thrive—so to speak. If he could do it, so could she.

And in this wide-open, apparently very tolerant country, she would have her chance at a new start. A chance to try and forget what circumstances had made of her in St. Louis. And to give thanks that no one, not even Simmons, knew what depths she had sunk to in order to survive.

Phoebe shot another glance at Miss Menken. The west was one place at least where a woman might run her own life. Make her own fortunes. And Phoebe intended to do just that—while remaining fully clothed, of course.

"Sit down, Miss Hightower," Riley said quietly. "Let's talk about this partnership thing."

She snapped out of her reveries instantly and turned to the chair he'd indicated a few minutes ago. Scooping up the papers haphazardly stacked on its seat, she dropped them onto the desk and sat down gingerly, half expecting the old chair to snap beneath her.

Riley lifted his other leg from the floor and crossed his feet at the ankles. He looked completely at ease here in this squalor and Phoebe almost resented it.

"Things have been kind of upside down here since Steve died," he said.

"For longer than that, by the looks of things," she said.

He nodded thoughtfully and began to rock his chair on its back legs. The screech of old wood straining stopped him in mid-rock and he slowly let the chair fall back to the floor. "Yeah, Steve wasn't much of a hand at the business end of things, was he?"

"Did you know Uncle Steven long?" Phoebe asked.

He looked at her. "About ten years, off and on. He made me a partner about five years back. Figured I'd always have a place to stay." He frowned thoughtfully. "Never actually planned on staying here permanent."

"You don't care for Rimshot?"

He grimaced slightly. "I grew up here, Miss Hightower. And as soon as I was old enough, I left here." He glanced around the room, then let his gaze drift back to her. "Came back occasionally to see family."

Family. His wife and child, no doubt.

"Then you didn't run the hotel with Uncle Steven?"

"Good God, no." Dropping his feet to the floor, Riley

leaned forward, bracing his elbows on his knees. "Hadn't been back in a couple of years when Steve died, leaving me the place."

"Half," she corrected quietly.

"Yeah," he said with a nod. "Half of this place. And that's what we've got to talk about, Miss Hightower."

The tone of his voice sent off little warning bells inside her mind. Phoebe braced herself and watched him. His clear blue eyes looked troubled and when he ran one hand tiredly over the rest of his sharply defined features, she was sure she wouldn't like what he had to say.

"This isn't going to work, y'know," he finally said, confirming her suspicion. "You and me. Here. Running this place together." He leaned back with a deceptively casual move and folded his hands atop his abdomen. Looking at her steadily, he asked, "Why don't you and your *butler* hop onto that train and go back where you belong?"

Where she belonged? Just where was that? she wondered. St. Louis? Where she had no home and no future? Only a past she was trying to bury? Or Rimshot, Nevada, where she clearly wasn't wanted and yet might be able to build a life of her own? The answer to those questions firmly in her mind, she said, "I belong here, Riley." It felt strange calling a veritable stranger by his first name, but he had insisted. "This . . . *hotel* is half mine. I intend to stay and work with you."

He shook his head slowly and let his gaze run over her thoroughly. "Ma'am, don't you be stubborn about this. You and me both know you have no business trying to run a saloon. Hell, excuse me, anybody with half an eye could see that."

"Be that as it may—" she started to say.

"Heck, I'm just learning how to do things myself," he admitted. "But at least I've *been* in good saloons. I know what they *should* be like."

"Good saloons?" she asked. "There are different types of saloons?"

"See? That's what I'm talkin' about!" He slapped the edge of the cluttered desktop for emphasis. "Miss Hightower—"

"Please call me Phoebe," she interrupted. After all, they were partners. Better that she establish that relationship right now.

"Fine. Phoebe, an unmarried lady like yourself doesn't know beans about saloons, admit it."

She sniffed. "Naturally, I would have to learn—"

"Too much," he finished for her. "And with both of us learning at the same time, nothing around here will work right."

This wasn't going at all well. Impatience nagging at her, she also began to notice that she had passed beyond warm to downright uncomfortable. Either the heat of the stove was making itself felt, or the temper she'd struggled for years to overcome was beginning to assert itself.

Hoping it was the former, she reached for her cape's clasp at the base of her throat. As Phoebe shrugged out of the worn but heavy material, she missed the look of stunned surprise that etched itself briefly on Riley's features.

He damn near toppled over in his chair. With that blasted gray cape off, her body was neatly outlined for anyone to see. And a figure like hers was going to be noticed.

Hell, it was like finding a rock, only to knock the dirt off it and recognize a lump of gold.

Riley almost laughed at the mental image he had had of Phoebe Hightower. Small, dried-up crone of a woman? This was more woman than he'd seen in years. *Ample* was the first word that leaped to mind. Tall, she was a little on the thin side but for her full, heavy breasts. Breasts that were enough to bring sweet dreams to any red-blooded man.

Or nightmares to the man forced to be her business partner.

Altogether, Phoebe Hightower wasn't at all what he'd

expected. Except for one thing. She was definitely, a city woman. And, like a lake trout thrown onto a dry bank, she had small chance of thriving in her new home. He'd seen the way she looked at the saloon. Like she was afraid there was dirt leaping off the floor to cling to her skirt. Well, fine. He'd be the first to admit that the place didn't look like much. What he didn't need was a city-bred female coming in and trying to run roughshod over everything just when he was trying to make sense of the new life he'd been tossed into.

No matter *what* she looked like.

"Riley," she said sharply, and from her tone, he guessed it wasn't the first time she'd called his name.

His attention snapped back to the moment at hand and, reluctantly, he lifted his gaze to meet hers.

"I don't know what you hope to accomplish by trying to drive me away," she said, her now-dark-blue eyes drilling into his. "But it won't work. I've come to stay and I've no intention of leaving."

"What if I buy you out?" He blurted out the question without even thinking it through. Suppose she took him up on it? What would he use for money? His bank account wouldn't tempt a self-respecting bank robber.

"I'm not interested," she said flatly.

"Phoebe," he said, leaning forward again, "if you'd just stop a minute, you'd admit that this is no place for a lady like you."

"Like me?" she repeated, one eyebrow lifting in a high arch.

"Yeah." For the first time, he noticed how fine her skin looked with a faint flush on it. Smooth. Soft. He shook himself and abruptly stood up. The softness of her skin was just another indication of the easy life she must have lived before coming here. A life that wouldn't have prepared her at all for what she'd find in high-desert Nevada.

Looking down at her, he told himself to keep his mind focused. Just like when he used to be on the hunt for some outlaw trying to lose him, he needed his concentration. "Rimshot ain't exactly St. Louis, in case you hadn't noticed."

"I noticed," she said and stood up to face him. "That's precisely what I like about it."

Perfect. Tall, he noted again, realizing that if he grabbed her and pulled her close, her head would rest comfortably on his shoulder. And he wouldn't be getting a crick in his neck from bending almost in half to kiss her either.

Kiss her?

Damn it.

He had to get her away from here.

From him.

"This is no place for you."

"That is up to me."

So much for good starts. "Damn it, Phoebe."

"There's no reason to resort to profanity."

He laughed out loud at that and had the satisfaction of seeing her eyes darken even further. "Honey, if one little *damn* upsets you, how're you going to stand a saloon full of drunks on a Saturday night?"

She stiffened and he could see what it cost her to say, "I don't have to approve of my customers to see that they're served well." Then, as an afterthought, she added, "And don't call me honey."

He inhaled sharply and blew the air out in a rush of impatience. "Phoebe, what is so all-fired important to you about this place?"

She lifted her chin and squared her shoulders, a movement that drew his attention once again to her truly magnificent breasts. Instantly, as if very aware of the direction of his gaze, she crossed her arms in front of her and tapped the toe of her shoe against the floor.

Slowly, leisurely, Riley lifted his gaze to meet hers. He smiled, letting her know that he knew she knew where he'd been looking and didn't mind in the slightest. If she was bound and determined to stay in Rimshot, then she'd damn well better get used to men looking at her.

Why the hell she was a spinster, he couldn't figure out. Unless of course, the smart men in St. Louis had decided that her prickly personality wasn't worth putting up with just to get at her delectable body.

He was losing focus again.

"Well, Phoebe?" he demanded. "*Why?*"

"Because," she said as she turned and snatched up her cape, "this is my home now. Every bit as much as it is yours."

Home.

Something he'd never really wanted and now resented the hell out of, she apparently wanted very much. Enough to put up with not only the Horseshoe itself, but him as well.

She stopped with her hand on the doorknob and glanced at him over her shoulder. "I'm curious."

"Naturally. You're a woman, aren't ya?"

She ignored that. "You said earlier that you're rarely in town. Even with a young daughter, you haven't been here in two years."

He stiffened slightly at the unspoken criticism. "So?"

"If you're never here, why do you care that I will be?"

"I won't be leaving again. I'm here for good." Or bad, he added silently.

One of her eyebrows lifted. "My sympathies to your wife."

A stab of something cold, hard, and ugly sliced at him. He met her gaze squarely. "My wife's dead."

Phoebe flopped down onto the mattress and her eyes widened at the resulting screech and groan of the bedsprings. When the noise had died away, she looked up at her butler and said, "Did we make a mistake coming here, to this . . . this . . ." Words failed her.

Simmons, who was never at a loss for words, finished her sentence for her. "Hellhole?"

In spite of her grim thoughts, Phoebe laughed and lay

back on the bed, one arm flung across her forehead. "It's awful, isn't it?"

Simmons shook the wrinkles from her gray dress then hung it in the armoire. "In a word," he said, *"yes."*

She turned her head to glance around her dismal room. Here, faded wallpaper in what had once been a truly garish sunflower pattern adorned the walls. Two grimy windows, naturally naked of curtains, fronted the main street, allowing in only a trickle of whatever daylight was left. A kerosene lamp stood on a rickety table beside the narrow bed. There was a washstand with a bowl, pitcher, and even a small oval mirror. The only other furniture was the armoire and a lone stuffed chair, drawn up close to a fireplace that now boasted a cherry blaze in its hearth.

As grim as this place was, it was still better than St. Louis and her life of quiet desperation.

Desperation. Was that something she had in common with her new partner? The memory of his cold, flat voice as he'd said, *My wife is dead,* rose up in her mind. He'd looked as though heavy shutters had slid down over his eyes. He'd been standing within a foot of her and yet she'd felt the sudden, wide distance separating them and recognized it for what it was.

He, too, was shielding his past.

Perhaps that was for the best. If neither of them encouraged familiarity, they would both be safe.

Looking straight up, Phoebe sighed and closed her eyes so she wouldn't have to see the water stains on the ceiling.

"Simmons?" she said. "There's something I didn't tell you before we left home." Even as she said it, she wondered if she should be telling him now either.

"What's that?" he asked and lifted her deep blue dress from the trunk.

She took a deep breath and said it before she could think better of it. "I think I *wished* us here."

"What?"

Phoebe opened one eye and saw him staring at her. No, she shouldn't have said anything. But she hadn't been able to help herself. Ever since receiving that telegram the morning after her wish, she'd been thinking about the tinker and the four wishes he'd granted her. Foolish maybe. But the coincidence of inheriting this place was just too much.

"You *wished* us here?" he repeated.

"I think so."

Propping herself up on one elbow, she watched Simmons's face as she briefly told him about her encounter with the tinker and her subsequent wish. When she was finished, he didn't laugh outright, but she was sure she saw a sparkle of amusement in his eyes.

"And you believe our arrival in Rimshot is due to your wish for a new life someplace warm."

"Well . . ." When you said it out loud like that, it did sound ridiculous. "How else do you explain it?"

"Bad luck?" he inquired and hung the blue dress up in the armoire as well.

"So you hate it here too."

"I haven't been here long enough to hate it," he reminded her. "However, I have already formed a powerful dislike for the place."

"What are we going to do?" she asked in a whisper.

"We're going to work," he told her gently. "Your hotel doesn't look like much now. But that can be fixed."

Looking into his eyes, she found the approval she'd always counted on. "You're right, Simmons. There's no reason on earth why the Horseshoe can't become a first-rate hotel."

Something small scurried across the floor at just that moment and Phoebe quickly drew her legs up onto the mattress.

A mouse? Or was it *mice*?

"Oh, Simmons," she said, hugging her knees to her chest. "Why wasn't I more specific with that wish? We might have ended up on a tropical island somewhere."

"Oh, my, yes, much better," he said wryly, with a glance at the floor. "Snakes, bugs, Barbary pirates."

Now Phoebe laughed. "There aren't pirates anymore."

"I daresay we'd have found some."

She nodded slowly. "Probably."

Simmons sighed and sat down on the edge of the bed. He gave her hand a pat, then said, "Miss Phoebe, a wish is not what brought us here."

"Then what?"

He shrugged. "Fate?"

"I suppose you're right," she said and pushed herself into a sitting position. "After all, I wished to be warm and it's snowing here."

"True," Simmons said and stood up to finish unpacking. "But I have a feeling that when summer finally arrives in this benighted country, you'll have more warmth than if you had wished to take up residence in hell."

"C'mon now," Riley said quietly. "Lay down and close your eyes."

It was a struggle every night. He couldn't really blame the child. Couldn't be easy falling asleep to the sounds of piano music and loud laughter drifting up the stairs from the saloon. But he'd thought she would get used to the noise. Here it had been more than a month and his daughter—Lord, it felt strange even to *think* that word— still made a battle out of bedtime.

Tonight was no different.

Riley sat on the edge of her bed and winced when a particularly loud, raucous laugh seemed to roll up through the floorboards to echo in the room. What kind of father was he anyway? Trying to bring up a kid over a saloon?

Becky's giggle brought him out of his thoughts. He looked down at the spot where she'd been only a moment before to find her bed empty.

The giggle sounded again and Riley turned his head toward the door just in time to see Becky, her tattered blue blanket tucked under her left arm, scoot through the doorway headed for the stairs.

"Damn it," he muttered. "Not again." Resigned now to the coming chase, he stood up and hurried after the quickly moving little girl. "Becky! You get back here right now."

She laughed again, the delicate sound somehow carrying over the hullaballoo from downstairs, and Riley groaned. Nearly every night, he ended up having to chase her up and down stairs and all over the damn saloon and hotel. Just that afternoon, he learned that the boys in the saloon were now taking bets on how long it would take him to catch up with the tiny cyclone at bedtime.

Becky was halfway down the stairs and gaining ground with every step. Amazing how fast the little devil was when she wanted to be.

Riley dove down the staircase after her and tried to ignore the shouts from his audience of nearly drunk cowhands.

"Toss a rope at her," one man called.

"Hell, he can't hogtie a child," another voice said.

"Look at that little thing go!"

"Get a move on, Riley," someone shouted. "My money's on you!"

He sent a quick scowl at the crowded room. Damn fools had nothing better to do?

"Feeb!" Becky shouted as she hit the bottom of the stairs and turned for the door leading into the hotel.

Feeb? Riley hurried after her. The kid wouldn't say *Papa* but she called for Phoebe? The woman hadn't been in town a full day and already his daughter liked her better than him?

Blast that female anyway. Didn't he have enough problems?

He raced through the doorway into the hotel and came to a sliding stop at the foot of the stairs. Taking a tight grip on the banister's newel post, he looked up and saw

Phoebe Hightower, halfway down the stairs, his daughter perched on one hip.

Becky laughed delightedly at her little joke.

Riley met Phoebe's gaze and saw that even she was enjoying him playing the fool.

"Lose something?" she inquired sweetly.

His teeth ground together. "Only my mind, ma'am. Only my mind."

Chapter Four

❦

If ever a man looked to be completely at the end of his rope, it was Riley Burnett. His daughter, however, seemed to be enjoying herself. Phoebe shot a quick look at the little girl's face and felt her heart twist slightly at the impish smile that met her.

A beautiful child, she thought, despite her poor hair. Knotted and tangled, it stood out in odd tufts from her head like a misshapen blond halo. Too, the girl's nightdress was nearly threadbare and her naked toes looked blue with cold.

"Thanks for catchin' her," Riley said, forcing Phoebe's attention from the girl in her arms to the man at the foot of the stairs.

Catching her hadn't been a problem. The child had come running directly to her, then practically flew into Phoebe's arms. "Why was she running away from you?"

Riley climbed the steps and stopped just below Phoebe. "When she can't fall asleep, she likes to run me ragged for a while."

Becky giggled again and the sound seemed to ripple through Phoebe in a pleasant wave of sensation. Then, Riley's words sunk in.

"Sleep? But she came in from the saloon—" She broke off and looked at him, appalled. "You don't mean to say you're trying to make her sleep through all that noise?"

"Look, lady," Riley said and reached for his daughter. Phoebe twisted Becky away from him and he sighed, nodding his head. "Fine. I know she don't belong there. But where else could I put her?" he demanded. "An empty hotel? I have to run that saloon, remember? How could I hear her if she was way over here by herself?"

All right, that made sense, she admitted silently. "But," she asked, "how can you hear her over that noise anyway?"

The clashing sounds from the room next door almost seemed to grow to emphasize her point.

"I don't know," he said. "But I do. So why don't you just hand her over and I'll take her back to bed?"

Phoebe frowned at him even as Becky's fingers tightened their grip on her shoulder. It wasn't any of her business how Riley Burnett raised his child. Besides, since learning of his wife's death, she had a bit more sympathy for him. He was obviously out of his depth, but at least he was trying.

A burst of wild laughter shot through the open doorway. The noise was going to take getting used to for all of them.

"Why don't you let her stay here tonight?" she suggested. "With me. Surely the hotel will be quieter than the saloon."

Riley looked at her long and hard. He hadn't expected this and didn't know what to make of the offer now that it had been made. Sure, it'd be a sight easier on him if he knew that Becky was safe and there was somebody close by in case of an emergency. But damn it, he didn't want to be obliged to his new partner in any way.

He was a man used to taking care of his own problems, sorting out his own troubles, and it came hard to accept help from anyone. Let alone Phoebe Hightower. A woman he was still trying to figure out how to get rid of.

A kicked spittoon hurtled through the open doorway behind him and he whirled around to watch the scratched-up brass object scuttle along the floor before it smacked into the far wall. Its dark brown contents splashed over the faded wallpaper, then spilled onto the floor as the spittoon toppled onto its side.

Son of a bitch, he thought. This is what his life had come to? Playing nursemaid to a bunch of drunks who thought nothing of breaking up a place just for the sheer hell of it?

For the thousandth time in the month since giving up his badge for a damn bar apron, Riley cursed Fate for landing him in this situation. What he wouldn't give to be able to hop onto his horse and ride hell for leather across the desert. To lose himself in high country or on the Texas plains where a man could ride for days and never see a living soul.

What the hell was he doing here? This wasn't working. None of it was. He couldn't take proper care of a child. Hell, he couldn't even keep peace in his own saloon!

A single gunshot cracked in the air. Furious cursing sprang up in its wake and following that came the distinct sounds of furniture breaking and the loud, scuffling thuds of a fight in progress.

Anger blistered inside Riley. Anger at himself. The saloon. His customers. Becky's mother, Tess. Fate. And at the woman whose gaze was boring a hole into his back at that very moment. Frustration rolled through his body like a boulder slamming its way down a steep incline. It picked up speed steadily until his whole body fairly shook with it.

Why was he even *trying* to do this? Everybody in town knew he wasn't up to it. He'd heard the whispers. The local gossips were laying bets on just how long he'd stick it out—and the long shot was another month.

Damn it, he'd never signed on for this. And pretending different wasn't going to change anything. He could play at the role of father. Businessman. But at heart, he knew this life wasn't for him. If he had any sense at all, he'd quit now.

Quit. Even the word turned his stomach. But didn't Becky deserve better than a half-assed father?

Another gunshot exploded.

His teeth clenched against a rising tide of sudden fury, he swiveled his head to look at Phoebe. He wasn't surprised to see her expression mirroring the shock she felt for this place, the men in the saloon . . . and no doubt, him.

And she was right, damn it. Hell, everybody in town was right. He had no business being in charge of an innocent child. *This* was where Riley Burnett belonged. In a bar fight, with drunks, thieves, and no-accounts. *This* was the world he felt comfortable in.

And maybe it was time he just admitted that to himself and did what was best for all of them.

"All right," he said. "You keep Becky here tonight. I'll clear out the rowdies from inside before they tear the place down around our ears."

"Alone?" she asked, clearly stunned. "But that's foolishness," she said, taking one step down the stairs toward him. "Someone in there has a gun."

"Phoebe," he said, already turning and starting back down the stairs, "*everybody* in there has a gun."

"Except you," she pointed out quickly.

At the foot of the stairs, he turned and looked up at her for a long, thoughtful moment. Crashes, thuds, and the sounds of splintering wood rent the air.

He glanced into the melee and back again to her. "Phoebe, this is what I'm good at," he said, and somewhere inside him, he regretted that piece of truth. But before he could examine that feeling, he turned and stalked into the center of the barroom brawl.

Someone threw a punch at him and he instinctively ducked just before driving his own fist into his opponent's fleshy belly. Air rushed from the man's lungs and he dropped face-first onto the floor. But Riley didn't pause to watch him fall.

Instead, he turned to the next man, throwing himself

into the battle like a man possessed. He moved from one combatant to the next with a mindless fury that fed on the frustration that had been building inside him for the past month or more.

Fractured chairs flew through the air above his head. Battle raged around him and for the first time in too long, Riley felt good. In control. He took a hard left on his chin that snapped his head back and set bells to ringing in his ears. But it also set off the powder keg inside him. He gave himself up to the raw, powerful rush of strength and eagerness that swept through him.

From the corner of his eye, he saw Mick, his bartender, wading into the crowd swinging a thick branch and sending men sprawling. Then the bartender yelled a warning and Riley turned, bringing his fist up to flatten a man coming in at him low and mean. The force of the blow rattled up the length of his arm, but he shook it off and made a grab for a short fella about to throw half a chair through the front window. Wrenching the man around, Riley tossed him into the middle of the fight, then turned again, looking for more. Needing more.

He'd had every intention of simply trying to stop the fight. But like every other saloon fracas he'd ever seen, what had begun as a small disagreement had quickly become a free-for-all, where no one man could stop it without jumping right in and becoming a part of it.

Which worked out fine for him, tonight of all nights. Tonight, when the constrictions of his new life had tightened around him until he felt as though he were smothering in the close confines of four walls and a roof.

Telling himself this was the only way, Riley plunged on, charging into the worst of it and laying low anyone who had the misfortune of coming at him. A couple of heavy blows shook him to the soles of his feet, but he shook them off, remembering other fights, other battles.

He fought until there was no one left to face him. Until the few men left standing were swaying on their feet, exhausted both from the fight and too much bad whiskey.

It was all over.

Breathing hard, Riley turned in a slow circle, letting his gaze slide over what was left of his saloon. The fallen were sprawled all across the floor and over tables and upended chairs. The piano lay on its side, broken whiskey bottles littered the floor—the shards of wet glass shining in the reflection of the overhead lamps—and the mirror behind the bar was shattered.

He looked at his own mirror image, crisscrossed with spidery cracks in the glass, and laughed. Instantly, pain shot through his split lip. Seven years' bad luck, he told himself and wasn't surprised in the least. He lifted one hand and touched the corner of his mouth gingerly. He didn't even glance at the smear of blood he wiped away.

"Good thing the theriff'th outa town," Mick said. "Theemths to me thith here fight might get uth all locked up."

Chuckling, Riley asked, "What the hell's wrong with you?"

"Ah," Mick said, disgusted. "One of them fellath thneaked up on me and got in a thucker punch. Bit my tongue near clean off. Now it'h all thwole up."

Riley laughed out loud, then took a deep breath before heading toward the bar. "I know just the thing to cure your swollen tongue and my aching head," he said and reached over the bar-top to pull a liquor bottle out from underneath it. Yanking the cork free, he took a long pull at the whiskey, shuddered, and handed it to Mick who did the same.

"Mick," he said firmly, "first thing we got to do around here is find some decent liquor."

The bartender tipped his head back, took another long drink, and handed the bottle back to Riley. "You thed it, mithter."

"Great thundering heaven," Phoebe whispered and took a half step backward, keeping to one side of the double doors. She'd gone unnoticed throughout the fight and had no intention of being discovered now.

Her gaze flew around the room, noting the sprawled men, a few of whom were beginning to stir restively, their moans and soft grunts rustling through the air. But she wasn't interested in the vanquished warriors. Instead, she turned her gaze back to Riley Burnett, still standing beside the bar.

Naturally, she'd paid no attention when he'd ordered her to stay upstairs. She'd retreated only long enough to deliver Becky into Simmons's care before racing back to watch the fight.

Now that it was all over, she remembered the fear that had held her rooted in place as she watched, horrified by the shock of witnessing such raw, wild violence acted out only a few feet away from her. Her gaze locked on Riley, she'd winced every time someone struck him. But then, she'd noticed that he'd almost seemed to be enjoying himself.

But even more surprising than that discovery was the tiny thrill of pride Phoebe'd experienced when the fight ended and Riley was left standing alone in the center of the destruction. Like some heroic figure in an ancient tale, he'd stood, undefeated, the bodies of his enemies strewn around him.

An odd stirring of something unusual swirled in the pit of her stomach and Phoebe swallowed heavily as she watched Riley share another drink with his bartender.

Apparently, she thought as she shook off the sensation, life in a western town hadn't changed very much since she was a girl and reading all of the lurid stories she could buy on her allowance. She turned thoughtfully toward the staircase. As she climbed the steps to the second floor, her fingers curled tightly around the banister, her mind raced with images of Riley. Images that continued to plague her long after she'd dropped into an exhausted sleep.

*   *   *

Weak winter sunlight filtered through the dirty front windows, splashing across the mess littering the saloon's floor. Nothing had been cleaned up yet, and as Phoebe glanced around her, she noted that the destruction looked far worse in the daylight.

It might take weeks before they were ready to reopen for business again.

"We can afford to hire some help," Riley said flatly as if reading her mind.

Phoebe glanced at him over her morning coffee and tried not to wince at the discoloration surrounding his right eye or his puffy, split bottom lip. If he was determined to behave as if nothing were wrong, then she wouldn't be the first to mention his battle scars.

"We can?" she asked.

He half smiled, then grimaced and lifted one hand to touch his lip gingerly. "Yeah. The hotel hasn't been run in a few months, but the saloon's been doing good business right along."

Amazing. Even before the fight she'd witnessed the night before, the Horseshoe Saloon had not exactly looked like a prosperous business.

"I know it don't look like much," Riley conceded and picked up his own cup of coffee. "But Steve did pretty well once the railroad crews started coming into town."

"You mean the train station in town is new?"

He nodded, then winced. "Railroad crews have been working in these parts for a couple of years. The train's only been stopping here for about a month or so. Already, though, the place has changed since the last time I saw it a couple of years ago. Rimshot's growing."

And he didn't sound happy about it.

Naturally, Phoebe had always read the newspapers back home, so she was well aware of just what the railroad's arrival could do for a small town. In no time at all, businesses were booming. Since the train made travel so much easier, more people went west, taking their ideas and their money with them. Within months, a tiny town, if chosen as a railway stop, could become the center of commerce for miles in any direction.

Apparently, that was what was happening in Rimshot.

And she was going to be in on the very beginning of its growth. A flash of excitement shot down her spine. Imagine, she thought. Just a few weeks ago, she was worried about surviving the winter in St. Louis. Now, she was on the other side of the country, about to witness the birth of what could be, one day, a fine city.

"Do you suppose," she said, her mind racing with one idea after another, "there will be other hotels built? Other saloons?"

"Count on it," he said grimly, his fingers tightening around the handle of his coffee cup.

"Then we'd do well to get a jump on our competition."

"What?"

"Competition," she repeated and let her gaze move across the saloon again, this time with a more than critical eye. "With more hotels coming, we'll have to make ours stand out from the crowd in order to draw in customers. We'll need to make it as fine as possible, with the best beds, the best service, excellent meals—"

"Meals?" Riley interrupted her flow of words and she frowned as her thoughts were forced to a shuddering halt. "You mean to open a restaurant too?"

Why did he look so surprised? She'd inspected the kitchen herself and, though filthy, it boasted a huge pantry, a bigger stove than she'd ever seen before, and plenty of workspace. "Of course," she said. "The kitchen—"

"Hasn't been used in years." He pushed back from the table and his chair's legs screeched against the floorboards. Jumping to his feet, he said, "Blast it, Phoebe, look around you. The whole damn place is falling apart."

"It can be fixed."

He stared at her as if he couldn't believe he was hearing her right. "If you aren't the stubbornest woman I've ever met. Why in the sam hill are you so blasted determined to stay here?"

"Uncle Steven left me this place." She took a breath and steadied her voice. "It's mine and I intend to make it work. You'll see."

"Don't you ever give up?"

"No." She stood up and faced him. "Why do you want me to so badly?"

He opened his mouth as if to speak, then snapped it shut again. After a long moment, he spoke again, but apparently he had decided to ignore her questions. "I don't suppose it matters to you what I think, does it?"

"Of course it matters," she said. "You are my partner in this, after all."

"Yeah." He shoved one hand through his hair in an impatient gesture, then shot her a steely look. "With all those big plans you're hatchin'," Riley said as he grabbed hold of the chairback and leaned in toward her, "you'd do well to remember that not everything that happens in a boomtown is a good thing."

"I know that," she tried to interrupt. "I've read—"

"Books. But books don't tell the whole story, Phoebe. Trains bring just as many charlatans, thieves, and killers as they do fine, upstanding citizens."

She blinked, but couldn't look away. The strength of his gaze captured her and held her fast. When she tried to speak again, he rushed right on, drowning her out.

"I've seen boomtowns spring up and then disappear again almost overnight."

"But the train—" she managed to say.

"The train will keep right on rolling, whether it stops in Rimshot or rushes right past where we used to be." He shook his head and his blue eyes glittered darkly. "This ain't a nice, quiet city like St. Louis, Phoebe. It's a wide-open place where anything can happen and generally does. Men around here don't call a policeman when they've got a problem. Hell, the sheriff ain't even always in town. Folks here settle things themselves. Usually with guns, sometimes with their fists."

"I understand all of that," she said before he could cut her off again.

"No, Phoebe, I don't think you do. I think you're standin' on the cliff's edge of danger and you haven't even noticed you've run out of road."

She glared up at him. He might think she was making a mistake, but it was *her* mistake to make. Not his. She wasn't asking him to hold her hand and protect her from danger. She was only asking for what was her due. Respect as his partner.

"I'm not a child," she said tightly.

"Oh, I can see that, believe me," he interrupted her neatly. His gaze ran her up and down a couple of times before he looked back into her eyes. "And so will other men. Some of them not what anybody would call gentlemen. Are you ready for that too?"

She almost laughed at him.

All right, she could admit, at least to herself, that he had been worrying her. Everything he'd said had painted a few mental images that were disquieting to say the least. A few niggling doubts had burst into life inside her, urging her to rethink her decision to stay in Rimshot.

He had been doing very well in his attempt to scare her off.

Until that last statement.

He must think her very foolish, indeed, if he thought she could be swayed into believing that any man would take one look at her and lose his mind to passion. She'd been on the shelf too long to be deceived by insincere flattery. In an instant, unwanted memories crowded her mind.

Images of her father, bringing home a succession of unattached men, in the vain hope that one of them would notice Phoebe. Though he had no doubt meant well, all her father had succeeded in doing was proving to Phoebe that she was a born spinster. Though usually polite, the men her father had paraded past her had taken no more interest in her than they would have an unremarkable stone statue.

Not that she'd found any of them worthy of more than a passing notice.

All Phoebe had ever really wanted was love. And, once she'd realized that she wasn't going to find it, she'd accepted that fact and let her romantic dreams die quietly.

So, having survived countless hours of strained conversations and the hurried escapes of would-be suitors, Phoebe knew her limitations well.

"I'm not stupid enough to believe compliments from a man who is only trying to scare me away. I do own a mirror, you know. And a calendar. I'm perfectly aware of my appearance and my age."

"Phoebe—"

"We're business partners, Riley. The fact that you're a man and I'm a woman has nothing to do with anything."

Riley stared at her and shook his head.

Footsteps interrupted whatever he might have said. They both turned to look as Mick walked into the saloon from the back room. The bartender stopped whistling abruptly when he caught sight of the glare Riley shot at him.

"Oopth. 'Thcuthe me!" He backed out of the room again, and closed the storeroom door behind him.

Riley slowly swiveled his head to look at the woman standing opposite him. A hard head, a figure to make a grown man weep, and a tongue sharp enough to slice meat.

His new life just kept getting better and better.

Next morning, a small noise woke him. Riley turned his head and saw Becky, sitting in the center of a puddle of morning sunshine. Clutching her beloved blanket to her chest, she looked at him as he pushed himself up and off the narrow bed he'd slept in last night.

Even knowing that Phoebe and that butler were close

by in case she needed anything, Riley hadn't been able to turn responsibility completely over to them. So, when the saloon was closed for the night, he'd found Becky's room and claimed the extra bed for himself.

And he had the kinks in his back to prove it, he thought as he moved across the way and took a seat on his daughter's bed.

"How'd you sleep over here, missy?" he asked, not expecting an answer. Becky surprised him by crawling into his lap and settling down as if easing into a comfortable, familiar chair.

He smiled and ran one hand gently over her tangled hair. A tug at his heart warred with the incessant doubt that continued to plague him. Memories of Tess throwing her other men in his face, laughing at his fury. Her rounded belly and the gossips who had first whispered the notion Becky might not be his.

The little girl leaned into him trustingly and he deliberately pushed those doubts aside. By law, she was his daughter. If his heart wasn't so sure, only he had to know it.

Shaking his head, he lifted the hem of Becky's nightgown and pulled it off. She shoved her hair out of her eyes, then tipped her face up toward him and asked, "Feeb?"

"Yeah," he muttered, still oddly bothered by the fact that Becky would say Phoebe's name and wouldn't call him a damn thing. "She's here. Somewhere. And not likely to be leaving either." Phoebe Hightower was just as stubborn as the day was long and even Riley knew when to quit beating a dead horse.

"Feeb!" Becky shouted and tried to scramble off her father's lap. But Riley was too quick for her and snaked one arm around her middle.

"No you don't, missy. First you get some clothes on, then you can go find Phoebe."

Becky folded her arms across her chest and stuck her bottom lip out in a perfect pout. In spite of everything,

Riley chuckled as he watched his daughter's sour expression and glaring eyes.

How many times in his life had he run into a female giving him *that* look?

"Who teaches you women how to do that, huh?" he asked and tugged a blue calico dress on over her head. As he took each of her arms in turn and shoved them into the sleeves, he went on. "All of you know how to turn on those big ol' eyes and that lip that sticks out far enough to tuck a penny in."

She glowered at him and the lip stuck out even farther. With her honey-blond hair all snarled and tangled and that stormy shine to her eyes, she looked as if she'd just gone a round or two with a mountain lion.

And come out the winner.

"Becky Burnett, you're a sight, you are." He shook his head and buttoned up the back of her dress, then pulled her against him so he could deal with her shoes and socks. But as he grabbed for her foot, she laughed and yanked it out of his reach.

"Becky . . ." he warned in a low voice.

She giggled and squirmed in his lap.

He'd caught greased pigs that were easier to hang on to. Riley sighed. "Becky, you got to wear shoes and socks. Now hand over that foot."

Like a snake, her body went all limp and curvy on him. In an instant, she'd slithered down between his legs to make a dash for the door. Well, he might have to spend his nights chasing his daughter to hell and back all over a hotel and saloon, but he damn sure wasn't going to start a new *morning* tradition.

Leaping off the bed, he moved across the floor in a few long strides and snatched her up before she could escape. Her slight weight tucked against him, her chubby little legs kicked at him and she planted both hands on his chest to try and push herself out of his grasp. A giggle bubbled up her throat, telling Riley that she was having a fine old time. She whipped her long, tangled hair out of her eyes to look up at him and he noticed how her eyes sparkled when she was enjoying herself.

A pang of something sharp and sweet settled in the pit of his stomach as he looked into his daughter's upturned face. Such a pretty little thing. And so damn full of spirit. Jesus, but she deserved more out of life than a not-so-capable father and a run-down saloon.

Duty warred with common sense inside him. He'd come home to take care of his child, as he should. But damn it, he just wasn't any good at it. Hell, he couldn't even brush her hair!

Was it right to force her to live like this? To force himself to give up the one thing he was good at—being a marshal—just so he could say he had done what was expected of him?

Responsibility was a two-edged sword. Staring down into that face, he realized that he could stay here, be responsible for her, and end up completely ruining her life. Or, he could swallow his pride, admit defeat, and turn her over to someone who could give her everything she should have.

His thoughts immediately shifted to Tess's folks. Living fine in San Francisco, they could do right by their only granddaughter. They could see to it that she had schooling and fine clothes. She'd be a helluva lot better off than living in a backwater like Rimshot with a father who didn't know shit about children.

The fact that he would then be free to go back to marshaling, he told himself, was just a side benefit.

"Missy," he said softly, and waited until Becky's gaze was locked with his to continue. "I'm gonna do what I should've done from the start."

She rubbed her eyes, then grinned up at him.

His heart felt as though a giant fist had tightened around it.

"I'm sorry, Becky," he said and felt his throat tighten around the unfamiliar words. There were folks scattered all across Nevada, New Mexico, and Texas who could tell Becky that her father didn't apologize often. Riley rubbed one hand across his face. He'd always prided himself on doing right. Not making mistakes you could avoid making. He grimaced tightly before continuing. "You deserve better than me, missy. And I'm gonna see that you get it."

He'd send a wire to San Francisco that very day. With any luck, Tess's folks would be here in a few weeks to collect their granddaughter and he could return to the life he knew. The life he understood.

This way would be best for all of them. Even for Phoebe. Then she could have this whole damn place all to herself. Run it any way she wanted to.

Becky's gaze slipped away to look past his shoulder. "Feeb!"

Hell, he thought, the girl'd probably miss Phoebe more than she would him.

"I already told you," he said, "Phoebe's around here somewhere."

"Right here, actually," a familiar voice said from the doorway.

"Feeb!"

Damn. He wondered just how long she'd been standing there. Riley slowly turned around to look at her. Her hair was all tucked up nice and neat, the long sleeves of an ugly brown dress were rolled to above her elbows, and she wore a fresh white apron tied around her waist. Her eyes shining, a soft smile on her face, she looked ready and raring to go.

And too damn good.

Damn. Why didn't she look like a spinster was supposed to? All dried up and forgotten. Instead, she had the look of a tasty fruit left long enough on the vine to ripen to sweet perfection. The fact that she didn't seem to believe that only added to the attraction, somehow.

Riley found himself wishing he could be the man to show her that she was wrong about herself. To prove to her just how tempting a female she was. But if his plan worked out, he'd be leaving soon. And that was for the best, he reckoned. Phoebe Hightower was the marryin' kind of woman.

And Riley had already proven without a doubt that he made a godawful husband and a near-useless father.

Still, he thought, with a last, lingering look at her full, generous mouth, never seeing her again was going to be surprisingly hard.

"What did you mean . . . doing what you should have done from the start?"

He stiffened slightly. Hearing his own words echo back to him only strengthened his resolve. He was doing the right thing. For Becky. For him. For all of them.

"Privacy works better if the door is closed," she said, obviously in response to his expression.

"I'll remember that," he said tightly.

Phoebe smoothed her hands down the front of her apron. "I didn't mean to eavesdrop," she said.

"It's all right," Riley told her and meant it. She'd have to know sooner or later. Although he'd just as soon it was later. He was in no mood to listen to advice from a woman who didn't know him *or* his daughter well enough to have an opinion.

"What exactly did you mean?" Phoebe asked.

"I'll explain later," he said shortly. As for now, he wanted to get over to the telegraph office and send that wire. The sooner he got this mess straightened out, the better off everybody would be. Crossing the room to where she stood, he thrust Becky into her arms and said, "Watch her for a while, will ya? Got something I have to do."

He stomped off down the hall, boot heels slamming into the floor. He didn't look back.

Chapter Five

✤

Guidry Yates squinted at the telegraph form in his hand, then lifted his gaze to the man standing on the opposite side of the counter. "You sure you want to send this, Riley?"

Snatching off his hat, he slapped it against his thighs. "I wouldn't have written it out if I didn't want to send it, now would I?"

The older man muttered something low, then reached up to carefully scratch the top of his head without disturbing the two long strands of white hair witch-hazeled to his scalp. "Folks around here ain't gonna be too happy to hear the Harrises are comin' back to town," he said, shooting Riley a disapproving glance.

"If folks hear about this," Riley told him in a low, firm voice, "it'll be because the telegrapher broke the law."

"Here now," Guidry protested, his Adam's apple wobbling in his scrawny throat.

"No, you listen to me," Riley warned him, leaning in close. "Telegrams are private and you damn well know it. One word of this gets out and I'll see to it you lose this job, Guidry."

"Ain't no call to take on so," the older man said with a sniff.

"I keep my business my business," Riley said. "Understood?"

"Folks'll find out soon enough," the other man said. "And they ain't gonna be happy about it."

All right, so the Harrises didn't have many friends in town. They'd been the wealthiest people around and hadn't bothered hiding the fact that they looked down their noses at most everyone else. It had about choked Frank Harris to see Riley Burnett marry Tess. But with Becky on the way, the man hadn't had much choice but to go along.

Although the minute the ceremony was over, Frank and Elizabeth Harris had left town so they wouldn't have to actually associate with their new son-in-law. He could just imagine the kind of things Becky would grow up hearing about her pa. There was a bitter pill.

"They won't be staying long," Riley told him.

"Reckon not," Guidry allowed, pursing his lips like he'd taken a bite out of a lemon. "Just long enough to take your daughter and hightail it back to California."

Glaring at the man, Riley snapped, "Just send the wire, Guidry. Today."

"I'll do 'er right now. You want to wait for an answer?"

"No," he said, settling his hat back on his head. "If there's an answer, send it over to the saloon." Then he flipped a coin onto the counter and left.

Guidry's disapproval was just the beginning, he knew. Oh, he'd keep his mouth shut, but the little man was right. Sooner or later everyone would know. Then, no doubt, folks would be lining up to give him what-for. And something told him Phoebe would be at the head of that line. Well, it didn't matter what they said. What anyone said. His mind was made up. Decision reached. Becky was leaving and that was that.

Gritting his teeth, Riley stepped off the boardwalk and headed for the saloon. He might as well get some work done before he left. The least he could do was leave Phoebe a place that wouldn't fall down in a stiff wind.

*   *   *

"Ma'am." A short man with very thinning hair stood in the open doorway of the hotel.

"Yes?"

"Telegram here for Riley. You know where he is?"

"I'll take it to him," Phoebe offered and accepted the yellow envelope.

"Much obliged," the little man said and scuttled away again.

She watched him go, then shifted her gaze to the telegram. Not so long ago, one just like this had changed her life forever. She couldn't help wondering if the same thing was going to happen to Riley.

Hurrying into the saloon, she glanced around, noted the open storeroom door, and walked toward it. Inside, a single lamp burned in the corner, spilling a soft light across the darkened room. Riley stood on the far side, rearranging bottles of liquor and counting out loud to himself.

"Riley," she said and he turned toward her. "There's a telegram for you."

In the shadowy light, his features seemed to tighten slightly, but she couldn't be sure. "Just leave it there, Phoebe. On that crate."

Surprised, she glanced down at the envelope. "Aren't you going to open it?"

"I know what it says."

"But how can you . . ."

Grumbling under his breath, he stepped away from the cluttered shelves, marched across the room to her, and snatched the telegram.

This close to him, Phoebe saw that his eyes were as shadowed as the room. His jaw tight, shoulders rigid, he took a step away as if purposely distancing himself from her. Something was going on. A small tendril of anxiety unwound along her spine.

He tore the envelope open, read the wire, then darted a look at her. "I told you. I knew what it would say."

Instinctively, she laid one hand on his arm and instantly felt a spark of sensation that shot along her nerve endings. He must have felt it too, because he stared at her in surprise before taking another step back.

"Bad news?" she asked and hoped her voice didn't sound as forced to him as it did to her.

"No." Slowly, deliberately, he crumpled the telegram in his fist. His long fingers squeezed the paper into a tight wad and then he shoved it into his pocket. Taking a deep breath, he said, "I've got to finish this inventory."

"But what about the telegram?" she asked, hoping he'd explain.

"What about it?"

"Are you sure everything is all right?"

"Everything's fine," he said shortly, already turning back to the shelves. With his face averted, she couldn't read his expression, but his voice was tight, hard, and filled with an emotion she couldn't quite identify. "Becky's grandparents are coming for a visit. Be here in a month."

Relief washed over her. Silly to have been so worried by a telegram.

"Is that all?"

Watching her, Riley recalled the brief message he'd just read. *Impossible to leave now. Social obligations to be met. Be there late November. Have Becky ready.* A warm-hearted response to his wire indeed. He gave Phoebe a halfhearted smile and said, "Yeah. That's all."

A week later, some progress had been made on both the saloon and the hotel. Thanks in large part to Phoebe, who threw herself into the daunting job with enthusiasm and single-mindedness.

She was concentrating her efforts on the lobby and bedrooms. Of course, the first order of business had been to get rid of the mice. She'd hired two boys, Henry and Joe Weatherby, the ten-year-old twin sons of the black-smith, to supervise their cat Jumbo's excellent hunting abilities.

Simmons had taken on the job of restoring the hotel's kitchen to some sort of order. It wasn't easy, what with having to go out the back door every few minutes to draw water from the well that stood at least fifty paces from the building. Uncle Steven, along with being disorganized, hadn't been too concerned with the niceties.

"I do wish there was water right inside the kitchen," she muttered, just thinking about how difficult it would be to go to and from that well in heavier snow.

Still, Simmons had the stove working again, the cupboards fixed, and the cast-iron cookware down at the blacksmith's being repaired. Though how he had managed to get anything done with little Becky attached to his right leg was a wonder. The girl had adopted Simmons and clung to him with the same grip she reserved for her beloved blanket.

Mick Dennis, the bartender, was busy in the saloon and Riley . . . Phoebe sighed. Well, Riley Burnett was acting like a caged tiger.

He was doing his share of the work, helping to ready the hotel for his in-laws' arrival, but Phoebe saw the restlessness in him. She'd caught him unawares several times during the last week and watched him staring off into the distance, like a hungry man looking at the last bite of food in the country.

Only two days ago, she'd found him behind the saloon, facing into the wind, his gaze trained on the far horizon. The land stretched out forever, unmarked by houses or wagons or new buildings being erected. If she hadn't been aware of the noise coming from the town behind her, Phoebe would have thought there wasn't a soul for miles.

Stands of pine and aspen reached up from the snow-dotted brown winter grass. The land itself dipped and rolled into small valleys and crests. A cold wind rushed across the open spaces and grabbed at them. Phoebe shivered and took a step closer to Riley.

A long lock of her hair twisted free of its knot and

flew across her eyes. She reached up to brush it aside, then took a moment to study him. There was more than hunger on his features—there was also a deep sadness, regret. But for what? she wondered even as she instinctively reached out to try to comfort him somehow. But she didn't have the right, so she stopped short of actually touching him and reluctantly let her hand fall back to her side.

She should leave him to his dark thoughts, she knew. Yet she couldn't make herself turn and leave him alone.

"What do you see out there?"

Riley swiveled his head to look at her briefly before returning his gaze to the wild, untamed land that seemed to hold him captive. He inhaled sharply, drawing the cold air deep inside his lungs. "Open spaces," he said quietly. "Freedom."

The longing in his voice said far more than his few words.

Phoebe's gaze swept across the empty stretches of land and she felt dwarfed by its sheer size. For a woman who had lived her entire life in the confines of a city, the broad, sweeping landscape seemed intimidating. Dangerous. "It looks lonely to me."

"Lonely's not always a bad thing, Phoebe."

"I don't think I would like it," she admitted, her voice soft, thoughtful. "No one to talk to. To laugh with."

"No one to betray you. Disappoint you."

She glanced up at him. His features tight, his eyes had a haunted look that she instinctively wanted to banish.

"All people aren't like that."

His lips quirked in a sad, wry smile. "Sure they are," he said quietly. "Given enough time."

Who was it? she wanted to ask. Who had let him down so badly that he still felt the ache of an old pain? But she didn't have the right to ask and she knew it, so the silence between them stretched on for several more minutes.

Finally, he said, almost to himself, "Best not to expect

too much of folks. Then you got nothing to lose."

"Or to gain," she added.

He shot her a quick, guarded look. Then suddenly, he pointed off to the right. "Snow coming."

The abrupt shift in subject startled her momentarily. Phoebe turned her head and saw granite-colored clouds gathering on the far horizon like a dark army waiting for its strength to grow before attacking. "How soon?" she asked, already mentally saying good-bye to the weak winter sunshine playing on her back.

"Few days," he said shortly, then abruptly turned for the ladder propped against the side of the building. "Better get back to those shingles before the next snow."

And the moment between them was shattered, as if it had never been.

Phoebe inhaled sharply and released the memory of that day. Since then, she'd hardly seen her partner alone for more than a few minutes. It was almost as if he were avoiding her on purpose. As though he were regretting their short conversation and trying to ensure it didn't happen again.

As that thought drifted through her mind, the crash of Riley's hammer sounded out again. She tossed a look at the ceiling. "Who is it you're hitting up there?" she wondered aloud. "You? Or me?"

But there were no answers to that question. Just as she couldn't understand why every night, after tucking Becky into bed, Phoebe would lie awake until she heard Riley's footsteps echoing along the hall. Her dreams lately were studded with images of his face. Echoes of his voice. Reflections of his eyes.

A flicker of sensation tickled the base of her spine and Phoebe forced herself to ignore it. She was too old now to indulge herself in fancies. Turning her mind away from thoughts of Riley Burnett, she stepped out onto the boardwalk and crossed to the edge of the porch. She shivered slightly in the chill, but after working all day inside the heated rooms of the hotel, she almost welcomed a breath of cool air. Squinting into the afternoon sunlight, she let her gaze wander across the small town she now called home.

A jumble of buildings were clustered together on either side of a narrow, muddy track that the citizens of Rimshot referred to as Main Street. Mostly wood-framed and badly in need of paint, some of the stores looked as though they were leaning against each other for strength. A dusting of dirty snow still lay in the shadows along the rooftops and beside the edges of the uneven boardwalks that rolled up and down the length of the street like waves on the ocean.

From the far end of town came the clash of the blacksmith's hammer on an anvil, and closer by, a dog howled mournfully until someone shouted, "Shut up, you!"

"Ma'am," a man said with a tip of his hat as he walked by, and Phoebe smiled just as a tight group of children darted past her. They leaped off the boardwalk and landed very nearly under the wheels of a huge lumber wagon rumbling down the street. The driver shouted, the children laughed, and life went on.

She smiled to herself. There was so much going on here. A bustle of noise and activity that somehow seemed important. Phoebe felt, for the first time in her life, as though she were a part of something grand. Something substantial. She was helping give birth to a town that would hopefully one day be a great city.

" 'Scuse me, ma'am," a deep voice asked from behind her. "Did you want all them walls painted yellow?"

Phoebe jumped, startled, and turned around. Creek Jackson, one of the men hired by Riley to help out, was at least fifty. A former prospector, deep creases lined the corners of his dark brown eyes, a fringe of salt-and-pepper hair ringed his bald pate, and his hands were callused and scarred. But his hard appearance hid a friendly soul.

"Yes, thank you," she said. "All of them."

"Up to you," he answered with a shrug. "Seems awful bright to me, though."

"That's just what I want, Mr. Jackson," she said. Bright, clean, cheerful-looking color to rejuvenate the sadly stained, dingy walls. Appearances were everything, after all. And a dark, depressing hotel wouldn't draw many customers.

He cringed. "Creek, ma'am," he said. "Just Creek."

She smiled at him as another freight wagon rolled down the street. Phoebe half turned to look. Only that morning, she'd counted at least four wagons, all loaded with building supplies brought in by train. And each of those wagons headed straight for the edge of town. "They certainly are busy," she murmured.

"Yes, ma'am," Creek said, joining her briefly for a look toward the new structures going up. "Guess they figured to not wait for spring. Long as the weather's hold-in', why not build now? Sorta get the jump on the late-comers." He shot a quick look at the sky and the lowering dark clouds scuttling in. " 'Course, looks like it's comin' on to snow again, so they'll have to quit soon enough."

"What exactly are they building?" she asked. She hadn't had time yet to explore her surroundings and Creek Jackson quite frankly seemed to be an expert on whatever was happening in Rimshot.

"Two saloons, a bakery, a dress shop, of all things, and a boarding house," he said, confirming her belief in him.

Boarding house. The first competition for her—*their*—hotel. Well, she'd known it would be coming. And a bakery. That reminded Phoebe that she would soon have to think about hiring a cook for the restaurant she hoped to open. There was so much to do, she thought. And life here seemed to rush at a pace she hadn't really expected but was actually enjoying. She had no time anymore to sit around wondering about how she would live.

She was too busy living.

Creek reached up to rub one hand across his scalp. "This place is gettin' so crowded a man can't get drunk anymore, 'cause there's just no place to fall down." He sighed and added in the same, sorrowful tone, "Can't even have a good fight no more now, prob'ly."

"Why's that?"

"Sheriff's back, and he ain't the sort to be putting up with a lot of shenanigans."

"Do you know him?" she asked.

"Sure enough," Creek said. "Tom grew up here. Just like Riley and most of the folks on Main Street. Known him since he was a boy. Good man. Tough. But good."

She nodded thoughtfully. Those were just the words she would have used to describe Riley Burnett. Tough, but good.

"Guess I'll get back to the paintin'."

As Creek walked back inside, Phoebe turned slowly to watch the crowds. There was a sudden heaviness to the air. From the coming storm? No. It was something else.

Her gaze sharp, she studied the flow of people streaming up and down Main Street searching for . . . *something*. Or *someone*. She should get back to work, but for some reason, she didn't move. An odd, creeping sensation settled at the base of her spine until the hairs at the back of her neck stood straight up in response. She had the distinct impression she was being watched. She could almost *feel* someone's stare on her.

Mouth dry, nerves jangling, she stepped down onto the street to get a better look in both directions. A strange sense of anticipation gripped her and she narrowed her gaze, slowly raking the town and the people, looking for . . . *who*?

Then she saw him.

Outside the General Mercantile store was a small, battered wagon. And on the bench seat, staring at her, sat a man she hadn't thought to see again.

The tinker.

* * *

Riley slammed the hammer down onto his thumb. In the second or two before the pain started, he had the time to know it was coming and brace for it.

"Damn it!" he shouted and dropped the hammer onto his lap while shaking his injured hand violently. He hit his blasted thumb more often than he did the roofing nails. The throbbing ache quickly settled into a low hum of discomfort that he was getting far too used to. "It's a damn good thing you're leaving here soon," he muttered thickly.

He needed to get going. To get back to doing what he did best. He might be no good at living in town and taking care of a child . . . but put him out on a cold trail and within a few hours he'd be on the right track to finding whoever or whatever was lost. He could read sign in any kind of weather and had been known to find his way in a blinding snowstorm. There was one particular thief he'd caught up with who'd sworn later in court that Riley could track a snake across a flat rock.

But with a hammer in his hands, he was dangerous.

Riley looked around the roof and noted the new shingles. They didn't look any too good, but they should keep the rain and snow out. And hell, that's all that mattered, wasn't it?

He shifted slightly on the steep pitch of the roof and made a grab for a stack of shingles as they slid out of reach to tumble off the edge of the roof to the ground.

"That's just great," he snarled and threw a quick look at the approaching storm clouds. Running out of time and he throws the damn shingles off the damn roof.

Disgusted, he stared off into the distance and tried to imagine being out there again. Alone. No uppity butler. No loud saloon customers. No big-eyed Phoebe looking at him and making him think things he had no business thinking. And no Becky, curling up on his lap.

Something inside him shifted, tightened uncomfortably. He ignored the discomfort.

"Hey, Riley?"

His thoughts dissolved instantly as he turned toward the voice and saw young Henry Weatherby's face peeking up over the lip of the roof. No one had trouble telling him and his twin apart. The only thing the boys were alike in was their ability to find trouble.

Like now, climbing up a ladder that had more shakes than rungs.

"Henry, what in the hell are you doin' up here?"

The kid's eyebrows shot up at Riley's growl. That's good. Now he was yelling at kids.

"Brought you these," the boy said and lifted one arm to lay the spilled shingles on the roof.

"Thanks," Riley told him. "Now get down before you fall down and your ma skins me alive for killing you."

"Heck," the boy said and flipped his too-long dark brown hair out of his eyes. "She'd prob'ly thank ya!"

Riley chuckled in spite of the irritation still clawing at his insides. "Yeah, well, get down anyway," he said and moved carefully toward the boy to pick up the shingles.

"Yes, sir," the kid said and started down the ladder. Then he paused. "Oh, yeah, Miss Phoebe says to tell ya she'll be back soon."

Back? Riley thought, staring at the spot where Henry had dropped from sight. From where? "Henry!"

Instantly, the boy's face appeared again. He squinted into the afternoon sunlight. "Yeah?"

"What do you mean, be back soon? Where'd she go?"

"I dunno. Joe seen her. Said she jumped off the porch and started runnin' off down the street. Told him she'd be back and to tell you. So I did."

"Running down the street?" Riley repeated.

"What Joe says."

"To where?"

"I dunno," Henry said, a bit louder this time, then started back down the ladder.

This time, Riley let him go. Forgetting all about the shingles, he made his way carefully back up to the crest of the roof. Bracing one hand on the stone chimney, he looked down into the street, trying to pick Phoebe out of the crowd. From this angle, though, it was downright impossible.

"Son of a bitch," he muttered and started back for the ladder. Where the heck did Phoebe go and why was she running? Was there a problem somewhere that she didn't have time to tell him about? No. She would have said something to Joe, wouldn't she? Or sent for him?

His gaze raked the street again, even though he knew he wouldn't be able to find her from here. Hell, he didn't know what Phoebe would do in an emergency. Maybe she'd just trot off and try to handle a problem on her own. There was no telling with that woman.

Emergency? Now why assume there was some sort of problem? Maybe she just decided to do some shopping all of a sudden. Yeah. And she had to *run* to the Mercantile. Nope. Something was up and he didn't have the slightest idea what that something was.

But he'd find out. He'd put his famous tracking skills to good use, hunt down Miss Phoebe Hightower, and find out what was going on. He didn't bother to ask himself why her running off was bothering him. He didn't care to know why the thought of Phoebe being in trouble scared the hell out of him.

He figured the answers to those questions would really terrify him.

"It *is* you," Phoebe said as she trudged through the muck to stop alongside the tinker's wagon. She looked up and was instantly lost in the power of the gray eyes she remembered so clearly.

He tipped his floppy-brimmed hat and smiled. "It's good to see you again."

The musical quality of his voice filled her and seemed to drown out the noise and bustle of the street.

"What are you doing here, of all places?"

"I have come to see you," he said, and extended a

hand, inviting her up to the seat beside him.

Phoebe hesitated. His simple words had sent a ripple of uneasiness through her and she wasn't sure why. Nor did she know why he would come all this way just to see her—if indeed he had.

She hadn't been afraid of him in St. Louis. Why was she so leery of him now?

Phoebe sensed no danger from him and yet a part of her was reluctant to go closer. Ridiculous, to be wary of and yet drawn to this strange little man.

He smiled again, and in that smile, she read understanding and something else . . . what, she couldn't quite say. But he held her spellbound now, just as he had a month ago in St. Louis.

"Come, my friend," he said softly, still holding his hand out to her.

Phoebe swallowed heavily and took his hand. Then in a clumsy movement, she climbed onto the wagon and settled herself beside him.

Riley came around the edge of the hotel at a run and went on into the street, ignoring the horses and the lumbering wagons plodding through the thick mud. Turning his head one way, then the other, he looked for her. He tried to spot the soft brown of her hair or even to catch a glimpse of one of those ugly dresses she was always wearing. All of the concentration he had been known to show on the trail of some outlaw he now focused on Phoebe.

Crowds shifted, wagons rolled, children laughed.

His sharp, trained gaze swept across faces, both familiar and unknown. He didn't acknowledge any of them. He ignored shouts of greeting from people passing him and tried also to ignore a growing sense of apprehension. Where could she have gone so quickly? Even in this crowd, she shouldn't have been able to lose herself in such a short amount of time.

He looked harder, watching for her tall, shapely figure,

searching for a certain pair of blue eyes. Something tight and hard settled in the pit of his stomach. He was overreacting and he knew it. Damn it, there was nothing wrong. Didn't Phoebe have the right to go to a store without him running around like a crazy man?

And still, he felt that flicker of urgency.

Suddenly, the crowd parted and he spotted her, standing just outside the Mercantile. But even before he could relish the feeling of relief swamping him, she was gone.

In the blink of an eye, Phoebe Hightower had simply disappeared.

Chapter Six

❦

"Whatcha doin'?"

Joe stabbed the edge of the shovel deep into the dirt, rested his forearm atop the splintery end of the handle, and looked at his brother. Using one filthy hand to brush a hank of dark brown hair out of his eyes, he asked, "Now, what's it look like I'm doin'?"

Henry squatted beside the small hill of shoveled dirt and looked down into the pit where Joe stood. "Diggin' a hole."

"Shows all you know," Joe said with a snort. "I'm prospectin'."

"Henry?" Henry turned to glance at the hotel's kitchen door, just a few feet away. "What'd *he* say?"

Simmons. Joe's face screwed up. He didn't mind working for Miss Phoebe, even if she did have him and Henry doing cleaning up and such that everybody knew was women's work. She was real nice and she paid good too.

But that butler of hers was a sore pain in the backside.

Of course, what man wouldn't be with a baby hangin' on his leg every day so's he had to walk around all stiff so she wouldn't fall off his foot? Joe couldn't figure out why little Becky was so darn fond of the old sourpuss anyhow.

Shrugging the problem of Simmons aside for the moment, Joe picked up his shovel again, looked at his twin, and said, "He ain't seen it yet."

Henry nodded sagely. "He won't like it."

"That's too bad," Joe said and forked up another shovelful of dirt. "This here's a free country, Pa says."

"True, but how come you're prospectin' here?"

"Shoot, I asked Creek and he said it looked like a likely spot." Joe shot his brother another quick look and directed his next shovelful at Henry's feet. "He knows more about prospectin' than you, I reckon."

"Reckon so." Henry allowed and stood up to shake the dirt off his shoes. "Want some help?"

Joe smiled to himself. He'd been counting on Henry helping with the digging. Nobody'd told him that being a gold miner could be such hard work. "Guess so," he said, since it wouldn't do to sound too eager. "There's another shovel yonder." He jerked his head toward the second shovel he'd left propped outside the hotel.

Grinning, Henry ran for the tool, then hurried back to the "gold mine." Jumping into the hole beside his brother, he asked, "What're you gonna buy with your share?"

Joe smiled, lost in the dreams of fortune and fame.

It was as if she were in a giant soap bubble.

Phoebe watched the people hurrying past the tinker's wagon, but there seemed to be almost a milky haze covering her view. Main Street was still there. The crowds hadn't disappeared. But she looked at them through a wavering shield of some sort that muffled the everyday sounds of Rimshot and distorted her vision.

"What's going on?" she asked, shifting on the seat to face the tinker.

He smiled.

"Who are you?"

"A friend."

Perhaps, she thought, narrowing her gaze to study the man's silver-gray eyes. He might be a friend, but he was certainly no ordinary tinker. A thread of fear began to spiral in the bottom of her stomach and slowly unwound to snake through her limbs.

What if this *soap bubble* worked both ways? What if no one on Main Street could see her? Gripping her hands together tightly in her lap, she anxiously studied the faces of the people walking past. Not a soul paid the slightest attention to the tinker, his wagon . . . or her.

Her heartbeat skittered slightly. She hadn't been afraid in St. Louis. But then, people had been able to see the tinker. The boys taunting him. The curious people hurrying past.

This was different. She was as alone with this man as if she were in a deserted cabin in the middle of nowhere. How could she have stepped aboard a wagon and disappeared?

Swallowing heavily, she turned her head slowly to look at the man beside her. There was certainly nothing threatening in his appearance. But then, a sleeping lion looked like nothing more than an overgrown cat.

"You're not really a tinker, are you?" she forced herself to ask and then braced for his answer.

He shrugged. "At times, yes. Most times, no."

She'd been afraid of that. Phoebe scuttled closer to the edge of her seat and wondered wildly if she could jump through that soap bubble. Would something stop her?

"Please," he said quickly and reached for her, only to have her lurch backward away from his touch. Instantly, he pulled his hand back. "Don't be afraid."

"Afraid?" she repeated and tried for a lighthearted chuckle. It scratched past her throat with a choked-off sound. Squaring her shoulders, Phoebe kept to the far edge of the bench seat and said, in a slightly quavering voice, "I'm not afraid."

He smiled and she could see in his eyes that he didn't believe her.

"I'm not here to harm you."

Warmth streamed from the centers of his silvery eyes

and Phoebe's heartbeat slowly returned to normal. Though no man intending harm would actually *admit* it to his victim, for some odd reason, she believed him. For now.

"Why are you here, then?"

He shrugged. "To see you. To assure myself that all is well."

Phoebe frowned slightly. "Why? You don't even know me."

The tinker chuckled and the light, lilting quality of his laughter rose up like the softest music and settled down around her, warming her through. How very odd.

"I know you far better than you might think."

Worry slithered up her spine. How much did he know? Did he know about the things she'd stolen? Did he know that she was no better than a common thief? Shame flushed her cheeks. She'd so hoped to leave all of that behind her. But what if the tinker was here because he'd just discovered her ugly little secret? What if he was here to take her wishes away and send her back to the life she'd had before?

Fear and anger twisted together in the pit of her stomach and, a moment later, the anger won. She wouldn't go back. She couldn't. Tossing a glance at the street beyond the soap bubble, she knew she would stay in Rimshot no matter what. Her future was here. She felt it. And she wouldn't give it up. Not for anything.

"What do you want from me?" she demanded, still keeping to the edge of her seat in case she was forced to jump.

"Ah," he said with a tilt of his head. "I see your fears have vanished behind a greater need . . . curiosity."

"Curiosity is what a child feels on Christmas morning," she told him hotly. "I want to know exactly who you are and why you're watching me."

"It's what I do," he said with another shrug that sent his simple clothes into a ripple of movement.

"Follow women?" she asked, outraged. "Spy on them?"

"No, no, no." he said, and smiled again.

Phoebe frowned. Really, the man's smile and his eyes were designed to put a person at ease. She almost resented it.

"I am a Watcher," he said simply as if that one phrase explained all.

"You'll have to do better than that, I'm afraid."

"And I shall," he said gently.

But first things first, she told herself. "How well do you know me?"

"Very," he said simply, and his gaze deepened into hers.

Instantly, Phoebe knew that he was privy to all of her secrets. What he would do with that knowledge, she wasn't sure.

"Your . . . secrets are safe."

Oh, she wanted to believe that. If the people in Rimshot found out she was a thief, her new life would end in a flurry of gossip and innuendo.

"I am here only to help."

"As a Watcher," she said.

"Yes." He sounded pleased, like a schoolmaster with a particularly difficult student.

"What exactly is that?"

He inhaled deeply and exhaled on a thoughtful sigh. "It's hard to explain to a mortal . . ."

"Mortal?" Was he saying he wasn't mortal? What did that make him, then? Immortal? Or dangerously insane? She scooted even closer to the edge of the seat and felt as though one stiff wind would push her the rest of the way off, landing her . . . where?

He smiled. "Watchers guide humans. Helping when we can, comforting when we cannot."

Oh, my. The swirling gray and silver of his eyes took on an entirely new meaning. This man had to be crazy.

Didn't he?

She chanced a look at Main Street, only a breath away, and saw again the vaporous cloud that seemed to separate her from the rest of the world. What if he wasn't crazy at all, but actually who he said he was?

Riley hurried down Main Street, his steps dragging in the mud. People waved to him, called to him, but he paid no attention. Instead, he focused on the spot where he'd last seen Phoebe.

He could have sworn there was an old wagon outside the Mercantile and that Phoebe was standing right beside it. But there was nothing there now. And wagons just didn't up and disappear. So where was it? And more importantly, where was Phoebe?

"Hey, Riley," someone called from nearby.

Grumbling under his breath, he shot a look at the caller. Dave Hawkins, town deputy. Tall, thin, with long black hair he usually wore pulled into a tail that hung down between his shoulder blades. His brown eyes were too old and wise to be in such a young face, but like most of the men who'd fought in the bloody Civil War, he'd come out much older than he'd gone in.

"Dave," Riley said with a nod.

"What's your rush?" Dave asked and stepped off the boardwalk into the muck.

"I thought I saw . . ." He shook his head. "I was looking for Phoebe."

"Ah." Dave nodded and smiled. "Your new partner. Saw her yesterday, coming out of the blacksmith's."

Yesterday did him no good. "Seen her today? A few minutes ago?"

"Nope," Dave said as he stopped alongside him. "But then, I've been in the office all morning with the sheriff."

Riley's gaze shot to the building just behind the man. The sheriff's office stood huddled between the Bathhouse and the dentist's office. "Heard Tom was back."

"Yep," Dave said, tilting his hat back on his head. "And he's already wearing me out."

Riley shifted his gaze back to his friend. "You tell him about the fool that's been busting my windows for the last few weeks?"

"Yeah. Said to tell you we'd keep an eye out, but that it's prob'ly just some kids."

Hell, Riley knew that. He was just tired of replacing window glass. Although, in the week or so since Phoebe's arrival, the vandalism had actually stopped.

But he wasn't worried about destructive kids at the moment. Right now, he just wanted to find Phoebe. He didn't ask himself why.

"Thanks," he said, "I'll see ya later, Dave. Come by for a drink tonight. Bring Tom."

"You buyin'?"

"Yeah," Riley said and slapped Dave's shoulder as he started walking again. "I'm buying."

"I'll be there," Dave called. "Hey, want some help lookin' for your lost female? That's a real handsome woman there."

Riley's mouth tightened into a grim slash. Just what he needed. Some other man noticing that Phoebe's striking features came together to make quite a picture.

"No, thanks," he yelled over his shoulder. He'd just as soon Dave kept his distance from Phoebe. The deputy had a well-deserved reputation with the ladies and he didn't want the man practicing his charm on Phoebe Hightower.

Not that it mattered a bit to Riley if men found her attractive. He just didn't want to see her get hurt was all. Although, in a few weeks he'd be gone and Rimshot would be just a memory. Then he wouldn't be around to protect her from the men who'd come sniffin' around her. But it couldn't be helped. Besides, Phoebe was a grown woman. Could look after herself. Wasn't anything to him if she got hooked up with some slick-talking no-good.

Hell, he thought, reaching up to yank his hat down lower over his brow, even he didn't believe that.

* * *

"Are you saying you're some sort of . . . Guardian Angel?"

The tinker blinked at her and then laughed, a full, rich sound that seemed to echo within the tight bubble. When he stopped laughing, he shook his head. "Certainly not. Some Watchers are hardly angelic creatures. They spend eternity seeking out mortals bent on self-destruction in order to enjoy their foibles." Sadly, he admitted, "There are, unfortunately, many such humans from which to choose."

"Is that why you're here?" she asked, though she'd never thought of herself as self-destructive, by an immortal's standards, one never knew.

"Oh my, no," he said quickly, reassuringly.

"Then why me?"

"Why not you?"

Despite the unusual situation, a spurt of annoyance shot through her. "Can't you answer a simple question?"

"I could," he told her gently. "But I won't."

"Whyever not?"

"Sometimes it's better not to know."

Exasperating. Talking in circles. Her former fears forgotten now, she gave in to the impatience rising within.

"I don't care for riddles, Mr. . . ." She paused. "What exactly should I call you?"

"Tinker will do."

"Tinker, then," she said, at last releasing the white-knuckled grip of her hands. "If you won't explain anything else, at least tell me why you're here. In Rimshot."

He simply stared at her, as if waiting for her to answer her own question.

And a moment later, she did.

"My wish," Phoebe said softly. "I wished myself here, didn't I?"

"I did warn you to be careful."

"I only wished for a new start. And to be warm," she reminded him.

"And has that wish come true?"

Hmm. Her mouth snapped shut. Even with the varying weather, Phoebe had to admit that, yes, she was much warmer in her new home. There was always wood for the fireplaces. And a new beginning, where no one knew the old Phoebe, was just what she'd wanted.

"Then the wishes are real," she murmured.

"And now two of them are gone," he said gently. "I only wanted to remind you to be careful with the others."

"Two?"

She frowned, her brows drawing together, as she tried to remember when she'd made a second wish. And suddenly, it came to her. Phoebe gasped, horrified. "Blast and thunder," she whispered. "*Water.*"

The tinker nodded sagely.

Appalled, Phoebe told herself that if wishing for warmth had brought her to Nevada, wishing for water inside the kitchen might very well cause a flood.

"I have to go," she said and gathered her skirt.

"Certainly."

Perched uncertainly on the edge of the seat, Phoebe paused, looked back at the tinker and asked, "How do I leave this . . . ?" She waved one hand at the surrounding bubble.

He laughed again. "Simply step down from the wagon."

As simple as it had been to enter. She moved on the seat and turned around to climb out. Then she looked up at him, her heart in her eyes. "Does this mean you're not going to tell anyone about . . . you know." Shame colored her cheeks at the very notion of people finding out that she'd been a thief.

He shook his head. "There is nothing to tell, my friend. A wrong choice is sometimes the *only* one to be made."

That was how she'd felt at the time, she knew. Desperation could cause anyone to do something they ordinarily wouldn't consider. But desperation didn't excuse her.

"Remember, my friend. Your choices now must be made with care. Even to the words you speak. Make your wishes wisely." His eyes shone like two bright stars on a black night. "Or you may not have them when they are most desperately needed."

Riley made it all the way to the end of the street without seeing a trace of either her or the wagon. What the hell was going on? Where could she possibly have gone? No one he'd asked had seen her. And the town wasn't so big that he could have walked right past her and not noticed.

And why the hell did he feel like he *had* to find her?

Cursing under his breath, Riley tore his gaze from the peeling white paint of the little church at the end of the road and turned again to look back the way he'd come.

People. Scores of people, scurrying back and forth across the street, darting in front of wagons, skirting horses and riders, all intent on whatever was driving them.

And not a one of them had soft brown hair tied up in an ugly knot at the top of her head. Not a one of them was walking in that straight-backed, prideful stride Phoebe had.

Damn it all. Where was she?

"Stop! Thief!"

Riley's head swiveled around at the shout. A young boy scurried through the crowd with an irate shopkeeper hot on his heels.

Bang! Bang, bang, bang, bang!

A loud series of shots ricocheted through the air and it was as if the entire town came to a shuddering halt. From the far end of the street, Riley heard gunfire erupt again. And following right after came the loud whoops and hollers of cowboys out to "hurrah" the place.

Instantly, the people in the street sprang to life again, rushing for the boardwalks, scrambling for safety. Mothers dragged children, men sprinted through the mud, even a stray dog had enough sense to bolt for cover.

In seconds, the street was clear.

But for one woman.

Phoebe.

Riley's gut twisted. She'd appeared out of nowhere and now stood rooted in the middle of the road, staring at the six riders bearing down on her.

"Phoebe," he yelled, but his voice was lost in the crash of gunshots erupting from the cowboys' pistols as they fired repeatedly into the air.

Riley started running. Toward her. Toward the rushing cowboys and their horses. Mud sucked and pulled at his boots, as if the very ground was trying to hold him back. Keep him from reaching her in time. But he wouldn't be stopped. Heart pounding against the wall of his chest, blood drumming in his ears, Riley pushed harder, desperation fueling every long stride. His gaze locked on her back, he looked away only long enough to judge the distance between Phoebe and the coming cowboys. They had to be drunk. Or blind. Or sure she would run out of the way at the last minute.

But he knew different. He felt it deep in his soul. She was frozen. Whether from fear or surprise, her feet were locked in that mud and she would still be there when those horses knocked her into the ground and trampled her.

Sound died.

The air was so silent, he heard his own straining breath as he came close to her. Stretching out his arms, he grabbed her around the middle and threw them both to one side just as the riders went past, the horses' hooves tearing up the mud, slashing at the ground.

Riley twisted in midair, so that his body would take the brunt of the fall. They hit hard. He heard her breath rush from her lungs as they rolled to safety. His arms wrapped tightly around her, he pressed her body close and levered himself above her. He didn't let go for a long minute after the danger was past.

Finally, still breathing hard, he went up on one elbow

and looked down into her mud-covered face. "You all right, Phoebe?"

She looked at him blankly for a second or two, then nodded. "I think so," she whispered, and winced as she tried to move beneath him.

Riley sucked in air when her hips rocked against his, and he muttered, "Lie still for a minute. Make sure you're all right."

"I'm fine," she insisted and squeezed one hand from between their bodies to wipe at the mud gathered at her mouth. "What happened?"

"You almost got yourself trampled into the road," he said.

"Those cowboys," she said, drawing her head back into the mud to look at him. "I thought sure they'd stop when they saw me. I kept waiting. I couldn't seem to move. Didn't know which way to run."

"Why the hell'd you stop in the middle of the street like that, anyway?" he asked, his gaze sweeping over her, assuring himself again that she was whole, in one piece.

"I heard someone shouting," Phoebe muttered and beneath the mud mask she wore, he noticed small patches of her skin were blushing a fiery scarlet.

"You mean that storekeeper shouting at the kid?"

"Kid?" she asked, her gaze locked with his.

"Yeah." He reached up and pushed some of her hair back from her forehead. "Some boy must have snatched something. Old man Fisher was chasing after him with a rolling pin."

"Oh," she whispered and her features seemed to relax a bit.

What in the hell was going on here? he wondered.

"Is she all right?" someone above them asked.

"Yeah," Riley answered, somehow reluctant to get up and off her.

"Something ought to be done about those durn cowboys," one man said, clearly disgusted.

"Can't stop young fellas from hurrahing towns."

"Somebody's gonna get hurt. Like her."

Riley paid no attention to them. Their voices swirled around him, but his entire concentration was fixed on the woman lying tucked beneath him. He wanted to know why a thieving kid could affect her so. But more than that, he wanted to enjoy this moment, with her so close to him. Each breath she took seemed to shudder through him. Holding her like this only fed the urge to hold her more closely. More privately. He wanted to caress her cheek. Feel the soft creaminess of her skin. He wanted to smooth his hand up and over her breasts, cupping their fullness. To watch her eyes cloud with sudden, overwhelming passion. To hear her whisper his name as he entered her.

A wellspring of sadness suddenly roared up within him as he realized that he would never do any of those things. He was leaving this place . . . and her . . . far behind him. Regret simmered in his bloodstream and he wished heartily that things could have been different. That he had been a different sort of man.

Phoebe's gaze locked with his. He stared down into her eyes and wondered if she knew what he was thinking. Then he wondered what thoughts were going through her mind. Was she feeling the same stirrings as he? Would she, if she knew of his plans, feel the same regrets?

Sweet Jesus, he hadn't counted on this.

"She's all right," someone spoke up again. "Riley said so."

"You sure?" another man asked. "She ain't movin'."

"Well, now," a woman snapped, "it can't be easy to move with a man lying on top of you like that."

A snort of laughter erupted at that remark and Riley watched a flush of embarrassment warm Phoebe's cheeks. The magic between them had effectively splintered; he should have been grateful. But he wasn't. He only hoped the damn mud covering him would also hide any sign of the desire still pulsing through his body. He slowly rolled to one side of her, stood up, then held out a hand to pull her to her feet.

She was a sight. Mud from the top of her head to the tips of her shoes. Her face was spattered with it. Her dress was soaked through. Her hair hung in filthy strands along both sides of her head. But as he watched her, she wiped mud from her face with a furious embarrassment that made her look as if she could bite the head off a nail.

And Riley wanted her so bad, his knees shook with the need.

Phoebe straightened her spine and lifted her chin, shaking her hair back out of her face, she heard the *plop* of mud as it flew off her head to land on the street. She gave the people staring at her a quick look, then shifted her gaze to Riley Burnett.

His hat was gone, lying somewhere in the muck. Mud covered him, head to toe. His eyes shone like two sapphires dropped onto a square of black velvet.

He looked wonderful.

And every bit as much a hero to her as any of the fictional characters she used to read about in dime novels.

It had all happened so fast. The moment she'd stepped off the tinker's wagon, she'd heard someone shout, "Stop, thief!" and her whole body had gone rigid. Ridiculous as it seemed now, she'd reacted as though the voice were accusing *her*. And before she'd been able to recover from the instinctive reaction, those cowboys had been thundering down on her, guns blazing, horses charging.

She'd tried to move. But it was as if someone had nailed her feet to the ground. She had no doubt at all that if not for Riley, she would have been run down in the street, pummeled into the mud.

Riley. Wrapping his arms around her and flying through the air to safety. It was as though those few seconds had lasted an eternity. She could still feel the warm, solid length of him pressed along her body. The strength of his arms. The gentle sureness of his grip. And his eyes as he looked down at her when it was all over. As if he was reaching inside her soul, touching her where she'd never been touched before.

Good heavens. Heat shot through her body with the crackling intensity of a lightning bolt. And like a lightning-struck tree, she felt aflame from the inside out.

"Everything all right?" a new voice asked.

Phoebe gasped, startled out of her wild thoughts, and turned to look at the man speaking. Of average height, he wore a cream-colored, wide-brimmed hat pulled low over dark eyes. Dressed in jeans, a white shirt, and a black vest, the badge pinned to it glittered in the afternoon sun.

"Everything's fine, Tom." Riley spoke up and the man slanted a look at him.

"Hell, Riley," the sheriff said on a laugh, "I wish we had one of those photographers in town. I'd surely love to have a tintype of this!"

Several people behind them laughed and Riley nodded slowly. He and Tom had grown up together, and Riley'd never known a better man. Or had a better friend. At least, until Tess had stirred things up between them. Then there'd been a fight or two until Tess finally chose Riley and Tom had regretfully accepted her decision.

Still grinning, Tom turned to Phoebe. "Ma'am? I want you to know, I'll speak to those cowboys and see to it we don't have any more gunplay in the streets."

Phoebe smiled at him and felt the mud drying on her face crack slightly. "Thank you, Sheriff . . ."

"Wills, ma'am. Tom Wills." He gave her a slow, lopsided grin. "If you don't mind my saying so, mud suits you lots better than it does ol' Riley here."

In spite of the situation, Phoebe chuckled at the bizarre compliment before looking at Riley. He wasn't smiling.

"Good to see you, Tom," Riley said and took her elbow in a firm grip.

"I'll come by the saloon," the sheriff said to Phoebe. "Give me a chance to catch up with an old friend and hopefully," he added with a smile, "make a new one?"

Phoebe's gaze darted from one man to the other. They appeared to be talking to her, but were actually speaking to each other, she was sure. Now if she only knew what they weren't saying.

Begrudgingly, Riley said, "See ya tonight. For now, I'm gettin' Phoebe back to the hotel so she can—"

Oh, good heavens! Yanking her arm free of his grip, Phoebe gasped and shouted, "Blast and thunder, the hotel! The kitchen!" She hitched up her muddy skirts and ran off down the street.

Chapter Seven

❧

Phoebe stopped dead after she hurtled through the hall door and into the kitchen. The first thing she noticed was that her feet were underwater. Sighing, she looked down. At least three inches of water covered the wide pine-plank floorboards.

"Blast and thunder," she muttered as she remembered the wish she'd made without thinking. *I wish we had water inside the kitchen.* Well, now they did, although she'd been thinking more along the lines of a pump.

The tinker had a decidedly unfunny sense of humor.

For heaven's sake, if wishes were going to be this much trouble for a person, why grant them at all? But then, she thought, maybe he was enjoying watching her stumble. Hadn't he said himself that certain Watchers entertained themselves by observing mortals self-destruct? After all, she only had his word for it that he wasn't one of *those*.

Simmons, carrying a broom, strode into the kitchen through the back door. His pants rolled up, his pale white legs, now turning blue with cold, jutted up from black socks and black shoes. Phoebe'd never seen him looking quite so . . . undignified. He stopped dead when he spotted her and she watched his gray eyebrows lift high on his forehead.

Right behind him were the Weatherby twins, looking

surprisingly subdued, and on their heels was Creek Jackson, Becky Burnett perched on one of his beefy arms.

"Feeb!" the girl crowed and waved her blanket like a flag.

"What happened to you?" Simmons asked, his gaze raking her up and down.

"What happened here?" Phoebe countered, dismissing his curiosity over her mud shroud.

For answer, Simmons half turned and shot the twins a look that Phoebe remembered well from her own childhood. And, like her, the boys couldn't withstand the power of that glare.

"We did it," Henry said sullenly, dipping his head and risking a look at Simmons.

"Not on purpose," Joe piped up, shooting a rebellious look at the butler. "We was prospectin'."

Simmons shook his head as if it pained him.

"Prospecting?" she asked, and stepped farther into the room, creating a wave that crested against the table leg as she walked. "In here?"

Joe scowled at her.

Simmons answered for him. "No. Right outside the doorway." He set the straw end of the broom into the water and added, "Apparently, the young Weatherbys decided the hotel is resting atop the infamous Mother Lode."

"Creek said it looked a likely spot." Obviously Joe was unwilling to concede defeat just yet.

Phoebe turned her gaze on the old forty-niner.

He shrugged. "Looked as good as any. Figured they'd dig a hole, get tired, and fill it in again." A sheepish expression crossed his face. "Who knew they'd hit a wellspring?"

"Perhaps they should dig another hole. Maybe they'll find hot water as well as cold," Simmons suggested wryly.

"Ya know," Joe told him hotly, "there's no tellin' where a spring is until you dig."

"How fortunate for you to have found one on your first attempt," the butler said.

A spring. Phoebe shook her head, crossed to the table, and sat down hard on one of the chairs. Her feet were cold. The water had seeped right through her shoes and stockings and she felt as if her toes were freezing over.

Staring down at the floor, she noted three cookies, a mousetrap, and a collar button float by. Water inside the kitchen. Good heavens.

Riley burst into the room a moment later and everyone looked up. "What in the hell?"

"Is it raining mud outside?" Simmons asked, looking from Riley to Phoebe.

"Joe and Henry went prospecting," Phoebe said when Riley turned toward her. "They struck water."

Slowly, he swiveled his head to stare at the twins.

"You don't have to say nothin' about this to our ma, do ya?" Henry asked.

Patches of lamplight glistened on tiny puddles of half-frozen mud. The soft color lay like golden nuggets ready to be picked up. Phoebe smiled at the thought and wondered if the Weatherby boys had been cured of their gold fever.

After spending hours cleaning the kitchen and then fashioning a cover for their newly discovered well, Joe and Henry had stumbled home, exhausted. She rolled her shoulders and felt the tense muscles there stretch and pull. Just as tired as the boys must be, Phoebe couldn't seem to rest.

Between the excitement with the kitchen and the memories of her chat with the Tinker—not to mention the incident with Riley running to her rescue—her nerves were as taut as her aching shoulders.

Wishes.

She shook her head and focused her unseeing gaze on a particularly bright patch of frozen lamplight. It was so impossible. So ridiculous. And yet . . . here she was in Nevada. With a water-logged kitchen.

Why me? she wondered. Was she being punished or rewarded? And what was she supposed to do now that she knew she was being observed? Well, beyond of course, minding her stray thoughts and never allowing the word *wish* to enter her brain.

Was she supposed to be different? Changed in some way because of an immortal's intervention in her life?

She frowned and reached up to rub her forehead, hoping to ease the beginnings of what promised to be a monstrous headache. A brief gust of chill air swept along the street, bringing the scent of a coming storm. Phoebe rubbed her upper arms absently, thinking back to her first encounter with the tinker. It seemed so long ago and yet it was hardly more than a month.

So much had happened in that time. So much in her life had already changed.

But what was it he'd said when he'd bestowed those blasted wishes on her and she'd so blindly accepted them?

A price?

No. He'd said, *Heaven demands a price.*

She shivered again and this time the cold settling over her had nothing to do with the icy night air.

"Quite a day."

Phoebe jumped, one hand shooting to the base of her throat as she spun around.

"Didn't mean to spook you," Riley said as he stepped onto the boardwalk and crossed to her side.

She laughed shortly. "It's all right. I guess my mind was wandering."

"Like I said, quite a day." He smiled at her and Phoebe realized just how seldom that one particular expression crossed his face. A shame, since he had a very nice smile.

"Yes," she said, "it was."

"Fancy those boys trying to find gold practically under the porch."

She chuckled, turned her back on the darkened street,

and braced her hip against the porch rail. "According to Creek, gold's been found in stranger places."

"Suppose so," he said, studying her profile in the dim light cast through the hotel's front windows. He'd already discovered gold, he thought, staring at the golden glow lying on her hair as it shimmered gently, tempting him to pull the pins free and run his fingers through the thick, long mass.

Riley sucked in a gulp of cold night air and told himself to quit thinking along such lines. He had no business entertaining any notions at all about Phoebe. She was staying and he was going and never the twain would meet.

To divert his own thoughts, he said, "I talked with one of the men from the construction sites."

She looked at him, waiting.

"He said he'd come by tomorrow. Take a look at the spring. Said he could probably lay a pipe and hook up a pump."

Phoebe laughed under her breath. "Water inside the kitchen, then."

"Yeah," he agreed. "Steve should have done it a while back. But what with the well being so far from the hotel, the cost would have been too dear."

"Well, at least *that* problem's been solved."

Riley gave her a half-smile. "No wonder Mrs. Weatherby let us hire those two. She probably would have paid *us* just to get them out of her hair for a while."

"They're good boys," Phoebe said, defending them.

It warmed him to hear her stick up for the pair who had submerged her kitchen. Phoebe Hightower had a big heart. He'd known folks who would have beaten the tar out of those two for a lot less.

"Oh, there's no meanness in them," he said. "But there sure is double the mischief."

For a long moment, neither of them spoke and the only sounds came from the saloon just a few steps away. Piano music, laughter, and snatches of songs only half remembered by the drunks crooning them.

Riley wished briefly that he and Phoebe were far away from there. Alone in the darkness with only the sound of their own heartbeats murmuring in the stillness.

He'd like to see her bathed in the soft silvery cast of the moon's light. He'd like to spend long, slow hours exploring her body. And when the exploration was finished, he'd like to begin again. And again.

His body stirred and he cursed his own wandering mind.

She shivered and he snapped himself free of the mental images crowding his mind. Shrugging out of his coat, he draped it across her shoulders. The back of his fingers brushed the nape of her neck and an arc of heat linked them briefly before Riley took a step back, rubbing his fingertips together as if they'd been burned.

"Thank you," she said and her voice carried a raw huskiness that poked and prodded at him.

He nodded stiffly, shoved his hands into his pockets, and glanced up at the heavens. No stars shone there. Heavy storm clouds covered the moon and draped the sky in a winter blanket.

"Snow before morning," he said and leaned one shoulder on the newel post beside her. His pose was casual, but the hands he kept hidden in his pockets were fisted.

"Certainly cold enough," she replied, tugging the edges of his coat more tightly around her.

A hoot of laughter burst into life from inside the saloon and they both glanced toward the lamplit windows.

"Sounds busy," she said.

He shrugged. "Saloons are always busy. Plenty of men willing to spend money to drink the night and their cares away."

"Shouldn't you be in there?"

Riley half smiled. "Trying to get rid of me?"

"No," she said quickly.

Too quickly.

Damn. He sucked in a breath. It probably would have been better for both of them if she'd said yes. If she'd just come out and asked him to leave. Instead of looking at him through those wide blue eyes. He saw his own reflection in their depths and wondered what she saw when she looked at him.

And what she would say when she found out he was leaving.

"Thank you again," Phoebe said. "For today, I mean. You saved my life."

"My pleasure." And it had been. Especially lying with her in the mud and muck, looking down into sky-blue eyes lined with dark, curling lashes.

"The sheriff?" she asked in a thoughtful tone.

The warm feeling inside him withered just a bit. He'd seen the way Tom had looked at Phoebe. Had she been looking back? "What about him?"

"Is that the kind of lawman you were?"

A spurt of relief coursed through him and he called himself all kinds of a fool. Hell, it'd be better for Phoebe if she was interested in Tom Wills. At least, there was a settled man. A good man. With a steady job. A man who obviously *liked* town life.

So why was he so damn pleased it was curiosity about *him* that had prompted her question?

"No. I was a Federal Marshal," he said, then asked, "Who told you?"

"I don't even remember," she admitted. "Creek, maybe."

He nodded and stared out toward the edge of town. He couldn't actually see much, as dark as it was. But he didn't have to see wild country to know it was out there. Soon, he'd be a part of it again. Yet, as that thought whispered through his mind, he didn't feel the tug of eager anticipation he expected to feel.

"You do that a lot, you know," Phoebe said, her voice a soft contrast to the boisterousness coming from the saloon.

With an effort, he dragged his gaze away from the unknown darkness and the confusion of his thoughts and looked at her again. "Do what?"

"Stare off into space," she said and turned around to look into the blackness herself. "Into the distance. As if you're looking at something the rest of us can't see."

"Old habit, I guess."

"I think there's more to it than that."

She took a step closer and Riley caught the slightest whiff of lavender drifting from her. He inhaled it, drawing it deeply within him, capturing it in his lungs as if he might later be able to draw on it, bring her close again. Why he might *want* that memory was a question he preferred to ignore.

"I've never been much on towns," he said, half hoping she'd accept that explanation—half hoping she wouldn't. "Even when I was a kid, I was always stealin' off to explore new ground. To look over the next hill and the one beyond that."

"If you don't care for towns," Phoebe asked, turning her face up to his, "why are you here? Did you hate being a marshal so much that running a saloon seemed a better choice?"

He actually laughed at that notion, but the laughter was strained and squeezed past his throat grudgingly.

"No," he said, looking down into her face, bathed now in a square of mottled, muted lamplight. Instinctively, he pulled his hands from his pockets and almost reached for her. He stopped himself just in time to keep from stroking the line of her jaw, testing the softness of her skin. The temptation to touch her was so strong, Riley pushed away from the newel post and took a step or two past her, farther from the saloon, into the deeper shadows afforded on the opposite side of the windows.

There was no safety there, though.

He should have known that Phoebe would follow him, silently refusing to be put off. And in those shadows, it was as if they were in a private, dangerous world—just the two of them.

"Riley?"

He shoved one hand through his hair, tunneling his fingers along his scalp. Anything to keep from grabbing hold of her. "I liked being a marshal," he finally said, training his gaze on the far-distant darkness. He ignored the occasional bright patches in windows, shining like quilt squares of lamplight, and concentrated on the night world beyond Rimshot.

Out where he'd always felt most comfortable.

"But more than that," he added, "I was good at it. It was the one thing in my life I did well. Maybe better than anyone." Somehow, it was important to him that she understand.

She touched him briefly and he felt the pulsing heat of each fingertip burn right through his shirt, into his flesh and still deeper, until it settled in his bones. He should move, he knew. Pull away. But he didn't.

Couldn't.

"Then why did you quit?" she asked simply.

"Because of Becky," he answered.

"Ah . . ."

Sympathy. He heard it in her voice and, because he knew he didn't deserve it, felt shame crowd him.

Riley turned his head to look at her, forcing himself to meet her gaze. In the dim light, he saw kindness etched on her features and the sympathy he'd heard in her voice shining in her eyes.

"Don't look at me like that," he said quietly.

"Like what?" Tiny lines etched between her brows.

"Like I did something noble in giving up marshaling to be a saloonkeeper."

She smiled slightly and he was struck again by how the simple act of curving her lips made her damn near beautiful.

"You don't consider giving up something you love for the sake of someone else noble?"

Noble. Jesus. Just wait until she found out he was leaving. That Mr. Noble had handed his kid off to her grandparents. Again. "Nothin' noble about it, Phoebe. Believe me." Deliberately looking away, he said softly, "My folks were raising Becky up till a couple of months ago. They died in a carriage accident, so I was called back home. Until then, I hadn't seen Becky but a few times in her whole life."

"I'm so sorry," she said, laying one hand on his forearm again.

He closed his eyes tightly, briefly, enjoying the feel of her touch. Then he buried that sensation in the back of his mind and went on. "Erma, over at the Mercantile, took care of Becky until I could get back here."

"I'm sorry," Phoebe whispered. "I didn't mean to pry."

"You didn't," he assured her and turned his head away from her, until he was once again staring off into the night shadows.

Phoebe perched gingerly on the porch rail, her back to the night, her gaze locked on Riley. He felt the power of her stare and schooled himself not to return it.

"So, until recently, you didn't really know your daughter?"

"That's right. Real noble, huh?" There, he'd said it out loud. He'd admitted to remaining a stranger to his own child.

"And yet," she said quietly, "you altered your entire life for her."

Didn't she get it? Didn't she understand? Hell, he'd admitted to ignoring his own child's existence the first two and a half years of her life and still Phoebe wanted to grant him nobility?

If he hadn't been so stunned, he would have laughed.

"I didn't have much choice," he told her, finally forcing himself to turn and meet her gaze.

"Of course you did," Phoebe said, shaking her head and *smiling* at him.

"What?"

She stood up beside him and laid one hand on his forearm again. The quick flash of heat ricocheted throughout his body like a bullet gone wild, tearing at everything in its path. He knew he should pull away from her, but God help him, he craved the heat like a man freezing to death in a snowdrift. Riley stood stock-still, afraid the slightest movement from him would cause her to step back and away from him.

Phoebe's fingertips tingled. Warmth sparkled in her veins like the tiny bubbles in champagne. She looked up into his stony features and wanted to smooth the deep furrow from between his eyes.

She was finally beginning to understand this man who was her partner. Guilt drove him. Guilt over his dead wife and the child he was only now coming to know. The haunted look in his eyes pulled at her.

Odd. She'd known him little more than a week and yet, at this moment, she felt closer to Riley Burnett than she would have thought possible. And the urge to somehow ease the pain lurking beneath his shadowed blue gaze compelled her to speak.

Deliberately leaning in closer to him, she said softly, "I think you're being too hard on yourself, Riley."

He snorted a choked laugh. "Now Phoebe, that just goes to show how little you know me."

"You're doing everything you can. And Becky is healthy and happy." She tightened her grip on his forearm slightly before releasing him. Strange, but the tingling sensation continued. "You've thrown away your own dreams in favor of your child. I think that's very noble. Almost heroic."

"Stop it!" He grabbed her shoulders in a firm grip. "Jesus, Phoebe, stop looking at me like I'm some damned saint." Clearly frustrated, his voice ground out from between clenched teeth. "If I'm doin' such a fine job of taking care of Becky, how come it is the child's hair's standin' on end 'cause I can't brush it without makin' her scream?"

"I can fix her hair, if you'd like."

He sighed heavily and let her go. "She'll scream at you too."

"I won't hurt her," Phoebe promised.

"Hell," Riley said, swiveling his head to look at her again. "I know that, Phoebe."

The dim reflection of lamplight flickered in his eyes. Phoebe's breath caught. Her chest tightened until it felt as though a giant hand held her in a powerful grip. From the corner of her eye, she noticed a few fat, lazy snowflakes drifting toward the ground.

"Phoebe . . ." Her name whispered from him in a hush. "It's not just her hair," he said, shaking his head. "It's her livin' in a saloon. It's me trying to figure out what to do for a little girl. It's this town. This place . . ."

A small frown creased her brow even as a twinge of worry eased up inside her. "What are you trying to say?"

Reaching up, he shoved both hands through his hair, squeezing his scalp as if trying to hold his head onto his shoulders. Then he took a deep breath and said, "Nothin'. Just . . . nothin'." He couldn't tell her. Not now. Not like this. Despite what she thought of him, he was a selfish man. Selfish enough to turn his child over to others so that he could go back to the life he loved. And selfish enough to keep the truth from a woman who looked at him as if he were something special—just because he hated to see the light in her eyes dim.

Because even if it was only this once, he wanted to kiss her. Needed to kiss her, hold her, pretend, if only briefly, that this was more than just a stolen moment in the shadows.

She stared up at him, their gazes locked, and all around her, the world suddenly seemed to hush. As if even God was holding His breath.

"Phoebe," Riley murmured just before he slowly lowered his head, angling his lips toward hers.

Anticipation shot through her. At last, she was going to be kissed. Phoebe had long ago given up any hope of experiencing the feel of a man's mouth on hers. She'd resigned herself to the knowledge that she would live and die, untouched by a man's passions.

Now, it seemed that finally she would know the thrill of being held in a man's arms as his lips claimed what her books described as the "sweet, juicy fruit of a woman's heart."

Breathlessly, she tilted her head back and puckered her lips in readiness. Her eyes slid shut and she leaned into him, hoping that she wouldn't make a mistake.

"Ah, Phoebe," he whispered and she felt him rub the pad of his thumb across her mouth, relaxing the tight purse of her mouth.

Disappointed, she opened her eyes to find his face only a breath away from her own. "I thought . . ."

"What?" His gaze moved over her features like the softest of caresses.

Embarrassment flooded her and she quietly gave thanks that the light was too poor to see the red flush staining her cheeks. "I'm sorry," she said tightly, forcing the words past her throat. "I thought you—" No, she wouldn't say it out loud. Bad enough to be wrong silently. "I'm sorry," she said again. She tried to take a step back from him, but his left hand snaked around her waist, his palm flattened against the small of her back.

Phoebe drew in a shaky breath and tried to ignore the wild, swirling sensations twisting inside her.

Then his thumb slid across her trembling lower lip and his breath fanned her cheek as he said, "You thought I was going to kiss you?"

Oh, Lord, she prayed fervently, please, if You're a just and loving God, let the ground open up and swallow me whole. She waited a heartbeat for a miracle that wasn't coming before bowing her head and admitting, "Yes."

"Well, Phoebe," he said, a smile in his voice, "you were right."

She gasped in surprise just as his mouth dusted across hers. The tingling warmth that simply touching him inspired was nothing compared to this.

Skyrockets went off inside her. She felt them explode behind her closed eyes, showering her world with brilliant flashes of color.

Soft, she thought. Yet strong. Tender, yet persuasive. Once, twice, three times, his lips brushed across hers, as if he were tasting her in tiny increments. Her breath caught after each contact and she felt herself leaning closer to him, instinctively, silently, asking for more. She'd never expected this. She'd had no way of knowing just what a man's kiss could do to a woman's soul. How it could reach down beyond the years of loneliness and stir the ashes of long-dead hopes and dreams.

Her mind whirled. Her spirit soared.

He groaned and held her tighter, pressing his mouth more firmly to hers.

Phoebe heard quiet whimpering, then realized that *she* was making that sound. But she couldn't seem to stop it. His lips caressed hers. The tip of his tongue traced the seam of her mouth and she was deliciously scandalized. Her heart raced, fluttering wildly in her chest. She didn't know what to do, so she let him silently tell her.

Once more, his tongue smoothed across her closed mouth and this time she opened slightly, hesitantly, for him. He kissed her more intimately and her quick intake of breath seemed to spark something in him. He groaned tightly and lifted one hand to cup her face.

This was what had been missing from her life. This urgency. This need to become a part of something bigger than oneself.

His arm around her waist tightened, drawing her close. His strength wove itself around her until she felt as though she were wrapped in a soft blanket shot with threads of steel.

Time was lost. What might have been seconds or minutes or hours flew past and Phoebe didn't care. All that mattered to her was exploring the glorious wonders so unexpectedly offered her.

" 'Evening, Riley," an amused, deep voice said from somewhere to her left. "Miss Phoebe."

Phoebe jumped in Riley's arms, startled out of a private world to come crashing back into reality. Keeping her face averted, she pulled away and faced the falling snow. She suddenly felt as cold and aimless as the small bits of white fluff twisting and dancing in the night air.

"Damn it," she heard Riley whisper just before saying in a harsh, strained voice, "Tom."

"Didn't mean to interrupt," Sheriff Wills went on. "But you did invite me in for a drink tonight."

"I did, didn't I?" Riley said. "Why don't you go on into the saloon and I'll join you there in a minute or two?"

"All right." A pause, then, "Good night, Miss Phoebe."

She didn't speak. She couldn't. If it had meant her life, she wouldn't have been able to squeeze a single word past the hard, tight knot in her throat. She heard the sheriff move off, his boot heels scraping on the wood planks, and she and Riley were alone again.

"Phoebe," he said and laid one hand on her shoulder. She shook her head. Humiliating. To at last discover the joys to be found in a kiss only to have that essentially private moment interrupted.

He said her name again and this time turned her around to face him. Tipping her chin up with the tips of his fingers, he didn't speak again until their gazes were locked.

"I'm sorry," he said then, and her heart broke.

He regretted the single most exciting moment in her life. She wrapped her arms about her waist and held on tight. She wouldn't let him know how deeply he'd affected her. She would spare herself that particular indignity.

"Don't be sorry," she managed to say, congratulating

herself silently on finding her voice. Then, determined to sound casually dismissive of the entire incident, she added, "Accidents happen."

He actually chuckled.

She blinked up at him. Was he laughing at her? Had she been so dismal a kisser that laughter was his only response?

Shaking his head, Riley said, "I didn't 'accidentally' fall and land with my mouth on yours."

Phoebe shivered. Oh, Lord. Just talking about it sent ribbons of excitement glittering up her spine.

He lifted one hand to cup her cheek again. His thumb caressed her skin as he went on. "I'm only sorry for starting something I had no right to even think about."

"No right?" she repeated, confused. If she allowed him leave to kiss her, what other "right" was required?

"None at all," he said, and even in the dim light, she saw his features tighten as his gaze moved over her.

And before she could say anything more, he left her in the shadows and walked toward the saloon.

Chapter Eight

Riley didn't know whether to be mad or grateful that the sheriff had interrupted them when he had.

His body hard and uncomfortable, he ached with the need to return to Phoebe, to pull her into his arms and taste her sweet mouth again. But he'd been honest with her when he'd said he had no right to touch her. So he forced himself to keep walking toward the saloon and the safety found in a roomful of drunks.

Damn it, *this* he hadn't planned on. He didn't want to care about Phoebe. He didn't want her looking at him with stars in her eyes and dreams in her soul. Because then he'd have to hurt her.

Not that he wanted to, mind you. But it would happen, all the same. And there was no way to escape it. If he pulled away now and told her he wasn't interested, she'd be hurt. If he let things go on and then left as planned in just a few weeks, her hurt would be deeper and harder.

Maybe he should just tell her the truth about himself and be done with it. He could start with admitting that he was handing his own daughter over to grandparents who couldn't be bothered to put off social obligations to come and get her. Or maybe tell her all about how he'd sent his wife away right after Becky's birth. About *paying* her to leave and then finding out she'd been killed in a train wreck when a trestle bridge collapsed.

Hell. Maybe he should just look deep into Phoebe's big blue eyes and tell her that he was running. Running away from the risk of failure.

How noble would she think him then?

He paused just outside the twin half doors and looked to the shadows where Phoebe had been only moments before. Where he'd touched her and found something he hadn't expected.

A soft, sad smile briefly crossed his face as he remembered her tightly puckered lips and the rigid tension of her body as she awaited what had to have been her first kiss.

First kiss. Jesus, were none of the men in St. Louis worth their salt? Were they all looking for some tiny blond-haired dimwit? Had no one ever noticed her striking looks? Her sharp, intelligent gaze? And if not, *why* not? Why hadn't someone courted and married her? Then she wouldn't have come west and he wouldn't be left wanting something he could never have.

His gaze narrowed as he looked at the empty porch. She must have left right after he'd walked away from her. Oh, he'd handled that real well, he told himself in disgust. The shadowy corner was deserted. As if they'd never stood there together. As if she'd never been.

He frowned thoughtfully, suddenly remembering that he never had found out where she'd been that afternoon. When she seemed to have disappeared right in front of him.

But then, it wasn't any of his business where she'd gone. And he'd do well to remember that.

"Aw, hell," he muttered.

With the scent of lavender still clinging to him, he angrily pushed through the swinging doors. Blue-gray smoke twisted with a stray gust of air and wreathed itself into ghostly halos over the heads of the card players seated at the tables. Tinny music competed with the laughter and shouts from the winners and losers. The smells of whiskey, unwashed bodies, and the ever-present mud blended together into a rank odor he'd come to think of as his own personal hell.

And the faint trace of lavender was obliterated.

A few of the gamblers looked up as he passed. Nods, smiles, and sometimes grunts of welcome rose up and fell behind him as he made his way through the teeming crowd. At the bar, a glass of beer in his hand, Sheriff Tom Wills watched him approach.

Riley's gaze flicked to the star on the man's vest and he tried to stifle the instant ache of envy. He still wasn't used to the emptiness over his left shirt pocket. But in a few weeks, his badge would be back, pinned over the place where his heart used to be.

He finally reached the bar, propped one boot on the brass foot-rail, and leaned an elbow on the gleaming pine bar-top.

"Sorry I interrupted," Tom said loud enough to be heard over the clatter.

"You didn't," Riley said shortly.

The man grinned and took a sip of beer. "Not what it looked like to me."

A slow flush of irritation rode him. They'd known each other long enough for Tom to poke fun at him. But Phoebe didn't need folks in town getting the wrong idea about her. "Let it be, Tom."

"Sure."

Impatiently, Riley turned toward the bartender. "Mick, that new order of whiskey come in yet?"

The beefy bartender nodded.

"Then pour me one. A double." If he couldn't get Phoebe out of his mind, the least he could do was cloud her image.

"Can't do it, boss."

Was nobody going to give him a little peace tonight? "Why the hell not?"

"Ain't got any."

Riley inhaled slowly, deeply, refusing to feed the temper riding him. He'd learned years ago that the fastest way to get yourself killed was to get mad. Once a man let anger take charge of his mind, he didn't think. Didn't react. And more times than he'd like to remember, his ability to control his temper had saved his hide.

Now, staying calm around here might not mean life and death, but it could prevent another bar fight. And he'd just spent the last week cleaning up the mess from the last fracas. He wasn't ready to deal with another.

So with more patience than he was feeling at the moment, Riley reminded him, "You just said—"

"I said the order came in," Mick interrupted him and continued drying clean glasses with a spotless white bar towel. Absently, Riley guessed that the towel was due to Phoebe. He'd never seen a clean cloth in the bar until she hit town.

"I *didn't* say what shape the whiskey was in," Mick finished.

Riley rubbed one hand hard across his face. "Just spit it out."

"Malloy, down at the train depot?" Mick set the towel and glass aside, leaned both burly forearms on the bar and continued. "He sent word telling me to pick up the order. Had it set out waiting for me. By the time I got there, somebody'd smashed every last bottle."

"Smashed?"

Mick nodded. "Just like they'd jumped up and down on the crates. Wood and glass everywhere, the station platform smelling like a whorehouse on a Saturday night, and some of the passengers sniffin' like they was fit to die from the stench."

"Wonderful," Riley muttered. He'd ordered that damn whiskey in from San Francisco. Now all they had left to serve was the blasted "Indian" whiskey that about ate its way through a man's stomach lining.

But more important than that was the question of who had smashed the liquor. And why. Was this something new? Or had his vandals decided not to give up harassing him after all?

"Malloy see anything?" Tom asked, and Mick's gaze shifted to him.

"Nope, but that ain't surprising. Only time Pete steps out of his little office is when he absolutely has to."

"Well," the sheriff went on, now turning his attention to Riley. "Someone must have seen something. I'll ask around."

"Thanks." Damn. He'd been hoping the vandalism was over. Nobody'd pitched a rock through his window since Phoebe had arrived.

"Dave told me your problems were over," Tom said, his features now schooled into his professional mask.

"Yeah. I thought so too." Riley glanced at Mick. "Get me a drink."

"All we got is—"

"I know," Riley snapped, and a small part of him was even looking forward to the liquid fire that nasty whiskey would create. Since he and Mick had made this last batch, he should know better than to drink it. But a man made do with what he had or he did without.

And he'd learned long ago that in place of real whiskey, men with a thirst would swallow just about anything.

The liquor he and Mick had concocted a couple of weeks ago tasted worse than some but a helluva lot better than others. The recipe was pretty basic, but the flavor changed according to whatever the brewer happened to have on hand. Starting with a couple of gallons of cheap wine he'd found in the Mercantile, Riley'd added shaved-up black chewing tobacco, a few dozen red peppers for bite, and then let the mess boil for a while. Then they strained it, dumped the liquid into forty gallons of spring water, and added a quart or two of molasses for flavoring.

Yeah, he sure had been looking forward to store-bought whiskey. Once his drink was poured, Riley tossed the poisonous-looking liquid down his throat and, instantly, his eyes watered. Slamming the glass back onto the bar, he gasped, "Fill it again."

Tom chuckled and picked up his beer. "Hell, Riley, that stuff'll kill ya."

"Sure as you're born, *something*'ll kill ya sooner or later." Curling his right hand around the jigger glass, he glanced at his old friend, cleared his throat, and said, "Things have been quiet around here for more than a week. Thought whoever it was, was finished playing around."

"Guess not," Wills said and took another sip of beer. "What about the hotel?" he asked. "And Miss Phoebe? Everything all right there?"

Riley's grip on the small glass tightened at the thought. But he told himself there were no worries there. "Why wouldn't she be all right? This trouble started before she got here. It has nothing to do with her."

Who was he trying to convince? Wills? Or himself? What if whoever was riding him decided to switch targets? Something black and hard settled in the pit of his stomach. What if the next rock came hurtling through a hotel window? What if the vandals didn't stop at breakage and went right on to actually hurt Phoebe?

Or Becky.

Son of a bitch.

Riley lifted his glass and drank the contents in one swallow. The resulting heat did little to offset the sudden chill building deep in his gut. He was worrying over nothing, he told himself. In the west, good women were as safe as a babe in a cradle. It was only on the rarest occasions that a woman found herself in danger from anything other than Indian raids, fire, flood, snake bite, and blizzards.

Hell, nature might try to kill a woman, but otherwise, she was pretty much on safe ground.

Still, it wouldn't hurt to be on his guard more. At least

until he could discover exactly who was behind the mischief aimed at him.

Riley shot the man beside him a look. "You're the sheriff, Tom. Find out who's doing this."

Tom Wills gave him a slow, confident smile. "Have I ever let you down before?"

Phoebe stared out the window into the snow-covered darkness. Gently falling flakes had given way to gust-driven bits of white that slapped at the glass panes, making her grateful for the fire blazing cheerfully in the hearth.

But even the heat from the carefully banked flames didn't quite reach the small spot of coldness nestled deep within her. Rubbing her upper arms with both hands, Phoebe asked herself again just what she had done to make Riley change so abruptly.

Each time she remembered that scene on the porch, a wave of heat engulfed her. Even now, her lips burned with a tingling sensation as if she could still feel his mouth pressed to hers. Her nipples ached as though she still held tightly to him and her heart quickened until she thought it might fly from her chest.

A knock at her door startled her and she half turned from the window. "Come in."

"The incoming tide has been quashed," Simmons announced as he stepped into her room. "And just in time, I might add," he said with a nod in the direction of the falling snow outside. "By morning, we might have had to ice-skate our way across the kitchen."

Phoebe smiled and ducked her head. "I'm sorry about the water, Simmons," she said.

"Why on earth would you be sorry?" he asked, walking about the room and straightening objects that didn't require it. "Those two young . . . *boys* were behind the near-biblical flood we experienced."

She couldn't let the Weatherby twins accept the entire blame for what had happened. "What would you say if

I told you the flood was another wish gone wrong?"

He stopped dead, cocked his head to one side, and studied her. A small pool of lamplight lay in a soft, glimmering circle behind her. Her features in shadow, it was impossible for Simmons to see her expression—and yet, he knew what it would be.

All of her life, he'd taken care of her, guided her, loved her. When her own father was too involved in his work, lost in the translation of yet another Greek text to notice his daughter, Simmons had been there.

He'd been the one to keep her secrets, to dry her tears, to foster her sense of worth and independence. He'd read her fairy tales and, later, had procured the dime novels she'd kept hidden within the pages of her lesson books. She was the child he'd never had and he couldn't have loved her more had she been his own.

Still, that didn't prohibit him from acknowledging her faults. Such as this recent propensity to believe in wishes coming true.

"Don't frown," he said. "Your face will soon be as wrinkled as an old map."

She laughed shortly. "Doesn't really matter, does it?"

"It does to me," he replied, pleased that for the moment at least, she was smiling.

"Simmons, I saw the tinker today."

"Where?" he asked and crossed the room to her side. "*Here.*"

"At the hotel?" Impossible. He hadn't seen anyone.

"No. On the street. Outside the Mercantile."

He didn't know what to think. It seemed too much of a coincidence for the same tinker to show himself in both St. Louis and Rimshot, of all places. Now that he was close enough to her, he saw the worry in her eyes. The soft, pale light reflected off the falling snow outside the window gave Phoebe's features an ivory cast, making her look more like a fine porcelain statue than a woman.

Or was she pale for another reason entirely?

"Did you speak to him?"

"Yes." She flopped down onto the nearby chair and stared up at him.

Impatience stirred within him. "Are you going to relate the conversation to me?" he asked. "Or would you prefer that I go into the snow, find the bloody tinker, and ask him?"

She leaped to her feet again. "He said he's been watching me."

"Watching you?" Oh, he didn't like the sound of that. Perhaps he *would* go in search of this mysterious tinker. And he would be carrying something heavy. "For what purpose?"

She shook her head. "It's what he does, he says. He's a Watcher."

Ambiguous enough to mean almost anything. "And just what, precisely, is a Watcher?"

Breathlessly, Phoebe told him everything the tinker had said. Simmons listened with a distracted air. He didn't know what part of all this worried him more. The tinker's obvious instability—or the fact that Phoebe clearly believed him. When she'd finished, she added, "So you see, if what he's saying is true, he's not even human."

Human enough to respond to a sound thrashing, he'd wager. "I thought he was a tinker."

"Apparently, he's both."

"Ah," Simmons said, with more levity than he felt. "A master of all trades."

She didn't rise to his teasing tone.

He inhaled slowly, deeply. "Phoebe, surely you see that this is nonsense. That this man, for whatever reason, has taken it upon himself to lie to you in a very creative manner?"

"I suppose that's possible," she said, though her voice said very clearly that she doubted it.

"Phoebe," Simmons said, his tone firm, "you're a grown woman. And this fantasy is one a child would have difficulty believing."

She scowled at him. "The water in the kitchen was my

fault. I inadvertently *wished* it so. Just like I wished us here."

"Phoebe—"

"No," she interrupted. "I did. I actually wished that we had water inside the kitchen. Of course, I *meant* piped-in water with a pump."

"Naturally," he said. "Why would you have wished for a flood?"

"Don't you see? That's two wishes. One brought us here and one—"

"Nearly washed us away." He nodded. "Yes, I see. But you have no proof at all that either of these things have anything to do with you making a wish."

"It makes sense, though. Doesn't it?"

"None at all." And even if it had, he wouldn't have admitted it. He didn't want her worried over random thoughts and stray wishes. "Phoebe, *wishing* for something doesn't make it so."

"But," she whispered, turning her gaze from him to the window. Phoebe stared at the snowflakes as they twisted and danced in the cold wind rattling the glass panes. "What if it did?"

"I beg your pardon?"

She smiled, despite the nagging worry at the back of her mind. Simmons's voice was always at its most British when trying to win an argument. Flicking a glance his way, she said, "What if wishing *did* make things so? What then?"

"Then, to borrow from the poet, 'Beggars would ride.' "

"Simmons," she whispered, ignoring his sarcasm. "Don't you see? If these wishes are real, then I have an extraordinary chance here. It's the sort of thing people dream of."

"Phoebe," he said quietly, and she turned to look at him.

His features schooled into a mask of patience, he went on. "Tinkers do not grant wishes. Nor are they otherworldly beings. This man, for whatever reason, is lying to you. Don't believe him."

She stared into his familiar face, creased by lines of concern, and wished she could make him understand. The tinker was real. The wishes were real. And she didn't know what to do next.

For the first time in her life, Simmons couldn't help her with a problem.

Her mind raced with possibilities. She had to be careful of everything she said now. Even of her thoughts, since she had no way of knowing if an unspoken wish could be granted as easily as one said aloud. Good heavens, there were any number of things that could go wrong.

She could inadvertently wipe out a town!

And Riley, she thought suddenly. Clearly, he hadn't *wanted* to kiss her. What if she had unconsciously wished him to? Oh, blast and damnation. Her mind immediately unleashed the memory of his kiss and the unknown fires that the brushing of lips had created.

"Phoebe?" Simmons said, taking her by the arm and gently lowering her into a chair. "Are you all right?"

She swallowed heavily, grateful that she'd been able to sit down before her watery knees had collapsed. "I'm fine," she whispered, not even looking at the man kneeling by her side.

"Oh, yes," he said. "Splendid. You always turn that lovely shade of hot pink when you're feeling in the glow of good health."

She shook her head, uncertain if she could speak at the moment. Her mind and soul were too filled with the memory of kisses in the shadows and the thrum of some unfamiliar ache deep within her.

"It's the tinker, isn't it?" he demanded. "You've remembered something else. Something that frightened you. What is it?"

She looked into his dear face and read the concern shimmering in his eyes. But she couldn't very well ask his opinion on stolen kisses, now could she? No. She knew what she had to do. The same thing she'd done all those months in St. Louis when she'd pretended to be out "shopping" for groceries and was instead stealing milk or bread or whatever else she could find.

Meeting his gaze squarely, she looked him dead in the eye and lied through her teeth. "There's nothing else, Simmons. Really."

"Hmmm . . ."

It wasn't a complete lie, she told herself. Something *had* frightened her. It simply wasn't the tinker. It was the realization that even the memory of Riley Burnett's mouth on hers had the ability to turn her mind to mush and her body into a bubbling cauldron of sensation.

And for the moment, the memory of that kiss wiped away even the notion of having two more wishes at her beck and call.

Chapter Nine

❦

The snowstorm thickened during the night, becoming a blizzard that blanketed the town in a swirling cloud of white. By late the next morning, the snow showed no sign of letting up and Riley paced the inside of the saloon restlessly.

Back and forth he walked, his boot heels sounding like a heartbeat, ticking away the seconds of his life. He paused at one of the front windows to stare out at Main Street. At least, he guessed the street was still there. With the howling wind and the flying snow, he could hardly see beyond the end of the boardwalk.

Which meant that even his most die-hard customers wouldn't be coming in today. No doubt every soul for miles around was holed up, waiting out the storm. And most of them were probably enjoying this time in front of their own fires. No work to do. Nowhere to go. No one to bother them.

He snorted and viciously rubbed the back of his neck.

On the one day when he desperately wanted to be surrounded by crowds, he was alone. Alone with the thoughts that had plagued him all last night.

Riley suddenly kicked the doorjamb, then winced as a well-deserved stab of pain shot up from his foot along his leg. Limping slightly, he started pacing again. Anything. Even the sound of his own boots against the floor was better than the silence crowding in on him.

But while he walked, his mind was free to race. With images of Phoebe. Her eyes. Her figure. Her hair. Her *mouth*.

He groaned.

All through the sleepless hours of the night, he'd tortured himself with the memory of her kiss. The taste of her. The soft brush of her breath against his cheek. The feel of her beneath his hands and the hunger that had rocked him to his soul.

Riley shoved both hands through his hair and squeezed his skull as if trying to destroy the memories before they could destroy him.

But it was no use.

That kiss was burned into his mind and heart for eternity. It had touched him in a way he'd never thought to experience. *She* had touched him.

And in touching him, reminded him that he had no right to touch her in return.

"Riley?"

As if his wayward thoughts had conjured her out of thin air, Phoebe stood in the doorway separating the saloon from the hotel.

Even in that ugly gray dress of hers, she looked too damn good.

"What is it?" he asked, more harshly than he'd intended.

She blinked in surprise. "Perhaps now isn't a good time."

"As good a time as any," he said, waving one hand to indicate the empty saloon. "As you can see, I'm not real busy."

Her expression didn't soften. "Still, I'll come back later."

Forcing a more conversational tone to his voice, he said quickly, "I'm sorry for snarling at you. It's the storm, I guess. Makes a man jumpy when he can't even see past his front door."

"Really?" She shot a glance at the wall of white outside the front windows. "I rather like it. With the fires burning in the hearths and the world so still, it feels . . . cozy."

"Cozy." He repeated the word as if he didn't recognize it. And actually, he had very little experience with anything cozy. The word implied family and warm feelings and kids playing and supper simmering on the stove. He laughed inwardly. Nope. Hadn't been any cozy in his life since he was a boy.

And for the first time ever, that admission depressed hell out of him.

Phoebe, her gaze locked on his face, took a step closer to him and something in his chest hitched. He thought it might be his heart.

She smiled and Riley's body sat up and took notice.

Damn it.

"I didn't come in here to talk about the snow," she said.

Speaking tightly through clenched teeth, he asked, "What is it, then?"

One dark eyebrow lifted into an arch at his tone, but she didn't comment further on it. Instead, she said, "Becky wants to show you something."

Becky. His daughter. Damn. Rather than feeling sorry for himself, he should have been spending this time with Becky. But in the last week or so, he'd become accustomed to either Phoebe or Simmons riding herd on her. All right, he could at least be honest with himself, if no one else.

He was enjoying having someone else look after Becky. It was far easier than trying to pretend he knew what he was doing. Lately, all he'd had to do was get her dressed in the morning, which was a feat in itself, then turn her over to that stuffy butler.

But it wasn't just easier on him. It was better for the girl too. No sense her getting attached to him when he was going to be pulling up stakes in a few short weeks.

Instead, let Becky get accustomed to strangers taking care of her, he reasoned. Then maybe it wouldn't be so hard on her when two more strangers showed up and took her off to a place she'd never been before and tried to convince her it was *home*.

Pain slashed at him and the force of it surprised him. He was doing the right thing, wasn't he? For him. For Becky. He raked his fingers through his hair again and muttered, "Sorry. Shouldn't have left her with you again."

Phoebe frowned at him. "Whyever not? She's a pleasure."

Maybe for everyone else. But for her papa, little Becky Burnett was still about as pleasurable as a mountain lion with a nasty disposition and a sore foot to boot.

Of course, maybe that was his fault. Maybe he just hadn't spent enough time with her. If he just didn't feel so blasted stupid around her. But what did he know about kids? All he'd ever learned was how to track a fugitive, how to shoot, and how to hold his liquor.

Not the things you want to teach a little girl.

Phoebe turned to one side and held out her hand. "Come on, Becky. Let's show your papa how pretty you look."

Riley pushed his doubts and worries aside, determined to concentrate on his daughter. For the few weeks he had left with her, he could at least *try* to be a decent father.

Then Becky ran to Phoebe. The little girl scurried across the hallway, disregarded the woman's outstretched hand, and instead wrapped herself around Phoebe's leg, fists clenching the gray fabric of her skirt. Only when she was firmly settled, did his daughter turn her face toward him.

Riley looked at her for a long moment, then slowly shifted his gaze to Phoebe's proud, pleased expression.

"What the hell did you do to her?" he demanded.

*   *   *

Well! That certainly wasn't the reaction she'd expected. Phoebe looked down at Becky, admiring the shining cap of blond curls that hugged the child's scalp, framing her elfin face. But even as she watched, Becky's bottom lip began to tremble and her wide blue eyes filled with a sheen of tears.

Turning her gaze on Riley's outraged expression, Phoebe said flatly, "I cut her hair."

"I can see that," he growled. "Why?"

"Because you allowed her hair to get so snarled, there was no other answer."

"You said you'd fix it."

"I did."

"Hell, *I* could have scalped her!"

Becky hiccuped and began to cry, softly at first, the sound rising with the promise of a real screech in a few minutes.

"Then you should have," Phoebe pointed out and bent down to pick up Becky, perching the child on her hip.

"If I'd wanted her to look like a boy, I would have."

"I don't understand why you're so upset. It's only hair," Phoebe said sharply, jiggling the baby in hopes of stemming the coming screams. "It will grow back."

"That's not the point," he argued, but didn't bother to reveal just exactly what his point *was*. Stomping across the few feet of space separating them, Riley reached for his daughter. "Give her to me."

The tiny girl wailed and dug her hands and feet into Phoebe's body, shaking her head wildly.

"I don't think she wants to go to you," Phoebe said. "And quite frankly, I don't blame her."

"She's *my* daughter."

"And you're scaring her with the tone of your voice."

He took a deep breath, clearly searching for calm. "Fine," he said after a long moment, a forced smile plastered on his grim face. "I'm *happy* now. See?"

Becky's little fingers dug into the shoulders of Phoebe's gray dress with surprising strength. The child stared at her father through watery eyes and yet still managed to give him a hard, mutinous stare.

An expression that reminded Phoebe of one she'd seen on Riley's own face fairly often.

"You know," Riley said grimly, as his empty arms fell to his sides, "just because I've been leaving her in your care a lot lately, that don't make her *your* child."

Of all the . . . Phoebe sucked in a gulp of air to feed the sudden burst of outrage welling in her bosom. She felt red flames of anger race up her neck and blossom on her cheeks. Perhaps she *had* become a bit too attached to Becky. But that was understandable, wasn't it? She hadn't tried to keep father and daughter apart in any way . . . she had simply been feeding her own long-denied urge for children. And too, perhaps, by lavishing attention on Becky, she somehow hoped to make it up to whatever St. Louis children she might have deprived with her thievery. With those thoughts racing through her mind, she kept her voice calm and even as she met his challenge.

"Riley Burnett, that is, without doubt, the most . . ." Her mouth opened and closed several times. She couldn't think of a word strong enough to describe the feelings swamping her at the moment.

Blast and damnation! The perfect scathing retort would probably occur to her hours from now. When it wouldn't do her the slightest amount of good.

"Stupid?" Riley offered suddenly and threw both hands up like a man reaching for a lifeline. "Foolish?" he went on, shaking his head in self-disgust. "Idiotic? Loco? Downright ungrateful?"

Phoebe almost smiled. Almost. The fact that he obviously recognized his mistake didn't really take the sting out of his accusation. Especially when she considered how she might have been contributing to its cause. When he paused, though, apparently at a loss for more invectives, she urged, "Oh, do go on. You're doing so nicely."

"Suppose I had that coming," he muttered and had the good grace to give her a rather sheepish look. "But you didn't. I shouldn't be yelling at you for doing what had to be done. Hell, I'm not mad at you. I'm mad at me."

His apology forced one of her own. "Maybe I have been taking too much of Becky's time."

"No," he said quickly, then added, his gaze locked on his daughter's face, "It's my fault she looks like that now. And no wonder she doesn't want to come to me. Why should she? Hell, that butler of yours has been more of a father to her in the last week or so than I have since she got here."

Phoebe studied him for a long moment and couldn't help feeling that he looked . . . defeated, somehow. And strangely enough, that bothered her. It was a hard thing to see a strong, proud man question his own worth.

"It's not a disaster, Riley," she said.

"No," he agreed softly. "But it does show just how bad a daddy I would be."

Would be? she thought, wondering over his choice of words. A worrisome chord was struck within her and she felt the ripple effect of it spreading.

"You're doing much better than you think you are," Phoebe told him and spared a glance at the little girl who had stopped crying but was still eyeing her father warily.

"Oh, yeah," Riley snorted. "You can see she's real fond of me. Hell, if looks could kill, I'd be six feet under at the edge of town."

"At least you care if you're doing well by her or not," Phoebe said.

"Well, of course I care. She's mine to look after."

"The two things don't necessarily go together," she said and lowered her gaze to Becky. Gently, Phoebe smoothed the blond curls back from the girl's forehead and smiled when Becky leaned into her.

How easily she'd become accustomed to the feel of this child in her arms. At twenty-seven, Phoebe had long since abandoned any dreams of one day having a baby of her own to love and nurture. Now, having Becky Burnett in her life was like a gift. One she cherished.

No, things weren't going smoothly for Riley and his daughter. At the moment. But that would change, given time. Riley was a man determined to do right by his child. And one day, Becky would realize that. This little girl would never know the pain of discovering, as Phoebe had, that her father cared more for his work and his studies than he did for his daughter.

A wistful old pain struggled to life in her chest before she fought it down with the ease of long years of practice.

Phoebe took another long look at the little girl before shifting her gaze to Riley. She laughed out loud when she realized the two of them were wearing identically mulish expressions.

"What's so funny?"

"The two of you," she said, shaking her head. "You look so much alike, it's startling."

"We do?" he asked and stared at his daughter as if looking to find the resemblance himself.

Phoebe frowned a bit, then found herself pointing out the obvious. "She has your eyes and definitely your scowl."

His eyebrows lifted at that.

"And I think her hair will probably darken to just your shade of blond when she's older."

"Maybe." He shoved his hands into his pockets. "As for the other, her mother had blue eyes too, so that doesn't prove anything." He paused thoughtfully. "Suppose it doesn't matter, really."

Phoebe wrapped her arms a little more tightly around the child. That sense of unease thickened inside her until it felt as though even her air were being choked off. "What are you talking about?"

He shot her a closed, guarded look. "Nothing."

There was more, she could see it in his face. But he obviously wasn't going to tell her what it was. And maybe that was for the best. Judging by his expression, she wasn't at all sure she wanted to know what he was holding inside. After a long moment, she tried to steer the conversation back to safer ground.

"Things will get easier for both of you," she said, giving Becky a brief smile. "The longer she's here—"

"She's not stayin'."

Her breath caught and lodged in her throat. Phoebe slowly turned to look at him, not surprised at all to see his eyes still tightly shuttered and his features locked into a stony expression.

Squeezing the words out, she asked, "What do you mean, she's not staying?"

"Just that," he said flatly, as if discussing nothing more than discarding an old pair of shoes.

"But . . . she's your *daughter*," Phoebe said, as a sense of outrage began to trickle through her.

"And I'm doin' what's best for her," Riley countered. "My in-laws'll be here to get her by the end of the month."

He couldn't be serious. Mouth dry, arms clutched protectively around Becky, she started talking, words tumbling from her mouth. "Riley, you gave up your job for her. You've started a business. A life. You can't just walk away now."

Jaw tight, Riley yanked his hands from his pockets, raked his hair impatiently, then let his hands fall to his sides. Staring first at his daughter, then at Phoebe, he said, "I have to do the best thing for her. Can't you see that?"

No. All she saw was a man turning his back on his daughter. And that scene stung too much. Reminded her too much of her father who had ignored her. Oh, he hadn't sent her off to live with someone else. But he might as well have. They'd lived together in the same house for years and had been utter strangers.

She'd thought Riley was different.

"The best thing for her is to be with you."

"Oh, yeah," he practically snarled at her. "Livin' here.

In a saloon. With a man who doesn't know the least little thing about kids. Hell, I couldn't even comb her damn hair!"

Frustration simmered in his tone and Phoebe knew it, but that didn't stop the torrent of words spilling from her.

"No one cared about her hair," she said, even though the rat's nest had bothered her terribly. It was such a small thing. So insignificant.

"*I* care," he snapped, leaning in toward her. Then, noticing Becky's mouth tremble, he lowered his voice by sheer strength of will. "And I'm the one who decides her future." With that, he turned and walked toward the front windows. One hand braced on the wall, he stared out into the whiteness like a man looking for answers he couldn't find anywhere else.

Never taking her eyes off his broad back, Phoebe set Becky down, gave her behind a gentle pat, and said, "Go find Simmons, sweetie. He'll give you some candy."

"Cannee!" Becky shrieked and ran off down the hallway. Phoebe smiled to herself; the girl's upset was already forgotten. Couldn't Riley see that a child could and would put up with anything as long as she was loved?

When they were alone again and the only sound in the room came from the wind-driven snow pelting against the glass, Phoebe crossed to his side. He didn't acknowledge her when she stopped just inches from him. He didn't turn his head to look at her when she stared at him, waiting expectantly. He simply kept his gaze trained on the storm as if his life . . . his sanity . . . depended on it.

Swallowing back her anger . . . and her disappointment in him, Phoebe tried desperately to keep her voice even as she said, "You can't do this, Riley. Don't send her away." That ripple of uneasiness inside her had risen like floodwaters pushing against an unstable levee. Reaching out, she took hold of his arm, her fingers tightening around the corded muscles hidden beneath his shirt. "Riley . . ."

He glanced down at her hand, then briefly looked into her eyes before shifting his gaze back to the storm. If anything, his expression had hardened. As if he were steeling himself.

"This town," he said so softly she had to strain to hear him. "This place . . ." He shook his head as his voice faded off. The tiny slap of snowflakes against the glass sounded overly loud. "When I was growin' up here, all I could think of was gettin' out. Gettin' away. Off to the high country." He paused for a deep breath, then went on. "After the war, I only came back here a time or two. Hell, even after Tess and I got married, I was never here more than a few times a year."

She couldn't imagine a life so unconnected. So alone. But she wanted to keep him talking, if only to give herself a chance to change his mind for him, so she said only, "That must have been hard."

He shot her a quick look. "Hard for Tess. Not for me." Turning away from the window, pulling free of her hold, he grabbed both of her shoulders and said, "Don't you get it, Phoebe? I'm not the stayin' kind. I don't know what to do for Becky. Or for the damned saloon. Or for you."

Phoebe pulled away from him and took an extra step back. She would not let him use *her* presence as an excuse for quitting. "I didn't ask you to do anything for me," she said hotly.

"Don't you think I know that?" he said just as sharply. "Do ya think I like knowin' that you're settlin' in here easier than I am? Hell, woman, I grew up here! My folks are buried in the town cemetery. I *belong* here and you fit in better than me. What's that say to ya?" He laughed shortly, harshly, and the sound grated on her ears. "Damn it, even that British butler of yours makes a better pa to Becky than me."

"So you're saying this is *our* fault?" Her voice rose

along with the tide of rage sweeping through her blood-stream. If he was going to let his child drift out of his life, that was his choice. But by thunder, he wouldn't one day look back and say with regret, *It was all that Phoebe's fault. Her and the butler. If they hadn't shown up in town, everything would have been different.*

"It's nobody's *fault*," he snapped. "It just *is*."

"The only thing that *is,* is you're giving a little girl away. Taking her from her home and everything she knows and sending her off without a care!"

At that, his features hardened into a mask of tightly controlled fury. "That's what you think? That I don't care?"

No, he cared. She saw it in him every time he looked at Becky. Every time he tried to pull on her little socks and shoes. Every time he used his enormous store of patience to chase her through the hotel just before bedtime so she could giggle and laugh her way into sleep.

Why couldn't *he* see how good he was with her? For her? How good the two of them were together and how much he would miss that child if he gave her up? How much he would lose over the years by not being a part of Becky's life?

But she didn't say any of that. Instead, she said, "I know you care. That's why you can't do this. I can't believe you're going to quit on the most important job you will ever have!"

"Oh, no, ma'am," he said, taking a step toward her and shaking his head. Lamplight flickered in his eyes. "You do not get to sit in judgment on me. You know nothing about me. About Becky. You sail in here and inside of two weeks you think you've got all the answers? Well, you don't, Phoebe. So don't go throwin' accusations at me. I have to do what I think best for Becky."

"You're what's best," Phoebe argued, unwilling to give up just yet. "She's *your* responsibility. *Your* daughter."

"I don't *know* that!" he shouted.

Stunned, Phoebe inhaled sharply and stared at him. He

looked just as surprised by his outburst as she was.

Rubbing one hand across his face as if he could somehow erase the words he'd just shouted, he muttered
thickly, "I've gotta go do inventory . . . or some damn
thing." Then, without looking at her again, he left the
room. The echoes of his boot heels thundered around her
in the silence.

He couldn't sleep.

Riley turned his head on the pillow and glanced at
Becky's sleeping form. The moon had finally fought free
of the layer of clouds and now shone a gentle light
through the windows. In the soft glow of that light, Riley
watched her and thought again about what he'd said to
Phoebe hours ago.

Damn it all to hell and back.

Never once had he admitted to *anyone* his doubts
about Becky's parentage. His insides seized up and he
threw one arm behind his head and stared at the ceiling.
Instead of the freshly whitewashed wood, though, he
again saw the expression on Phoebe's face when he'd
blurted out the secret he'd lived with for years.

Damn, but she'd been something, standing toe to toe
with him, matching him shout for shout. The fire in her
eyes had sparked a like fire deep inside him that not even
his shame at his own stupidity could quench.

Blast it all, he *cared* what Phoebe thought of him. He
cared for Phoebe. But at that thought, he shook his head
in disgust. *Care* was a weak word for what he was starting to feel for the sharp-tongued spinster.

And if there was one more thing he didn't need now,
it was that particular feeling.

"Shit." Swinging his legs off the bed, Riley snatched
up his pants and tugged them on. Donning a shirt, he let
the edges hang open as he quietly crossed the room and
let himself out.

Might as well go down and have a drink. Do some
thinking. Anything to get his mind off Phoebe for a while.

He backed into the shadowed hallway and gently closed the door after him.

"You can't sleep, either?" Phoebe's whisper shattered the silence.

He shot a glare heavenward. Nothing like tossing temptation to a man already headed for hell.

Chapter Ten

❦

Riley turned around and felt his heart stop.

She held a kerosene lamp high in her right hand and a golden puddle of lamplight streamed around her like a sunbeam straight from heaven. Which should have warned him right off. What right did an old devil like him have admiring a woman like her? But devil or not, he was only human.

Her soft brown hair, finally freed of that bun she was forever tying it up in, fell across her shoulders in gentle waves that ended in curls atop her breasts. Her floor-length white cotton nightdress surely wasn't the most alluring thing he'd ever seen, but somehow, with Phoebe in it, the blasted thing was more erotic than black silk.

She'd tossed an old blue shawl around her shoulders and looped the ends together in a knot between her breasts, hiding their shape and outline. Only in his imagination did he see her small nipples pucker and stiffen in response to his gaze. But according to the hard discomfort of his body, his imagination was all that was required.

Her eyes looked wide and darker than usual, despite the faint flicker of the oil lamp dancing in their depths. He wanted to know what she was thinking. What she was feeling.

If she was remembering his outburst and wondering

what kind of man it was who denied his own child.

Phoebe was reeling. She tightened her grip on the lamp in her hand and squeezed until her fingers ached. She hadn't seen him since their confrontation in the saloon. And now, seeing him like *this* was almost too much for her.

In the small pool of lamplight shimmering around them, Riley's bare chest gleamed like finely polished oak. Not a spare ounce of flesh on him, his upper body was one hard, sculpted muscle. A narrow thatch of dark gold hair dusted his skin and tapered into a thin shadow, until it disappeared beneath the waistband of his jeans. She drew in a long, shuddering breath and deliberately lowered her gaze to the floor.

But there was no help there.

Something deep inside her curled tight, like a coiled spring about to pop. Ridiculous as it sounded, the sight of his bare feet made this accidental meeting seem even more . . . intimate.

She pulled in a deep breath and lifted her gaze until she was looking deep into his eyes. "I, uh . . ." What? What had she been about to say? What was she doing here again?

"Couldn't sleep?" Riley prompted.

"Yes," she agreed quickly. "I mean, no. I mean—" Blast and damnation, just what *did* she mean? Steady, Phoebe, she told herself. She'd known that their first meeting after their . . . conversation . . . would be a difficult one. After all, they'd both said things that, once uttered, couldn't be taken back. But to meet him like this . . . oh, Lord. "That's right. I couldn't." She nodded stiffly, forced a smile, and added, "So I thought I'd go down and have a cup of muscles."

He frowned at her. "What?"

"Coffee!" she whispered quickly and scurried past him.

Muscles, huh? Riley grinned. But as he watched her go, that smile faded and he told himself not to follow.

Nothing good could come of this, he warned silently.

Moving quietly to the head of the stairs, he glanced down. The shimmer of lamplight enveloped her as she walked quickly along the hall toward the kitchen. He gritted his teeth and curled his fingers along the banister. Squeezing the cool, dark wood until even his shoulders hurt with the effort, he tried to convince himself to go back to his room. To forget the look in Phoebe's eyes. To keep his damn distance from the woman. Only a fool would go walking clear-eyed right into trouble.

In the silence he heard the gentle swish of the swinging door as she entered the kitchen, and before that door had swung back into place, he was on his way downstairs.

The fool's eyes were wide open.

"Muscles," she muttered and hurriedly filled the coffee-pot with well water from her brand-new kitchen pump. How humiliating it was to be so at a loss around the man.

As she scooped coffee grounds into the pot, she thought back over the years. She'd never before experienced the mind-numbing sensation of staring into a man's eyes and reading her own wants and desires written there.

On the contrary. The men who came to study with her father more or less ignored her presence until she served them something to eat. And even then, their attention was grudging as they hurried to get back to their professor.

As time passed, Phoebe had more or less accepted that she simply wasn't the type of woman to inspire romantic notions. After all, she wasn't tiny, blond, or especially circumspect in her opinions.

No doubt it was her lack of experience with men that prompted her peculiar bursts of warmth toward Riley Burnett. He was the first man to have looked at her and really seen her. Phoebe.

She lifted one hand to touch her lips in memory of that one amazing kiss. He saw her as she really was, and had kissed her anyway. No wonder she was so flustered.

Of course, nothing would come of any of this, now

that she knew he intended to give his own child away. All afternoon, she'd thought of nothing else and had arrived at one very obvious conclusion.

With Becky gone, Riley would have no need to stay. So in a couple of very short weeks, the child she'd grown to love and the man who turned her insides to hot mush would be gone.

And she'd be alone. Again.

"Phoebe?"

She set the coffeepot down onto the still-hot stove. "I'm making coffee."

"Sounds good."

A strained, forced laugh shot from her throat before she could bite it back. "I hope so," she said. "Simmons usually makes the coffee, you know. And everything else, for that matter." She took a short breath and rattled on, aware that she was babbling, but somehow unable to stop herself. "My father always loved Simmons's coffee, and when our cook quit unexpectedly, Father simply put Simmons in charge of the entire kitchen. Which worked out well," she added quickly, lacing her fingers in front of her and squeezing tightly. "Because he really is a wonderful cook. But then, he's actually wonderful at almost everything he does. I've known him my whole life, you know."

"Phoebe . . ."

"Well," she corrected, whipping around to face him. "Not my *whole* life. But at least from the time I was five or six, which is practically the same thing."

Riley frowned and took a step closer.

She nervously backed up a pace. "I know it really doesn't matter how long I've known him, and you probably don't really care, but I did want to warn you that I'm not very good at making coffee, so you'll be taking your chances, I'm afraid . . ." She paused for breath again, shot him a wild look, and muttered helplessly, "Good Lord, help me to stop talking!"

One corner of his mouth tilted slightly before evening

out into the flat line she was most accustomed to seeing on his features. He shook his head and said, "Do I make you that nervous, Phoebe?"

"Of course not," she said too quickly, and was sure he'd spot it for the lie it was. Not only did she have the embarrassing memory of their earlier conversation running through her mind. But now she was faced with his naked chest—*Oh heavens, naked*—which probably accounted for the muddle her brain seemed to be in at the moment.

"I'm sorry," he said, and her gaze lifted from the tanned expanse of muscled flesh to stare into blue eyes that seemed to look deep into her soul.

"Sorry?" she asked.

"For earlier. Yelling at you like that."

"Oh." *Think, Phoebe, think*. "Well, as I remember, we both did more shouting than listening."

"Yeah." He shook his head, then let it fall back on his neck. "But only one of us said something that should have been left unsaid."

Instantly, she remembered the look on his face when he'd blurted out the doubts that had obviously haunted him for years. "You mean about not knowing if you're Becky's father?" she whispered and watched him as he straightened up to look at her again.

"That's what I mean."

Lamplight flickered as the flame danced on the wick, casting writhing shadows on the whitewashed walls. An old pain flashed across Riley's features and tugged at Phoebe's heart. How those doubts must plague him and how he must regret admitting to them aloud.

"Riley," she said softly as he turned and took a seat at the table behind them. "You can't really think Becky isn't yours. She looks so much like you, it would be obvious to a blind man."

"Maybe." His shoulders stiffened as if in anticipation of a blow. Not looking at her, he said, "Hard not to wonder, when Tess planted the thought herself."

Phoebe blinked, walked to the seat closest to him and sat down. "Your wife?"

"Yeah." A tight smile twisted his lips slightly. He shot Phoebe a look, then said, "As she was leavin' town, she told me she wasn't at all sure Becky was mine. Then wished me luck and climbed aboard the stage." His gaze shifted. "Last time I saw her."

And good riddance, Phoebe couldn't help thinking. "Why would she say something like that?"

He rocked his chair onto its back legs, planted his hands on his thighs, and stared at the ceiling. "Tess wasn't a woman to suffer in silence."

"Suffer?"

"Loneliness," he muttered. "With my job taking me away so much of the time, Tess looked for company wherever she could find it." As soon as the words were out of his mouth, he shook his head again and stared at the wall opposite as if looking deeply into his own past. "Everybody in town knew. Hell, her own folks moved to Frisco to escape the talk."

What a foolish woman, she thought. She had had everything. A husband. A home. A child. And she'd thrown it all away. Difficult to feel any sympathy for a woman as stupid as that.

Yet, Phoebe knew how vicious gossip could be. Hadn't she spent the last year of her life trying desperately to keep up appearances just so she wouldn't be a topic of whispered conversations?

"By the time Becky was born, any number of men could have claimed her."

"But you did," she pointed out.

"Don't make me into some sort of hero, Phoebe. Yeah, I claimed her. But then I told Tess to leave town. Gave her some money and told her to get out. I'd had enough of the men and the whispering." He shoved one hand through his hair and rocked the chair faster. "Didn't want Becky growing up listening to folks talking about her mother."

"Where did she go?"

"Nowhere," he said, his features blank. "On the way into Reno, her stage overturned. She died."

Phoebe felt his anger and frustration simmering in the air. Along with the guilt that must still plague him. She sensed that her sympathy wouldn't be appreciated. "And yet," she said cautiously, "you didn't give Becky to her grandparents then."

He laughed shortly, a sound that scraped into the stillness like a raw wound. "Wrong, Phoebe. I handed her to *my* parents. They took care of her until they died a few months back. So ya see? I'm not the good father you think I am."

No, he wasn't perfect. Perhaps he might have done some things differently. But he'd claimed a child many men wouldn't have and seen to it that Becky was well cared for. And now, he'd given up everything for the girl.

"You're the only father she knows. You accepted her, Riley."

He tore his gaze from the past to look at her. The wildly shifting shadows kept her from reading his expression as he said, "She was born to my wife. That makes her my daughter."

"She *is* your daughter. You've only to really look at her to see it."

"That doesn't even matter to me, Phoebe. Not anymore."

"Yet you're willing to send her away now," she said softly.

"Like I told you earlier, it's for her own good."

"Is it?" she prodded, her hands gripping the edge of the table. "Is it really?"

He let the chair slam to the floor and then smacked one hand down onto the tabletop. The salt and pepper shakers teetered, then fell onto their sides. Carefully, Phoebe turned them upright.

He took a long, deep breath before speaking again.

"Tess's folks will do right by her." His gaze shifted her way, then aside again.

"What can they do that you can't?" she demanded.

"They're rich, for one thing," he snapped. "She can live in a house instead of a saloon."

"Can they buy her a father's love?" One part of Phoebe heard her arguing with him and was appalled. What right did she have to interfere with this man and his daughter? She wasn't a part of their family. She had no claims on either of them. And yet . . . she knew all too well what it was like to grow up without a father's love. To know that your father was more interested in his own life than yours. To wonder what you had done wrong that kept him from loving you.

She didn't want Becky to know the same unhappiness. And, too, even if Riley was unaware of it now, she *knew* he would regret giving up his child one day.

Tears rose up in her eyes and she dashed them away with the backs of her hands.

His voice tight and harsh, he muttered thickly, stubbornly, "She'll be better off with them."

"Will she? They raised your wife, you know." She gasped and her eyes widened. Covering her mouth with one hand, she futilely tried to drag the words back.

He shoved away from the table and looked down at her. "They're not bad folks. Tess was always wild. It's not their fault things turned out like they did."

"But it's *your* fault?"

"No, it's my fault Tess is dead. I sent her away."

"She made her own choices, Riley. Besides, what happened was an accident," she replied, standing up to face him. "What you're doing now isn't."

"Damn it," he said, "don't you see? This isn't about fault. This is about what's best for Becky."

"*You're* what's best for Becky. She loves you."

He seemed to pale and Phoebe knew her words had hit home.

"Sometimes love just ain't enough, Phoebe," he said tightly.

Outside, the wind moaned like a tormented soul, rattling the windowpanes as if trying to force its way past heaven's gate. The perking coffee bubbled and jumped in the pot, sending its aroma through the room.

"Can a father's love feed her?" Riley asked quietly, speaking more to himself than to her. "Buy her fancy dresses? Send her to good schools?" He shook his head. "I don't know a damn thing about kids, Phoebe. What could I teach her? How to hunt down a thievin' murderer? How to get handcuffs just tight enough? How to shoot your way out of trouble? No. I'm no good at this. It's better this way, Phoebe. For Becky. For me. For you."

Better? How could this empty feeling inside be better for anyone?

"You'll be leaving too, won't you?" she asked and didn't want to hear his answer.

"Yes." He paused, then added, "I'll sign the place over to you when I go. It'll all be yours, Phoebe. You can do what you want to with the place."

A deep, hollow ache pulsed through her. With every beat of her heart it only sharpened, dug deeper. And she knew it was only a pale foreshadowing of the pain she would experience when this man and his daughter were gone. All of the idle dreams she'd indulged in were crumbling around her.

How could this be happening? How could she have formed such a strong attachment to these people in just a couple of weeks? And how could she stop?

Long seconds passed. Eternity filled seconds when Riley stared at the woman so close to him and briefly indulged in a fool's paradise of dreams. But dreams weren't made for men like him. He'd learned that the hard way. He had no part in Phoebe's—or Becky's—life.

He was now what he'd always been. A man whose future lay in unbroken trails and across empty land. If that future suddenly looked bleaker than it had a couple of weeks ago, it didn't matter. He knew what he had to do. For all their sakes.

Leave.

The coffee boiled over. Dark brown foam erupted from the pot's spout and sizzled across the stove, sounding more like an old man's hoarse chuckling.

"Blast!" Phoebe raced to the stove and snatched at the pot handle. Instantly, she yelped, dropped it, and cupped her singed hand with the other.

Riley grabbed her, dragged her to the sink and held her still while he pumped cold well water over her burned palm.

A sigh of relief escaped her as she sagged against him. "That was stupid," she muttered and winced when he paused to inspect her hand.

"You'll be all right," he said, smoothing one finger across her palm. Soft, he thought. No calluses. No blisters, no scars of any kind caused by the type of hard work that had defined his life. Phoebe was different. In so many ways, he couldn't even begin to count them all.

She shivered slightly and he felt the tremor course through his own body as well. All right, here was trouble.

Slowly, he swiveled his head to look down at her. He liked that she was so tall. Put her mouth in nice and easy kissing range. His gaze locked on that mouth. The curve of her lips, their soft fullness, the pale pink color. He bent his head, easing closer to her, devouring the scent of lavender that seemed to fill up every empty corner of his heart.

She gasped, whether from desire or surprise, he wasn't sure.

But that one small sound stopped him cold.

Riley straightened up, released her hand, and said gruffly, "Why don't you go sit down? I'll pour the coffee. If you still want some."

She nodded and he turned away from the question in her eyes. Only when he'd poured two cups of the thick black brew did he take a seat opposite from her, determined to keep the safety of the table's width between them.

"Riley, I . . ."

Her voice trailed off. A hint of color stained her cheeks and her eyes . . . her eyes held a confusion he knew he'd put there.

Damn. What had he been thinking? The answer to that, of course, was that he hadn't been thinking at all. Just feeling. Feeling things he'd never expected. Things he couldn't have and shouldn't want.

He took a sip of the scalding hot, bitter brew. It burned his tongue before he swallowed it like a penance. Grimacing, he said, "You make lousy coffee."

"I did warn you."

"So you did," he said, forcing another swallow down. Get onto a safe subject, he thought. School your thoughts away from the fact that she's sitting there, half-dressed, within arm's reach. And damn, she looked good with her hair all soft and pretty in the lamplight.

Deliberately, he looked away from her. "You've made some progress in here," he said, taking in the white-washed walls, the scrubbed table, the blackened stove, and the still-damp floor.

"Yes," she answered, obviously as eager as he for the shift in conversation. "But I need to find a cook. Simmons refuses to be a chef, he says."

"Just as well. That butler of yours wouldn't know how to cook the kind of food folks around here like anyway. I doubt he's ever sat down to a bowl of chuckwagon stew or fried rabbit, or even a decent dish of chili."

Not much of a conversation, he thought. But it was surely a safe one.

"Is there a newspaper in town? I could advertise."

"No paper," Riley said. "Just go to the Mercantile. Ivy Talbot runs the place and practically everything else in town. She should know somebody who needs a job."

Phoebe nodded and something else occurred to him. "Speaking of the Mercantile," he started and leaned toward her, planting both elbows on the table. "The other day, when you nearly got run down in the street?"

"Yes?"

"Where the hell were you? You seemed to show up out of nowhere right in the path of those horses."

Her gaze dropped to the tabletop. Her fingers twirled her coffee cup in the ring of moisture it had created. "I was just talking to someone. Didn't pay attention to what was happening."

"Talking where?" Riley stared at her, willing her gaze to meet his. But she didn't look up. What wasn't she saying? "I didn't see a sign of you on the street until it was almost too late."

"It was crowded." She shook her head. "You probably just missed me."

"Uh-uh." He hadn't missed her. He had a sharp enough eye to spot her no matter how thick the crowds. A moment or two passed as he waited, hoping she'd say more, wondering what in the devil was so mysterious that she couldn't tell him about it.

When she didn't speak, though, he told himself it was just as well. Better he get used to not worrying about Phoebe Hightower. Because in a couple of weeks, she'd be out of his life forever.

Strange, but that thought brought him no comfort at all.

Riley abruptly downed the last of his coffee and stood up, his chair legs scraping against the wooden floor. Best for all concerned if he just kept a comfortable distance between them. And that surely meant no more late-night chats in lonely kitchens.

"Good night, Phoebe."

He left, his bare feet soundless as he moved through the hotel and up the stairs. Phoebe drew in a long, shuddering breath. She could still feel the power of his eyes as he'd watched her. She closed her own eyes now and sat stock-still for several long minutes, thinking about everything that had just passed between them. And what hadn't.

There had been a moment, at the sink, when she'd thought for sure he was going to kiss her again. And everything inside her had strained for it. Reached for it. She'd wanted so much to feel that sparkle of life rush through her veins again. Even knowing that he was planning to leave couldn't quite diminish her own need to touch him and be touched.

Yet he'd stopped. Why?

And why, she asked herself, did he have so many questions about that day on the street? She'd wanted to tell him about the tinker. But how could she explain something to him that she didn't understand herself? Besides, if even Simmons, who'd known her forever, didn't believe her, why should Riley?

He paused at the head of the stairs and looked back down as if he could see through the walls and into the kitchen where Phoebe sat, alone. An ache settled around his heart as he realized that, for the first time in his life, he found himself wishing things were different.

But wishing for something didn't make it so.

Abruptly, he turned and stalked down the hall. He opened the door to his room to hear Becky whimpering softly in her sleep. In the wash of moonlight spread across her bed, she lay twisted in a tangle of blankets, her little head turning this way and that on her pillow.

Nightmare.

Though he had no idea what kind of dreams a two-year-old could conjure up, he knew enough about haunted sleep that her distress tore at him. How many nights had he himself come sharply awake, gasping for air, eyes wild?

Quietly, he walked to her, sat down on the edge of the mattress, and hesitantly reached out to stroke her short curls. "Hush now, Becky," he whispered. "It's all right now. You're fine." He swallowed heavily as her lips moved into a pout and her eyes squeezed shut, a single tear escaping to roll down her plump cheek.

That tear worked its way right into his soul.

A stab of pain hit him hard and low. He wondered if Tess's folks would think to check on her at night. He wondered what Becky would be like next year. Or the year after. Would she even remember him? Probably not, he told himself, and that would be for the best.

Wouldn't it?

"Papa's here," he said, his voice tight as he stroked her back in long, gentle motions.

She sniffled in her troubled sleep, one hand reaching out blindly for the blanket she carried everywhere like a shield.

So small, he thought. So defenseless.

His heart ached for her misfortune as having him as a father. A man less suited to the task had never been born. Awkwardly, he patted her again, scowling as her whimpers only increased.

Damn, he hated this helpless feeling. With Phoebe. With his daughter. How was a man supposed to know how to deal with females when the only women he'd had any experience with at all were the ones who charged a man by the hour?

Becky's eyes flew open suddenly and she stared at him.

"See there," he said softly, "everything's fine."

She sniffed and rubbed one hand across teary eyes. Clutching her blanket to her chest, she hiccuped and launched herself at him unexpectedly. Stunned, Riley sat completely still while she burrowed into his chest, snuggling her little head beneath his chin.

Her teary face pressed against him, Riley felt a small speck of warmth begin to burn deep inside him. She crawled farther into his lap and settled in, that ratty blanket draped across both of them.

Still unsure of himself, Riley wrapped his arms around her and was rewarded when she tipped her head back and gave him a watery smile. He looked down into those tear-washed blue eyes—so much like his own—and his breath hitched.

"Papa," she said, then splayed one tiny hand against his chest.

Jesus.

Riley pulled in a deep, shuddering breath, cupped her small head with the palm of his hand, and drew her close. With that one word, she'd beaten him. With her trust-filled eyes, she'd conquered him. Struggling to breathe past the hard knot lodged in his chest, he held her tenderly, carefully, until her measured, even breathing assured him she'd fallen asleep again, secure in his arms.

And the walls around his heart cracked a bit, letting in a trickle of warmth that seemed almost painful.

Chapter Eleven

❦

He woke up late and realized by the strength of the sunshine pouring in the window to smack him dead in the face that half the morning was gone. He turned his head slightly on the pillow.

Becky was gone too.

Riley dressed hurriedly and went downstairs, drawn to the kitchen by the lure of voices. Only last night, he'd fled the room like the hounds of hell were on his heels. Yet now, he headed toward the sounds of laughter and easy conversation like a man dying of thirst in the desert and spotting a mirage in the distance.

Outside the swinging door, he stopped. Gently, he eased it open an inch or so and looked into the room.

Phoebe, Simmons, Creek, Becky, and the two Weatherby boys were seated around the table, laughing and talking with each other as if they were long-lost cousins at a family reunion.

A wistful smile crossed his face briefly as he realized Creek was telling another one of his tall tales. The scent of coffee and fried bacon drifted to him and his stomach grumbled, demanding that he take himself inside and feed it.

He almost did, but something held him back.

The very thing that had called him to this spot.

His gaze locked on Phoebe, bright-eyed this morning,

wearing her dark blue dress, her long hair tucked up into a bun. She laughed at something Creek said and turned to spoon some oatmeal into . Becky's open, birdlike mouth.

Joe Weatherby reached for another biscuit to stack on his already full plate and Simmons smacked his hand. Henry laughed and Creek stole one of *his* biscuits.

It was the kind of easy, family-type setting that had eluded him for most of his adult life. He couldn't count the times over the last several years that he had passed well-lit windows, sparing glances at the families living there. As a young man, he'd run from the town and the house he'd grown up in. As a husband, he'd been more interested in the open road and tracking fugitives than in spending time with a wife who'd become a stranger to him.

But now . . . now that he actually had the chance to be more than a passing stranger, it was too late. He was too set in his lonely ways. And too old, he figured, to learn.

Riley's teeth clenched. He heard them, he watched them, and despite all of his effort, he felt a spurt of envy rattle through him with the subtlety of a runaway train.

That fragile warmth he'd felt the night before when Becky had called him *papa*, when Phoebe had looked at him through dazzled eyes, awaiting his kiss, that hadn't been real. *Those* moments had been the aberration.

This was the reality.

And though his heart told him to try . . . to go into that room and join in their fun . . . his head told him to back off. To know his place and stay in it.

On the outside, looking in.

Before he could weaken, he let the door slide closed and started for the front door. He'd find him a cup of coffee somewhere else.

Hell. *Anywhere* else.

*   *   *

Laughter rose up around Phoebe as Creek finished telling
one of his more colorful prospecting stories, but she hardly heard it. Her gaze locked on the door where she'd spied
Riley peering in at them, she fought down a sense of disappointment.

Why hadn't he joined them? Why did he insist on
keeping himself separate? Was he just avoiding *her*? Or
was he afraid to spend time with her and Becky? Afraid
that he might change his mind about leaving, about giving his daughter to her grandparents?

Becky slapped her palms down on the tabletop and
shouted, "More!"

"Here now, there'll be no shouting at table," Simmons
said firmly, but his smile softened his tone. He handed
her a piece of biscuit, still warm from the oven. While
the baby tore it into tiny bits, he looked at Phoebe.
"Something wrong?" he asked quietly.

"No," she said and shook her head. "Not a thing.
Everything's . . . fine."

But she couldn't help sending one last look at the
closed door separating her from Riley and so didn't see
the worried expression in Simmons's eyes.

She knew there was another door that was closed to
her too. The door to Riley's heart. And since he was determined to leave in a couple of weeks, she knew she
would never be able to open it.

Phoebe reached up to adjust the tilt of her hat, then
walked into the General Mercantile. A cowbell attached
to the top of the door bounced and clanged to announce
her presence. She stepped quickly to one side and paused
just over the threshold to look around.

General Merchandise, the sign outside read, and the
inside of the store delivered on that promise. A long,
curved counter wrapped around the interior and in the
center aisle were three tables, laden with everything from
hair ribbons to knitting yarn to hunting knives. One wall
boasted coats of every size and shape hanging from doz-

ens of wooden pegs pounded into the walls.

Opposite was what looked to be a mile of shelving. Dresses, overalls, long johns, and saddles were each stacked in different niches along the shelves. Huge barrels took up space in front of the counter, with signs posted that read, *Pickles, Crackers, Flour, Sugar.*

The entire store was spotless. Even the pine flooring shone from a high polish and reflected the overhead lamplight.

"Howdy-do," a deep, female voice shouted from somewhere on her right.

Phoebe turned. Eyes wide, she smiled as a huge woman came around the edge of the counter, hand extended, a warm smile on her broad face.

"You'd be Phoebe Hightower," the woman said and took Phoebe's hand in a bone-crushing, but thankfully brief handshake.

"How did you know?" she asked and resisted the impulse to shake life back into her numb fingers.

"Shoot, hon'," the woman said with a snort of laughter, "I know everything that goes on in this town!"

Then she *had* come to the right place.

"The name's Ivy Talbot and this is my place. Good to meet you finally."

Ivy Talbot stood six foot one in her stocking feet, as she liked to brag. Her heavy breasts strained against the spotless white bib apron she wore over a particularly gaudy yellow and green flowered dress. Her dark brown hair was twisted into a knot on top of her head and two pencils jutted up from the mass like twin horns. Her face was faintly lined, putting her age at about thirty-five, and her green eyes flashed with curiosity and warmth.

Phoebe liked her instantly.

"Been here nigh on two weeks already," Ivy said, planting her hands on her hips. "Expected you long before now. I know what a mess your uncle, God rest his soul, left that hotel in. And that Riley, though he's a charmer by half, he's just a man and couldn't have made much difference in the place on his own." Ivy reached to one side and flicked a nonexistent speck of dust from the gleaming countertop. She clucked her head, clapped her hands together in a violent brushing motion, and went on. " 'Course, I meant to get over to the hotel to welcome you proper with some cakes and such, but business is so durn busy, ain't hardly had time to sit, let alone go for a visit."

"I've been busy too," Phoebe managed to say when Ivy drew breath. "But I do need to buy a few things for the hotel and—"

Ivy looked her up and down quickly. "And a couple two or three things for yourself, I'll wager."

"Oh, no," Phoebe said. She didn't have enough money to go shopping for anything but necessities.

"Nonsense," Ivy told her emphatically. "You're durn near as blue as that dress you're wearing. Got to have a decent coat." Two big fingers plucked at Phoebe's cape. "This little thing won't do for Nevada snows."

It didn't do for St. Louis snows either, but it was all she had.

Ivy drew Phoebe in her wake as she headed down the main aisle. "That butler of yours? He come in the other day. A honest-to-God *butler* of all things!" she added with a shake of her head. "Bought some hard candy and, before we had a chance to chat, was off again like a stiff wind."

Candy. That explained why Becky was so fond of the older man. As a girl, Phoebe had always been able to find candy in Simmons's coat pockets. Apparently, her soft-hearted butler was continuing the tradition with Becky.

"Fine-lookin' man," Ivy was saying. "He got a wife somewhere?"

Phoebe nearly ran to keep up with the much bigger woman. "Simmons?" she repeated, astonished at the thought. A wife?

"That his name?" Ivy asked. "Simmons what?"

"Just Simmons."

"Got to have a Christian name, don't he?" Ivy demanded, turning her head briefly to stare into Phoebe's eyes.

"I . . . suppose."

Ivy shrugged massive shoulders, dismissing Phoebe's ignorance. "Don't matter. Simmons'll do, I reckon. You know, as my third husband was wont to say, 'a rose by any other name would smell as sweet.' "

Amazed, Phoebe smiled. "Your third husband said that?"

"Yep," Ivy told her with a proud shake of her head. "He was a real smart little fella. Always coming up with pretty sayings and such. He should have wrote 'em down. Bet he could have made 'em into a book."

Phoebe bit the inside of her cheek. If Ivy wanted to believe her husband had coined the phrase, she wouldn't tell her differently. Besides, what Shakespeare didn't know wouldn't hurt him.

The cowbell jangled again, announcing another customer. A veritable mountain of merchandise blocked their view of the front of the store, so Ivy shouted, "Be right there!"

When no one answered, Ivy frowned, gave Phoebe an absent pat, and muttered, "Be back in a minute, hon'." Then she sidled down the aisle toward the front counter.

Considering her size, Ivy moved with a silent stealth worthy of Apaches mounting a surprise attack. Curious, Phoebe followed as quietly as possible. She thought she heard the quiet scrape of wood on wood, but before she could decide, Ivy, a good three feet ahead of her, suddenly shouted, "Hey, there! Put that right back!"

Startled, Phoebe hurried to catch up and was just in time to see a young boy, running as if the seat of his pants were afire, race through the front door, a brown paper sack tucked beneath one arm.

"The little thief's gettin' quicker every day, I swear it," Ivy muttered with a shake of her head.

"Thief?" Phoebe echoed and felt a guilty flush steal

over her. Ridiculous, she knew. She hadn't stolen anything. And yet, memories of her own short-lived criminal career were far too close to be comfortable. "Are you going after him?"

Ivy swiveled her head and gave Phoebe a thoughtful look before saying, "No, I ain't." She drew a breath and folded her hands beneath her impressive bosom. "That boy's got his reasons, I reckon, for what he's doin'. And he never takes more than he needs."

Surprised at the woman's understanding, Phoebe couldn't help asking, "Then you know who he is and still don't say anything?"

Leading the way back to the far side of the store, Ivy talked as she moved. "I know that might sound funny to city people, but around here . . . well, let's just say that boy and me have an understanding. He keeps his thievin' small so I don't have to chase him."

Finished explaining, Ivy stopped at the wall of coats, snatched Phoebe's cloak from her shoulders, and reached up to grab down a dark brown wool coat. "Try this one on," she ordered in a tone that brooked no arguments, and Phoebe did as she was told.

"Good," Ivy muttered, stepping back to consider, "but not quite." She turned to the wall again, rummaging through the coats hanging there for just the right one. "Now my second husband," she went on as she searched, "Earl. He wasn't one for talking. Not like Zeb with his pretty speeches and sad eyes. But Lord, that Earl could kiss."

"Kiss?" Phoebe repeated, instantly flashing to the one kiss she'd shared with Riley. She wondered if Earl had been half as talented.

"Oh my, yes," Ivy said in fond memory. "Used to curl my toes. That man had a mouth on him straight from heaven." She sighed heavily and shrugged again. "But he passed on and I met up with Zeb, my third husband. He talked so pretty, I just had to have him."

Fascinating. Phoebe had learned more about Ivy Talbot in less than five minutes than she knew about the St. Louis neighbors she'd lived beside for twenty-some years. Her curiosity aroused, she asked, "And your first husband?"

"John Henry," Ivy said on a deeper sigh and turned around, a black coat with sheepskin lining in her hands. She plucked the rejected coat off Phoebe and helped her into the new one. She smoothed the fit, nearly squashing Phoebe into the ground with her strong hands. But as she worked, she talked. "John Henry was a bad sort, God love him. Scoundrel of the worst water. Stole my heart at the same time he stole my daddy's best horse." Ivy paused to lay one hand against her abundant breasts. "He had a way about him, no doubt about it. Now, Riley Burnett reminds me some of poor ol' John Henry, though Riley's always been on the healthy side of the law. But he's got the same look in his eye that sent me over the moon for John Henry when I was a girl."

"Have you known Riley long?" Phoebe prompted during a pause in the woman's conversation.

"Since he was a boy, but he don't talk much," Ivy allowed.

Phoebe was willing to bet that not many people around Ivy were given the chance to talk much.

"But that's a cute youngster he's got, despite the wife who gave her to him. But back to my first husband . . ." She stepped around, buttoned up the coat, then adjusted the collar. "Only fourteen when I first saw him. Took one look at John Henry and when he said 'Come with me,' I did." She grinned broadly in memory. "Love at first sight, I guess." Ivy shook her head, reached up to pluck a pencil from her hair, and produced a small tablet from her apron pocket. She scribbled something, then tucked everything away again. "'Course," she went on, "a posse strung him up not long after we got married, but oh, Lordy, those were three of the best months of my life."

"They *hanged* him?"

Ivy looked at her, surprised. "Well, sure, honey. He *was* a horse thief after all. It wasn't only my daddy's horses he took. Oh, John Henry was a caution, all right." She took a step back, looked Phoebe up and down, and nodded. "How's that one feel? Must say, it looks a durn sight better than that ol' cape."

"It feels wonderful," Phoebe admitted, tearing her concentration away from Ivy's fascinating life story to admire the coat. Smoothing her hands up and down the heavy woolen fabric, she luxuriated briefly in the soft caress of lamb's wool up against her neck. "But," she said reluctantly, "I'm afraid I can't really afford this right now."

"Now's when ya need it," Ivy pointed out. "It's cold out there, girl. You take it, and I'll put it on your bill."

"But I don't know when I'll be able to pay for it."

"Honey, the way this town's growin' in leaps and bounds, we'll both have plenty of money come next summer. Why, folks'll be flockin' to that hotel of yours. You wait and see."

"I hope you're right," Phoebe said.

"You know me a while longer," Ivy told her with a grin, "you'll see I'm *always* right. Ask anybody in Rimshot."

Obviously, Riley's advice had been good. Ivy Talbot was definitely the woman to ask for help. "Speaking of the town growing, Riley suggested I ask you who I might hire as a cook for the restaurant I'm opening."

"Restaurant? Shoot, honey. Where you gonna put tables for customers?"

Phoebe opened her mouth and then slammed it shut again. She hadn't really considered that problem yet. But a problem it was. Of course, she told herself with a silent sigh, it wouldn't be for much longer. Riley would be leaving. Signing the hotel over to her completely. If she wanted to, she could convert the entire saloon into a dining hall for a nice-sized restaurant.

Strange to realize she would much prefer the saloon with Riley running it.

Giving her a hearty slap on the back that nearly sent her sprawling, Ivy said on a short laugh, "Now, don't you fret, hon'. We'll think of something."

Smarting from the stinging, yet well-meant blow, Phoebe looked up at her new friend. Somehow, she had the feeling that Ivy Talbot could indeed find a solution to almost any problem. Just maybe, she could help Phoebe find a way to convince Riley to not only stay in town, but keep his daughter with him as well.

"Now, about that cook . . ." Ivy shot her a look. "You do still want one, don't ya?"

"Yes," Phoebe said quickly. She would find a way to open a restaurant. And until then, her new cook could teach Phoebe how to cook and start setting up the kitchen.

"Atta girl! I know just the woman." Ivy gave her a broad smile. "Mary O'Rourke. Husband took off to do some prospecting three years back—hasn't been seen since. He was a good sort, Danny was. He'd come back if he was able, so I figure he's dead. But Mary, she don't believe it for a minute. Still, she and her kids could sure use the money." Pausing, she gave a quick look around the store as if to make sure no one else would hear her. "It's one of her boys that's stealin' my crackers all the time. Mary helps out here a few days a week, but it ain't enough to keep body and soul together. And it'd break her heart to know her boy was helpin' himself to my goods."

As it would break Simmons's if he ever knew that she, too, had had to resort to theft just to survive.

"She sounds perfect," Phoebe said. Not only would she hire Mary, she would find a job or two for the little would-be thief. At least in this one small way, she could try to make up for all of the stealing she'd done.

Ivy picked up the small gold watch pinned to her shirt-front and checked the time. "Mary's due in a little bit.

Why don't we go have a nice talk over some cake?" She took Phoebe's elbow and started across the floor in long, purposeful strides. "You can tell me all about yourself—and," she added with a sly wink, "that butler of yours. My goodness, that's a fine-lookin' man."

It was all Phoebe could do to keep up as she was dragged in Ivy's wake. She had a fleeting thought of somehow trying to dissuade her new friend from looking at Simmons as husband number four. But Simmons could take care of himself.

Besides, Phoebe told herself as Ivy plopped her down in a chair, life had taken so many changes of late, maybe the butler would enjoy the big woman's attentions.

She loosened her hat ribbons and let the bonnet fall down onto her back. In a few short minutes, the older woman had two cups of coffee poured and two thick slabs of chocolate cake set out on the table.

"So, you going to fill me in on that butler of yours?"

"All right," Phoebe said, looking up into warm green eyes. "I'll tell you about Simmons, if you'll tell me all you know about Riley Burnett."

Ivy's eyebrows rose high on her forehead. She sat down across from Phoebe and whistled. "So, that's how the wind blows, eh? You don't mind my sayin' so, you've got your work cut out for you with Riley. It's a wonder that wife of his didn't turn him against all women forever. A bad sort, Tess was." She winked and added, "But I'm thinkin' he's worth the trouble."

Phoebe shrugged out of her coat, letting it fall across the back of her chair. As she took a bite of cake, she said, "Ivy, I think you're right."

After all, until Riley actually left, *anything* could happen.

"Like I said before, hon'," Ivy confided with a knowing smile. "I usually am."

Steam covered the windows in the saloon, making it nearly impossible to see outside.

Riley reached up and ran his fingertips across the cold glass. Moisture clung to his skin and he looked at the world through a watery lens. Familiar shapes wavered, as if the people outside were trembling or swaying in a fierce wind.

The sun beat down on Rimshot from a cloudless blue sky and reflected off the fresh snow with glinting, almost blinding, light. If the ground hadn't been covered by more than a foot of fresh snow, you wouldn't even know yesterday's storm had happened.

Restlessness rode him hard. He itched to be outside, away from the four walls and the people who surrounded him. He wanted to hop on his horse and ride straight out until it was too dark to see. Until he was miles from this town and the two females who had him so confused he hardly knew which way was up anymore.

Phoebe's relentless questions and arguments nagged at his mind even when she wasn't planted firmly in front of him. And Becky . . . hell, he didn't know how the kid knew that she'd be leaving soon, but she seemed to have picked up on something in the air. All day, she'd been hanging on him, turning those trusting blue eyes on him. Calling him papa.

Driving an invisible stake deep into his heart.

Head pounding, he suddenly snatched his sheepskin coat off a nearby peg, shrugged into it, and stomped to the door.

"Hey, boss," Mick yelled, "where you headed?"

Riley didn't even look at the man. Instead, he stepped through the front door and closed it behind him. Crossing the wide porch in a couple of steps, he stopped just at the edge.

Looking first one way, then the other, his gaze raked the main street of Rimshot. Strange, but he was almost getting used to the hustle and noise of town life. When he'd first come home, he'd thought he would lose his sanity. But now, there was a familiarity to the sounds around him. The blacksmith's hammer, the barber's wife shouting at him from down the street. The friendly yap of dogs as they chased alongside a group of kids.

A farm wagon lumbered along the street, drawing Riley's eye. As the heavy dray rolled past, its wheels screeching, he noticed, for the first time, a smaller wagon that had been obscured behind the larger one.

Damn familiar, he told himself, his gaze narrowing thoughtfully. A flicker of memory teased his mind and he fought to nail it down. To identify it. As he watched, concentrating, a small man appeared alongside that two-wheeled cart and scrambled up to the bench seat, disappearing behind the white canvas wagon covering.

Scowling now, Riley stepped off the boardwalk and into the muddy, slushy street. The small hairs at the back of his neck rippled as if in warning. He knew that cart, and its driver.

The last time he'd seen it had been more than a month ago.

In New Mexico territory.

The tinker.

Chapter Twelve

What the hell was *he* doing here?

Riley's teeth ground together. His boots crunched on the snow as he hurried forward. He fought the soggy ground for purchase and nimbly dodged the horses and pedestrians in his way.

A sense of urgency ate at him.

Something was wrong, here. He felt it, bone deep. Logically, he knew there was no reason why a traveling tinker shouldn't be in Rimshot. But this particular tinker had struck Riley strange right from the get-go.

For him to show up here and now seemed a bit too coincidental.

"Riley!"

He paid no mind to the shout. At the moment, all he was interested in was reaching the tinker before the man had a chance to leave town. And by the look of things, Riley thought as he spotted the leather reins lifted high off the horses' backs, that's just what the little man had in mind.

"Hey, Riley, hold up there a minute!"

He cursed under his breath and kept going. But it felt as though the soggy ground was holding him back purposely. As if even the earth was grabbing at his feet, slowing his progress.

Halfway to his destination, the tinker's cart started

rolling. "Damn it," Riley muttered. He was going to lose him.

"Hey," that voice called out, nearer this time. "You deaf or something?"

The tinker's wagon rolled around the corner of Main Street and trundled off into the crowds.

A horse. That's what Riley needed. A horse. He'd go to the stables, saddle up, and follow the little fella. Instantly, he spun around to go back the way he'd come and crashed right into Dave Hawkins.

"Steady on," the deputy said with a laugh and staggered slightly as his footing shifted in the precarious slush and mud. "What's your hurry?"

"No hurry," Riley snapped and tried to step around the younger man. "Just want to see a man about . . . something."

He wasn't about to start explaining the situation with the tinker. Who'd believe him, anyway?

"I want to talk to you about something," Dave said as he moved to block Riley's path.

"Later."

"It'll only take a minute."

Riley tossed a quick glance over his left shoulder at the spot where he'd seen the tinker's cart disappear. How fast could the man possibly travel in that thing? He wouldn't have any trouble catching up on horseback. Fine. He'd spare a minute for the deputy and then be on his way.

"What is it?" he asked, swiveling his head around to look at the dark-haired man in front of him.

"It's about Miss Hightower. Phoebe."

Riley's gaze narrowed as he took in the anticipation on the deputy's features. Like a hungry dog staring at a meaty bone. His insides twisted into a knot as he asked, "What about her?"

"Wanted to ask you a question," Dave said with a thoughtful look at the other man's fierce expression. "But it appears I already have my answer."

"I don't have time for this, Hawkins," Riley said

quickly. Nor did he want to encourage what had to be Dave's interest in Phoebe. Best to just have this done and over. "What's your question? Ask it fast."

"Well . . ." The man's dark-eyed gaze shifted to a point just beyond Riley's shoulder. "I was wonderin' . . ."

"What?" he nearly shouted and immediately searched inwardly for the patience he'd always prided himself on. Unfortunately, he couldn't seem to find it.

"Hell." Hawkins looked at him for a long minute. "I want to know, have you staked a claim on Phoebe?"

Well, son of a bitch. Of course, he should have been expecting this. It had only been a matter of time before the men around here started taking an interest in Phoebe. He was only surprised that it was the usually shy Hawkins to get the ball rolling.

Damn his eyes anyway.

"So," Dave said, starting to show a bit of impatience himself. "Are you interested in her?"

Now there was a loaded question.

One he wasn't ready to acknowledge.

"What's it to you?"

Hawkins shrugged and a slice of sunlight glanced off his badge to streak across Riley's eyes. "I figured if she was fair game, I'd make my play."

"Fair game?" Riley repeated darkly.

"Yeah. She ain't married and, except for you, I ain't seen her spending time with any particular fella."

"Maybe there's a reason for that."

"Well, now that's why I'm askin'."

Fair game. Phoebe.

An invisible fist tightened around Riley's chest and squeezed.

"Look," Hawkins snapped. Clearly his own temper was starting to kick in. "It's a simple question. Is there something between you two or not?"

Two different questions, Riley noted silently. Was he interested? And was there something between him and Phoebe?

As to the first, he'd have to say he didn't know. Lord knew there was interest aplenty, but his brain was still functioning enough to let him know constantly that there shouldn't be. As to something being between the two of them . . . hell, yes, there was something.

One amazing kiss and a lot of confusion.

"Well?" Hawkins prompted.

But did he want Phoebe considered "fair game" by every man in town? Hell, no. Though since he'd be leaving in a couple of weeks, he guessed he really didn't have much to say about it either way. And that thought bothered him plenty.

"Stay the hell away from Phoebe, Hawkins," Riley shot back.

Those brown eyes became slits and anger spat at him from their depths. "I came to you 'cause it seemed the decent thing to do," the deputy said softly. "But if you ain't willing to slap a brand on that woman, then you'd best step aside for someone who is."

"And I'm telling you I don't want you sniffin' around Phoebe. You stay clear of her."

"Burnett," Hawkins said as he reached up to pull his hat brim down lower over his eyes, "don't you make me sorry we've been friends." Then he pushed past Riley and continued off down the street.

Riley watched him go for a moment or two and almost felt a twinge of regret. He hadn't had so many friends in his lifetime that he could afford to lose one. And maybe he didn't have the right to keep men away from Phoebe.

He turned around again and headed for the livery stable, in long, determined strides.

But damn it, he just didn't have the stomach for watching other men come to claim what he couldn't.

If that made him a bastard, well, he'd just have to live with that.

Mary O'Rourke looked far older than her thirty-five years. Until she smiled. Then the lines on her face shifted into familiar patterns and her green eyes sparkled with good humor. Her clothes were worn but clean, and when she spoke, her voice still carried the faintest traces of the Ireland she'd left behind nearly twenty years before.

Ginger-colored hair neatly twisted into a braid that hung down between her shoulders, swung about her hips with her rapid, sure movements.

The moment Ivy introduced the two women, Phoebe had sensed a kindred spirit. Though their lives were different in many ways, both she and Mary had found ways to survive in difficult circumstances.

Phoebe watched, fascinated, as the other woman peeked into every cupboard, inspected the pantry, and considered the store of pots, pans, and dishware.

"Well," the redhead finally announced, turning to face her new employer, "you're fairly well set up. You'll need to stock more supplies, of course, but what we have on hand will do for now."

"And you're sure you can teach me to cook?" Phoebe asked, remembering the pot of undrinkable coffee she'd brewed just the other night when she and Riley had sat together in the shadowed darkness.

As to the other memory from that night, the moment when he'd held her singed hand and very nearly kissed her again . . . Phoebe tried not to think about it.

"Of course I can," Mary said, and dumped a scoopful of flour into a bowl. "Just takes practice is all, and with running a restaurant, there'll be plenty of that!"

"True," Phoebe said and leaned her elbows on the table. Concentrating every thought on the here and now— and the future of her business.

While Mary worked, Phoebe thought through an idea that had occurred to her only a while ago. Dragging one fingertip through the fine dust of flour on the table, she said, "I've been thinking . . ."

"Yes?" Mary looked at the younger woman and waited, ready to do whatever Phoebe Hightower wanted. Being offered this job was like the answer to all of her countless prayers. With Danny gone, life was harder than it ever had been.

Feeding three children and trying to keep them warm and clothed as well, all on the bits of money she managed to make from the odd jobs she found about town wasn't easy. Worse than that, though, was the knowledge that one of her children was stealing bits and pieces just to help out and she couldn't afford to make him stop. But now, working for Phoebe, with regular money coming in, perhaps she could stop bending Saint Jude's ear every bloody night.

Oh, yes, she owed Phoebe Hightower a debt of gratitude, and whatever she wanted done, would get done, or Mary O'Rourke would know the reason why not.

Phoebe looked up at her, a considering smile on her face. "What would you say to opening a bakery right now? I mean, I know they're building a new one up the road, but it won't be open before spring. Why shouldn't we get the jump on them?"

"A bakery?"

"Yes." The idea had been simmering in the back of her mind ever since she'd realized she had no dining room for a restaurant. As Ivy had pointed out, come summer, the hotel would likely be full of paying guests. But until then, she needed a way to make the money they'd need to fix up the old hotel—and perhaps enough to build a dining room adjacent to the place. Just in case she could convince Riley to stay.

Warming to her idea, Phoebe stood up, walked to the far wall, and pulled a second apron down to tie around her waist. "I mean, with all of the construction going on, I'm sure we could sell whatever you baked to the workers without any problem at all."

Mary grinned and said, "Why not? With the appetites of those men, you'll likely find yourself in the midst of a gold mine."

"*We* will," Phoebe told her and stepped up to the other woman, holding out her right hand. Mary took it in a brief, floury grip. The two women took each other's measure and both seemed pleased with what they saw.

"Feeb!"

Phoebe turned to see Becky Burnett race into the kitchen, stark naked.

"Becky!"

Mary O'Rourke laughed aloud and Becky grinned up at her like an actor thanking her audience for their appreciation.

"Where are your clothes?" Phoebe asked and scooped the girl up into her arms. Becky's flesh was alive with goose bumps and her bare toes looked purple.

The child clapped her hands, then threw them wide, shaking her head wildly.

"Yes," Phoebe laughed. "I can see they're gone. You're turning into a little blond icicle!"

"Cookie!" Becky shouted.

"Clothes," Phoebe countered and moved closer to the heat flowing from the fire in the big stove.

"She's a cute one," Mary said, still chuckling under her breath. "Riley Burnett's, is she?"

"Yes." Phoebe looked over her shoulder at the other woman even as she lifted her apron to wrap it around the child in her arms. "Her name's Becky and apparently she's decided to stop wearing clothes."

Mary reached past her to pat the baby's cheek gently. "Ah, they all do that around this age," she said, shaking her head. "My Shane? When he was near three, I found him stridin' down the middle of Main Street, naked as a jaybird, with his da's hat perched on his head."

"Oh, my," Phoebe laughed.

"Oh, yes," Mary told her on a chuckle. "And me threatenin' to tell that story to his friends is sometimes the only way to bring young Shane to heel now."

"Cookie!" Becky crowed again when it seemed no one was paying attention to her demands. Phoebe snatched an oatmeal cookie from the table and handed it to the baby to ensure peace for a few minutes.

"How old is Shane now?" she asked and hefted the girl a bit higher on her hip.

"Ah, well," Mary said, turning back to the bread bowl. "Shane is nine"—she winked—"a terrible age for worryin' over what his friends think of him. Danny junior is near eleven and little Molly is five."

"Three children," Phoebe whispered and cuddled the warm, solid weight of Becky Burnett closer. She thought briefly what her own life might have been like if she'd been blessed with a husband and family of her own. She'd always wanted a houseful of children.

Being an only child herself, she understood the loneliness of having no one to share your secrets with. No one to get into trouble with. No one to dream with.

A swift, brief pang of regret shot through her and she tightened her hold on Becky. Not her child, but as close as she was likely to come to knowing the wonders of being a mother.

And she was going to lose her.

Bending her head slightly, Phoebe rubbed her cheek over Becky's sweet-smelling curls, cherishing the soft caress and tucking the memory of this moment into a corner of her heart. Years from now, she would pull out this memory, dust it off and relive the precious warmth of it.

Just as she would relive the kiss she'd shared with Riley and all of the silly dreams that kiss had inspired.

"Aye," Mary was saying and paused in her work to smile at the thought of her children. "Three, though late at night they cause enough of a row and eruption to be a dozen."

Phoebe smiled wistfully, imagining the scene.

"Of course, when my Danny gets home," Mary went on, "they'll settle to right away. There's something about the sound of a man's deep voice that'll put a quick stop to shenanigans."

A deep, heartfelt yearning colored her tone and it pulled at Phoebe as she remembered Ivy's words. *If Danny could come home, he would. Must be dead.*

"It must be hard," she said carefully. "Being mother and father."

Mary buried both of her hands in the bread dough and began to knead it with a vengeance. "It'll all be worth it," she muttered, as if she'd repeated the words often to herself, "when Danny comes home. Won't be long now."

"Ivy says he's been gone three years?"

"Aye," Mary told her, keeping her head down, her gaze fixed on the dough. "He went to the gold fields, looking to find our fortune, he said. Last I heard, he was somewhere in Idaho." A year or more now it's been," she continued with a sniff. "But, then, Danny doesn't read or write. And in the gold fields it's probably not an easy task to find someone who can."

"I'm sure it is . . ." Phoebe's voice was gentle, yet her pessimism must have rung through.

"Oh," the other woman said with a nod. "I know what you're thinkin'. What everyone in town is thinkin'."

"I didn't mean to—"

"It's all right," Mary said softly. "You're not the first to think I should give up waiting." She straightened up for a minute, looked Phoebe dead in the eye, and said simply, "But my Danny *will* be back."

"How can you be so sure?" Phoebe asked, deeply moved by the woman's certainty despite all logic.

"Because," Mary answered with a wink and a strained half-smile, "he told me so when he left. And Danny's never lied to me."

What must it feel like, Phoebe couldn't help wondering, to be loved so fiercely and loyally as that?

"Folks say he could be dead." Mary winced tightly and even Phoebe felt a pang for a man she'd never heard of until today. "But he's not." The woman shook her head and tapped her chest with one doughy fingertip. "If he was, I'd feel it. Inside me. And I don't," she added firmly, as if daring Phoebe to argue the point. When she didn't, Mary smiled grimly. "Not even the devil himself could stand between me and my Danny. He'll be back. You'll see."

Phoebe smiled, but didn't know what to say. The other woman's words still echoed in the warm room and she felt an odd ache deep in her soul, only to recognize the sensation as envy. Despite Mary's hard life and the uncertainty that must plague her day and night, she had an unshakable belief in her husband. A bond with him that couldn't be severed by time or distance. Despite the passing years, her faith was unwavering.

Instantly, Riley's face rose up in her mind. Was what she felt for him the first stirrings of love? Or was she simply deluding herself into building dreams on the misty foundations of one magical kiss? Dreams that were destined to end in two short weeks when he rode out of her life forever.

The kitchen door opened and Phoebe turned her back to the gust of cool air that rocketed around the room, protecting Becky as best she could.

"What are you up to, Dave Hawkins?" Mary asked.

Phoebe glanced over her shoulder at the deputy and watched him drag his hat off. His warm brown gaze locked with hers even as he answered Mary. "I was hopin' to beg a cup of coffee. It's cold out there."

"Help yourself," she said, smiling. "I'll just go get Becky dressed. Be back in a minute." Then she stepped through the swinging door and hurried down the hallway.

When the quick taps of her heels against the floorboards died away, Mary said quietly, "It's more than coffee you're after, I'm thinkin'."

Dave walked across the room, poured himself a cup, then took a seat at the table. Looking up at her, he grinned. "Can't blame a man for trying," he said.

"No," she said lightly, but was remembering the look on Phoebe's face when she greeted the deputy. There'd been no instant flash of awareness. No spark of something hot and fine. For all the notice she'd taken of him,

Phoebe might have been welcoming a maiden aunt.

Dave Hawkins could try all he wanted, Mary thought. But there was no magic between him and Phoebe. And without magic, she reflected as Danny's image rose up in her mind, the world was an empty place.

And love, just another word.

Riley pulled back on the reins and scowled at the long, winding road that led back to town. He'd ridden miles along the narrow track and seen nothing more than two jackrabbits bounding over the snow-covered ground.

Where the hell could he have got to?

Why was the tinker here at all, for that matter?

But most especially, why did it feel so important that he find out?

Riley should have been able to catch up with that little cart with no trouble at all. But it was as if the tinker and his horse and wagon had rolled right off the end of the earth and disappeared. A chill that had nothing to do with the temperature crawled up his spine at the thought, even as his rational mind assured him that was impossible.

Turning in the the saddle, Riley looked around the open stretch of land that lay on either side of the road. No sign of a wagon. There were no tracks to be found and in the fresh snow there damn well should have been.

What was going on around here?

Blast Dave Hawkins for slowing him down.

His horse snorted, puffs of steam rising up around its muzzle in the cold air.

"Yeah, I know," he muttered, reaching down to stroke the animal's neck. "You're just as itchy as I am to be on the move." Briefly, he glanced behind him at the road that led to Carson City and beyond that, anywhere.

He hadn't found the tinker, but he had found the old restlessness clawing at his insides. Soon, he'd be back on that road, or one like it. Headed into empty territory, with Rimshot, Becky, and Phoebe tucked neatly away into memory.

Yet surprisingly enough, that thought didn't bring the comfort it might have once upon a time.

He was doing the right thing, though. Wasn't he? Becky deserved better than he could give her. And as for Phoebe . . . maybe it didn't set right, leaving before she had the hotel up and running . . . but at least this way, she could have it the way she wanted it right from the start.

So if he was doing all the right things, why did he feel so damn bad about it?

Chapter Thirteen

"What's he doin' in there?" Henry asked.

His twin, Joe, eased up slowly in front of the window and stopped when he was just high enough to get a look into the kitchen. Scraping hair out of his eyes with one furtive hand, he scowled, then eased back down before stepping to one side and facing his twin. "He's just settin' there drinkin' coffee and makin' stupid faces at Phoebe."

"Faces?" Henry brightened right up. Heck, if Deputy Dave was playing games with Phoebe and Mary, maybe they could get in on the fun. "What kind of faces? Scary?"

"I said stupid, didn't I?" Joe asked. Giving his brother a disgusted snort, he went on. "He looks like this . . ." Then he cocked his head, rolled his eyes, and simpered.

Henry's features screwed up and he took a step backward as if the deputy's affliction might be catching. Didn't seem like fun to him. Dave must look like a fool. "What's he want to do that for? Is he sick?"

"Might as well be," Joe said, clearly disgusted with the man. "Reckon he's sweet on Phoebe." He stepped off the back porch and kicked at a rock half buried in the mud.

"Well, heck, if Dave's sweet on her, he's gonna be hangin' around here all the time! How're we gonna bail out our mine and get back to prospectin'?"

They'd been shut up in the house during the storm and

now they were anxious to get back to their interrupted gold hunt. But now that the storm was over, they had other problems. Too many durn folks around, for one. Not to forget the water.

Joe slid a glance to the hole in question. Beneath a layer of dirty snow, only two loose planks covered what had been a promising gold mine. Hell, even Creek had said it was a good spot for treasure. Damn shame, he thought. All those riches lying down there under gallons of water.

There had to be a way . . .

"What're you boys up to?"

Both boys jumped, startled, and whipped around to look at Riley as he walked up behind them.

Recovering quickly, Joe said, "Nothin'."

Riley looked from one to the other of them and could almost see the wheels of mischief turning in their minds. There was just no telling what the Weatherby boys would do next. Just remembering what he himself and their pa had been like as kids was enough to scare the hell out of him. "You stay away from that well, you understand?"

Henry shoved his hands into his pants pockets, tipped his head back, and whistled at the sky, in a useless bid for an innocent air.

"Yes, sir," Joe muttered, then dipped his head and looked at Riley from underneath a hank of dark hair. "You goin' inside?"

"Why?" He shot a look from Henry's unconvincing act to the calculating gleam in Joe's eyes.

The boy shrugged. "Just thought you ought to know Phoebe's entertainin'."

"Entertaining?" Riley flicked a glance at the kitchen door as if he could see through the wood to the room beyond. He was in no mood for playing games with these children.

"Dave Hawkins is in there," Henry told him, "goin' like this . . ." And he repeated the act his brother had shown him.

"What do you know?" Joe demanded. "You didn't see a durn thing. You wouldn't even go peek in the window. You was scared."

"Was not!"

"Was too!"

The twins started in on what looked to be a promising argument and Riley took a step away from them, concentrating on the kitchen where Phoebe was *entertaining*.

Dave Hawkins.

Something small and cold settled in his belly. Riley's features tightened as he stepped up close to the window. Keeping to one side, he glanced in, feeling like the peeping Tom he was.

Phoebe's back was to him, Mary stood at the table kneading bread dough, and Dave sat opposite Phoebe. The three of them made quite a little picture as they laughed together.

At least she wasn't alone with him, he thought, though that was small enough consolation. A corner of his mind noted and approved that Dave was facing the door so as to be ready for trouble. But just because the man seemed to be a decent enough lawman didn't mean that Riley cared for his calling on Phoebe.

At the thought of her, Riley's gaze shifted until he was staring at her back. She held herself straight and proud. There was an elegance to the way she tilted her head and his gaze caressed the column of her throat. Her hair, though still confined to its usual bun, looked a bit looser today. There were a few stray wisps of hair that had worked themselves free of the knot to dangle gently along the nape of her neck.

His fingers itched to touch them and he curled his hands into empty fists. Unbidden, the memory of the kiss they'd shared in the first fall of snow came rushing back at him, weakening his knees and sending a rush of blood to a part of him that needed no encouragement.

Jesus. Why torture yourself? he demanded silently. He was leaving in a couple of weeks. There was simply no point in allowing foolish notions to race through his mind. But for some reason, he couldn't seem to stop them.

Even as his gaze moved over Phoebe to rest briefly on Dave Hawkins's animated face, he asked himself, Isn't this for the best? Wasn't it better for both of them if Phoebe formed an affection for some other man? But that thought caused the cold hard knot in his guts to twist violently. It didn't seem to matter if it would be best or not. The idea of Phoebe in another man's arms was enough to turn Riley as icy as the piles of dirty snow stacked up along the edges of the buildings.

Abruptly, he pushed away from the wall and stole one last glance at the woman he couldn't have, yet didn't want to lose. Separated from him by something much more impassable than a windowpane, Phoebe was out of his reach and he'd best learn to deal with it.

One hand lifted slowly, hesitantly, and his fingertips touched the window and that's when it struck him. Here he was, standing outside a room he longed to enter. Apart from the person he most wanted to be with. Staring through the glass like a kid in front of a candy-shop window.

Just like always. On the outside, looking in.

A week passed and cold, starry nights followed cool, clear days. The snow melted beneath the persistent rays of a weak winter sun.

The only news was a brief telegram from his in-laws. *Delayed another week.* Riley stood in the open doorway and braced one hand on the doorjamb as he wondered again if he was doing the right thing.

Naturally, when the telegram had arrived, Phoebe had taken the opportunity to point out that Becky's grandparents certainly didn't seem eager to claim her. When he'd tried to argue, she'd simply asked, "If they're this disinterested in her now, what will her life be like living with them, do you think?"

His back teeth ground together and his hand fisted helplessly. Thanks to Phoebe, that's all he'd been thinking about since. What *would* her life be like? Would she be forgotten? Lonely? Or spoiled by overindulgent grandparents with too much money and not enough time for her?

Shoving away from the wall, he ordered himself to stop second-guessing himself. The decision about Becky had been made. There were other things to think about. Things like the vandalism against the saloon that had so mysteriously stopped. Though he should be grateful that no more rocks had been thrown through his windows and no more shipments of whiskey had been smashed, he couldn't help wondering if the trouble was really over. After all, they'd never caught the fella responsible.

And something in Riley's gut told him his vandal wasn't finished. There was no reason to believe the trouble would start up again. Yet, it felt as though something, somewhere, were building to a head. Every instinct in his body told him to be ready. Alert. Watchful.

And he'd learned long ago not to ignore his instincts. Once a lawman always a lawman. Couldn't be helped, he supposed. When a man was used to living his life a certain way, it was bound to color the way he looked at the world and the people around him.

"Riley?"

He closed his eyes briefly at the sound of her voice. He'd done his best to avoid Phoebe during the past week. Dave Hawkins had come calling several times. Riley had stayed clear of the hotel, surrounding himself with the safety in numbers to be found in the saloon every night. And taking care of Becky himself during the days.

It wasn't cowardly, he told himself. It only made sense. He had nothing to offer her. And though it pained him to even think of it, he didn't have the right to keep her from looking for happiness elsewhere.

But he didn't have to watch it either.

Riley half turned to look at her as she stepped into the room.

She wore a new blue and white striped dress that detailed her figure to a point that had Riley's breath catching in his chest. Her hair, still in its damn bun, looked fuller, softer, today and there was one stray wisp of hair that lay along her cheek like a caress.

He swallowed heavily. " 'Morning, Phoebe," he said finally. "You're looking fine."

She flushed with pleasure and gave him a smile that hit him like a punch to the gut.

"Thank you," she said, running one hand down the front of her skirt. "I probably shouldn't have bought it, but Ivy convinced me that I needed some new dresses."

"It suits you." Now there was an understatement. She looked as shiny and fresh as a brand-new twenty-dollar gold piece.

She walked toward him, holding out a cup and saucer. "I brought you some coffee," she said and, at his disconcerted expression, added with a laugh, "Don't worry. Mary made it."

He hadn't been worried about what it tasted like. He was simply surprised that she'd thought of him. Riley accepted the coffee and tried to ignore a rush of pleasure. Stupid, really. It was such a little thing. A kindness she probably thought nothing of. But he couldn't remember the last time someone had done something . . . unexpectedly *nice* for him.

"Thanks," he said softly.

He must have been staring because Phoebe cleared her throat, linked her hands behind her back, and turned to peer out the doorway. "What were you staring at?"

"Nothing. Just looking."

She shot him a sidelong glance. "Your expression was so serious. You're sure nothing's wrong?"

He took a sip, shook his head, then shifted his gaze back to the street. He couldn't keep looking at Phoebe and maintain concentration at the same time. "I'm just trying to work on the puzzle of who's behind all the trouble we were having."

"Oh, that," she said and moved up closer beside him.

Riley inhaled deeply, deliberately, knowing the scent of lavender would invade his lungs and paint another memory of Phoebe.

He silently called himself all kinds of a fool.

"Dave thinks the trouble's past."

"Really?" It irritated the hell out of him the way she said that. Just like, *Oh, by the way, God told me the weather will be just dandy on Sunday.*

"Yes." She leaned past him, craning her neck to look up and down the boardwalk. Then she drew back inside and shivered. "Still chilly out there, even with the sun."

"Uh-huh," he said, not interested at all in talking about the weather. "What else did Deputy Dave have to say?"

"Oh." She turned and smiled up at him.

Really, her eyes were the most incredible shade of blue he could remember seeing. Dark one moment, light the next, it was as if he were watching the surface of a lake while the sun played hide-and-seek in the clouds.

Jesus, he was in trouble here. And he was missing whatever it was she was saying.

". . . so he thinks the kids probably lost interest and moved on to something else."

Hawkins had worked it all out, had he? And made sure he shared all of his seasoned insights with Phoebe. Irritation rode him hard and Riley had to draw rein on a temper that was building like a forest fire rushing over dry tinder.

"So Dave thinks it was just some kids." Sarcasm colored his tone despite the fact that Riley himself had been thinking the same thing just a few minutes ago.

"Of course," she said, her gaze locked with his. "Who else could it be?"

Damned if he was going to stand there and pretend along with her that Dave Hawkins was some kind of ancient soothsayer, holder of all truths, knower of all things. The man might be a halfway decent deputy, but he damn sure wasn't the be-all and end-all of the whole damn world!

He set his coffee cup down on its saucer with a clatter that made her blink. "Hell, Phoebe, it could be anybody!"

"Dave says . . ."

Riley was getting almighty tired of hearing what *Dave* said. What had happened here? Phoebe Hightower had never struck him as the kind of woman to parrot whatever some man told her. Was she so besotted with *Dave* that she actually believed the man was as good as he obviously thought himself to be? "What makes you so sure he's right?"

One of her eyebrows lifted slightly at his tone and Riley winced.

All right, he told himself. Calm down. Else she'll see you for the fool you're behaving.

"Why are you so determined to prove him wrong?" she asked finally. "I thought you liked Dave Hawkins."

Riley turned and headed for the nearest table. He set the cup and saucer down carefully despite the urge in him to throw it against a wall just to hear it break. Damn, he hadn't been at all prepared to hear her defending another man to him. Did she already care that much for Dave? Had the deputy somehow won her heart in little more than a week?

A sharp, stinging pain slashed at his soul and Riley realized that this was what he would be feeling in the coming years. The ache of knowing that Phoebe's loyalties, her *love,* had been given to some other man.

Foolishness to grieve for something you never really had. Yet there it was. Logically, he knew it was stupid. Unfortunately, logic had little to do with what a man felt.

What a man dreamed.

He swung around to look at her again and somehow wasn't surprised that she was standing right alongside him. His gaze moved over her in a heartbeat and he couldn't help wondering what might have been. But trains of thought like that were destined to derail, leaving a man's mind and soul in ashes. So he pushed them aside and got back to the business at hand.

"Liking him has nothing to do with anything," Riley said, trying to ignore the shift of color in her eyes. "I was marshaling long before Dave Hawkins and I'm telling you I don't think it was kids."

The high pink flush in her cheeks faded a bit and Riley bit back an oath. Good going, he told himself. Dave had her calm and untroubled and he'd just managed to throw worry back into her lap.

Phoebe sat down and looked up at him. "Why not?"

Riley yanked a chair out from under the table, its legs screeching on the plank floor. He sat down, propped his forearms on his thighs, and met her gaze squarely, evenly. He didn't want her to be scared, but he did want her to be careful.

"Lots of reasons. Mostly, though, because a kid wouldn't think to ruin a shipment of whiskey. A rock through a window, that's easy. The other, too much trouble. No. It has to be an adult. A man," he corrected, since he didn't believe a woman would be any more likely to jump up and down on whiskey bottles than a kid would.

"Dave said—"

"Damn it, Phoebe," he snapped, interrupting her before she could quote the great and powerful Hawkins to his face again. "Pinning a badge on a man doesn't make him infallible!"

"I didn't say he was," she argued.

Riley reached out, picked up one of her hands from her lap, and enveloped it between both of his. His fingertips smoothed across her soft flesh and every touch was like a brand, sending scorching heat into all the dark spots within him. He relished that warmth for a long minute and a part of him wanted to claim it for his own.

To claim her.

But that was a dream and he had always dealt in the cold, hard realities of life.

She gave a feeble effort to pull away but he strengthened his hold on her, reluctant to let her go just yet.

"A badge only gives a man the right to look. It doesn't make him *see*."

"But you *do* see."

"I think so."

"How much?"

"What?"

She sucked in a deep breath, looked at their joined hands briefly, then lifted her gaze to his again. "I mean, do you see that what you're doing about Becky is wrong? That leaving Rimshot is a mistake?"

He released her abruptly and sat back, hands on his thighs. "We're talking about vandals here. Not me."

She missed his touch, though she could still feel the tingling sensation where their flesh had met. She'd never experienced anything like that before Riley and she didn't want to lose it. "We're talking about people seeing what they want to see."

"What I *see* is that my daughter will be taken care of better than I could hope to do it."

Did he really believe that? Or was he just telling himself so to make it easier to let her go?

"Will they love her?" she asked quietly.

"They're her grandparents, for God's sake!"

"That's no guarantee," she said quickly. "If they were truly concerned about her, they would have come for her already."

A muscle in his tight jaw twitched. "Christ, Phoebe," he said, "let it go."

Despite the urge to ease away the lines of tension etched between his eyebrows, she couldn't give him what he wanted. She couldn't watch him turn away from his daughter when she *knew* he would regret it one day.

"I can't. I know what growing up without love is like." She hesitated briefly, wondering if she should say any more, but then her determination prodded her on. "My father was more interested in his studies than he ever was in me. And that's a lonely way to grow up, Riley."

He sighed heavily, and kneaded his thigh muscles with his fingers as if looking for someone to strangle. "I'm sorry, but—"

"I don't want your sympathy," Phoebe countered. "I only want you to think about this. Becky would be much happier with someone who *loves* her."

Jumping to his feet, Riley looked down at her through eyes glittering with frustrated anger. "You think this is easy for me? I've spent most of my life doing my duty. Don't you think I know where my duty here lies? But sometimes, duty isn't what's most important." He shoved both hands through his hair, squeezing his skull until his knuckles shone white. "What is important is that Becky have everything she should. Love don't buy groceries, Phoebe. You come from a different place. You don't know what it would be like for a kid to grow up in a *saloon,* for God's sake."

"Hotel."

"Whatever you want to call it, if it doesn't make money, then what? Do I tell Becky, Sorry you're hungry, honey. I could have sent you to live with rich grandparents, but at least I love you. No," he went on, shaking his head. "You don't get an opinion here, 'cause you don't know a damn thing about this." He took a deep breath and added, "I know you mean well. But stay out of it."

She stared into his eyes and felt her own fury mount. He was talking to her as though she were a dimwitted child. As though she'd spent her life being waited on hand and foot. Of course, a still-reasonable corner of her mind admitted, what else could he think? She'd brought her butler with her.

But she wasn't interested in reason at the moment. He was dismissing her because he thought she was too protected to know what kind of fears haunted him. Well, she wouldn't allow that. "You're so wrong, Riley." Tears filled her eyes but she blinked them back, refusing to let them fall. "Have you ever been so hungry or so cold that you had to resort to *stealing* to survive?" She laughed shortly, harshly, at his surprised expression. "No. You were too busy arresting people for doing that." Poking his chest with her index finger, she went on. "Well, let me tell you something, Riley Burnett, I *do* know what it's like to follow wealthy strangers like a vulture, hovering close, waiting for a chance to steal something . . . anything that could be sold to buy food. I know what it's like to strip a house of everything of value and then sell it to a junk dealer hoping he'll be *fair*, if not generous. And I know what it's like to watch someone you love shivering from cold and have no furniture left to burn in the fireplace."

"Phoebe . . ." His voice choked into the room.

But she wasn't listening. She started pacing, her heels tapping furiously on the wooden floor. She couldn't have stopped now even if she'd wanted to. It was as if talking about her secret shame had lanced a boil on her soul and the poison she'd bottled up had come pouring out.

"You're the one who doesn't know what it's like. Try finding work as a woman," she muttered with a violent shake of her head. "The jobs a woman can get don't pay enough to support a half-starved child. She can be a teacher, if no man wants the job. She can be a governess, if she's alone with no one else to look out for." Phoebe shook her head fiercely again and this time her hair tumbled free of its knot, falling down around her shoulders. Grumbling, she reached up and shoved it back from her face before snapping him a look that should have seared him.

Pulse pounding, heart racing, a part of her couldn't believe she was telling him all this. Yet it felt so good to get it all into the open at last, she ignored the sudden sense of humiliation beginning to throb inside her and finished.

Stopping dead in her tracks, she said, "Or you can surrender the last shreds of your dignity and self-respect and barter your body on a street corner."

His eyes narrowed as the implications of that statement sunk in.

"Jesus, Phoebe." He started for her, but she stopped him with an upraised hand.

"No," she said flatly and paused for breath. But as she drew in the chill air, the action seemed to calm her and her voice was less strident when she added, "It didn't come to that." She swallowed heavily past the knot that seemed lodged in her throat. "Thankfully, I received word of Uncle Steven's legacy before I became that desperate." Wrapping her arms around herself, she whispered, "God, it seemed like a miracle."

"I'm sorry, Phoebe," he said softly. "Sorry you went through that and sorry I made you relive it."

"I didn't tell you to gain your sympathy," she said quietly, her voice faint now that the inner storm had passed.

"Don't you think I know that?" He started toward her again.

Phoebe backed up. Taking a deep, steadying breath, she said, "I'd appreciate it if you wouldn't say anything about this to anyone."

"Damn it, Phoebe," Riley snapped. "Did you really think I'd run into the street spreading your story all over town?"

"No." She smiled briefly, but he saw there was no humor in it and the sadness welling in her eyes tugged at him.

Damn, he was a fool. He'd assumed Phoebe had led a privileged life just because she traveled with a butler, came from St. Louis, and her hands were unmarked by labor. He should have known better than anyone just how many ways there were to suffer quiet hurts and small miseries.

"Does Simmons know?"

"Oh, good God, no!"

"He won't hear it from me."

"Thank you."

Polite strangers separated by embarrassment and shame.

He took another step toward her, and swallowed his disappointment when she began edging more quickly in the direction of the doorway.

"Phoebe, don't go yet." He spoke quickly, holding out one hand toward her.

"I have to go help Mary in the kitchen," she said just as quickly and only gave his outstretched hand one regretful look before turning and leaving the room.

He left the saloon a moment later and hit the boardwalk at a fast trot. Jumping off the edge, he kept on down the muddy street, dodging wagons, horses with riders, and the occasional fool like himself who chose to struggle through mud for the sheer cussedness of it.

Phoebe's eyes swam in the front of his mind and Riley fought doggedly to dismiss the image. Anger and frustration rattled through him, putting him on edge; he was a man looking for somewhere to release the tension that crowded him.

He had two choices.

A woman or a fight.

In the past, he might have sought out the local whorehouse and found solace for a few hours in the arms of a woman who cared for nothing but his wallet. But that notion didn't hold the appeal it once had. Not when the only woman he wanted was Phoebe.

So he was left with the latter.

All he needed now was an opponent.

His gaze shot from one side of the street to the other as he slogged his way down the muddy track. But it was as if even Fate was working against him. No sign of the tough cowhands who generally killed time by holding up a porch post looking for trouble. Instead, he was surrounded by townsmen. Merchants who were interested only in the kind of battles to be fought with their ledgerbooks.

"It's a sad time in the west," Riley muttered to himself, "when a man can't find a good fight when he needs one."

Then he stopped dead in his tracks. Up ahead, parked beside the tiny church that came to life only once a week, was a small, two-wheeled cart.

A swell of anticipation rose in his chest.

Fine. If he couldn't get a good fistfight, he'd settle for questioning that damn tinker and finding out just what in hell was going on around here.

Chapter Fourteen

❧

Phoebe stopped in the hallway just outside the kitchen. She couldn't face Mary yet. Her cheeks aflame with embarrassment, she lifted both hands to her face in a vain attempt to cool the hot blood racing through her.

Her heart pounding as though she'd run a race, Phoebe snatched up the length of her hair and quickly plaited it into a long, thick braid. Her hairpins were scattered somewhere in the saloon, and she wasn't willing to go in there to look for them. Not if it meant facing Riley again so soon after her confession.

She slumped back against the wall and closed her eyes. Instantly, though, his face rose up in her mind and she saw again his stunned expression as she admitted to being no more than a common thief. What had she been thinking?

She hadn't thought at all, that was the problem.

Instead, she'd surrendered to a heated moment and let slip every secret she'd been guarding for months. What must he think of her? A quiet groan escaped her throat. Rather than convincing him to stay, she'd probably just given him another reason to leave. After all, what man would willingly want a partner who admitted to being a thief?

The sweet, unrealistic daydreams she'd been indulging in splintered at her feet. The memory of the one kiss she'd shared with Riley flitted through her mind, filling her with sadness as she realized she would likely never experience *that* again.

But perhaps, she told herself as she let go of her dreams, perhaps it wasn't *Riley's* kiss that had affected her so. Maybe it was simply being kissed. Maybe any other man's touch would do the same incredible things to her.

Yet it was more than likely she'd never have that question answered either.

"You all right, Phoebe?"

She turned abruptly to find Dave Hawkins standing right in front of her. "Excuse me?"

He grinned. "I asked if you were all right."

"Oh! I'm fine, thank you."

"Glad to hear it," he said. "Passed the hotel and saw you standin' there like a statue or something."

She glanced around them at the empty foyer and hall. The whole room glistened and shone in the late afternoon sunshine pouring through the windowpanes. So different, she thought, from the first time she'd seen it. The wood floors and mahogany registration desk gleamed from the coats of beeswax rubbed into their surfaces. The freshly painted lemon-yellow walls seemed to capture the warmth of the sun and gave the entryway a welcoming air.

Yes, different. But no more different than she herself was. She'd arrived in Rimshot with little more than hope and now found herself a part of this town, with a business and a future.

A future without Riley . . . but a future.

And even more importantly, she'd left behind her shame and outgrown the notions of spinsterhood that had defined her life in St. Louis. Here, she could do anything, be anything, she set her mind to. Here, she'd even found that she wasn't too old or too long on the shelf to long for . . . love.

Dave let his gaze drift leisurely over her before saying, "You sure look pretty today."

"Thank you," Phoebe said and waited for the same rush of pleasure that had accompanied Riley's compliment. She frowned thoughtfully when it didn't come.

"Somethin' wrong?"

"No, nothing." At least, nothing she could talk over with him.

"Good." He nodded, glanced along the hallway as if to ensure they were alone, then turned back to her. "I was wondering if you might want to step out with me tonight," he said. "Take a walk down to the lake . . ." He paused, shrugged his shoulders and added on a laugh, "I'd offer to buy you a cup of coffee too, but you own the only place in town that sells it."

Phoebe smiled. He really was a nice man. Her gaze moved over his familiar features. Handsome too. In fact, his long hair, the badge on his vest, and the gun on his hip added up to make him the very image of her childhood fantasies. And yet . . .

When she looked into his dark brown eyes, she found herself thinking more about a certain pair of blue eyes instead. When he laughed, she remembered Riley's infrequent chuckles. When he touched her, she compared the warmth he inspired with the inferno Riley Burnett created within her.

"Phoebe?"

She blinked away her thoughts and took a deep breath. It wasn't fair to any of them to keep comparing one man to the other. Especially if one of those men was determined to leave town. Still, perhaps here was her chance to discover if it was Riley or the very act of kissing itself that turned her insides to melted butter.

"Dave," she said quietly, before she could lose her nerve, "would you mind very much kissing me?"

"Ma'am?" Confusion etched itself into his features, yet she caught a flicker of anticipation in his eyes.

"Would you kiss me?" she repeated. "Please?"

"Phoebe," Dave said and yanked off his hat to toss it onto the nearby registry desk. "You'll never have to say *please* to me. I've been wanting to kiss you since almost the first day I saw you."

Amazing, she thought absently and held very still as Dave's hands came up to frame her face. She looked into his eyes as he studied her. She took a short breath and closed her eyes when he lowered his head to hers, covering her mouth with his own.

Nice. Warm and soft and . . . nice. But there was no overwhelming tide of sensation cresting within her. She told herself perhaps it was because she wasn't concentrating. If she was to be fair, she had to give him all the encouragement she'd given Riley the night he'd kissed her. Deliberately, she banished all thoughts from her mind and focused on Dave Hawkins.

His lips moved on her's with quiet confidence and practiced skill. Soft, tender, yet somehow compelling as he silently urged her to surrender to him, to feel what he wanted her to feel. To melt beneath his touch.

Phoebe tried.

She kissed him back and, though she was certainly no expert, thought she was doing a good job of it under the circumstances. And still there were no sparkles of light and heat dancing through her veins. Her knees were steady as rocks and her balance quite unaffected.

After another few disheartening seconds, she pulled back from him and he let her go.

"It's not there, is it?" Dave whispered and his fingertips trailed along her cheek before he dropped his hands to his sides.

"No," she said simply, buoyed somehow by the knowledge that she hadn't been the only one unaffected by their kiss.

"Shame," he replied and gave her a brief, halfhearted smile.

"Dave," she started to say, then broke off, shaking her head. Lost, Phoebe had never in her life imagined being in the position of having to tell a man that she wasn't interested in him romantically.

He took a step closer and lifted one hand to cup her cheek briefly. "Don't, Phoebe. There's nothing to be sorry about." He shrugged good-naturedly. "It's either there, or it ain't. Simple, really."

"Not always, I'm afraid," she said.

He gave her a rueful smile. "It's Riley, then?"

"How did you know?"

"Not a hard guess," he told her with a chuckle. "I've seen how he looks at you. Hell, when I told him I was plannin' to come calling on you, he damn near tore my head off."

"He did?"

"Uh-huh." He stepped past her, reached for his hat, then put it on. Tugging the brim down low over his eyes, he said, "I hope this doesn't mean I can't come by for coffee and some of Mary's doughnuts from time to time."

"You're always welcome here," Phoebe said and meant it.

"Good." He walked to the open doorway, where he paused and looked back at her. "I wish you luck with Riley, Phoebe. I really do."

"Thank you," she said, but he was already gone.

Alone in a puddle of sunshine, Phoebe wrapped her arms around her middle and held on.

Now she knew.

It wasn't just being kissed that caused all of those wild, indescribable sensations.

It was being kissed by Riley.

And he would be leaving town all too soon.

At first, he didn't notice anything odd.

It was only as Riley drew closer to the tinker's cart that he became aware of a subtle difference in the air around him. The chill breeze had stopped. Not a breath was moving.

Then he realized the everyday noises of downtown

Rimshot, not twenty feet away, were muffled, as if coming from a great distance.

He stopped and looked from the cart to the street behind him and, for the first time, felt a twinge of uneasiness. Some sort of filmy screen separated him from the town. He could see all right, but it was like staring into a mirror lying at the bottom of a water-filled pot. The image was there, it was just a touch out of focus.

As he watched, a farm wagon backed into a freight wagon and the drivers shouted curses at each other. He saw it and knew he should be able to hear every cuss word clear as a bell. Instead, though, the two men's mouths moved and their angry shouts sounded like distant muttering.

He sucked in a long gulp of air and swiveled his head around to look at the back of the cart. It hadn't moved, even though a part of him had expected the damn thing to disappear before he reached it.

Riley rubbed one hand across his mouth, then hitched the gun on his hip into a more comfortable position. Old habits die hard, though he was beginning to have his doubts about how much good a pistol would do him.
— Something damn peculiar was happening here.

As ready as he'd ever be, Riley marched up to the front of the wagon, stopped alongside the bench seat, and looked directly into the little fella's silvery gray eyes.

"Hello, my friend," the tinker said. "I've been waiting for you."

Well, now. Was that good? Or bad?

"What the hell's goin' on here?" Riley blurted.

"What do you mean?"

He shot a glance over his shoulder at the blurry film between him and the town and waved one hand at it. "That," he said. "What is that thing keeping me shut in here?"

"Oh," the tinker said with a nod. "Don't worry. You may leave anytime you like."

Maybe, Riley told himself. And maybe the tinker was more used to lying than telling the truth.

"I simply wanted us to be able to talk privately."

Riley's gaze narrowed thoughtfully. The last time he'd seen this little man, he'd ridden away as fast as he could. There'd been something odd about the tinker then, and as far as he could see, nothing had changed.

"If you're so anxious to talk to me," Riley said, "why'd you disappear the other day when I chased after you? And as to that . . . where'd you disappear *to*?"

"I left because it wasn't time for us to speak." The tinker smiled and shook his head. "Where I went is of no importance, my friend. What is important is that we talk together now."

Riddles. The man still talked in riddles. Well, this time, Riley wouldn't be put off with talk of gifts and prices and regrets. "Just who are you, mister?" he asked. "And what are you doing here?"

A smile crossed the man's long, narrow face and those eyes of his glittered like he was staring into the sun. Which he wasn't.

"A friend."

"I pick my own friends."

"And not many of them," the tinker observed.

"I don't see that that's any of your business," Riley countered, unwilling to admit how the truth of that observation stung.

"*You* are my business," he said, shrugging in a way that made Riley want to reach up and pluck him from that bench seat for a good shaking.

"I don't have time for your games, little fella," he said instead. "But I do have a question for you. And I want a direct answer. Are you the one pitching rocks through my windows?"

He'd clearly surprised the tinker, who stared at him for a long moment before giving an amused laugh. "No, indeed, my friend. Your troubles are your own. They are not my doing."

Riley believed him. He wasn't sure why, but he did.

"Then what do you want? You're no ordinary tinker, are you?"

"Ordinary . . ." He seemed to consider this before shaking his head. "No." .

"Is this about that gift you offered me before?" Riley asked. "Because if it is, I can tell you, I want nothing from you. You can keep your gift and ride out of town."

Those silver-gray eyes sparkled again and Riley had a feeling the man was disappointed in him somehow. Ridiculous.

"You've already received my gift," he said.

"Yeah?" Riley countered. "If I did, I haven't noticed. All I've got here lately are troubles. More than I care to deal with and certainly enough that I don't want more from you."

"My friend," the tinker said and leaned forward. His gaze bored into Riley's until he felt as though the tinker were examining his soul and coming up short. "The gift is yours for the taking. I am here now to remind you of the price to be paid."

A dark shadow fell across Riley and he fought the urge to shiver under the other man's penetrating stare. "Mister," he started, "I don't know what you think you're doin'—"

"Pay the price, my. friend," the tinker said, his voice bereft of music and strained with urgency. "Else all the regret in the world will not buy back for you what you might have had."

A tight, cold fist squeezed Riley's heart until he felt as though his chest might explode from the pressure. His ears rang with the odd, strained silence surrounding him. The world around him swam, shapes and colors blending together until nothing looked real. The tinker's voice chanted over and over again in his mind as Riley staggered blindly back and away from the cart.

Pay the price, pay the price, pay the price . . .

He cupped both hands over his ears and squeezed his

eyes tightly shut against the mounting pressure building within him. And when he thought he would never draw another easy breath, it all stopped.

Riley cautiously opened his eyes to find everything around him returned to normal. Sounds rushed at him from Main Street. The blurred images were sharp now, as they should be.

The tinker was gone.

The saloon had been closed for an hour and still Riley hadn't come upstairs. Phoebe waited in the darkened hallway, in a chair she'd dragged from her room. She had to talk to him.

This wasn't about her confession—or even about the still-lingering sense of humiliation she'd experienced in blurting out the truth. All afternoon, her mind had raced with the implications of Dave's kiss and what she'd felt . . . or rather, what she hadn't felt.

Phoebe clasped her hands together in her lap and squeezed tightly. All around her, the hotel was silent, Becky and Simmons sleeping soundly in their rooms. But sleep eluded her. Every time she closed her eyes, her brain conjured up images of Riley. Laughing. Frowning. And his most favored expression . . . scowling.

She turned her head and shot a quick look at the head of the stairs, just a few feet away. A glimmer of light from below shone in the dark, illuminating the stairwell and the tall, carved newel post. In the silence, she heard her own rapid heartbeat and willed herself to calm down. It didn't help.

She inhaled sharply, let her head fall against the back of the chair, and focused her gaze on the overhead beams. So much had happened to her in the last few weeks. She'd left the only home she'd ever known. Come halfway across the country. Inherited a business and a partner. Fallen in love with a child.

And that child's father.

"Oh, my," she whispered, laying one hand against her

stomach where dozens of butterflies were soaring, batting their fragile wings frantically.

Love? Was this really love? She had no way of knowing for sure. And no one to ask. What she wouldn't give right now to be able to talk to someone about what was happening to her. But she couldn't imagine broaching such a subject with Simmons. Or even Ivy Talbot, who would no doubt advise her to "throw a rope on the man."

"Phoebe?"

She jumped to her feet and turned toward the staircase where Riley stood, a tall, dark shadow in a night filled with them.

"What are you doing, sitting here in the dark?" he demanded, his voice harsh and strained as he came toward her.

"Waiting for you," she blurted out and saw his steps falter slightly.

"This isn't a good idea, Phoebe," he said quietly.

No, it was terrifying, she thought. But at the same time she had no intention of leaving just yet.

"If this is about what you told me earlier . . . your secrets are safe with me, Phoebe."

"I know that." Somehow, she'd always known.

He sighed in the darkness, and when he spoke again, his voice was a low hush of sound in the stillness. "Look. It's late. I'm tired." He walked past her and stopped at the door to his and Becky's room.

The doorknob turned beneath his hand. A slice of pale lamplight stabbed through the shadowy darkness as he opened the door.

She had to say something fast. Something to make him stay and talk to her. Something . . .

"Dave Hawkins kissed me today."

Riley stopped dead.

Everything in him went cold and still. His grip on the knob tightened until he was sure the brass ball would break off in his hand. Hawkins and Phoebe. Kissing.

A heartbeat later, he eased the door closed and quietly shut it. He turned around and took another step or two closer to her. "He kissed you?" he asked, wanting to find the young deputy and beat him into the ground.

"I asked him to."

So Dave would live and Riley would die.

He didn't say anything for a long minute, and when he did speak, it sounded as though the words had been squeezed past his throat. "Well, then. Thanks for tellin' me."

His hands dropped from her shoulders and Phoebe felt suddenly adrift. To fill the painful silence, she asked, "Would you like to know *why* I asked him to?"

He snorted a choked-off chuckle. Oh, yeah, that's just what he wanted to hear. Why Phoebe found Dave Hawkins so damned appealing that she'd gone begging for a kiss. "No, I believe I'll pass."

Phoebe stepped up close to him and laid one hand on his forearm. Beneath the fabric of his white shirt, she felt his muscles tense in response to her touch. It gave her all the encouragement she needed.

"I had to know," she said.

He hesitated. "What?"

"If all kisses were alike. If my response to Dave's kiss would be the same as my response to yours."

She heard his quick intake of breath, a hiss of sound, followed by a thundering silence.

"Phoebe," he finally whispered, "don't—"

"Do you know what I discovered?"

"No, but I get the feeling you're fixin' to tell me whether you should or not."

Phoebe tilted her head back slightly to look up into his face. His features tight, he stared back at her, and only a trick of the moonlight let her see the shine in his eyes as he watched her.

"I found out," she said, taking another half-step closer, "that it's only *your* kiss that causes fireworks to light up inside me."

He groaned and Phoebe's breath caught on a quickly buried groan of her own.

"When Dave kissed me," she went on, thinking bizarrely that it had been a full day as far as confessions went, "it was very nice. Tender. Strong."

"Jesus, Phoebe," he said thickly, and reached for her, his hands at either side of her waist. "Do you think I want to hear what Dave Hawkins's kisses are like?" He gave her a small shake and his grip on her tightened until Phoebe was sure she could feel the hot, separate imprint of each of his fingers burning through her dress to mark her flesh. "Do you really think I want to even *know* that another man's been kissing you? Tasting you?"

Her stomach flip-flopped and Phoebe leaned in toward him in an instinctive bid for something to steady herself against.

"Sweet God, Phoebe," he whispered and lifted one hand to touch her face, her cheek, her mouth, with a feather-light caress that sent brilliant, white-hot shooting stars through her bloodstream. "Don't you know that all I think about is holding you, kissing you so long and so deep neither of us can breathe?"

The pulsebeat at her throat threatened to strangle her.

He lowered his head until their lips were just a breath apart. Cupping her face between his palms, he went on in a voice ragged with desire. "Why the hell do you think I've been keeping my distance from you?"

"I didn't know," she said softly. "But I've missed seeing you all week. Talking to you." She took a slow breath. "Then today, after I told you about what I'd done . . ." Her gaze lowered.

His grip on her loosened slightly. "You did what you had to do," he said, his voice tight. "I can't fault you for that. Neither should you. It has nothin' to do with what's between us."

"What is between us, Riley?"

"Too much, honey," he said quietly. "It's killing me to stay away from you, Phoebe, but being with you is even harder. Because then all I can think about is how I want to lay you down in a sweet-smelling meadow and watch the play of summer sunshine on your naked body."

Phoebe trembled and her knees gave out.

Riley steadied her as he continued to torture them both with vivid word pictures. "I want to run my hands over your flesh until I know every inch of you. And then I want to start over, this time with my mouth doing the exploring. I want your taste on my lips. I want your scent buried so deeply inside me that I'll never be without you. And finally," he ground out, letting his forehead rest against hers, "I want to bury my body in yours. I want to feel your body cradle mine and I want to look down into your eyes as pleasure rocks through you."

"Oh, my." Scandalous! That's what he was, *scandalous*. The things he was saying. The look in his eyes. But what was far more shocking was her reaction. Liquid heat formed at her center, filling her with an ache she didn't recognize and had no idea how to assuage.

"I want to claim you, Phoebe," he whispered on a tight groan, "body and soul. But I can't. I won't."

Her quickening heartbeat staggered as an aching sense of loss opened up inside her. He was still planning to leave. She'd finally found the kind of love—the kind of man—she used to dream about and he was going to leave her.

"Do us both a favor, Phoebe," he said and closed his eyes briefly as if in terrible pain. "Go to your room and close the door."

"You want me to make it easier for you to leave?"

"Nothing about this is easy," he said through gritted teeth.

"I don't want it to be," she whispered.

"Then you win," he told her.

From down the hall, a creak of wood splintered the private cocoon surrounding them. Riley turned his head and stared off into the darkness, the spell between them shattered.

"What?"

"Shh . . ." he whispered. "I heard something."

She listened for a long moment, struggling to hear over the pounding of her heart. But no other sound came.

"There's nothing," she said, cursing the timing of that phantom noise.

"Maybe," he said, tearing his gaze from the far end of the hall to look down at her. Taking a deep breath, he said, "It's late, Phoebe. You best go to your room now."

Her room? No. That wasn't what she wanted. She wanted to stand here in the darkness with him. She wanted him to kiss her again. She wanted to feel her insides melt and her toes curl.

If that was shameless, she didn't care. She wasn't a young girl anymore. She was an adult. Capable of making her own decisions and answerable to no one. And if the man she loved was bent on leaving her, then she wanted to at least once know the joys that other women took for granted.

Swallowing hard, she said, "Don't you want to kiss me, Riley?"

"Jesus, woman!" He took another step back from her as if needing a safe distance, then stared at her like a man at the edge of reason. "For God's sake, don't make this harder. Just"—he shook his head—"forget about tonight. I plan to."

Chapter Fifteen

❧

Morning sunshine filtered softly through the hotel's front windows and spilled across the shining wooden floor, laying a shimmering path leading to where Phoebe stood behind the registry desk, dust cloth in hand. She'd been up and working for hours already, trying to keep herself too busy to think. To remember.

It wasn't working.

Simmons came in from the saloon and walked stiffly across the floor. He stopped in front of the desk and waited until she met his gaze before speaking. "The surly cowboy seems more sullen than usual this morning." Speculatively, he watched her as he added, "Is there a reason for his churlishness?"

Phoebe shifted slightly, then concentrated her attention on a spot of dust. Rubbing her cloth at it viciously she tried for a casual tone—and failed. "I wouldn't know, I'm afraid."

"Hmm . . ." Simmons continued to stare at her. She felt his gaze despite the fact that she was avoiding meeting it. "Perhaps there's a problem," he ventured.

"Perhaps," she said and half turned to run the cloth across the curve of the desk.

"Shall I inquire?"

Phoebe spun around sharply and looked at him aghast. "No!"

His eyes narrowed thoughtfully at her outburst.

"I mean . . ." She tried to soften her response, but she knew it was too late. Simmons was no fool. "I'll take care of it."

"I offer only because you, too, seem a bit out of sorts today . . ."

Oh, blast and thunderation. Having a butler who knows you this well could be a real trial, Phoebe thought. The gleam in his eyes assured her he suspected something.

"I'm fine," she said, and hoped to heaven he'd leave it at that. She should have known better.

"Really?" he said. "And did you sleep well?"

She shot him a sidelong glance and thought back to the creaking that had interrupted her and Riley the night before. Had it been Simmons, opening his door? Had he seen them?

"Miss Phoebe?" he prompted.

"Actually," she admitted on the off chance he hadn't seen them and that this would excuse her mood, "I didn't sleep much at all."

"Bad dreams?" he asked, too casually.

Tempting dreams, she answered silently. Tempting, haunting, frustrating dreams that had finally forced her out of bed. Her body humming with a nervous energy she'd never experienced before, she'd paced the confines of her room, remembering every moment with Riley. Imagining his touch, his caress. Until at last, half-crazed, Phoebe had gotten dressed and gone downstairs to work.

But even then she'd found no peace. While pushing a broom or using a dust cloth, her mind was free to wander and wander it did.

Straight back to that darkened hallway.

And what might have happened.

"Is there anything you'd like to discuss with me, Phoebe?" Simmons asked gently.

His voice drew her away from the mental images that continued to torment her and she looked up at him. More father to her than her own father had ever been, Simmons was the one man she'd always confided in. Trusted. And yet she couldn't bring herself to talk about this with him. It was all too new. Her feelings still too raw for exploration.

"No," she said, and tried to ignore the flash of hurt that shone briefly in his eyes. Instinctively, she reached out and grabbed one of his hands. "Please," she said softly. "Understand. I can't . . ." Her voice trailed off.

He patted her hand gently. "I believe I do understand, Phoebe," he said. "But know that I'm here if you need me."

"Just as you've always been." Like the sun rising every morning. Like the tides. Like snow in winter and flowers in spring, Simmons was the one constant in her life.

As he started to draw away, she tightened her hold on his hand and he looked at her, a question in his eyes. For the first time, Phoebe really noticed the lines in his face, the silver in his hair, and something inside her tightened painfully. Before now, he'd always seemed the same to her. Unchanged. Ageless. Immortal.

She'd spent her lifetime knowing that he would always be there. That she was never truly alone. Secure in the knowledge of his love, she'd grown up never telling him just what his presence in her life had meant to her.

Now, when she was discovering so many emotions and feelings she'd never dreamed of experiencing, she realized what hearing those words might mean to a person.

"What is it?" Simmons asked quietly, concern etched into his features.

She stared at their joined hands for a long minute and thought of how many times over the years he'd soothed her hurts and wiped away her tears. The hands that now seemed somehow fragile had been strong yet tender as he guided her into adulthood and Phoebe couldn't imagine her life without this one very precious man.

"I should have told you this years ago," she said, capturing his gaze with her own. "I realize you've always known how I feel about you . . ."

His eyes widened abruptly, giving him a wild look. He cleared his throat unnecessarily, a sure sign of discomfort. Phoebe plunged ahead, though, determined to at last say the words to a man who'd more than earned the right to hear them.

She took a deep breath and in the hush of early morning quiet said, "I love you, Simmons."

The calm, stoic butler blinked rapidly and lifted his chin to its normal position of hauteur. "Miss Phoebe . . ."

She came around the edge of the desk, keeping a tight hold on his hand so he couldn't escape. When she was right in front of him, she went up on her toes, locked her arms around his neck, and squeezed tight. After a long moment, she felt his arms slide around her for a brief, but heartfelt hug.

Tears sprang to her eyes and the room in front of her blurred. "Thank you, Simmons," she whispered, "thank you for everything you've given me."

He reached up to loosen her hold on him. He had never been a man to wallow in sentimentality and Phoebe knew how hard this was for him, but there was one thing more she had to say.

"You've been a wonderful father." Drawing her head back, she looked up at him. "I couldn't have asked for better."

He gave a little start of surprise, then went completely still. A film of moisture clouded his eyes as he cleared his throat again and gave her an awkward pat before taking a step backward.

He sniffed and reached into his inner coat pocket for a handkerchief which he handed to Phoebe.

"Thank you."

"No," he said solemnly, "thank *you*." He inclined his head in an abbreviated bow. Taking back the handkerchief, he tucked it away, squared his shoulders, and lifted his chin before saying, "You've been a good daughter, Phoebe. All I could ever have hoped for."

A bubble of warmth spilled from the center of her

chest to encompass her whole body. A fresh sheen of tears swam in front of her eyes.

Sighing dramatically, Simmons reached once again for his handkerchief. "That will be quite enough tears, madam," he said, "else we'll no doubt have to suffer through another flood of biblical proportions."

Phoebe chuckled and dutifully dried her tears. "Right you are, Simmons."

He nodded in approval.

"Now, then," Phoebe said, shooting a glance at the open doorway leading to the saloon. "Perhaps it's time I talked with Riley."

"Indeed, madam," Simmons said, then reached out and laid one hand on her shoulder briefly. "I shall be in the kitchen if you require assistance."

"I don't think that will be necessary." Her gaze didn't shift from the doorway, her mind already racing ahead to the confrontation awaiting her. She wouldn't be ignored. She wouldn't be forgotten. And it was time to let Riley know that.

"I hope you're right," the butler said, and then she thought she heard him mutter, "for Mr. Burnett's sake."

But a moment later, Simmons was striding down the hallway and Phoebe herself headed for the saloon.

Riley sat at an empty poker table savoring the early morning quiet. Outside, the town was just coming to life and the first rays of the sun sparkled through the front windows, making his sleep-deprived eyes ache.

He told himself it was thoughts of that blasted tinker that had kept him up all night. After all, it wasn't every day that a man disappeared into a bubble of silence. That tinker was too strange by half to dismiss readily and there was no telling what he was up to.

But his sleeplessness was due solely to Phoebe, of course.

A deck of well-used playing cards lay beside two black leather-bound ledgers at his elbow. His mind wasn't sharp enough to deal with the neat columns of figures just yet, so he'd been fiddling with the cards. Grabbing up his cup of cooling coffee, he took a swallow and winced at the lukewarm bitter flavor.

"No more than you deserve," he muttered thickly.

"Talking to yourself?"

Phoebe's voice, too loud and too close by for comfort. "Shit."

Her rapid footsteps rang out in the empty room, tapping harshly against the wood-plank floor.

"There's something I need to talk to you about," she said as she came to a stop beside the table.

He shuffled and the flutter of the cards was the only sound in the room.

"Riley."

"Go away, Phoebe." He was in no mood for this. Hadn't he just had a go-around with that uppity butler of hers? Riley scowled to himself, remembering the creaking he'd heard last night. He was willing to bet that had been Simmons, peering out his open door. The man had made no secret of keeping a wary eye on Riley. And not without reason, he supposed, since all he really wanted to do was carry Phoebe into a bedroom and lock the door behind them.

Frowning up at her, he said again, "Go away."

"Not quite yet," she told him, then drew out a chair and sat down opposite him.

"Jesus," he grumbled, "what is it about women?"

"What?"

"Why do you all have to talk a thing to death?"

"It seems to me," she said in a voice sharp enough to draw his gaze away from the cards, "that *you're* the one talking."

He chuckled mirthlessly. "Only to try and head you off."

"It won't work."

"Naturally." In fact, he'd never known a woman to be put off track once her mind was made up.

"Riley, I think—"

"I know what you think," he interrupted her.

She huffed a bit. "Well, that's fascinating, Mr. Burnett. Why don't you tell me what I think?"

"Fine." He tossed the cards onto the table and leaned back in his chair, assuming what he hoped was a casual attitude. For the first time since she'd come in, he really looked at her and wasn't at all pleased with what he saw. Her eyes looked red and there were pale violet shadows beneath them. Apparently, she hadn't gotten any more sleep than he had.

But more than that, there was an air of hurt about her that cut him to the bone. He'd done that. But one day, she'd thank him for walking away, for keeping them from doing something really stupid.

With that thought firmly in mind, he started talking. "You're thinkin' that we should talk some more about me leavin' and you not wantin' me to. About what might have happened between us last night. You want to discuss it all to death and then pull it apart and talk about it some more."

Her mouth tightened and she sat up straighter in the chair. Her back was so stiff now, she looked as if she were tied to a pole.

"And you don't," she said, as prim as her posture.

"No, ma'am, I don't." He folded his arms across his chest. "What good could it do?" He paused, then answered his own question. "None."

"Well, *I* think—"

"You think that because we fire a few sparks off each other, that means we should settle down and build a real fire." He pushed away from the table suddenly, stood up and snatched his coffee cup. Crossing to the bar, he poured more of the hideous stuff, then turned around to look at her, bracing himself to withstand the pain he was sure he'd see in her eyes. "Well, sometimes, Phoebe, sparks are all there is. And a fire can do as much damage as it can good."

No pain, he thought absently, staring into blue eyes suddenly gone as cold and dark as the bottom of a lake.

Anger.

Hell, that was probably for the best.

She stood up slowly, regally, keeping her composure despite the temper he saw simmering within her. Riley felt a flash of pure admiration. A fine woman, Phoebe Hightower.

Too damn good for him.

"Blast and thunderation, you're a pigheaded man," she said.

"You're not the first to notice."

"I should think not." She set one pale, fine-boned hand on the bar as if for balance before continuing. "But you'll be surprised to know that I'm not here to talk about last night."

"Good."

She frowned at him and started to rethink the decision she'd only just made. Maybe it would be better if she simply left. Maybe she should hide her head in the sand as he seemed to prefer doing. Certainly that course of action would be far less humiliating than what she'd come in here prepared to do. But then, she would be running away from what lay between them, just as Riley was.

No. She wouldn't make it easier for him to leave. She wanted it to be the hardest thing he'd ever done. So hard as to be impossible.

"I—" She stopped, took a breath, and squeezed her hand together until her knuckles gleamed white. "Riley, I think I might be falling in—"

He jumped to his feet, sending his chair clattering to the floor. "Don't say it, Phoebe," he warned with a slow shake of his head.

"—love with you," she finished on a long exhalation of breath.

"Damn it," Riley snapped, "didn't I tell you not to say it?"

"Don't panic," she said. "I'm not a silly schoolgirl, ready to build castles in the air and wait for a handsome prince to come striding through the clouds."

"Phoebe—"

"I'm a grown woman," she said hotly. "I make my own decisions and my own mistakes."

"I can see that—" He couldn't get a damned word in.

"And I wanted you to know how I feel, even if you don't return the feelings." She felt the first rush of heated blood racing to fill her cheeks and knew her face was as red as a ripe apple. But there was no going back now.

"I don't know what you want me to say."

"Yes you do," she countered, then lifted her chin. "But wanting a thing doesn't mean I expect it."

"Phoebe," he said, and let his chin hit his chest. "In a few weeks, I'll be gone and you'll forget me."

"I know you want me to," she said, "but I won't."

"Goddammit, why are you doing this?"

"Because I don't want you to leave."

Damn, this woman got to him like no other ever had.

"Last night," she said, "you told me that you planned to forget what happened—or didn't happen—between us. I don't think you can."

"I'm sure as hell gonna try." His back teeth ground together and something hard and cold tightened around his heart. She loved him.

Besides, she was only doing what he wanted her to, right?

Phoebe flashed him a quick, unreadable look, then turned and poured herself a cup of coffee.

"Don't drink that," he warned. "It's near poisonous."

She took a sip and gasped as it went down.

"You're a hardheaded woman, Phoebe," he said with a shake of his head.

"Why is that trait called determination in a man and stubbornness in a woman?" She set the cup down and looked at him again.

Those eyes of hers had an unnerving way of looking

right into the heart of him. He wondered if she could see how last night had affected him. How hearing that she loved him made him want to grab her up and hold her tight. If she was aware that everything he'd said to her about forgetting her had been a bluff. A dodge to cover up things he knew he shouldn't be feeling.

He wondered if she could see what this was costing him.

Riley inhaled the soft, sweet scent of lavender, despite knowing it would only make his hastily buried desire harder to hide. Dear God. She loved him.

This wasn't going well at all, she thought, and wondered just where exactly she'd gone wrong. But blast and thunderation, she had no experience with this. She didn't know what to say, how to act, what to think. All she knew was, she didn't want him to go. Didn't want him to forget her. And if he was still determined to go, she wouldn't help him.

"But," she said, "that wasn't my only reason for coming to see you."

He shot her a cautious look. "There's more?"

"Mary and I have an idea."

"Huh?" The abrupt shift in subject caught him off guard. Worse, he had a feeling she knew that and liked it.

"We'd like to sell some of our baked goods in here at night."

Amazing woman.

"Cookies?" he asked. "In the saloon?"

"Why not?" She shrugged. "When men are drinking, Mary assures me they work up an appetite."

So, he thought. This is what the hard-driving, ever relentless U.S. Marshal Riley Burnett had finally come to. Driven to distraction by a spinster, wet nurse to a baby girl, and selling cookies in a saloon.

Lord, how a man could veer off his chosen path.

Not for much longer, though.

"Fine," he said abruptly, turning back to the table and

picking up the cards. He'd agree to anything right now, if it meant she'd leave him the hell alone. He sat down again and, shuffling the deck, he started laying the cards out for a game of solitaire, hoping she'd take the hint.

"You don't care?" she asked, standing alongside him. "Then maybe you should know that when you leave, I'll be closing the saloon entirely to turn it into a dining hall."

So the moment he left town, there wouldn't even be a memory of him in this place. So much for love. That bothered him more than he cared to admit. Concentrate on the cards, he told himself. Don't look at her. She'll see the truth in your eyes. Red five on black six. "It doesn't matter, Phoebe. Do what you want." Black queen on red king.

She bent over, slapped her hand down on the cards, and swept them all right off the table. So much for ignoring her. He lifted his gaze and stared right back into shining, furious eyes.

"The saloon doesn't matter," she said tightly. "Clearly *I* don't matter."

He bit down hard on the inside of his cheek, grateful for the sharp stab of pain.

"Your own daughter doesn't matter," she said. "Exactly what *is* important to you, Riley?"

He stood up to face her and Phoebe almost took a step back from the hard, implacable man she saw in front of her. Almost. But whatever else he was, Riley wasn't a man to be afraid of. She knew that, bone-deep.

"Duty matters, Phoebe," he said tightly, his voice grating in the stillness. "Duty. Honor. Loyalty. They matter. They're all I know."

Her anger drained away like dirty water from a washtub. All he knew? Though certainly good things, duty, honor, and loyalty were hardly emotional ties. They spoke to a man's pride. Not his heart. She stared up into his eyes and looked for the man with whom she'd stood in the dark sharing dreams of a passion she'd never known before. But in the harsh light of day, that man was gone, shielded behind a mask of indifference.

"Isn't it your duty to take care of Becky? To hold up your end of this partnership?"

"I've seen to Becky's care. With her grandparents. As for you," he said, "you'll do fine without me."

"And love, Riley?" she asked, her tone softer. "Doesn't love matter to you at all?"

If anything, his features tightened further. "*Love*'s a word folks use too often and mean too seldom. It's something that's only brought me grief."

Pain rose up in her slowly, like a rising tide, and banked against her heart. Even in her sometimes lonely life, she'd known love. What must it be like to live in a world so empty that only duty filled it?

"No, I don't believe that."

He laughed, a strained, choked sound. "I'm not surprised."

"I've seen you with Becky. You love her."

"I'm her father. I'll do my best by her," he snapped and shoved both hands through his hair in a gesture she was becoming all too familiar with. "But as far as lovin' goes, Phoebe, I'm a poor bet. For *anyone*."

He sucked in a gulp of air and said tiredly, "Now if you'll excuse me, I've got to go over these ledgers." Then he picked up the leather-bound books and turned for the small office at the bottom of the staircase.

Phoebe watched him go and didn't try to stop him. She was too busy thinking about what he'd just said. Too filled with a sudden, raw hope that nestled in her chest and tried to take root.

Anyone else, he'd said. But he'd meant *her*, Phoebe. He was actually warning her away from him. For her own good, he was trying to tell her not to count on him. A small trickle of warmth spread through the coldness she'd felt since the night before.

It wasn't that he didn't want her.

He wanted her to have better than him.

Her mind dredged up images of Riley with his daughter—his gentle tenderness, his patience. And then her memories shifted to the night before and the exquisite sensation of standing in the shadows with him and only him.

He felt more for her than he was admitting to.

She wouldn't give up on Riley Burnett just yet.

"They bought everything," Mary crowed with delight. "Every last scrap!" She sailed into the kitchen and dropped an empty wooden tray onto the table. "Just look. Hardly a crumb left."

Phoebe glanced up from the bowl of chocolate frosting she was stirring and gave the other woman a distracted smile. "That's wonderful."

Mary frowned at her as she began loading up the empty tray again with cookies, cupcakes, and huge wedges of cake. "All right," she said firmly. "Tell me what it is."

"Hmm? What?" Phoebe tucked the ceramic bowl in the curve of her left arm and stirred even faster, the wooden spoon clicking against the ceramic in a rhythmic fashion.

"Don't make out you don't know what I'm sayin'," Mary warned. "You know bloody well you've been walking around here with your head in a fog for the last two days."

She kept her gaze fixed on the dark brown frosting, concentrating only on whipping the spoon through the confection until every last lump had been dissolved.

"So what is it?" the other woman asked, more gently this time. "Maybe I can help."

Help? The only help she needed was in convincing a certain stubborn ex-marshal that he loved her.

Since their talk in the saloon two days ago, Riley had been more distant than before. Just as he'd said he would, he seemed determined to ignore his own feelings and forget completely about Phoebe's.

"Ah," Mary was saying as she finished loading the tray. "It's himself, isn't it? Riley Burnett."

Phoebe nearly dropped the bowl of frosting. She looked up to meet the other woman's concerned, understanding gaze and was undone by the kindness she found there. "I don't know what to do," she blurted. "He hardly speaks to me anymore. Even when I asked him if he'd mind our selling baked goods in the saloon at night, he hardly turned a hair."

"And why should he?" Mary countered. "It's made him a nice bit of coin. And me as well." She stopped suddenly. "Do ya think it's because you've given me the lion's share of the saloon money?"

"No!" Phoebe said quickly. "That's only fair, Mary. You're the cook, we're only furnishing the supplies."

"Aye, but a seventy-thirty split seems a bit much to me still."

"Well, it's not." She knew how desperately Mary needed the extra money. Besides, even thirty percent would soon earn Phoebe enough money to outfit a good-sized dining room come spring. "No," she went on, determined to convince the other woman. "This has nothing to do with money, believe me."

"Ah." Mary smiled knowingly and came around the table to stand beside her. "Then 'tis love that's behind all of this."

"I told him I loved him," Phoebe muttered.

"Well, now, that's enough to give any man a good scare and himself more than most. That wife of his was no good, I hear. Led him a merry chase with half the men in town."

"So now he wants nothing to do with love at all."

"Well, isn't that like a man, though?" The redhead smiled fondly and her eyes softened as she retreated into what were clearly happy memories. "My own Danny, as stubborn a man as you'd care to meet. It took me two years to run him to ground, him complainin' all the while that he wasn't the marryin' kind."

"How did you win him over?" Phoebe asked. Now this kind of help she might be able to use.

Mary blushed a deep scarlet. The sprinkle of golden freckles across her nose stood out in sharp relief. "I—" She glanced behind her as if to make sure they were alone. "There's not many I'd say this to, Phoebe, but you've been a good friend to me."

Phoebe leaned in closer, eager to hear any secret that might assist her in reaching Riley's heart. "I won't say anything," she assured her friend.

"Ah." Mary smiled. "I know that. The thing is, it's not something I'd care to admit to just anyone . . ." She breathed deeply, leaned in close and whispered, "I took him into me bed and let him see just what he'd be missin' if he didn't carry me off to the priest."

Phoebe leaned back and stared at her.

"Oh, I can see what you're thinkin'," Mary said with a nod. "And 'tis true even me own mother used to say 'Why would a man buy a cow if he's gettin' the milk for free?', but *I* say, how's a man to know the milk is sweeter than all the rest if the cow's nowhere to be found?"

Phoebe's stomach fluttered with a sudden spasm of nerves, but she took a deep breath and fought it down. "And it worked? You convinced Danny?"

Mary held up her left hand and wiggled her ring finger so the simple band of gold sparkled in the overhead light. Smiling slyly, she said, "Once he'd had me, he couldn't live without me. And without a priest, he couldn't have me again."

"And you've been happy, you and your Danny?"

Her smile softened, her bottom lip trembled, and a single tear slipped from the corner of her eye. Quickly, though, Mary sniffed and brushed it away with the back of her hand. "Happier than I ever believed possible. And I'll be happier still when he's come home."

Phoebe felt a sharp pang of shame. Here she'd been drawing Mary into this talk about husbands and lovers all the while knowing that her friend's husband had been gone so long everyone but Mary had given him up for dead.

"I'm so sorry, Mary."

"Ah, don't be." She patted Phoebe's hand. "I do love talkin' about my Danny." She caught the worried look in Phoebe's eyes and said, "He'll be home soon, you'll see."

"I'm sure he will."

A knock on the back door sounded softly and both women turned. Mary reached it first and swung it wide. A little girl, a smaller, younger version of Mary, stood there, hopping from one foot to the other.

"Ma," she said, "Shane's sick and Mrs. Thompson says you should come and take us home."

"Mrs. Thompson?" Phoebe asked.

"She watches over the kids while I'm working." She turned and grabbed her black crocheted shawl off a nearby peg. To her daughter, she asked, "What's the matter with him? Same as always?"

"Yep. His tummy hurts and he's groaning something awful."

Even as she talked, Mary was stripping off her apron and turning toward Phoebe. "I'll have to go. Can you see to the tray?"

"Of course," she said. "You go on. I hope Shane is all right."

"I'm sure he is," Mary told her wryly. "The boy eats enough for a full-grown man, then complains about pains in his stomach. If Danny was here, he'd not be trying such foolishness."

Throwing her shawl around her shoulders, Mary stepped off the back porch and guided her daughter around the plank-covered well. They stopped dead, though, as the shadow of a man stepped free of the darker gloom in the narrow alley separating the hotel from the barbershop.

"Sweet Mother," Mary whispered as the man stepped into the slice of lamplight spilling from the open kitchen door. "Sheriff Wills, you scared ten years off my life."

"And mine," Phoebe piped up, one hand still clutching the base of her throat.

"Sorry, ladies," Tom said on a laugh. "Saw a couple of kids hiding in the alleyway, thought they might be up to something."

"And were they?" Phoebe asked, suddenly remembering all the little acts of vandalism they'd experienced not so long ago.

Tom Wills shrugged and shook his head. "Who knows? They took off when they heard me coming."

"Well," Mary said, "I'd best be off."

"Are you heading home?" Wills asked.

"First to Mrs. Thompson's," she said, nodding. "Then home. One of my boys is under the weather."

"I'll walk with you," he offered and scooped little Molly up into his arms. "Help you get the boy home."

"All right," Mary said, smiling at the man holding her daughter so easily. "That would be nice." Half turning, she called, "G'night, Phoebe, see you tomorrow."

She waved and continued to stare after them until the small group was lost in the moon-cast shadows.

But she didn't stop thinking of them. Mary worked so hard, she was wearing herself out. Between her job and her children and her home, she was worn to the bone and still she managed to find the energy to try and help Phoebe.

Maybe it was time to return the favor.

If her Danny wasn't coming home, perhaps it would be best if Mary found someone else to care for. Perhaps the sheriff.

Smiling to herself, Phoebe tilted her head back to stare up at the night sky. Thousands of glittering white stars lay across a velvet black plain that seemed to stretch on and on into eternity. A few threads of lavender-gray clouds unraveled along the sky, their ends twisting in a wind too high for her to feel.

Her gaze shifted to the pale glow of the half-moon

before she closed her eyes and thought for a long moment, wanting to phrase her wish perfectly. She'd already seen what a hastily made wish could do.

When she was sure, she whispered into the darkness, "I wish Mary and her children were safe and happy."

After a long moment, she opened her eyes again and sighed in satisfaction, sure that this time, she'd spent her wish well.

And in one of the darker shadows along the treeline, a small figure moved, darting back into the deep gloom, a pleased smile on his features. "Well done, my friend," the tinker murmured.

Chapter Sixteen

❧

She was still in the kitchen when the fire started.

Up to her elbows in a pan of hot, sudsy water, Phoebe washed muffin tins, baking sheets, and mixing bowls. While she worked, her mind wandered. She thought about Mary and the sheriff walking off together in the dark and wondered if her wish would bring the two people together.

She thought about the tidy profit she and Mary had made on the sale of baked goods in the saloon and idly planned the grand dining room she would build come spring.

And finally, she thought about Riley Burnett until heat rushed through her so swiftly, she was half surprised the dishwater didn't boil. Twenty-seven years old and finally in love.

With a man determined to leave her as quickly as possible.

She stared at her reflection, shining back at her from the windowpane over the sink. The light of a single oil lamp shared that reflection and made her own image waver and dance against the backdrop of the night. "I have one wish left," she reminded herself, but even as she said it, she knew she wouldn't wish Riley into loving her.

What good would that be?

If he was to love her, she wanted that love to come

from his heart, not from some wild stroke of magic granted by the tinker.

And judging from his expression when she'd confessed her love, the chances of his returning her affection were slim indeed.

Disgusted, she washed the last of the bowls, dipped it in the rinse water, then set it carefully on the drainboard before reaching for a dry towel. "You're too tired to think clearly, Phoebe. Just finish up and go to bed."

Her shoulders ached with weariness. From a distance, she heard the muffled roar of the rowdies in the saloon and knew it would be hours still before they'd be gone and the place fell into silence.

Her bare toes curled into the rag rug and she sighed as she lifted the first tray to be dried. Her feet were cold, but at least her tight shoes weren't pinching anymore.

From the corner of her eye, she noticed the reflection of the oil lamp flame in the window. She frowned and reached for a muffin tin. Odd, how the distortion of the glass could make a tiny flame seem so much larger.

Large flames.

She stopped, held her breath, then slowly turned back to the window. Weirdly flickering orange and red lights shimmered on the glass. A tight knot lodged in her throat. She took a half-step closer to the window. It wasn't an oil lamp's reflection glowing so brightly.

The hotel was afire.

Even as she watched, wind-whipped flames crept stealthily, hungrily up the side of the building, edging upward, feeding on the weathered boards like starving men at a banquet.

"Fire!" A shout from outside.

She took a sharp, horrified breath and the acrid taste of smoke invaded her mouth and lungs. Why hadn't she noticed the odor before?

In seconds, the world around her exploded in noise. Men shouted. A woman screamed. The wild, heavy thump of running boots pounded along the boardwalk and the icy ground as the citizens of Rimshot raced to the fire. In a town built of wood, flames were a threat to the entire community. Especially when the buildings along Main Street were each connected to the other, but for an occasional alleyway too narrow to keep eager flames from reaching across and lighting the next roof and then the next.

Phoebe raced to the back door and threw it open, nearly colliding with a man she didn't know as he rushed blindly past her. Men bumped and jostled her as she fought her way through the milling, shouting crowd to get a look at the fire.

Finally, a small patch of snowy ground. She whirled around and gasped, horrified at the long finger of flames working its way over the wooden plank siding. Someone nearby shouted for a bucket brigade and shoved her out of the way when she was too frozen in shock to move.

Booted feet thundered around her. She curled her naked toes into the snow as if holding onto the earth itself.

Upstairs! her brain screamed. The fire licked at the glass of a bedroom window.

Upstairs.

Bedroom.

Becky.

Oh, God. She'd tucked the little girl in herself several hours ago. Instantly, a mental image of the sleeping child rose up in Phoebe's brain. Taunting her. Torturing her. She saw it all so clearly. Becky, curled up in bed, hugging her little blanket to her, innocently sleeping while flames fed on the floors and walls and ceiling of her room.

The fire became a living thing.

A monster, intent on destroying all in its path.

A demon to be defeated before it was too late.

"Becky!" Phoebe shouted and lunged for the back door. She had to get to her. Had to reach her before the fire did.

"Hey, lady," someone yelled and grabbed her, throwing her backward into the snow. "You can't go in there!"

Phoebe sprawled in the slushy mud and the cold went deep, stabbing into her bones and stealing her breath. Her gray cotton dress soaked up the wet like a sponge and weighed her down as she tried to move. Still, she pushed blindly at the forest of denim-covered legs that crowded around her. Finally, she gained her feet again and started for the door, determined to get through this time.

One step after another.

Shove the men out of her way.

Almost there.

"Phoebe!" Riley came out of nowhere, grabbed her from behind, and swung her around to face him. In the weird light, his eyes looked wild. "Are you loco? Don't go back in there."

He didn't know. How could he know? He'd been in the saloon. He probably thought she'd already taken his daughter to safety—as she should have. Oh, God . . . why had she gone outside at all without first racing for the little girl? Dear Lord, if anything happened to her, Phoebe would never forgive herself.

Tears she didn't have time to shed filled her eyes and spilled over onto her cheeks anyway, drawing clean streaks in the mud that coated her hair and face.

The light of the fire played across Riley's features and she forced herself to look up into his eyes and shout to be heard over the din of confusion around her. "Becky!" Grabbing his shirtfront in both muddy fists, she screamed, "Becky's in there! In her room!"

His gaze shot from her face to the trail of fire already eating its way through the wall. In the strange light, his face paled and guilt jabbed at Phoebe again.

Her fault.

All her fault.

Please, God. Please, God.

"Jesus!" he said on a hiss of breath, then yanked her back and away from the door. "Stay here," he ordered in a tone that brooked no argument. "I'll get her and meet you out here."

She nodded, her eyes frantic as she shot another look at the rapidly spreading fire. It blossomed like some hideous flower, stretching its petals across the side of the hotel, streaking across one upper window, then another and another. The building groaned like an old woman rising from a bathtub.

"Simmons," she gasped, horrified anew, "Simmons is in there too."

"I'll find him." He grabbed her shoulders and shook her until she tore her gaze from the mesmerizing flames to look at him. "Damn it, Phoebe, listen to me. Stay *here*."

She nodded. Anything. She'd agree to anything if he would only just hurry. Becky. Simmons. Becky. Simmons. Their names played over and over again in her mind. Like a chant. A prayer. As if saying their names would keep them safe. Alive.

Horrid, crackling, eager sounds rushed at her from the heart of the fire. Dancing flames licked at the wood, wavering in the wind, sparks lifting from its heat and twisting in the air, glittering like lightning bugs in summer.

A long line of men stretched out from the side of the hotel around to the front of the building. At least a dozen buckets were being passed, hand over hand from the water trough. Sheets of water tossed at the blaze sent searing smoke swirling around the heads of the defenders.

The fire seemed to laugh at their pitiful efforts and, if anything, grew brighter.

Hotter.

Phoebe coughed, her eyes watered, and still she wouldn't move. Couldn't move.

Heavy, booted feet stomped all around her. Someone stepped on her bare feet and she barely acknowledged it. A scrape of wood registered in the back of her mind and she vaguely heard someone shout a warning.

About what, she didn't know. Didn't care.

Becky. Simmons. Becky. Simmons.

Empty buckets passed from hand to hand along the

line of men, to be refilled and sent back to the front. The fire hissed at its attackers like some ancient dragon cornered in its lair, fighting for its life. Orange-yellow light leaped and fell, pulsing over the faces of the men gathered together in a common cause and gave them all the look of lost souls writhing in hell.

Phoebe concentrated her entire being on those upper windows now sparkling and cracking from the heat.

Becky. Simmons. And now Riley.

All of them, inside a building slowly being engulfed by a raging beast that wouldn't be stopped.

If only she could *do* something. Anything. Horrible to stand here, watching. Useless.

She wished she could—

Phoebe stopped herself.

A wish!

She had one wish left.

Instantly, she closed her eyes, concentrated, and whispered aloud into the noise-filled night, "I wish Riley, Becky, and Simmons to safety." And in case that wasn't enough, she said it again. And again. And again.

A man staggered backward, crashing into her. Her eyes flew open. Phoebe wobbled unsteadily on her frozen feet, flailing her arms in a futile attempt to stay upright. Her balance dissolved. She pitched back, falling, and braced herself for the crash into the hard ground.

A thud that didn't come.

Instead, icy water enveloped her, sucking her down into the well that everyone, including her, had forgotten in their panic to fight the fire.

The plank cover had apparently been kicked aside in the confusion, leaving the well a gaping hole of blackness awaiting the unwary.

Phoebe gasped helplessly as the cold shot through her and instantly realized her mistake as water poured into her lungs. Her sodden skirt wrapped itself around her legs like a giant, frozen hand, intent on keeping her there in the dark, icy water. Eyes wide, terrified, she looked at the blackness surrounding her and instinctively fought her way up, up toward the fiery night that now looked more like heaven than hell.

Her frozen hands clawed at the muddy sides of the well and couldn't find purchase. She kicked violently, straining toward the surface, lungs bursting, head pounding, and stars exploding behind her eyes.

Fear kept him moving.

Complete, soul-chilling fear.

Riley darted up the staircase, keeping one eye on the rolling cloud of smoke creeping along the ceiling, sending tentative fingers of darkness down, as if probing just for him.

At the head of the stairs, he plunged along the hallway. Smoke was heavier here. Thicker. He coughed, bent low, and squinted into the grayness, and ran, aiming for Becky's room. First things first. He'd find his daughter, see her to safety, then come back for Phoebe's butler.

The air was heavy. Hot. It burned as it shot down his throat and gagged him. Fear rode him hard. A wild, nameless fear that he couldn't ever remember experiencing before.

He'd faced outlaws with guns, rampaging grizzlies, and once, even a nest of hibernating rattlers and none of that had even come close to causing what he felt at this moment.

Fear was a thing most men didn't talk about. No man wanted to be known as a coward. And yet, a man without fear was a fool, not a hero.

He was no fool.

He narrowed his gaze and went on, trusting to instinct now to guide him to the door he couldn't see through the pall of smoke. Guts churning, lungs clamoring for fresh air, Riley staggered on, unstoppable.

Finally. He bent his head and grabbed at the doorknob just as it turned and the door swung open.

Simmons, his face beet-red, eyes watering, held a quilt-covered Becky tightly to his chest. Riley felt a quick, encompassing surge of affection for the man who'd risked his life by going after Becky.

"I have her," the butler said quickly. "Now, I suggest we leave."

Simmons didn't look strong enough to stand up much longer, let alone carry a squirming, crying toddler to safety. The older man looked near the end of his strength. "I'll carry her," Riley said and grabbed his daughter. Becky wiggled against him, winding her tiny arms around his neck and burrowing her face into his shoulder. And even with the world exploding around him, Riley knew one exquisite moment of perfect joy. Settling one arm around his precious burden, he shouted, "Let's go," and started Simmons back down the hall toward the stairs and safety.

It was the longest few minutes of his life. From the moment he'd heard the word *fire* shouted until his race down the stairs, no more than three or four minutes had passed, and yet it felt as though eternity had ground to a standstill.

His heartbeat thudded in time with his boot steps on the long hall and staircase. He flicked an anxious glance at Simmons, but saw the man's color improve the farther they got from the heart of the fire.

Outside, his brain screamed.

He made a sharp left, pushing the butler ahead of him down the short hall leading to the kitchen.

Through the window, he saw the crowd and the glitter of flames on the glass. A few more steps. Out the door, off the porch, and into the snow. Shoving past the bucket brigade, his gaze sweeping the faces, looking for one in particular. The only face that could assure him all was well. That everything and everyone he cared about had survived.

But he couldn't find her.

* * *

Phoebe swung her arms high overhead, hoping someone would see. Notice that she was drowning in the midst of a crowd.

The cold pulled at her, numbing her limbs until she felt almost warm again. Tired. So tired.

Lungs bursting, she dug her bare toes into the mud-lined walls and shoved up. Her head broke the surface of the water briefly. She had time to gulp at the smoke-tinged air before her heavy skirts dragged her back, plunging her into the darkness again.

Above her, she could see the glitter of firelight on the rippled water. Shadows passed back and forth as the men in the crowd hurried about the business of saving their town, unaware she needed help.

Again and again, she tried to pull herself up, but the muddy walls fell apart under her touch, dissolving into the murky water.

"Phoebe!" Riley shouted her name, looking over the heads of the crowd, searching for her.

"Where is she?" Simmons asked.

"I don't know," Riley said, and handed Becky to him. "I left her right here. I told her not to move, damn it!"

"You don't think she went in there and we missed seeing her, do you?" Simmons sounded horrified as his gaze shifted over the burning wall.

"There's no telling what that damned woman would do," Riley shouted, fighting the fear that was reborn and growing at an extraordinary rate. He reached out with one hand and grabbed the man closest to him. "Did you see Phoebe go back inside?"

"Who the hell would go in there?" the man yelled.

"Phoebe would," Riley muttered. He should have known she wouldn't listen to him. Should have known that she would be willing to put her own life in danger to save Becky and Simmons. "Damn it," he whispered angrily, and the sound was caught and carried away in the frenzy noise around him. "Why didn't you trust me? Why didn't you just wait?"

"Stay here," he told Simmons, and with a last quick look at his daughter, turned on his heel, headed back into the hotel.

A boy's frantic shout stopped him.

"Help!"

Thin, reedy, the voice should have been lost in the surrounding noise, but somehow, it was heard.

An instant later, a man called out, "Over here! Hey, somebody, give us a hand!"

Riley turned again, facing the crowd. Something spurred him on, an instinct he'd learned long ago not to question sent him plunging into the midst of the gathered men, throwing them out of his way.

He knew Phoebe was the cause of the shouts.

"Jesus!" he heard. "Pull her up! Pull her up!"

"Is she breathin'?"

Breathing? Riley thought wildly, fighting through the mob of men.

"Don't know."

His blood iced over.

"Hell, when'd Riley dig a well?" someone shouted.

Sweet Jesus. The well.

"Fill up the buckets here, forget the brigade," another man called. "We can beat this damn thing now!"

"Get the woman out of there first!" still another voice called, and Riley shoved a man blocking him to one side. Heart pounding, throat cotton-dry, he looked down to see Phoebe, soaking wet, stretched out along the snowy ground beside the uncovered well.

Joe Weatherby, tears streaming down his face, sat beside her, patting her unmoving hand, muttering, "Phoebe, wake up. Please, Phoebe. Don't die."

"God!" Riley muttered thickly and vaulted over the open well to land in the dirt beside her.

Young Joe looked at him through wide, pain-filled eyes. "She ain't moved, Riley." His breath hitched painfully and his narrow shoulders slumped. Head shaking, voice quavering unsteadily, he said, "I think . . . she's dead or somethin'." His bottom lip quivered and more tears rained down his cheeks.

Dead? Phoebe?

Impossible.

Riley looked at her, so still. So quiet. And felt his soul wither. Her eyes, those incredible, color-changing eyes, were closed. Please, God, not forever. In his mind, he heard her voice. *I love you.* "What happened?"

"She musta got knocked into the well," someone behind him said loudly. "The boy there spotted her."

"Her hands," Joe said, and pulled in a long, struggling breath. "Stuck up out of the water. Wavin', like." He hiccuped harshly. "She fell in our prospectin' hole. We never meant nothin' like this to happen, Riley. Honest we didn't. We always liked Phoebe."

Liked, he thought grimly. The boy was talking as though she were already gone. *I love you.*

"I shoulda seen her sooner," Joe whimpered, shaking his head in time with the gentle pats he gave Phoebe.

Riley reached for her, unable to believe that she might have left him. Her cheeks were like finely polished stone. No warmth. *I love you.*

"Dear heaven, no," Simmons said, and Riley spared him a quick look. The older man's features twisted in a grimace of pain that tore at Riley, sharpening his own agony and forcing it down, deep into his chest, where it gnawed at his insides with razor-sharp teeth.

I love you.

No! his mind shouted as he turned his full attention on Phoebe. Goddammit, no! Pushing concerned hands aside, he hovered over her, running his hands up and down her icy body, roughly, hoping to shock her into wakefulness. Checking for a pulse, a heartbeat, a flicker of movement that would tell him she lived . . . so that he could too.

Her face was bloodless.

I love you.

Damn it, Phoebe, don't you die on me!

His mind screamed in rage and fear, but his teeth ground together, locking his jaw, keeping his panic bottled tightly inside.

Chalky white, her skin made the dirty snow look like coal in comparison. His heart stopped. He felt it. He stared hard at her chest, willing it to move, and when it didn't, felt something inside him snap and shatter into thousands of pieces.

I love you.

"Damn it, Phoebe," he shouted and lifted her by the shoulders. Her head fell back limply and he shook her, hard. Water dribbled from her mouth and a tiny spark of hope rose up in his chest. Of course. Have to get her emptied out. Must have swallowed half the well.

Instantly, he rolled her over onto her stomach and tipped her cold, expressionless face to one side. As the men of Rimshot fought the fire, he fought his own private battle.

I love you.

He heard those three little words over and over inside his head. Hearing them before had panicked him. Hearing them now taunted him. He didn't deserve her. He knew that. But damn it, he wanted her and wouldn't lose her without a fight.

Planting his hands in the middle of her back, he shoved down hard, trying to force the water out of her lungs. Her body gave beneath his hands and he imagined her hale and hearty. In his mind's eye, he saw her gaze full of spirit and spunk and clung to that image.

It was working, he thought. That small thread of hope blossomed into a wild, glorious thing. Sound, people, disappeared from his consciousness. His world now consisted of him and the woman he refused to allow to die. Again and again, he pushed down on her back.

I love you.

Water trickled from her mouth again, and Riley doubled his efforts, forcing her lungs to work. At last, when his arms and shoulders ached, when Joe was looking at him like he was a man crazed, Phoebe choked, coughed and gagged, bringing up the rest of the well water clogging her chest.

"She's breathin'!" Joe shouted, a wide grin on his tear-streaked face, but Riley hardly heard him.

Relieved beyond words, Riley picked her up, cradled her close to him, and ignored the shaft of ice that slid from her body into his. Each of her gasping, choking breaths felt like a celebration.

He spared a look at the fire and saw that the men were winning, though the hotel would be uninhabitable. The flames were beaten, but they'd devoured most of the wall on the second story. Didn't matter. Everyone was safe.

"Phoebe?" Simmons asked and stepped close.

Riley looked down at her and was the first to see her eyes open. She gave him a small, weak smile. "Cold."

Riley's arms tightened around her. "Damned right," he said. "You're frozen to the bone."

"I'll—"

Simmons never finished that sentence. No one was going to take Phoebe from Riley tonight. No one. "We'll all have to move to the rooms over the saloon for now. You take care of Becky," he told the older man. "I'll see to Phoebe."

The two men stared at each other for a long, tension-filled minute. Simmons's gaze locked with his and Riley met it squarely. He tightened his hold on Phoebe, and when she burrowed in closer to him, he knew the butler would have to shoot him to take Phoebe from him tonight.

Something in his eyes must have conveyed that thought because the butler nodded slowly. "Very well," Simmons said in a resigned tone. "I'll look after your daughter." He gave Phoebe a quick look before spearing Riley with his gaze. "See that you take good care of mine."

"Count on it."

Chapter Seventeen

He half ran up the stairs, his arms wrapped around her like iron bands. Charging down the hallway, his boot steps muffled on the carpet runner, Riley stopped in front of the room at the end of the hall. Bending slightly, he opened the door, stepped inside, and kicked it shut behind him.

Teeth chattering, Phoebe had never been so cold in her life. Every inch of her felt as though it was covered in ice and every breath she drew labored to fight its way into frozen lungs.

"You're gonna be all right, Phoebe," Riley muttered as he strode straight for the wide bed against the far wall.

She nodded and the top of her head clipped his chin. "So cold," she managed to say.

"I guess so," he told her and sat her down on the edge of the mattress. "Takin' a swim in a near frozen well is bound to do that to a body." He left her just long enough to strike a match and light the kerosene lamp standing on a nearby table.

She trembled violently from head to toe. "Didn't . . . didn't . . . do it on purpose."

"No." He knelt in front of her again and kept his head bent as his fingers worked the tiny buttons lining the front of her dress free of their holes. "Don't suppose you did at that."

Alive! his mind shouted. She's alive.

"Somebody bumped me," she said and fought to hold her head still. The tremors coursing through her made her vision wild, sending everything in the room into motion. "Fell. Couldn't get out. Tried." She held up her hands to prove it to him and saw the mud caked beneath her nails and ground into her skin. "Kept falling," she said around a series of short, sharp breaths. "Couldn't breathe. Couldn't see. Couldn't—"

"Shh . . ." Riley looked up and she stared into eyes filled with the remnants of a fear so deep, it shook her to the bone. "Don't think about it now," he said.

"Can't stop."

Forgetting about the stubborn buttons for a minute, he pulled her into his arms and held her tightly, as if to reassure her that she was free of the well.

So warm. His body radiated heat that drew her in close. "Scared, Riley," she said, her breath now hiccuping from her throat in loud, choking gulps. "So scared."

"I know just what you mean, darlin'," he whispered so faintly she almost missed it. Then pulling away from her again, he knelt down in front of her and went back to work on those buttons. "Damn things," he muttered darkly. "Why d'they make 'em so blasted small?"

She wanted to smile, but her face hurt. Her hands curled into tight fists in her lap. The cold went so deep now, Phoebe couldn't even remember a time when she was warm. Absently, she tried to dredge up memories of a hot St. Louis summer. Damp, cloying heat. Perspiration rolling down the back of her dress to pool uncomfortably at the small of her back. Tendrils of hair clinging to her forehead. Not a breath of air stirring the big trees outside her home and even the crickets too limp and drawn to sing at night.

Another shiver wracked her body. It wasn't working.

This time she tried to focus on her surroundings. Red flocked wallpaper, thick blood-red drapes at the windows, rag rugs on the floor, paintings of naked women in poses they should be ashamed of on the walls.

She trembled violently and watched those paintings dance before her eyes.

"Help, Riley," she said breathlessly. "Can't stop shaking."

"I know, honey," he said and gave up on the damn buttons. Taking the sodden fabric in both hands, he ripped her bodice open and Phoebe heard the tiny bone buttons skitter across the plank floor.

One small corner of her mind told her she should stop him. She shouldn't be sitting there like a stone statue while Riley Burnett undressed her. But she was too cold to care, and if the truth be known, the brush of his warm fingers against her bare, icy skin felt too good to complain about.

Besides, she thought absently, the ladies in the pictures were naked. Why shouldn't she be as well?

Vaguely, as if watching herself from a safe distance, she saw Riley push her chemise off her shoulders, baring her breasts. Shouldn't she be embarrassed?

But he didn't give her time to consider the question. Easing her off the bed, he quickly stripped her dress and nearly frozen white drawers down off her hips and legs, then tossed them to the floor. Snatching up two quilts from the end of the mattress, he wrapped them around her, then jumped to his feet and crossed the floor to the stove in the corner.

"I'll get a fire started, then clean you up. Make you some tea or something."

She nodded and realized that it was involuntary. Her entire body kept shaking. She couldn't stop. Gripping the edges of the quilts with both dirty hands, she watched him. He fed the stove with kindling and held a match to it until flames leaped up from the base, looking for more fuel. Carefully, he stacked more wood on the growing fire until it was well under way.

"Fire," she breathed as he closed the metal door on

the stove. "Strange. One fire terrifies, the other comforts."

"Yeah." He stood up and faced her from across the room. "It's been a real interesting night that way." Shoving one hand through his hair, he asked, "You be all right here for a minute? I want to go get a kettle full of water and some cloths."

"Yes," she said tightly. "I'm fine. Really."

"Yeah." He snorted. "I can see that."

A hurried knock at the door startled them both. Riley scowled and grumbled, "I told him I'd take care of you. We had a deal."

"Simmons?"

"Who else?" He stomped across the room, threw open the door ready to do battle, and had the wind knocked clean out of his sails. "Ivy?"

The huge woman looked past Riley to Phoebe and concern colored her voice when she said, "I heard what happened." She held out a large brown bottle. "Brought some brandy to warm her up some and a new nightdress."

"Thanks," he said and took them.

Ivy frowned at him. "You gonna step aside, or do I go right through ya?"

Riley stiffened slightly and looked squarely into the woman's sharp-eyed gaze. He was grateful for the brandy. And the nightgown. But damned if he was going to let Ivy Talbot march in and set up camp. "I'm taking care of Phoebe."

"That ain't fittin'," Ivy told him. "And you know it."

"Fitting or not, that's the way it's going to be."

"Riley," Phoebe said.

He didn't even turn around. "Keep still, Phoebe. Everything's fine."

"Yeah." She snorted in a good imitation of him. "I can see that."

He smiled inwardly. How he would have missed her if she'd gone and died on him.

"Riley Burnett," Ivy said, drawing herself up to her more than formidable, full height, "don't you be a damn fool. You let me care for her. You can come in again when she's decent."

His grip on the brandy bottle tightened. She was probably right. He should leave Phoebe to her care. But he wasn't going to. Images of Phoebe, still and white and cold, clouded his mind. He couldn't leave her. Not yet. Not while she still needed him.

"I don't care if it's decent or not," Riley told her. "I'm staying."

"You think folks won't care what goes on here tonight?" Ivy prodded him. "Once talk of the fire's past, they'll be talking about you and Phoebe here. Alone."

"Not if they don't know about it," he countered.

Ivy huffed and her bosom swelled with a sharp, indrawn breath. "Don't look at me like that. I'm no gossip."

"Then there's no problem."

"Riley . . ." Phoebe's voice again. Tired. Small.

He gritted his teeth. He was wasting time, he thought. Precious time. "I appreciate it, Ivy," he said, lowering his voice and hoping she'd take the hint to do likewise. "But I'm not leaving her tonight. And nothin' you can say is going to change that."

Ivy Talbot looked into dark blue eyes and knew she wasn't going to be able to budge him without a stick of dynamite. And maybe that was for the best. After all, she reflected, we rarely appreciate what we've got until we come close to losing it.

Seemed like Riley had gotten a good taste of "what if" tonight and it had gone down hard.

"So be it then," she said, her voice a low rumble. She half leaned in toward him and poked his chest with her index finger hard enough to draw blood. "But you mind yourself. That's a good woman in there. And I won't stand for a good woman being used lightly. You hear me?"

"I hear you, Ivy. And thanks for the brandy."

"Hmmph!" She shook her head at him, then looked past him to Phoebe. "You need anything, hon', you just give a holler and I'll come runnin'."

"Th-th-thank you."

"Mind what I said," Ivy warned Riley one last time, then turned and flounced off, her heavy steps echoing down the hall.

Riley watched her go, telling himself he was a fool. He should have listened to her. He had no right to endanger Phoebe's reputation just to satisfy his own need to care for her.

"I'm glad she's . . . gone," Phoebe said from behind him, and he turned around to look at her. "I don't want—want—to see anyone else right now."

That settled that, Riley thought and marched back to her side. Setting the brandy and the nightgown down on a nearby table, he said, "Sit still. I'll be back in a few minutes and we'll get you settled."

She gave him a jerky nod, but her color wasn't much better than it had been right after being pulled from the well. That put a fire under him and he hurried down the stairs and across to the hotel kitchen.

"Papa," Becky crowed when he entered the room.

Riley paused in the doorway and let his gaze fly around the kitchen. Amazing. It looked pretty much untouched, but for the trail of mud across the floor and a broken window.

Simmons lifted his head to stare hard at him, and Ivy Talbot, standing at the stove, shot him a look that should have curled his hair.

"How is she?" the butler asked as Riley took a quick moment to pick up his daughter and give her a squeeze. Another blessing. He'd been given two miracles in one night. Becky and Phoebe. Alive. Thank you, God.

"She'll be fine as soon as we warm her up." He noticed the older man's soot-streaked, weary expression and knew he himself looked no better. "How's the upstairs?"

"I took a peek," Ivy told him. "Place is a wreck. You have you a mountain of rebuilding to do on this side of the building. Most of the wall's gone and what was inside is soaked or covered in soot and smoke."

He nodded grimly.

"It's about ready," Ivy said and plucked Becky from his grasp before he could protest.

"What is?" he asked, puzzled by her shift in subject.

"Hot water." Ivy nodded at the butler. "Simmons there put some on to heat straight off. You can take it up now."

"Thanks."

Simmons only glared at him, as if regretting allowing Riley to care for Phoebe.

Becky waved her cookie in the air and slapped Ivy in the face with its gooey edge. The big woman grinned at her.

"I'll bring the tea up when it's ready," she told him.

"Ivy . . ."

She held up one hand to stop him from continuing. "I'll knock and leave it by the door. You lace it with some of that brandy, y'hear?"

Riley smiled at her. "Thanks. Thanks again."

Then he grabbed the pan of warm water and the small stack of towels beside it and headed upstairs again.

He stood with his back to her as she washed the mud off herself. Listening to the gentle splash of water in the pan and Phoebe's faint sighs was driving him to distraction.

"This'd be a sight faster and easier if you'd just let me do this for you."

"No," she said and her voice quavered.

Still trembling from the cold, he thought.

"I can . . . can do it myself."

Riley shifted from foot to foot, jammed his hands on

his hips, and stared sightlessly at the ugly wallpaper in front of him. There was enough of the color red in this room to blind a man. But then, he reminded himself, the men who used to visit the girls in these rooms weren't interested in the decorations.

"You nearly finished?" he asked. She was taking so long about this, he'd never get her under those quilts and warmed up.

"Yes, almost."

His gaze shifted, wandering over the room, looking for something to occupy his thoughts while he waited. He stopped dead, though, when he caught sight of the mirror on the other side of the room. Why hadn't he noticed it before? Hell, for that matter, why notice it *now*?

The full-length, brass-edged mirror was positioned just right to give him a tantalizing view of Phoebe.

Look away, he told himself, but his gaze never wavered.

She had a quilt half over her, hanging limply from her shoulders to lie along her sides. As he watched, Phoebe moved, stretching her right leg out in front of her and half bent to run the wet cloth over her skin.

Mouth dry, Riley swallowed hard, following the trail of that cloth down, over her calf, her ankle, then back up across her knee and up the outside of her thigh. His breath caught and lodged hard in his throat when she dragged that cloth to the inside of her thigh. But his torture wasn't over because she repeated the whole maneuver again on her left leg. When she straightened up, the quilt slipped, giving him an unimpeded view of her naked body.

Her loose, still-damp hair hung around her shoulders and dipped and swayed across the tops of her breasts, like a living curtain, shifting, seducing.

He directed his gaze at those lush, full breasts, their nipples peaked and hard from cold, and he wanted to cup them, explore them, taste them. Riley swallowed a groan as she ran that warm cloth across her upper body and then down her rounded hips, flat abdomen, and the small triangle of dark hair protecting her secrets.

His body came alive in a rush of sensation. He'd been so scared she was lost to him. So wrapped up in saving her, warming her, he hadn't, until this moment, had time to react to the simple pleasure of looking at her.

"Finished," she said softly, and gathered that quilt around her again, unaware that he'd seen everything she was trying to hide.

Turning around, he walked across the room to where she sat perched on the edge of the bed, the star quilt wrapped tightly around her.

"Did you drink some of the tea Ivy brought up?"

"Not yet."

He frowned. "Have some," he ordered and picked up the brandy bottle. "With a little of this for good measure," he added and splashed a large dollop of the liquor into her cup.

Dutifully, she lifted the cup, took a drink and frowned. "It's awful." Then she sat up straighter and whooshed out a breath. "But . . . but warm."

"Good." He knelt down in front of her. The only part of her visible besides her face were her feet. Lifting her right foot, he took it between his palms. "Your feet feel like blocks of ice."

She nodded jerkily. "Barefoot. In the snow."

Good God. He rubbed her toes briskly, then set her foot down and began on the other one. "Why weren't you wearing shoes?"

She shrugged halfheartedly. "Feet hurt."

"Jesus, Phoebe," he muttered, absorbing the cold of her skin into his hands, "you're lucky you don't have frostbite."

"Luck . . . lucky I'm alive."

His gaze shot to hers. He knew that all too well. He doubted very much if the image of her lying so still and lifeless in the snow would ever completely leave him. And he suspected that image would be haunting his dreams for years to come.

To cover the swift rush of emotion he felt, Riley spoke gruffly. "Get into that bed. Under the covers. Got to get you warm or you'll be looking at pneumonia next."

She blinked at his tone, but did as she was told, too cold or too tired, or both, to argue with him.

Once she'd stretched out on the mattress, Riley heaped blankets on her, then ran his hands up and down the fabric, trying to heat her up fast. It wasn't working, though. He could see it in the pallor of her face and feel it in the tremors still coursing through her body.

This was no good. It wasn't enough for a woman as down-deep frozen as Phoebe. Drastic situations called for drastic measures, he told himself.

"Phoebe," he said, and stood up. "There's only one sure way I know of warming you up fast."

She just looked at him. Her dark blue eyes looked even darker in the pale whiteness of her face.

Stripping off his shirt, he tossed it aside, then bent to yank off his boots.

Her eyes widened slightly and she seemed to burrow down deeper into her blankets.

"This is the only way, Phoebe," he said as he worked at the buttons of his jeans.

Quickly, she closed her eyes.

Riley grumbled to himself. This wasn't exactly the way he'd thought this moment might happen. All of those sleepless nights, when he'd entertained the notion of climbing naked into Phoebe's bed, he'd always imagined her just a bit more welcoming.

He pulled his jeans down and off his legs, and when he was naked, Riley lifted the edge of the quilt and slipped into the bed beside her. Instantly, she rolled onto her side and inched away from him.

"Damn it," he muttered and snaked out one arm toward her. Wrapping it around her waist, he pulled her against him, her back to his front.

A shocked breath hissed into his lungs at first contact with her icy body, but he held her close, despite her efforts to wriggle away.

Though he wished to heaven she'd stop moving her hips like that.

"You can't . . ."

"Yes I can," he grumbled close to her ear. "Nothin's going to happen, Phoebe," he added when she squirmed in his grasp again. "But it would be a sight easier on me if you'd lay still."

Instantly, Phoebe stopped moving. Eyes wide and staring at the wall opposite her, she lay pressed to him and tried not to think about what part of him was poking at her.

Indecent, that's what this was. She told herself to be shocked. Outraged. But in truth, his warmth felt so good, she only wanted to move closer. It was only the last ounce of sense she'd somehow managed to hold on to that kept her from doing just that.

The cold that seemed to have seeped right into her bones gradually slipped away in the shared heat of Riley's body.

One of his arms closed around her middle, pinning him to her, and she concentrated solely on that arm. The heavy, muscular feel of it lying against her naked flesh.

Naked.

Her mind played with that word. She was naked. In bed with Riley, who was also naked.

A nervous giggle bubbled in her chest and she struggled unsuccessfully to hold it in.

"What's so damn funny?" he asked and his voice came as a rumbling hush of sound carried on a warm breath that caressed her neck and sent goose bumps rippling up and down her body.

"We're naked."

He laughed shortly, harshly. "Nothin' funny about that, Phoebe. Believe me."

She shifted on the mattress and his hard body jabbed at her again. He groaned.

"Lord, woman, would you hold still? You keep moving like that, and you're liable to kill me."

"I'm sorry," she whispered.

"It's all right," he said tightly. "I guess I should be the one apologizing. But when you're around, my body just has a mind of its own."

A swirl of delight suddenly implanted itself low in her stomach. "You mean . . . *I* do that to you?" she asked quietly.

His arm around her waist tightened slightly. "Only constantly," he admitted.

"Oh, my." It was a heady sensation, she thought. Phoebe'd never considered herself the kind of woman to inspire such a reaction in a man. But the proof was right there in front of her—or rather, behind her. She laughed again, nervously.

"Y'know, Phoebe," he said, his voice lazy, "laughing at a naked man in your bed isn't always the best thing to do."

Well, she didn't want to insult him. Half turning her head on the pillow, she looked up at him. "I wasn't laughing at you," she said, staring into his eyes. "Just at the idea of *me* being the cause of your . . ." She lowered her gaze a bit. "Discomfort."

He shook his head as he looked at her, his gaze moving over her features like a touch. "Phoebe, don't ever doubt it."

Caught by the shine in his eyes, she whispered, "I know you liked kissing me . . ."

"Oh, yeah."

"But I didn't think that—" She broke off.

The fingers of his left hand played with her hair even as his right hand moved lightly across her skin, sliding gently over her rib cage to caress her just below her breasts.

She sighed and closed her eyes briefly at the almost indescribable sensations he aroused.

"I've been thinking about just this for some time now," he said softly, and his fingertips brushed the bottom of her breast.

Phoebe arched into his touch. "You have?"

"Oh, yes, ma'am," he told her, lowering his mouth until his breath dusted her ear. "Phoebe . . . when I saw you lying there beside the well, so still . . ." He dragged in a shuddering breath. "I've never been so scared in my life."

She frowned slightly, trying to concentrate both on his words and his fingers, now edging closer and closer to one of her nipples, which seemed to be aching unbearably.

"Riley . . ."

He kissed her cheek, her temple, and she felt each kiss touch her soul. Such gentleness. Such tenderness. He filled the hollow emptiness that she had carried around with her for most of her life. That place in her heart that had long been resigned to remaining untouched, unnourished. With his whispered words and soft caress, Riley Burnett had given her what she'd always craved.

To be needed.

To be loved.

Whether he said the words or not, she felt his love in his every touch. And now, she wanted—no, had—to have more.

She lifted his right hand and held it away from her body. Instantly, Riley stiffened.

"I'm sorry," he whispered. "You're right. I promised you nothing would happen and here I am—"

"Riley," she said, interrupting him neatly, "show me."

"Huh?"

She looked into his eyes again, losing herself in the blue depths. Taking a deep, steadying breath, she laid his hand atop her breast and held it there. He inhaled sharply and she said, "Make love to me, Riley."

"Phoebe . . ."

She shook her head. "I could have died tonight."

He groaned.

"I almost did." She pounded that thought home before adding, "If I had, I would have died never knowing what it was to be loved by a man." Unbidden, tears leaped into her eyes and she blinked them back determinedly. "I don't want to risk that again, Riley. I want to know what other women know. I want to feel like I'm a part of someone. Something. I want you to become a part of me."

He let his head fall forward until his forehead rested on hers. "Jesus, Phoebe. You don't know what you're asking."

"Yes I do." She sniffed and tightened her hold on his hand covering her breast. "I'm asking you to bring my soul to life—as you did my body just hours ago."

"Phoebe," he said through tightly gritted teeth, "I want you more than I've ever wanted anything in my life."

"And I love you," she said, relishing the feel of the words on her tongue.

A soft groan escaped him as he rested his forehead against hers. "You deserve more than me."

She bit back the disappointment at not hearing her words echoed back to her. For now, for this moment, it was enough to know he wanted her. Remembering Mary's advice earlier tonight, Phoebe told herself that perhaps with a taste of the milk, he would see that they deserved each other.

"Love me tonight, Riley," she answered and turned into him. "Just for tonight."

Chapter Eighteen

For tonight.

Those words echoed over and over in his mind as he looked into her eyes and he knew he was lost. Hell. He'd known it the moment he'd stripped and climbed into bed beside her.

It was more than wanting to care for her—warm her. Riley felt a deeply rooted need to simply hold her. To feel her breath, hear her heartbeat. To assure himself that she was safe.

Alive.

She stared up at him and he read the love in her eyes. A love that shook him to his soul.

"For tonight," he whispered, and bent his head to claim the first of many kisses. His lips touched hers briefly, as if testing, waiting for her to change her mind. He held his breath. If Phoebe said no, he would walk away now, though he'd be in agony for the rest of his life. But she welcomed him, opening her mouth slightly to invite a deeper kiss. He obliged, his tongue sweeping the inside of her mouth in a swirl of caresses that made her shiver in his arms.

So right, he thought. So perfect.

He could lie with her like this forever. Her body warmer now and aligned invitingly to his. Their mouths locked, their breathing in harmony, their hearts pounding.

Sweeping his right hand along her body, he explored her curves with a gentle, sure touch. Over her hips, along her thigh, as she drew her leg up to receive his caress. Then back up to her breasts and the hardened, dark pink nipples that demanded his attentions.

His thumb and forefinger tweaked the sensitive, rigid flesh and Phoebe moaned from the back of her throat. Riley smiled to himself and tore his mouth from hers reluctantly.

"Riley . . ."

"Shh . . ." His lips trailed damp, heated kisses along the line of her throat down and across her chest. Warm, soft, smooth, he couldn't get enough of her. He followed the swell of her breast with his lips until, finally, his mouth closed over her nipple and she arched high off the bed in response.

"Oh, my!"

He smiled against her skin, his tongue drawing lazy circles around the rigid tip of her breast. Every hitched breath she took, every sigh, every half-strangled moan, fed his own desire until he thought he would disgrace himself by exploding.

And still, he tortured them both.

Phoebe's head whipped from side to side on the pillow. She stared unseeing at the ceiling and waited breathlessly for the next wave of sensation to pour over her. How much more could she stand? How much more could there possibly be?

Then his mouth closed over her nipple.

She gasped.

He suckled her and she speared her fingers through his hair, holding him firmly to the breast she never wanted him to leave.

Phoebe's mind spun like a whirlwind in a flower garden, sending bright colors twisting wildly behind her eyes. How could she have lived her whole life never knowing such feelings existed? And how could she ever live without this closeness . . . this man . . . now that she'd found him?

His mouth tugged at her, dissolving her thoughts into nothing more than an urgent plea for more. Over and over again, drawing, pulling, his lips and tongue sent her spiraling out of control, headed for a shadowy abyss that seemed to stretch out for miles in front of her.

With each tug at her tender nipple, something happened lower in her body. An ache built, slowly, steadily. A burning need for something she'd never known—never thought to know.

And knew she had to have before her body splintered.

"Riley . . ." She managed to squeeze his name past her lips, though she wasn't sure just what she was asking for.

He only suckled harder, more firmly, his tongue, his lips, his teeth, dragging across skin more sensitive than she'd ever suspected.

Daringly, she shifted her gaze from the overhead beams to where Riley's head bent over her breast. He shot her a quick, knowing glance that should have colored her cheeks, but instead sparked yet another fire deep within her.

Heaven help her, she was completely shameless.

She held his head to her and almost moaned aloud when he pulled back anyway. But he only turned slightly, to attend her other breast, bringing her fresh waves of pleasure.

As his mouth tortured her, his hands began a torment of their own. Up and down the length of her body, he touched her, caressed her, stroked her until her flesh was humming, burning for a respite she didn't know how to find.

She twisted on the sheets, feeling them bunch beneath her. One of his hands swept down low, across her abdomen, to the damp, heated spot at her center.

Phoebe gasped aloud, lifting her head from the pillow in shocked surprise. "Easy, Phoebe," he soothed, in the same tone he might have used to a recalcitrant horse. "It's all right." He caught her gaze with his and held it while he continued to explore the deep intimacies of her body.

Once, twice, three times, his fingertips brushed across her sensitive flesh. And each time, she half jumped in response. But the gleam in his eyes held her captive as much as his touch, and at last, she lay quiet, allowing him to deepen his exploration.

He dipped one finger within her and Phoebe's eyes flew open wider at the unfamiliarity of it all. Riley Burnett was touching her from the *inside*.

Strange and exciting and so completely right.

She gathered that knowledge close and held it while she waited for his next caress.

"Ah, Phoebe," he whispered, and moved until he could plant a soft, tender kiss at the corner of her trembling mouth. "You're so beautiful. More than I dreamed. More than I deserve."

"Riley—" she started, then stopped suddenly as his fingers moved inside her again. "That feels—"

"Good?" he finished for her.

"Wonderful," she corrected.

He groaned tightly and when she parted her thighs to grant him easier access, he kissed her again, his teeth tugging at her bottom lip.

She'd waited her entire life for this night. And she wanted to enjoy every moment of it. Inscribe it deeply into the pages of her mind so that years from now, as an old woman, she could relive this magic and remember how it felt to be held and caressed by the man she loved.

Phoebe turned into him, pressing herself against him, wanting to feel his hard, muscled body along her own. She'd thought of nothing else since the night she'd seen his bared chest. Now, she indulged her fantasies and scraped her palms down, over hard, planed flesh, along his ribs and lower and around to the small of his back. Her short, neat nails dragged along his skin and she smiled at his ragged exhalation of breath. Apparently, he was as sensitive to her touch as she was to his.

Delighting in this new information, Phoebe gave her hands free rein to move, to discover his body in the same way he'd come to know hers.

"Sweet heaven, what you do to me," he murmured, and the words filled her, sweeping away her last insecurities.

Nearly growling, Riley pushed her back onto the mattress and held her there. He went up on his knees and moved to kneel between her parted thighs.

Every inch of her tingled in anticipation. Something hot and tight and prickly coiled in the depths of her core and she rocked her hips in silent invitation.

She wanted to feel everything. Experience everything. Finally, she would learn the secrets between man and woman.

For the first time in her life, Phoebe Hightower felt beautiful.

Wanted.

Desired.

It was so much more than she'd ever hoped for.

His thumb brushed across an especially sensitive nub of skin and Phoebe gasped, arching high off the bed. Lightning-like shocks of awareness sparkled within her and she silently begged him to touch her like that again. And again.

There was something there. Something blossoming. Something that lay just out of reach at the very center of the shadowy abyss that now surrounded her.

"Lovely," he murmured.

She practically purred at his words, his touch. His fingertips brushed that spot again and the tightness within her swelled until she thought she might burst and hoped it would happen soon.

"Riley, I need—"

"I know," he said softly. "I do too."

Then he scooped her up, his broad palms supporting her backside as he lifted her high off the mattress. Her legs dangled helplessly and she curled her fingers into the wrinkled sheet beneath her as she watched him, unable to look away.

"Is this how it happens?" she asked quietly, confused now. She'd thought she knew the basics of sexual joining. But she'd never imagined that her body would have to be in midair to complete it.

"It?" he asked, and his breath puffed against her center.

She squirmed a bit, but his hands held her firmly. "You know . . . *it*."

He smiled at her, a soft, small smile that touched her heart. "*It* comes later," he whispered. "First, there's *this*." And then he bent his head to her and covered her with his mouth.

"Blast and damnation," she muttered thickly, around the sudden, hard knot in her throat.

She'd never expected this.

Never even *imagined* this.

Liquid. She felt liquid.

Her bones dissolved beneath her skin. He licked at her and she quivered, knowing that if he let go of her now, she would simply slide right off the bed. And yet, at the same time, Phoebe felt as tightly strung as a violin being plucked by a master.

His tongue moved over her, teasing that special place, tossing her higher and higher over the abyss as she reached out blindly for the final secret she'd yet to learn.

Her eyes closed on the incredible things he was making her feel. The better to concentrate on every kiss. Every stroke of his tongue.

His fingers gently kneaded the soft flesh of her behind, his breath brushed across her and his mouth continued to spiral her toward a sky that seemed to glow with the light of a million suns.

Her breath caught.

She tightened her grasp on the bed beneath her.

Involuntarily, her body arched and jumped in his grasp.

On and on it went, those sensations, pushing her higher, faster, harder. Her breath staggered in her chest. Her heartbeat thundered in her ears. She reached out, almost touching what she needed so desperately.

She heard herself call his name on a gasping sigh, her body shattered under an onslaught of sensation too much to bear and then she willingly gave herself over to the pulsing throb of completion.

Instantly, even before the last shaking tremor had left her, Riley eased her down, knelt in front of her, and pushed his body into hers.

A quick, shocking pain shot through her and was as quickly gone.

"Are you all right?" he asked.

She looked up at him, his face just a breath away from hers. Phoebe rolled her hips from side to side, enjoying the feel of being locked with this man. Joined. Their bodies one. No end. No beginning.

Phoebe lifted one hand to cup his cheek. He'd already given her so much. She lifted her legs to wrap them around his waist, pulling him deeper within her, holding him more tightly to her, as if she would never let him leave her again.

"I'm so much more than all right," she said softly. "I never knew there could be so much between a man and a woman."

He grinned and she smiled back. Then he rocked his hips against hers, sending his body surging deeper into her warmth. "There's more," he whispered and bent his head to gently nibble at the base of her throat.

"More?" She sighed and tipped her head to one side.

More than he'd ever dreamed possible, Riley thought but didn't say. He'd been with his share of women over the years. But he'd never found anything to compare with what he'd just discovered in the arms of this one particular woman.

Pleasuring her had satisfied him in a deeper way than he'd ever known before. Watching satisfaction shimmer in her eyes and tremble through her body made him feel as though he was capable of conquering the world.

And holding her warm, soft body beneath his made him want to give it all to her.

Humbled and proud and terrified all at once, he claimed her in the only way he knew how.

Moving slowly at first, he led her once more on the path to completion. Hand in hand, they raced toward the top of the mountain and when they at last reached the precipice, he whispered her name like a prayer and gave her all that he was.

Then, joined together, they fell over the edge and tumbled into the magic that was theirs alone.

Early the next morning, Riley was up and gone before sunrise. Couldn't sleep. Couldn't stay in that bed another minute without waking Phoebe up and burying himself inside her again.

So instead, he dressed and went over to the hotel to check out the damage done by the fire.

He started in his and Becky's room.

Without benefit of a window, he looked through the half-charred wall directly at the rose-tinted clouds heralding the sun's arrival. Iced-over puddles of water dotted the floor and a crisp, cold wind shot through the open room to wrap itself around him.

Riley shuddered like someone had just stepped on his grave and shrugged deeper into his coat, jamming his hands into the pockets.

Christ, they'd been lucky. Sure, the hotel was a damned mess, but everybody was safe. His mind raced with the hundred or so grimmer possibilities they'd all escaped. He'd come close last night. Close to losing the precious few people who meant a damn to him.

And yet, hadn't he decided weeks ago to voluntarily lose them? Hadn't he sent for his in-laws to come and take his daughter away? The little girl he'd been so frantic to reach the night before. The child who had wrapped her arms around his neck and clung to him with a ferocious grip, expecting—no, *trusting*—him to keep her safe?

Jesus.

Remnants of last night's fear rose up in him, choking him as thoroughly as a hangman's noose. He remembered every minute of his dash through the smoky interior of the hotel. Recalled with perfect clarity the wild panic sweeping through him at the thought of Becky trapped by flames.

"God," he muttered, and ran one hand across his face in a futile attempt to blunt the memories crowding him. But it was no use. He'd go to his dying day remembering it all. And as he admitted that, he also had to wonder what might have happened if he hadn't been there. If he'd been gone, out on some trail, would anyone else have found Becky in time?

Hell, he wouldn't even have heard about the fire until weeks, maybe months, after the fact. He stared down at the charred floorboards so close to his little girl's bed. A small square of color at the corner of his eye caught his attention and he bent down to snatch up Becky's beloved blanket. Fingers curling into the ratty fabric, he came face-to-face with a sobering fact. He couldn't send his daughter away. Now or ever. She was a part of him. She'd wormed her way into his heart. He couldn't live not knowing if she was safe or not.

So he'd be staying in town, then.

A snort of laughter shot from his throat at his attempt at fooling himself. Hell, he could take Becky and go anywhere. They didn't have to stay in Rimshot.

There was only one reason for that. Phoebe.

And he wasn't staying to help her get the hotel in running order again either. He was staying because he couldn't bear to leave her. But with a woman like Phoebe, that would mean marriage. Was he ready to take that step again? Hell, yes. He could take his medicine as well as the next man.

"It seems, Riley," he said thoughtfully, quietly, "your wanderin' days are done."

"Talking to yourself now, are ya?"

Riley whirled around to face the speaker, then laughed shortly when he recognized the sheriff. "Jesus, Tom. You ought to know better than to sneak up on a man like that."

His old friend smiled sheepishly. "Sorry. Force of habit, I guess."

Riley understood. He'd done plenty of soft walking himself in his time.

Tom stepped into the room, his eyes smiling. "Couldn't help overhearing," he said. "Sounds like you've decided to stay then, huh?"

"Yeah." Riley held Becky's blanket more tightly as if to remind himself that he was doing the right thing. "Guess so. What with Becky and Phoebe . . ."

"Ah . . ." Tom nodded and picked his way through the mess littering the floor. "So that's how the wind blows."

"Surprised hell out of me too."

"Well, after Tess, I suppose you've earned it."

Riley's smile faded slightly. Tess. Lord, how he'd made a mess of marriage the first time. Starting with choosing the wrong woman. But Phoebe was different, he told himself. So this marriage would be different too.

Still, "Don't even know if she'll have me yet."

Tom shook his head. "She'll have you. Hell, everyone in town sees the way she looks at you. Just like Tess used to."

Uncomfortable talking about his late wife with a man who had also courted her, Riley changed the subject abruptly. "Got any ideas on the fire?"

Tom stuck his head out a charred section of wall to look straight down at the ground below, then pulled back and shot a glance at Riley. "Yeah, I do. Looked around some last night, when everyone had gone off. And again this morning."

"And?"

"Somebody used a slow fuse on this place."

That piece of news hit him hard, despite the fact that he'd had a horrible suspicion the fire was more than an accident. Rocks through the windows, smashed whiskey bottles. Irritating but basically harmless vandalism. But Jesus, a fire? The bastard could have wiped out an entire town.

"Soaked a couple of rags in kerosene, snaked 'em out along the ground, then lit 'em." Tom shook his head. "Probably took more than an hour for the building to catch fire."

"So you're saying it could be anybody in town." He already knew that too. A slow fuse was perfect for hiding the arsonist. All he had to do was light a cigar and lay it on the rags. In a while, the first rag would smolder and catch, burning slowly along its length to the next rag in the chain and so on until the small fire spread and began devouring whatever wood it found.

"Yeah. The fella might have been standing right there in your saloon when it finally caught."

Riley shoved one hand through his hair, dragging his fingers across his scalp painfully. Damn the son of a bitch, whoever he was. Phoebe and Becky could have been killed in that fire.

"Got any ideas about who might have it in for you?"

"Nope." He shook his head and stared down at the tattered blanket in his hand as if looking for answers.

"Well, think for a minute," Wills suggested, his voice low, helpful.

"It could be anybody," he acknowledged, with a sinking sensation that seemed to drop the floor right out from under his feet. A man didn't spend years as a marshal making friends—he made enemies. Lots of them.

"Hell, Riley," Tom said finally. "We'll catch him." He

walked across the room and stopped at the threshold. "How's Miss Phoebe today?"

"Sleeping." Riley glanced over his shoulder at the sheriff and saw him smile.

"A lucky thing, that." He shook his head, then reached up to tug the brim of his hat down low over his forehead again. "Saved from burning, near drowned in her own backyard."

"She was lucky," Riley agreed, then added, "But then, so was whoever started that fire."

Puzzled, Tom asked, "How so?"

"Because if Phoebe or Becky had been killed in that fire—or even badly hurt—I'd have to find that man and make him pay."

"Like I said," Tom told him, "we'll find him."

Riley listened to the man's footsteps fade away, then with a last, thoughtful look at the ruins around him, left and headed for the telegraph office. He had a wire to send, then it would be time to face Phoebe.

Chapter Nineteen

Phoebe woke slowly, lazily. Her mind in a fog, her body achy, yet somehow pleasantly so, she opened her eyes to gaudy red wallpaper and the instant awareness of what had happened the night before. After the fire.

Image after image flashed across her brain and she smiled to herself. She'd waited a lifetime to discover what most women her age had known for years. But it had been more than worth the wait.

She supposed she should be ashamed of herself. After all, a decent woman certainly wouldn't share a bed with a man who wasn't her husband. But she searched her heart and found only satisfaction. She'd spent her life following the rules society laid down for maidenly behavior and all she'd earned was loneliness. Well, propriety be damned, she thought. At twenty-seven, she was of an age to decide for herself how the rest of her life would go. And if society disapproved, blast them.

She smiled to herself, sat up and stretched, lifting her arms high over her head. The quilt dropped away and only then did she notice she'd slept nude for the first time in her life. But then just recently, there had been so many "firsts."

A brief knock on the door sounded just before that panel swung open. Eyes wide, she snatched up the quilt to cover herself. Riley walked into the room and she relaxed a bit, thankful it hadn't been Simmons.

But only a heartbeat later, she took a good look at Riley's expression and anxiety rushed through her again. This was not the face of a happy man.

A dark curl of worry settled in the pit of her stomach. Phoebe told herself she should have known. Should have guessed that nothing with this man would be easy. "Riley?"

He shot her a glance as he closed the door behind him and crossed the room to stand at the foot of the bed.

"What is it?" she asked, really beginning to worry now. Maybe someone had been hurt in the fire and he was trying to find a way to break it to her. "Is everyone all right?"

"Yeah," he said quickly. "Everyone's fine. The hotel's shot to hell. But everybody's all right."

"Good." She nodded. Her grip on the quilt tightened. If things were as fine as he claimed, why did he look like a condemned man? "Then what's wrong?"

He snorted a choked laugh, shook his head at her, and started pacing the room. Back and forth he walked, his boot heels clacking briskly against the wood. Morning sunlight poked golden fingers through the holes in the scarlet draperies, sprinkling him with dots of shimmering light. Waving one hand at her and the rumpled bedclothes, he said, "This is wrong, Phoebe."

She colored slightly. Felt the heat of blood staining her cheeks and wasn't sure herself if it was caused by embarrassment or anger. She might have expected to be chastised by Simmons. But *Riley*? Pushing her hair back from her face, she drew the quilt up higher until it rested just beneath her chin. "What exactly do you mean?" she asked and congratulated herself silently on the calm, even tone of her voice.

"You know exactly what I mean," he said and rubbed one hand across his face.

"What happened last night—"

"Shouldn't have," he interrupted, coming to a dead

stop at the foot of the bed. In the shadowy light, his features looked tight, grim.

The last few remnants of her pleasant mood evaporated. "How can you say that?" Anger churned inside her now like a bubbling cauldron of some foul-smelling brew. She'd thought, hoped, that last night had meant as much to him as it had to her. She'd assumed that he had been as moved as she. Apparently, she'd been wrong and that knowledge stung.

No, she told herself a heartbeat later, she wasn't wrong. Blast and damnation, why was he doing this? Last night, she had found something she'd never expected to find. These weeks in Nevada had given her a new life— and, so she'd thought, a new love. Why was he so determined to dismiss it? To turn his back on what they'd shared? What they might find together?

Riley knew he was going about this all wrong. Judging by the look in her eye, if she'd had a gun handy, he'd be a dead man. And damned if he could find it in him to blame her.

"Look, Phoebe," he tried again. "What we did was a mistake, but we can fix it."

"Mistake?" she repeated.

He'd thought this all out. Even had worked out the right words to say, but now they were gone. Pacing again, he fed the restless energy burning inside and decided to forget flowery speeches and just say what had to be said. "Hell, yes, a mistake. You're a good woman, Phoebe. This kind of thing just ain't done."

"I see," she muttered thickly.

"No, ma'am," he cut in again, "I don't think you do."

A short, choked-off laugh shot from her throat. "Well, then, by all means, enlighten me."

"Don't go gettin' all snippy, Phoebe," he said, reacting to the tone of her voice. "I ain't sayin' I didn't enjoy last night. All I'm sayin' is, we've got to do something about it. And I've got a plan."

She scooted off the edge of the bed, dragging the quilt

with her and wrapping it around her body tightly. Good. He didn't need the distraction of seeing her naked just now.

"I'm delighted to know that you enjoyed yourself, but I must say you've intrigued me. What sort of *plan*, Mr. Burnett?"

He winced at that. Hell, she sounded more prim than she had that first day he'd met her. Her long, loose hair streamed across her shoulders. She held the quilt up with one arm positioned under her breasts and her chin was tilted at a fighting angle. Well, hell. He hadn't expected this to be easy, right?

To keep his mind centered, he tore his gaze from her and started walking again. Movement helped him think. Always had. And right now, he needed all the help he could get.

"First off, you should know that I sent a wire to my in-laws. Told 'em not to bother coming because they can't have Becky." He risked another glance at her and noted that she looked a bit less murderous.

"That's wonderful, Riley," she said stiffly. "I'm glad for both of you."

Yeah. She sounded real happy. "Don't know what made me think I could give her away in the first place," he muttered, more to himself than to her. "But that ain't the point."

"What *is* your point, exactly?"

All right, then, he thought. Here it comes. Say it fast, Riley. "The point is," he said, coming to a stop directly in front of her. "I won't be leavin' town after all." He looked for a reaction from her and didn't get one. He didn't know if that was good or not. "The hotel's a mess, won't be ready for customers for who knows how long."

"And . . ." She started tapping one foot against the floor.

"And," he went on, his words tumbling from him in a rush. "Since we'll both be living here, in close quarters, and since we've already . . ."—he waved a hand at the bed "hell, Phoebe. We've made love. You could be pregnant right now."

She took a half-step backward and he knew she hadn't yet considered that possibility.

"So," he went on, taking advantage of her weakened condition, "I figure it only makes sense for us two to get married."

"Married." She said the word like it had been squeezed out of her throat.

"Hell, yes, married." He took a step toward her, grabbed her shoulders and pulled her close. Looking into her eyes, those amazing eyes that had always haunted him, he said firmly, "I got some money put by. Not a lot, but enough to get us started proper on the hotel. Now mind, you wouldn't be just taking me on, there's Becky too. But I think this plan makes sense, Phoebe. Married, we can enjoy each other and make a go of this place at the same time."

Several long moments ticked by and Riley started worrying. He spoke up again to fill the silence. "God knows, I'm no prize, Phoebe. I already failed at being a husband once. But I can promise you I'll try to do right by you."

Her jaw worked as if she was trying to speak but couldn't find her voice. A moment later, she did.

"What about love, Riley?" she asked tightly.

He let go of her as though he'd been burned. "What's love got to do with this?"

She advanced on him slowly, kicking the quilt out of her way as she walked. "Generally, when a man proposes marriage, there is some mention of the finer emotions."

He backed up a step or two. Not that he was nervous, mind you, but he had always been a cautious man.

"Well, Riley," she prodded, "do you love me?"

"I care for you, Phoebe. You know that."

"That isn't what I asked," she pointed out and took another step closer.

"I said I want to marry you, didn't I?"

Yes, he had, she thought, fury bubbling inside her like

the heart of a volcano, for all the wrong reasons. For business purposes. For Becky's sake. For the ease of being able to share a bed and a passion that had rocked her to her core.

But there'd been nothing about love in his words. No tenderness. No "I can't live without you, Phoebe." Well, she'd waited a lifetime to find this man and, by thunder, she wanted his love, not just his name. Not just his desire. And now that she knew what real love felt like, she wouldn't settle for less.

Strange, she thought, for so many years, she'd dreamed and hoped that a man would care enough to ask for her hand. And now that it had happened, she couldn't accept.

He *did* care for her, she knew that. Sensed it. But Phoebe needed to hear the words. To feel the truth behind them. To know that the love she gave Riley was given back in full measure. Without that, she would still be alone, even if they were married.

"Well, Phoebe," he asked, his gaze locked with hers. "Will you marry me?"

"No," she said simply and had the pleasure of seeing shock shining in his eyes just before she opened the bedroom door behind him and pushed him through it.

"I couldn't believe it though I was starin' straight at it," Mary said as she mixed another batch of cake batter. "Half the wall burned away as if it had never been there a'tall." She whipped the wooden spoon through the chocolate mixture until it was silky smooth. " 'Tis a miracle is what it is, that no one was killed."

"I know." Phoebe turned away from the window. Outside, storm clouds gathered and smashed into each other in their rush to pound Rimshot with more snow by nightfall. She touched her handkerchief to her nose again and walked across the room to take a seat at the table. The beginnings of a cold and a still–bone-deep chill were the only reminders of her time in the icy well water.

Instantly, images of wind-driven flames rose up in her

mind. She could almost hear the shouts of the men, hear herself using her last wish to keep the people she loved safe.

Love.

She frowned and stuffed her hanky into the pocket of her dress. Riley Burnett was safe. Her wish had kept him so, she was sure of it. Safe and more distant from her now than the first day they'd met, blast him.

"I'll bring more tea," her friend said, splintering her dark thoughts.

Phoebe sighed, propped her elbows on the table and her chin in her hands. "Much more tea and I'll float out of the hotel."

Mary clucked like an old hen over her last egg. "You did enough floatin' last night, I'm thinkin'. You shouldn't even be out of bed. After a night like you had, you must think about influenza. Pneumonia."

It was pointless to argue with Mary. Or with Simmons and Ivy Talbot, for that matter. She'd tried all day. They meant well, she knew, but between the three of them, she'd hardly been allowed to lift a finger all day. Giving her much too much time to think. Still, when they'd tried to insist she stay in bed, she'd rebelled. That particular bed was too crowded with memories for comfort.

Why was he being so stubborn? she asked herself for the hundredth time that day. Why couldn't he see that what they'd found together was worth everything? Why was he so determined to keep her out of his heart?

"Have you seen Riley today?" she asked abruptly and Mary turned from the pot of tea to look at her, frowning. "Mean as a troll he is," she said as she carried the teapot to the table and set it in front of Phoebe. "Upstairs now, cleanin' out the ruins left by the fire. I hope he's workin' off that temper of his."

"Good," Phoebe said softly, pleased to know that he'd been as upset as she after their argument.

"Ah . . ." Mary sighed and nodded her head. "So, *you're* the cause of Riley's black mood."

"No," Phoebe corrected with a smile. "He's the cause. I'm the reason."

"Well, now, that does sound interestin'."

"More infuriating than interesting."

"And isn't that just like a man, though?"

"Mary Shannon O'Rourke!" From outside, a deep, loud voice shook the walls and rattled the windows in their frames.

Color drained from Mary's face and Phoebe leaned toward her.

"Mary, me love!" the voice boomed again.

"Who in heaven is that?" Phoebe asked.

"You heard it too?" Mary pushed away from the table, her gaze locked with Phoebe's.

"Of course I heard it," she said, already standing and moving to the kitchen door. "He's loud enough to wake the dead."

"Then t'was real," Mary breathed as bright patches of pink stained her cheeks and dazzling sparks of excitement lit her eyes. "I've dreamed it so often, y'see," she muttered half to herself. "I hear his voice. I see his face. I can almost feel his big arms around me, and then I wake up. Alone."

"Your husband?"

Heavy footsteps sounded from outside and came to a stop on the kitchen porch.

Mary took a deep breath and held it. She turned toward the door and faced it with a wary, yet hopeful expression.

Phoebe twisted the knob and opened the door to reveal a mountain of a man standing on the threshold. Tall, broad-shouldered, he had wild-looking shoulder-length black hair and a week's worth of whiskers shadowed his jaws. His shining blue eyes were locked on Mary. A wide grin produced twin dimples in his cheeks and eagerness was etched into his features.

"Mary, me love," he demanded and swaggered into the room. "Have ya gone deaf in me absence?"

Even the air tingled with the sharpness of Mary's emotions. Phoebe's vision blurred as water sheened her eyes.

"Danny?" Mary's voice was a whisper. Tears rolled unheeded down her cheeks and her chest heaved with the effort to breathe. Her entire body trembled and she clasped her hands in front of her waist until her fingers whitened under the pressure. "Sweet Mother, is it really you?"

The big man's voice gentled into a low rumble of passion. "And who else would it be callin' you 'me love,' I want to know?"

She laughed, a little wildly, then screamed "*Danny!*" as she raced across the room and hurled herself at the giant's chest.

Big arms enfolded her, holding her tightly to him. He buried his face in the crook of her neck, and shook heavily as a man might when trying to strangle tears of joy.

Tears welled in Phoebe's eyes as she stood witness to a depth of feeling she'd never seen before.

As though there were only the two of them in the world, Danny O'Rourke pulled his head back, looked at his wife, and said, "I've been gone too long from ya, Mary me heart." He cupped her face in his hands and swore softly, "But never again, I swear to ya." Then he smiled again. "We're rich, darlin' girl. We're bloody well stinkin' rich."

Mary shook her head as she ran her hands over his face, his chest, as if assuring herself he was real. "As if that matters a damn to me, you big oaf. All I ever wanted was you."

He caught one of her hands in his and planted a kiss in the palm. "It mattered to me, Mary, love of me life. And now I'll never see another blister on your sweet hands." Then bending down, he swept her up for a kiss that left even Phoebe breathless.

Before she could silently slip away, giving them privacy, the O'Rourkes were hurrying out the kitchen door, without a glance in her direction. Completely wrapped up in each other, she doubted they even realized where they were.

Silently, she stood in the open doorway and watched them go, hugging her envy close to her heart. She'd wished Mary and her children to be safe and happy. That wish had no doubt brought Danny home where he belonged.

She didn't begrudge her friend the happiness she'd found, she simply wanted the same kind of happiness for herself. Wiping away a wayward tear, she straightened up and silently closed the door. Turning around, she faced the hallway and the stairs beyond.

She wanted Riley to look at her as Danny had his Mary. She wanted the soft words and whispered promises. She wanted to know that she was as important to him as he was to her.

With that thought in mind, she started across the room for the stairs.

Riley stared down at the wreckage of the bedroom and scowled fiercely. If he ever found out who had been behind this fire, he thought, heaven had better help him, because Riley wouldn't show him any mercy.

Stalking to the charred-out section of wall, he looked toward the edge of town and the open country beyond. Jesus, there was still a part of him that longed for the days when he could be out on a trail for weeks at a time and never see another person.

The good, uncomplicated days when all he'd had to worry about was getting shot by some damn fugitive or waylaid by an out-for-hair Comanche. Back then, all he'd had to think about was the job. Surviving another day.

Survival. That's all his life had ever been about. And had it ever been enough? His vision blurred as he turned his gaze inward, studying the past thirty-some years. He had loved his job, no doubt about that. And he still hated living in town—though he had to admit now it wasn't as bad as it had been at first.

He'd almost become accustomed to the same faces every day. To greeting a neighbor. To giving a helping hand when needed. There was, he guessed, something to be said for living among people. For having more in your life than just your horse and a destination.

But mostly, there was Phoebe. In a few short weeks, she'd slipped under his skin and into his heart, damn it. He'd been so sure she'd accept his proposal. He knew she loved him. Why the hell would she say no? And why the hell did it hurt so bad?

The cold wind bit deep, stabbing through the thin material of his shirt to slice away at his bones. He flicked a glance skyward and watched as black, ominous clouds bumped heads and rumbled.

She loved him.

All she'd wanted was to know he loved her too. Why hadn't he been able to give her that?

A shout from below caught his attention and he looked in time to see a huge man striding into the hotel kitchen. In moments, he heard Mary O'Rourke screech "Danny!" and Riley smiled. So the long-lost prospector wasn't dead after all.

Another minute or two passed and then Danny and Mary were walking off toward home, so entranced with each other, Riley could only hope they didn't walk in front of a freight wagon, because neither of them would notice it until it was too late.

A swift rush of envy filled him briefly before he buried it beneath his common sense. Best to let go of wants now that Phoebe'd made her choice.

"Riley." As if he'd conjured her with his thoughts, her voice came from close by and he steeled himself to face her. He turned. His stomach fisted. His breath left him in a rush.

Dressed in her old, faded dark blue dress, her long hair free of its bun and tied at the nape with a short piece of string, she looked every damn bit as desirable as she had stark naked. How in the hell was he supposed to live here with her and ignore what she did to him?

Shoving one hand through his hair in irritation, he asked, "Change your mind about my offer?"

"No," she said, and he didn't even acknowledge to himself just how deep that disappointment went. "Danny O'Rourke is home," she added quietly.

"I know. Saw them leave together." Turning away from her deliberately, he went back to the task of clearing away the rubble. Taking out his frustration on the mess around him, he ripped out piece after piece of charred wood, and tossed them through the opening in the wall to the alley below.

"I didn't tell you something this morning," she said, "when I refused your proposal."

He snorted a laugh and glanced at her. "Oh, you said plenty, Phoebe."

"I didn't tell you that even though I won't marry you, I do love you."

For one brief, heart-stopping moment, his soul soaked up the power of those words. Slowly, he straightened up and turned to face her. Her blue eyes looked soft in the afternoon light, but there was a strong, determined set to her jaw that boded him no good.

"If you love me so damn much, then marry me."

"I can't," she said with a shake of her head.

"Why the hell not?" he demanded, throwing his hands in the air. "You just said you love me."

"Because I want what Danny and Mary O'Rourke have," she said and took a step toward him.

He was willing to stay in town. Wanted to marry her. Why couldn't that be enough?

"Phoebe," he said, "you know I care for you."

"Last night," she said softly, as if he hadn't spoken, "was more than I ever dreamed it could be. I didn't know there was that much magic in the world. But you showed me differently. You gave me the magic, Riley."

Magic.

That was surely the right word to describe what had happened between them. Last night had been her first time, but in a way, it had also been his first. In Phoebe's arms, he'd discovered that sex and making *love* were two very different things. She'd given him more than he'd ever had before.

"Why do you want to let it go?" she asked.

"Me? You're the one who said no," he reminded her and felt the sting of her refusal again. If she didn't insist on being so damn stubborn . . .

She folded her arms in front of her and let her gaze slide from his. He wanted to grab her, hold her, rekindle that magic she'd talked about. Instead, he yanked another board free and tossed it with the others.

"I don't know why you're making this harder than it has to be." He shot her a quick look.

"It shouldn't be hard at all," she told him.

"That's what I'm sayin'," he snapped, disgusted and tired of talking in circles.

A moment or two of silence stretched out between them until finally Phoebe spoke. He was relieved when she changed the subject.

"I wonder how the fire started."

"It was no accident," he told her grimly and looked into her startled eyes. "Somebody set it. With a slow fuse."

A chill swept over her as she tried to imagine the kind of person who would set a building on fire, knowing that people were inside. "The vandal?"

"Vandal." He snorted and turned away, kicking at a loose plank. "Faint name for a man who'd set a slow fuse and then walk away to watch the fun."

"Slow fuse?"

Phoebe listened as Riley explained. Her complexion paled and her eyes widened as she realized that whoever had set the blaze had meant to do far more damage.

"It must have been those kids," she whispered to herself when he'd finished.

"What kids?" His gaze narrowed thoughtfully as he watched her and she instantly saw him as the marshal he had once been.

"Last night," she told him, "the sheriff saw someone in the alley, but they got away before he could catch them."

Scowling, Riley said, "He didn't say anything to me about 'em."

"Perhaps he wants to find them first."

"Maybe," he said and pulled in a slow, deep breath. When another blast of cold, snow-scented wind rushed at them, he turned away, saying, "You best get inside now, Phoebe. It's turning bitter."

"Riley."

"Let it go, Phoebe." Tearing at the charred wood, he added, "I asked, you said no. It's over."

She blinked, jolted by his casual, dismissive tone. Then she noticed the rigidity in his shoulders, the white-knuckled grip he had on the boards he was determined to rip from the floor. Whatever he was saying, she knew that what lay between them was far from over. For either of them.

But he was a hardheaded man, and she was unlikely to coax any more conversation from him for a while. Turning, she left him, went down the stairs, and through the front door. Needing time to herself, away from the concerned friends who hovered too closely today, she stepped onto the boardwalk and started walking toward the edge of town. She barely felt the stinging slap of the snow just beginning to whip through the air. Mind racing, she continued on, past the end of the boardwalk, stepping off onto the slushy ground. Mud and snow slipped beneath the tops of her shoes, but Phoebe paid no attention.

Her mind filled with thoughts of Riley Burnett, she didn't notice the people she passed or the horses and wagons that crowded the narrow street. Concentrating on the mess she found herself in, she jumped, startled, when a voice from close by said, "Miss Phoebe?"

She looked up to the man seated atop a big black horse and smiled. "Sheriff. I'm sorry. I didn't hear you."

He nodded. "Look to have a lot on your mind."

"I do indeed." She sighed and shook her head. "What can I do for you?"

"Riley sent me after you."

"He did?" Hope leaped into life in her chest.

"You don't mind my saying so," Tom told her, "you're asking for trouble, walking in the snow without a coat."

At his words, she suddenly realized just how cold she was. Good heavens, how long had she been walking? Her dress was soaked, the material catching and trapping each snowflake and hugging it close to her skin. Her toes felt like stones in her shoes, and when she drew a breath, the frigid air sliced into her chest like thousands of tiny knives.

Wrapping her arms around herself tightly, she shivered and glanced up at the man. "I think I'd better go home and change before seeing Riley. Thank you, though, for the message."

She turned back toward town and the sheriff wheeled his horse around too. "You don't understand, Phoebe. Riley's not at the hotel. I told him about those kids from last night. And where we could find them. He headed right out and asked me to bring you along."

Cold forgotten momentarily, she grinned up at the sheriff. Riley wanted her with him. That was all that mattered. "How far away is it?"

"Not far, ma'am. Not too far at all." He held out one hand to her. "You climb up behind me, we'll go settle this, then get you home and warm again."

Home.

With Riley.

Smiling through chattering teeth, she took the sheriff's hand and let him pull her up behind him on the horse.

"You hold on now," he said. "Don't want you falling off."

She nodded against his back and snuggled close to his heavy coat, wrapping her arms around his middle and clenching her teeth tight as the horse leaped into a canter.

Dave Hawkins stepped out of the livery, buttoning the collar of his coat. The blacksmith's place was the only warm spot in town this time of year, what with the glowing red forge and all.

Bitter cold outside, he thought, longing for the blistering-hot days of summer. He shoved his hands into the fleece-lined pockets of his coat and tucked his head down against the wind. A flicker of movement to the right caught his eye and he glanced up in time to see the sheriff, Phoebe sitting behind him, ride out of town.

He lifted one hand to wave, but the boss never looked at him. Just stared straight ahead, like a man focused on a hard task. Hawkins frowned to himself.

Now where the hell would the sheriff be taking Phoebe with a storm settling in?

"Burnett?" Ivy Talbot's deep, commanding voice rang out just a moment or two after Phoebe left.

"Damn women," Riley muttered darkly and tossed a look at the open doorway behind him.

"I want to talk to you," Ivy announced as she stepped into what was left of the room.

He shook his head in disgust when he noticed that Simmons, Becky attached to his leg, stood beside the woman, glaring daggers at him.

"Papa!" Becky crooned and his heart eased. At least someone wasn't mad at him.

He smiled at his daughter, then shifted his gaze to the big woman. "Not now, Ivy," Riley warned tightly, hoping the damn butler would leave with her. He should have known better.

"I warned you last night," Ivy said, walking into the

room with heavy, determined footsteps. "I won't stand for you treatin' Phoebe lightly."

"I'm not going to talk to you about this, Ivy." His back teeth ground together until his jaw ached.

"Then talk to me." Simmons spoke up, his British accent more clipped and snippy than usual.

"You neither," Riley said flatly. "Phoebe and I already talked it out."

"When's the wedding?" Ivy asked, folding her arms across her huge bosom.

"Not goin' to be one."

Simmons nearly smiled, but caught himself in time.

Riley shot him a glare hot enough to cook the soles of his shoes.

"Oh, yes there is," Ivy said, advancing on him, a glint in her eye that promised retribution to sinners.

"I know you mean well," Riley told her, though he couldn't quite stop himself from backing up a bit. "But stay out of this, Ivy."

"Yes," Simmons said, suddenly more agreeable. "If it's settled, perhaps we should stay out of it."

Figured, Riley thought. That butler never had liked him any.

"Oh, hush up, you old goat," Ivy told Simmons and the butler's eyebrows shot straight up. "You know durn well Phoebe loves this damn fool."

Riley stiffened. "Now hold on a minute here."

"No, sir, *you* hold on." Ivy pointed one finger at him as if it was a pistol barrel, and he was suddenly grateful she was unarmed. "I don't know what's put a burr under your saddle, boy, but you better fix it fast."

Riley held his tongue. He wouldn't shout at a woman who was only doing what she thought best. When she went on, however, it was a hard test of his resolve.

"I never thought you a half-wit, Burnett," Ivy said with a slow shake of her head. "But if you don't snatch that girl up and love her for all she's worth . . ." She paused for air, obviously trying to come up with something truly nasty for the finish. At last, she found it. "You'll never know another moment's peace, boy. You'll live the rest of your days knowing you could have been a happy man—if you hadn't been such a foolish one."

Hell, he knew that and sure as shootin' didn't need Ivy Talbot drawin' him a picture of what looked to be a damned empty future.

"Not that it's any of your business, Ivy," Riley practically snarled in his own defense, "but I asked Phoebe to marry me. She said no."

Any other time, the stunned expression on the big woman's face would have been downright entertaining.

"Well, then!" Simmons was gleeful, which only made Riley's mood blacker.

"I don't understand this at all," Ivy muttered.

"That makes two of us," Riley grumbled, and headed past them toward the saloon. He needed a drink.

Chapter Twenty

"Where are we?" Phoebe asked, and her voice was swallowed by the rising wind.

"Where we're supposed to be," Tom said and tied his horse's reins to a low-hanging pine branch.

Phoebe watched him, her arms wrapped tight around her in a vain attempt to keep warm. She was too cold now. She'd never be warm again. Couldn't even remember what it felt like to not have ice running through her bloodstream.

Where was Riley?

She inched closer to the tiny campfire the sheriff had built just inside a ring of boulders. The huge rocks blocked the wind slightly, but the wildly flickering flames were too small to fend off the deep cold settling inside her.

"When will Riley be here?" she asked through chattering teeth.

He shot her a quick glance. "Soon, I think. Shouldn't take him long, once Hawkins tells him he saw us leave town."

She frowned slightly. "What do you mean? You said we were meeting him."

"So we will," the man said as he walked toward her. He hunkered down on the opposite side of the fire and held his hands out to the flames. "As soon as Riley figures this out, he'll come running."

Tired, she thought. Cold and tired. It was as if her brain was icing over. She could hardly think anymore. Surely that's why what he was saying didn't make sense.

"Figures what out?"

He smiled at her and in the weird firelit shadows, his expression looked tight. "Why," he said pleasantly, "that I'm the one who set fire to the hotel."

She shook her head. Surely she hadn't heard him right. Why would a sheriff do something like that? "You?"

His smile faded as he stared into the flames like a man trying to see where he went wrong. "Found it too early. Should have used more kerosene," he said, nodding to himself. "But had to be away from the building when it went up." He paused, looked up at her and grinned. "Gave me quite a turn when you and Mary came out of the kitchen and found me slipping out of the alley."

Phoebe stared at him blankly. She had to think. She had to make her brain work despite the cold. Despite the urge to lie down in the snow and close her eyes, just for a minute or two.

"Why?" she asked, and the wind snatched her voice and carried it away.

Tom's gaze lifted briefly from the flames and touched hers with a hard, unforgiving stare far colder than the wintry afternoon. "Because he deserved it. He *earned* it."

She fought against the drowsiness, the lethargy invading her limbs and brain. "What . . . what are you going to do?"

He smiled again then and he looked like the friendly man she'd known these last few weeks. "Why, I'm going to kill him. By killing you."

Riley threw the bottle of whiskey against a far wall, but the shattering glass and splash of liquor did nothing to ease the hard knot inside him.

"Damn her," he grumbled, meaning Phoebe, not the

meddling merchant who'd looked him in the eye and called him for the fool he felt. "Why does she have to make this all so damn hard?"

Viciously, he rubbed the back of his neck. And how in hell could he ever live without her?

Heavy boot steps announced someone else's arrival and he only half turned as he shouted, "Saloon's closed!"

The doors swung open anyway and in the dwindling afternoon light, the deputy walked in.

"Didn't come for a drink," Dave said as he stepped inside. Reaching up, he yanked off his hat and slapped the snow off against his thigh. "Man, that wind's blowin' something fierce out there. Snow's already pilin' up."

Riley was in no mood for company. Especially the company of a man who'd once set his cap for Phoebe.

Practically snarling, he asked, "You come by to tell me it's snowin'? Well, thanks. Good-bye."

Dave glanced around the empty room quickly, noted the broken glass and spilled whiskey, then looked back at Riley through curious eyes. "Came to ask why Phoebe was ridin' out of town with the sheriff." He paused a beat, then added, " 'Course, maybe she's just trying to get away from that temper of yours. Can't hardly blame her for that. But she might have worn a coat."

Worry tugged at the back of his brain, but Riley fought against it. "You're wrong. Why would she leave town in this storm?"

Grimly, Dave looked at him. "Didn't say I knew why. Said I saw her ride out of town."

There had to be a reason, he told himself, his brain racing, trying to come up with one. In this weather, she'd freeze to death in a few hours without a coat. Why in the hell would she ride off like that? Where would Tom be taking her?

The sheriff.

What was it Phoebe'd said earlier? That the sheriff had been in the alley beside the hotel last night? Chasing some kids off?

The still-rational fraction of his mind insisted there was nothing wrong in that. Wasn't it Tom's job to be careful? To keep an eye out for trouble?

Yeah. But why hadn't he mentioned it to Riley?

"Kinda strange too," Dave added slowly, thoughtfully. "Sheriff was s'posed to be down at the bank for a meetin' with the town council."

A cold, tight fist closed around Riley's heart. His lungs clamored for air he couldn't seem to provide. Images and thoughts chased each other across his mind and Riley desperately tried to make sense of them all.

"Ain't like the sheriff to just take off like this." Dave paused. "And where would he be takin' Phoebe in this kind of weather? Her not even wearin' a coat?"

Dave kept talking, but Riley wasn't listening anymore. He'd heard enough. Enough to shake him to his boots.

He remembered little things. A certain look in Tom's eyes. His talk of the past. About Tess. Tom had taken it real bad when Tess chose Riley over him.

His mouth went dry. His fingers clenched and unclenched spasmodically. All of this was nothing, he knew. There wasn't a shred of evidence to prove that Tom was behind Riley's troubles. Yet . . . why would he have taken Phoebe out of town and into a storm?

"Riley?"

His gaze snapped to Dave's. It didn't make him feel a damn sight better to see the worried expression clouding the other man's face.

"This don't feel right."

Worse than that, Riley told himself. It felt horribly wrong. And he'd already wasted too much time trying to explain it all away. He'd learned long ago to trust his instincts and that's just what he was going to do.

"Let's go," he said sharply, already moving across the room.

"After them?" Dave asked, settling his hat back onto his head.

"Damn right, after them." Then he headed for the hotel kitchen, to get Phoebe's coat. He'd take it with him. He refused to entertain the notion that by the time he found her, she might not need it.

He studied the ground and the fear enveloping him got darker. Deeper.

Tom wasn't making any effort at all to hide his tracks. It was almost as if he *wanted* to be followed. To be found.

Why?

"What's he up to, you figure?" Dave asked.

Riley ignored him, needing to concentrate. To focus on the job at hand.

He'd always been good at that. Keeping his mind on his quarry. Not allowing distractions to pull him away from his goal. But this was different. This time, his heart and mind were with Phoebe.

Only his body was on the trail.

Gripping the reins in his left hand and his rifle tightly in his right, Riley stared off into the swirling clouds of snow in front of him. Already the soft powder was sifting down onto the tracks of Tom's horse. Filling them in. Obliterating them.

The wind tugged and pulled at his coat with frigid fingers and all he could think of was Phoebe . . . out in this with nothing to keep her warm. But the alternative was worse.

Please, God, let her be alive and cold and spitting mad.

Urgency rose up in him and he jabbed his mount's belly with his boot heels. The horse took off like a shot and Riley gathered himself for the fight he knew was coming.

Phoebe was in danger. He felt it in every bone of his body. He had to find her. Before it was too late. Before— He shut those thoughts off, refusing to even admit to the possibility that she might be taken from him.

His gaze continually raking the ground, following the fading remnants of tracks in the snow, he called himself the fool Ivy had named him. Nothing was worth being without Phoebe. Nothing.

And damned if he would live the next forty years without her.

"Somethin' strike you odd about this?" Dave asked, as he rode up alongside.

"You mean that he's not bothering to hide his trail?"

"Yeah. Almost like he's inviting us in."

"Me," Riley corrected the deputy. "He's inviting *me*."

Dave shot him a look through narrowed eyes. "Why?"

He was pretty sure he knew the answer to that one, but said only, "Find out soon enough."

Something bright flickered at the corner of his eye and he half turned to study the spot. A moment passed. Then two. And he saw it again. A flash of color in the swirling whiteness. A fire. Campfire. It had to be Tom and Phoebe. Who else would be out in this storm? "There." He pointed the rifle barrel at the ring of boulders.

"Yeah," Dave said softly. "I see it."

Riley looked at him for a long minute, as if measuring him before nodding. "You circle around. Come in behind them. I'm going in from here."

The deputy thought about it, then said, "Done. Watch yourself." A moment later, he was guiding his horse off to the right in a wide arc around the rocks. Hopefully, between the storm and his horse's quiet walk, he wouldn't be heard.

Riley stepped down, let his reins fall, knowing his horse would stay put as trained, and gripping the rifle, started for the rocks.

Someone slapped her, hard, and Phoebe came awake sputtering indignantly. She stared up into dark, empty eyes and immediately remembered exactly where she was. Dread squirmed in her stomach.

"Don't you go and die on me yet," Tom said pleasantly as he eased back to his spot on the far side of the fire.

Rubbing her cheek with one hand, Phoebe absently noted that she couldn't feel her own touch anymore. Even the stinging slap had been more surprising than painful. Almost completely numb, she wasn't even cold anymore. In fact, there was a curious warmth beginning to spread throughout her limbs. She might almost be comfortable. If she wasn't so tired. And frightened.

"Why are you doing all of this?" she asked.

Tom stared at her blankly when he answered. "To finally show Riley what it feels like to lose someone you love."

"I don't understand," she said, and reached up to rub her eyes.

"He will," Tom said with a nod. "He'll know why it has to be this way."

The sheriff fed a few more dry sticks to the fire and orange light moved across his features in a weird dance of shadows. "All his fault," he muttered. "He didn't really want her. If he'd just let her be, *I* could have made her happy."

"Who?" Phoebe determined to concentrate. To stay awake. Riley would come after her. She knew that as well as the sheriff did. And when he arrived, he might need her help. Opening and closing her white, stiff fingers, she forced her blood to move. To circulate. She had to be ready.

"Who are you talking about?" she asked again when Tom didn't answer.

"Tess." He looked at her then, and in his eyes, Phoebe read regret and just a hint of madness.

A sharp crack—a dry branch splintering—came from behind her and Wills leaped to his feet. Sparing her a brief sad smile, he pulled his pistol from its holster and pointed it at her casually, negligently.

Phoebe looked into the large, black hole of the barrel and instinctively tried to scoot away from the emptiness of it.

"Come on in, Riley," Tom shouted. "We've been waitin' on you."

"Riley, don't," she called weakly and heard the quiet click of the pistol's hammer being cocked.

"You don't," Tom yelled, "she dies now."

She closed her eyes and wished she still had a wish left. But there was no way for her to protect him. To keep him safe. Tom would kill her. Then turn his gun on Riley.

Tears swam in her eyes, tears for time lost, chances missed, lives unlived. Ridiculously, she thought about Riley's proposal and how she'd refused him because he hadn't spoken of love. Now, when it looked as though she'd never have another hour with him, she wanted to go back to that moment and say yes. Tell him that she would love him for the rest of her life and beyond.

But that chance, too, was lost as Riley stepped into the clearing, still holding his rifle. She looked her fill of him, determined to take his image with her to whatever eternity awaited her.

From the minute he'd heard her voice all Riley'd been able to think was, Thank God, she's alive. Nothing on earth could have kept him from walking into the circle of rocks to face the man who'd taken her from him. Nothing could keep him from her.

In the shelter of the boulders, the wild whistle of the wind softened, easing around the stones with a soft, keening sound. Like lost souls mourning the loss of heaven.

His gaze flicked instantly to Phoebe and everything in him raged in fury. Snow dusted her hair and dress. Her pale skin was milky white, making her eyes look even bigger and darker than normal. She was freezing to death and this bastard—he shifted his gaze to the man who had once been a friend—was responsible.

"Waited a long time for this," Tom said, his pistol never wavering from its aim.

One squeeze of the man's finger and Phoebe would be gone. Out of his reach forever. An icy calm dropped over him. He recognized it from his marshaling days. Once faced with the danger, his mind closed down and his instincts and reactions took over.

He had to protect Phoebe and trust that Dave would arrive in time to take care of Tom.

A part of him could hardly believe it had come to this. A man he'd called friend for most of his life holding a gun on a defenseless woman. But as he stared into Tom's eyes, Riley realized that the man he had known was gone. And in his place was a wild card.

"What the hell is this about?" Riley took a step farther into the ring of rocks, inching closer to Phoebe. If it came down to it, he wanted to be able to throw himself over her, block Wills's bullet with his own body.

"Don't you know?" Tom said, clearly disgusted with him. "It's about justice. About an eye for an eye."

Revenge, then.

"You want me, let's get to it," Riley told him, his voice low and deadly. "Leave her out of it."

"Can't." Tom shook his head and looked at him patiently. "She's the eye . . . don't you see yet?"

"Explain it to me," Riley said, stalling as he shifted a bit closer still to Phoebe. He didn't give two damns what Tom's reasons were. But he needed time. Time to get close enough to her. He couldn't look at her. Couldn't see the fear in her eyes or he would lose this battle. He had to watch for his chance and be ready to take it.

And he had to hope that Dave would hurry the hell up and get into position.

"You took her from me," Tom shouted. "Married her when it should have been me."

Of course. Tess. Somehow it didn't even surprise him to know that his late wife could reach out from the grave for one more act of misery.

"Tess made her choice." Another side step. Two.

"Yeah, she did." Tom gloated briefly when he added, "Every time you left on some damn trail or another, she came to *me*. We loved each other. She cried. She told me that you tricked her into marrying you when she really wanted me."

"Jesus! Nobody ever tricked Tess into anything, Tom."

"And then you sent her off and she died." Tom's features twisted into a grimace of remembered pain. "I loved her and you sent her away. If not for you, we would have been together." He waved his pistol wildly before turning the barrel back on Phoebe. "But you killed her and I can never have her now. All because of *you*."

So to get even, the man was going to kill Phoebe?

"Tom," Riley argued, even knowing it was pointless. The man was too wrapped up in his own grief and madness to listen to anyone's truth but his own. Still, he had to try. Had to give Dave time. He took another small step. "Tess made her own choices. You know that."

Tom shook his head, eyes wild. "Oh, no. You slick-talked her. Then got a baby on her when you knew she never wanted one. You didn't even love her. Not like I did. What we had was special. Pure. Now it's gone and it's *your* fault. All of it. But you're finally gonna see what it's like to lose the woman you love." He nodded at Riley and centered his aim on Phoebe. "You're gonna know how your soul dries up and shrivels away. You're gonna know all of it."

Crazy as a one-legged chicken, Riley thought, and knew there'd be no reasoning with the man.

"Kill her," he warned in a tone laced with steel, "and you're a dead man."

"Won't matter," Tom assured him. "You'll be alive. To suffer like I have."

Almost there. Just another foot or two.

"You're gonna find out how it feels to see the woman you love lying dead on the ground."

That image snaked through him like a spill of ink . . . blackness filled him at the thought. Years of emptiness stretched out ahead of him. She couldn't die.

He wouldn't allow it.

Riley sensed the man's readiness more than anything else. It was now or never. Instantly, Riley leaped at Phoebe, arms outstretched. He caught her up and rolled just as an explosion of sound ricocheted off the rocks. Something hard and hot jabbed into his shoulder, but he levered himself over Phoebe, unaware of anything but the icy feel of her body and the waxy pallor of her face.

He bent his head to the crook of her neck and held her tight, his body tensed, waiting for another shot.

"Damn you!" Tom shouted.

A blast of sound rolled down like thunder and even before Tom Wills's body hit the snowy ground with a muffled thump. Riley recognized it as rifle fire. Not a pistol this time. Dave had come through.

"Riley?" the deputy called as he crashed through the trees and across the clearing. "You two all right?"

Pushing himself up, Riley glanced at his fallen friend, lying dead in the snow, then up at Dave. "I'm hit, but Phoebe's frozen near solid. Got to get her back to town."

Dave took a step closer, looked into the woman's face, and shook his head. Grimly, he said, "You go ahead. I'll see to him."

Riley hadn't even waited for the deputy to finish. He lifted Phoebe into his arms, wincing a little at the pain in his shoulder, then headed for his horse. He staggered a bit, then righted himself again, forcing the pain from his wound to the back of his mind. All that mattered now was Phoebe.

She lay limply against him; the cold seeped from her body and dug into his, stealing his breath and scaring him right down to his boots. He held her tighter, closer, willing his own warmth into her. "Don't give up now, Phoebe," he whispered brokenly.

No response. She'd drifted into a deep sleep—a sleep she'd never wake up from if he didn't get her warm, fast. Wrapping her coat around her like a blanket, he climbed into the saddle and turned the horse for home.

By the time they reached Rimshot, she was hardly

breathing. His frantic shouts brought Simmons, Ivy, and Mary O'Rourke running. He carried her across the threshold and up the stairs. Only when she was in bed, being tended, did Riley allow the blackness hovering at the edges of his vision to swallow him and drag him down.

The longest week of his life crawled past, measured in each of Phoebe's labored breaths.

Riley hardly left her side.

Beads of sweat rolled down his back beneath his shirt. The fire in the hearth blazed night and day in their effort to warm her and to stave off the pneumonia that had finally settled into her lungs the night before.

The bullet wound in his shoulder ached miserably but he paid it no heed. Compared to the pain in his heart, that bullet hole was nothing. He reached out one hand and smoothed her hair back from her forehead. So hot. Her skin felt like parchment. Dry and lifeless.

She was slipping away from him and there wasn't a damn thing he could do about it. Why was he so damned helpless?

He'd face another madman with a gun. Charge a brush fire with a bucket of water. Stroll naked into an Apache camp. He'd do *anything* if it meant she would open her eyes and look at him. Tell him she loved him.

All week, he'd insisted that she'd be fine. He hadn't listened to the others when they'd whispered their fears. Instead he had waged a private war, beating back her fever with thousands of cool cloths, but again and again, the fever came back to claim her. Hotter. Fiercer. As if some damn beast had her in its jaws refusing to let go.

"Damn it, Phoebe," he whispered, leaning in toward her. "You can't leave me now. You can't show me what love is and then die on me. Come back, honey. Come back to me."

Nothing.

Not a flicker of her eyelashes.

She lay as still as death and just as unreachable.

Bracing his elbows on his knees, he buried his face in his hands and tried to stifle the groan building in his chest. Don't take her, he pleaded silently with a God he'd never really believed in before her. Sweet God, don't take her away from me. A tear rolled down his cheek.

"Riley?" Simmons spoke his name quietly from just behind him.

He sniffed and straightened up. "No change."

"I know," the butler said, pain quavering his voice. Walking around to the far side of the bed, the older man smoothed the unwrinkled quilts, then stood looking down at Phoebe. "Wishes," he muttered. "Where are the wishes now?"

"What're you talkin' about?"

Simmons glanced at him. "Phoebe believed a tinker had granted her four wishes." He smiled sadly at the memory.

"A tinker?" Riley's gaze shifted to Phoebe.

"If only she had saved a wish for herself," Simmons whispered, and bent down to lay his hand on Phoebe's brow.

The tinker. A brief flare of hope fired up inside him. It had to be the same fella. How many damn tinkers were wandering around handing out gifts and wishes? Why hadn't he thought of the tinker before?

Memories rushed through him and the tinker's words rattled inside his head like a death knell. *I offer you a gift. But with this gift comes the risk of pain. And a terrible price.*

What price? Phoebe's death?

"No." Jumping to his feet, he looked down at Phoebe and made a silent promise. I'll find him. And he'll make you well. I'll see to it. As he started for the door, he told Simmons, "Watch her. I'll be back."

*   *   *

The tinker was expecting him.

The little cart stood beside the church, as it had before, and the small man inside smiled when Riley yanked back the wagon canvas and glared at him.

"Welcome, my friend."

"I ain't your friend, mister," Riley said through gritted teeth. "I'm here to tell you to call off your dogs."

"What?"

Riley pulled himself into the cart and took a seat opposite the tinker. The air here was warm and smelled of applewood and summer. Surprising how much room there was, he thought, as his gaze instantly swept the place, noting the pillows and rugs spilled across the interior in a flood of jewellike color.

But he wasn't there to admire the man's doo-dads. "Phoebe was the 'gift' you promised me, wasn't she?"

He inclined his head. "She and all she brought you."

And she'd brought him plenty, Riley thought. Laughter. Love. Her smile. Her touch. A warmth he'd never known before. A sense of family. Hell, she'd even given him back his daughter.

And he was losing her.

A great, empty hole opened up inside him.

"If she's the gift, why is she paying the price?" Riley snapped, his voice harsh and filled with the pain that seemed to envelop him. "Take me," he said, leaning forward. "I'll pay. Not her."

"The price had been set."

"Change it!" he shouted desperately. "Phoebe's done nothing. Why should she die? There's no reason for it!"

The tinker only stared at him, sympathy shining from his silvery eyes. "My friend, why should this matter to you?"

He almost reached for the little man's throat, but he cooled the impulse. "Why should it matter? Are you loco?"

The tinker shrugged and his clothes rippled around him. "You do not love her," he pointed out reasonably.

"Who says?"

Again, the other man shrugged. "You do. By refusing her the words that mean all to her. You cling to a past rather than a future. You would lose my gift rather than risk your heart."

Heart pounding, sweat beading on his brow, Riley just stared at the tinker as his words rained down on him. Sweet Jesus, the son of a bitch was right. Why *hadn't* he said the words to Phoebe? Was there a part of him that believed if he didn't say *I love you,* he would still be free? Did freedom mean more to him than love? Than Phoebe? No. Nothing meant more than her. He finally knew that. Now, when it was too late.

"I am sorry for you, my friend," the tinker said softly, silver eyes glittering in the weird half-light.

Riley didn't want his pity. He wanted Phoebe. "Damn you," he said, his tone desperate as he fought for one last chance to make everything right. "You sent her to me. You let me see that a life without love in it is meaningless. A life without *her* isn't life at all. I *need* her." The words swirled inside him and he knew he needed Phoebe more than his next breath. That without her he wouldn't *want* his next breath. "I need what I found because of her. My daughter. This town. People."

"And your old life?" the tinker asked quietly, "What you valued most was your freedom. What about that?"

Wasn't he listening? Riley shook his head and ran both hands over his whisker-stubbled jaws. He'd held on so long to the notion that to be happy, all he required was a horse and open country. Why was it only now that he saw the truth? "That wasn't freedom," he whispered, lifting his gaze to meet the tinker's. "It was emptiness."

The little man gave him an understanding smile. "Go home, my friend. Hold to your gift. Hold her tightly and perhaps . . ." He lifted his narrow shoulders in a helpless shrug.

Hope. Hope and love were the only weapons left him in this fight for Phoebe's life. And armed with those two things, Riley would face down the devil himself if he had to.

Firelight and the yellow circles of light cast by kerosene lamps were all that stood against the darkness slowly invading her room. As if the very shadows were gathering, waiting to enfold her into their depths.

Riley's breath caught on each of hers. He stared at her, willing her to go on breathing. Willing her to open her eyes. To defeat the fever raging through her.

The rest of them had all given up, he knew.

They'd left him alone with her and for that he was grateful. But he wouldn't use this time to say good-bye. Instead, he clung to the tattered threads of hope and alternately threatened and pleaded with God.

From outside came the night sounds of life in Rimshot. People talking, the distant tinkling of a piano, the clop of horses' hooves. The world was going on without him. Without her.

Dave Hawkins had stopped by long enough to tell him the town council had elected Riley the new sheriff. Tom Wills had been buried and life in Rimshot carried on. And not a bit of it mattered.

Riley moved from his chair to stretch out on the bed beside her. Gathering Phoebe close, he inhaled the lavender scent that would be with him always. Heat poured from her body and each labored breath she drew rattled in her lungs as if it was her last.

"Don't go, Phoebe," he whispered, brushing a kiss against her hair. "Please don't go."

A shuddering breath was his only response.

Desperately, he spoke again, words tumbling from him in his haste to tell her everything he'd kept to himself for too long. "I was nothing before you, Phoebe. Alone. Empty. I wandered through life. Thought it was freedom. Thought it was all I needed." His hands moved over her face, his fingertips tracing every line, every curve, burning her image into his brain. A lone tear seeped from the corner of his eye, rolled down his cheek to fall on hers. It glittered in the lamplight, giving a false impression of life. "But all I need is you." He went on, his voice a tight thread, "Just you. Don't leave me alone again, Phoebe. Don't leave me."

She tried to reach him. Since the night in the clearing, she'd tried. But it was as if they were already separated by something determined to keep them apart. She couldn't break through the barrier between them despite all her efforts.

"I love you, Riley," she whispered, but no sound came. No comfort for the man who held her so tightly.

The shadows in the room crept closer, devouring the points of light one by one until the bed stood like an island in a pool of darkness.

Gift. Wishes. The two of them drawn together from opposite ends of the country. It all couldn't have been for nothing, he raged silently. His arms tightened around her slight, limp form. "Don't die, Phoebe. Don't die . . ."

She tried again to speak. To lift her hand to touch his face. So tired. So . . . tired . . .

She took a long, shuddering breath and released it slowly, the air sliding from her lungs like the last breeze of summer.

Then she was still and his world ended.

"No!" he shouted at heaven, his fury, his anguish, reaching beyond the shadows, beyond the veil that separates this life from the next. His cries echoed through the canyons of eternity. Clutching her to him, his hands fisting in the fabric of her nightgown, Riley bent his head to the crook of her neck and struggled to live without his heart. "Damn it, Phoebe," he crooned, "damn it, come back!"

In an agony so deep that tears burned in his throat but refused to spill from his eyes, Riley cradled the woman who'd brought him to life only to leave him. His heart breaking, he thought only of the endless days and weeks and years stretching out in front of him and wondered how he would ever survive without her.

"I love you, Phoebe," he whispered, squeezing the words past the hard knot in his throat. "I love you . . ."

"The price has been met, my friend." The tinker's voice rolled through Riley's mind. *"With the release of your old life to embrace the new, you have paid in full."*

The world went still. The shadows in the room seemed to slide back and away from the bed. An instant later, Phoebe suddenly jerked in his arms, dragging a deep, heaving breath into her lungs.

Astonished, Riley held her and stared unbelieving at the color rushing back into her cheeks. When her eyes slowly opened and she looked at him, his heart swelled until he thought it might burst from his chest.

"Phoebe . . ." He shook his head, grinning like an idiot, his gaze moving over her features again and again as if assuring himself he wasn't dreaming. But it was real. The fever was broken. And Phoebe lived.

"Riley." Smiling, she reached up to touch his cheek. "I love you," she said softly.

He turned his face into her palm and kissed her cool flesh. Then, smiling, he bent to press another kiss against her warm, pliant lips. Gently, tenderly, he tasted her, giving silent thanks to the God who had delivered him from his own stupidity. "I love you more than anything, Phoebe," he said, joy pushing the words from him in a tumble of emotion. "I'm not afraid to say it anymore." Touching her, caressing her, reveling in the glory of being alive and in love, he said, "Marry me. Tonight. Now. Don't let's waste another minute."

Phoebe smiled again and her eyes shimmered, dazzling him with their beauty. "Tonight," she whispered and lay against him, secure in the circle of his arms. Completion welled up within her and she closed her eyes to savor the wonder of this moment.

"It's magic, Riley," she said, burrowing closer still. "What we've found . . . it's simply magic."

His arms closed around her on his silent vow to never let her go again. He rested his chin on top of her head and his eyes slid shut as he whispered, "The best kind of magic, Phoebe. The very best kind."

Epilogue

In the distance, a one-story cabin spread out along the line of a swift-moving creek. Naked arms of the surrounding cottonwood trees rattled together and sounded like muttering old women. Smoke whirled from the chimney, twisted in the chill wind, and then rose up, sifting into the leaden sky.

The tinker straightened up on the bench seat of his cart and sighed. He'd only just completed his last assignment, quite satisfactorily, he thought. Yet here he was, awaiting his next command. Shifting his gaze from the cabin, he slowly lifted his face toward the heavens. He closed his silvery eyes and listened to the Voice only he could hear before slowly nodding in response.

"I understand," he said quietly, turning to look at the cabin once more. "A gift for the child, a choice for her mother."

He lifted the reins and tapped them against his horse's back. The beast plodded forward, crossed the creek, and dragged the cart to the cabin's front door.

That door opened slowly and a child, no more than eight years old, peered up at him. Dancer Hale's long blond braids framed an angelic face as she smiled. "Mama?" the girl called. "We got company."

A moment later, Corinne Hale, a young woman, stepped onto the porch. Lavender shadows lay beneath her eyes, but her welcome was warm, if cautious. "It's a cold night to be out."

"It is at that," the tinker agreed, his musical voice instantly putting the woman at ease.

She stepped closer, looking at him as if she thought she should know him. "Can I help you, mister?"

The tinker smiled.

Survey

TELL US WHAT YOU THINK AND YOU COULD WIN
A YEAR OF ROMANCE!
(That's 12 books!)

Fill out the survey below, send it back to us, and you'll be eligible to win a year's worth of romance novels. That's one book a month for a year—from St. Martin's Paperbacks.

Name _____

Street Address _____

City, State, Zip Code _____

Email address _____

1. How many romance books have you bought in the last year?
   (Check one.)
   __0-3
   __4-7
   __8-12
   __13-20
   __20 or more

2. Where do you MOST often buy books? *(limit to two choices)*
   __Independent bookstore
   __Chain stores *(Please specify)*
       __Barnes and Noble
       __B. Dalton
       __Books-a-Million
       __Borders
       __Crown
       __Lauriat's
       __Media Play
       __Waldenbooks
   __Supermarket
   __Department store *(Please specify)*
       __Caldor
       __Target
       __Kmart
       __Walmart
   __Pharmacy/Drug store
   __Warehouse Club
   __Airport

3. Which of the following promotions would MOST influence your decision to purchase a ROMANCE paperback? *(Check one.)*
       __Discount coupon

        __Free preview of the first chapter
        __Second book at half price
        __Contribution to charity
        __Sweepstakes or contest

4. Which promotions would LEAST influence your decision to purchase a ROMANCE book? (Check one.)
        __Discount coupon
        __Free preview of the first chapter
        __Second book at half price
        __Contribution to charity
        __Sweepstakes or contest

5. When a new ROMANCE paperback is released, what is MOST influential in your finding out about the book and in helping you to decide to buy the book? (Check one.)
        __TV advertisement
        __Radio advertisement
        __Print advertising in newspaper or magazine
        __Book review in newspaper or magazine
        __Author interview in newspaper or magazine
        __Author interview on radio
        __Author appearance on TV
        __Personal appearance by author at bookstore
        __In-store publicity (poster, flyer, floor display, etc.)
        __Online promotion (author feature, banner advertising, giveaway)
        __Word of Mouth
        __Other (please specify)_____

6. Have you ever purchased a book online?
        __Yes
        __No

7. Have you visited our website?
        __Yes
        __No

8. Would you visit our website in the future to find out about new releases or author interviews?
        __Yes
        __No

9. What publication do you read most?
        __Newspapers *(check one)*
          __*USA Today*
          __*New York Times*
          __Your local newspaper
        __Magazines *(check one)*

  __*People*
  __*Entertainment Weekly*
  __Women's magazine *(Please specify:_____)*
  __*Romantic Times*
  __Romance newsletters

10. What type of TV program do you watch most? *(Check one.)*
  __Morning News Programs (ie. "Today Show")
   (Please specify:_____)
  __Afternoon Talk Shows (ie. "Oprah")
   (Please specify: _____)
  __All news (such as CNN)
  __Soap operas *(Please specify: _____)*
  __Lifetime cable station
  __E! cable station
  __Evening magazine programs (ie. "Entertainment Tonight")
   (Please specify: _____)
  __Your local news

11. What radio stations do you listen to most? *(Check one.)*
  __Talk Radio
  __Easy Listening/Classical
  __Top 40
  __Country
  __Rock
  __Lite rock/Adult contemporary
  __CBS radio network
  __National Public Radio
  __WESTWOOD ONE radio network

12. What time of day do you listen to the radio MOST?
  __6am-10am
  __10am-noon
  __Noon-4pm
  __4pm-7pm
  __7pm-10pm
  __10pm-midnight
  __Midnight-6am

13. Would you like to receive email announcing new releases and special promotions?
  __Yes
  __No

14. Would you like to receive postcards announcing new releases and special promotions?
  __Yes
  __No

15. Who is your favorite romance author? _____

WIN A YEAR OF ROMANCE FROM SMP
(That's 12 Books!)
No Purchase Necessary

OFFICIAL RULES

1. To Enter: Complete the Official Entry Form and Survey and mail it to: Win a Year of Romance from SMP Sweepstakes, c/o St. Martin's Paperbacks, 175 Fifth Avenue, Suite 1615, New York, NY 10010-7848, Attention JP. For a copy of the Official Entry Form and Survey, send a self-addressed, stamped envelope to: Entry Form/Survey, c/o St. Martin's Paperbacks at the address stated above. Entries with the completed surveys must be received by February 1, 2000 (February 22, 2000 for entry forms requested by mail). Limit one entry per person. No mechanically reproduced or illegible entries accepted. Not responsible for lost, misdirected, mutilated or late entries.

2. Random Drawing. Winner will be determined in a random drawing to be held on or about March 1, 2000 from all eligible entries received. Odds of winning depend on the number of eligible entries received. Potential winner will be notified by mail on or about March 22, 2000 and will be asked to execute and return an Affidavit of Eligibility/Release/Prize Acceptance Form within fourteen (14) days of attempted notification. Non-compliance within this time may result in disqualification and the selection of an alternate winner. Return of any prize/prize notification as undeliverable will result in disqualification and an alternate winner will be selected.

3. Prize and approximate Retail Value: Winner will receive a copy of a different romance novel each month from April 2000 through March 2001. Approximate retail value $84.00 (U.S. dollars).

4. Eligibility. Open to U.S. and Canadian residents (excluding residents of the province of Quebec) who are 18 at the time of entry. Employees of St. Martin's and its parent, affiliates and subsidiaries, its and their directors, officers and agents, and their immediate families or those living in the same household, are ineligible to enter. Potential Canadian winners will be required to correctly answer a time-limited arithmetic skill question by mail. Void in Puerto Rico and wherever else prohibited by law.

5. General Conditions: Winner is responsible for all federal, state and local taxes. No substitution or cash redemption of prize permitted by winner. Prize is not transferable. Acceptance of prize constitutes permission to use the winner's name, photograph and likeness for purposes of advertising and promotion without additional compensation or permission, unless prohibited by law.

6. All entries become the property of sponsor, and will not be returned. By participating in this sweepstakes, entrants agree to be bound by these official rules and the decision of the judges, which are final in all respects.

7. For the name of the winner, available after March 22, 2000, send by May 1, 2000 a stamped, self-addressed envelope to Winner's List, Win a Year of Romance from SMP Sweepstakes, St. Martin's Paperbacks, 175 Fifth Avenue, Suite 1615, New York, NY 10010-7848, Attention JP.

KATHLEEN KANE

"[HAS] REMARKABLE TALENT FOR UNUSUAL, POIGNANT PLOTS AND CAPTIVATING CHARACTERS."

—*PUBLISHERS WEEKLY*

A Pocketful of Paradise

A spirit whose job it was to usher souls into the afterlife, Zach had angered the powers that be. Sent to Earth to live as a human for a month, Zach never expected the beautiful Rebecca to ignite in him such earthly emotions.

0-312-96090-5 _____ $5.99 U.S. _____ $7.99 Can.

This Time for Keeps

After eight disastrous lives, Tracy Hill is determined to get it right. But Heaven's "Resettlement Committee" has other plans—to send her to a 19th century cattle ranch, where a rugged cowboy makes her wonder if the ninth time is *finally* the charm.

0-312-96509-5 _____ $5.99 U.S. _____ $7.99 Can.

Still Close to Heaven

No man stood a ghost of a chance in Rachel Morgan's heart, for the man she loved was an angel who she hadn't seen in fifteen years. Jackson Tate has one more chance at heaven—if he finds a good husband for Rachel...and makes her forget a love that he himself still holds dear.

0-312-96268-1 _____ $5.99 U.S. _____ $7.99 Can.

Read Cheryl Anne Porter's
BOLD NEW SERIES
About Three Passionate Sisters
And The Men Who Capture Their Hearts!

HANNAH'S PROMISE
Nominee for the Bookstores That Care "Best Love & Laughter Romance" Category
After she finds her parents brutally murdered, Hannah Lawless travels to Boston, vowing revenge on their killers. When sexy Slade Garrett joins her crusade, Hannah may have found her soul-mate—or the heartless villain she seeks...
0-312-96170-7___$5.99 U.S.___$7.99 Can.

JACEY'S RECKLESS HEART
As Hannah heads East, Jacey Lawless makes her way to Tucson, in search of the scoundrel who left a spur behind at her parents' murder scene. When she meets up with dashing Zant Chapelo, a gunslinger whose father rode with hers, Jacey doesn't know whether to shoot...or surrender.
0-312-96332-7___$5.99 U.S.___$7.99 Can.

SEASONS OF GLORY
With Hannah and Jacey off to find their parents' killers, young Glory is left to tend the ranch. And with the help of handsome neighbor—and arch enemy—Riley Thorne, Glory might learn a thing or two about life...and love.
0-312-96625-3___$5.99 U.S.___$7.99 Can.